Always Yours

Book 2 of the Always Trilogy

9-19

CHERYL
HOLT

Praise for *New York Times* Bestselling Author
CHERYL HOLT

"Best storyteller of the year . . ."
Romantic Times Magazine

"A master writer . . ."
Fallen Angel Reviews

"The Queen of Erotic Romance . . ."
Book Cover Reviews

"Cheryl Holt is magnificent . . ."
Reader to Reader Reviews

"From cover to cover, I was spellbound. Truly outstanding . . ."
Romance Junkies

"A classic love story with hot, fiery passion dripping from every page. There's nothing better than curling up with a great book and this one totally qualifies."
Fresh Fiction

"This is a masterpiece of storytelling. A sensual delight scattered with rose petals that are divinely arousing. Oh my, yes indeedy!"
Reader to Reader Reviews

Praise for Cheryl Holt's "Lord Trent" trilogy

"A true guilty pleasure!"
Novels Alive TV

"LOVE'S PROMISE can't take the number one spot as my favorite by Ms. Holt— that belongs to her book NICHOLAS—but it's currently running a close second."
Manic Readers

"The book was brilliant . . . can't wait for Book #2."
Harlie's Book Reviews

"I guarantee you won't want to put this one down. Holt's fast-paced dialogue, paired with the emotional turmoil, will keep you turning the pages all the way to the end."
Susana's Parlour

". . . A great love story populated with many flawed characters. Highly recommend it."
Bookworm 2 Bookworm Reviews

BOOKS BY CHERYL HOLT

ALWAYS MINE

ALWAYS YOURS

ALWAYS

JILTED BY A ROGUE

JILTED BY A SCOUNDREL

JILTED BY A CAD

FOREVER

FOREVER AFTER

FOREVER MINE

FOREVER YOURS

ONLY MINE

ONLY YOU

HEART'S DEBT

SCOUNDREL

HEART'S DEMAND

HEART'S DESIRE

HEART'S DELIGHT

WONDERFUL

WANTON

WICKED

SEDUCING THE GROOM

LOVE'S PERIL

LOVE'S PRICE

LOVE'S PROMISE

SWEET SURRENDER

THE WEDDING

MUD CREEK

MARRY ME

LOVE ME

KISS ME

SEDUCE ME

KNIGHT OF SEDUCTION

NICHOLAS

DREAMS OF DESIRE

TASTE OF TEMPTATION

PROMISE OF PLEASURE

SLEEPING WITH THE DEVIL

DOUBLE FANTASY

FORBIDDEN FANTASY

SECRET FANTASY

TOO WICKED TO WED

TOO TEMPTING TO TOUCH

TOO HOT TO HANDLE

FURTHER THAN PASSION

DEEPER THAN DESIRE

MORE THAN SEDUCTION

COMPLETE ABANDON

ABSOLUTE PLEASURE

TOTAL SURRENDER

LOVE LESSONS

MOUNTAIN DREAMS

MY TRUE LOVE

MY ONLY LOVE

MEG'S SECRET ADMIRER

THE WAY OF THE HEART

ISBN: 978-1-64606-928-6 (Print version)

Cover Design Angela Waters
Interior format, Dayna Linton, Day Agency

Always Yours

PROLOGUE

SISSY WAS IN HER bedchamber, hiding in the corner by the bed. Her twin sister, Bec-Bec, was hiding with her. They were nose to nose and whispering. They talked in a language grownups didn't understand, but *they* understood it.

Scary events were happening. Mother and Father had flown up to Heaven, so she and Bec-Bec had spent hours looking out the window, wondering if they might be floating overhead, but they were never there.

Would they ever return? If not, why not?

Nanny wouldn't explain it. She was in her rocking chair, and she was weeping, dabbing at her eyes with a kerchief. The sight of her being so sad was frightening. They'd tried to comfort her, but she'd pushed them away.

A servant called from down the stairs, claiming it was time for them to leave. For days, there had been gossip that they would have to go and live elsewhere, but they couldn't figure out why they were departing. If they left, how would Mother and Father find them?

Nanny put down her knitting, and she bustled about, tying their bonnets and latching the clasps on their cloaks. Once they were ready, she grabbed their hands and started out, one of them on each side. Sissy kept peeking behind Nanny's legs to see Bec-Bec staring back.

They reached the foyer, and suddenly, a wicked witch swooped in and grabbed Sissy. Before she could blink, she was carried off. The move was so quick and so terrifying that she cried out with dismay. Bec-Bec cried out too, but where was she?

The witch was tall and wide, so she blocked Sissy's view. She and her sister were never separated. Everyone knew that, so why had they been jerked apart?

There was shouting and arguing, and for an instant, she had caught a glimpse of Brother as he demanded, "Where are you taking them? Why won't you say?"

She was wiggling and kicking, attempting to scoot down so she could run to Brother and Bec-Bec, so she'd be safe, but she couldn't scramble free. The witch tossed her in a carriage, and even though she meant to jump out and rush to Brother, a housemaid pressed her down on the seat so she couldn't escape.

Bec-Bec was screaming, Brother yelling at the adults, but over the past few weeks, she'd learned that adults didn't listen to children. She clapped her palms over her ears to drown out the awful sounds.

The witch loomed in and settled herself on the opposite seat. She spoke to the servants in the driveway, scolding Nanny for being lazy, scolding Brother for being so loud, then the driver cracked the whip, and they lurched away.

As the noises faded, the witch muttered, "Gad, that was dreadful."

In response, Sissy wrestled and kicked again, and the witch said to the maid, "Shut that urchin up. I've had enough caterwauling to last a century."

The maid pressed Sissy down even more firmly, and she was so heavy that Sissy couldn't breathe.

Where were they going? If the witch wouldn't tell Brother the destination—when he was a boy and six years old—she would never tell Sissy who was a girl and just three. Where was Bec-Bec? How could they leave her behind? How would Sissy find her again? Had she flown up to Heaven to be with their parents? If so, why couldn't Sissy have joined her?

They rattled through the city for a very long time, then finally, they lurched to a halt. The maid eased away and pulled Sissy to a sitting position.

Sissy glared at the witch, wanting her to know that she was being very cruel, but the witch didn't notice. Sissy might have been invisible.

The witch placed some papers in Sissy's hand, wrapping her fingers around them, showing Sissy how to squeeze them tight.

"Don't drop those," the witch told her. "They're important."

The door was opened, and the step lowered. The witch climbed out, and a footman lifted Sissy to the ground. They were next to a large building, and there was a big sign on the front, but she couldn't read, so she had no idea what it said.

The witch led her to the door, then she leaned down and hissed, "You stay right here until someone comes out to get you."

Sissy frowned at her, her gaze worried and alarmed.

"Did you hear me?" the witch barked. "You're not deaf, so don't be disobedient. You'll remain here until someone fetches you. Nod yes if you understand."

Sissy nodded.

"And don't you dare lose those papers," the witch commanded.

She knocked, three sharp raps that made Sissy flinch, then she went to the carriage and climbed in. The footman leapt into the box, the driver yanked on the reins, and the horses trotted away.

"Wait!" Sissy called to them, but they ignored her.

She stood on the cobbles, watching as they vanished. She was all alone in a strange spot—but without Nanny to tell her what was supposed to happen. People hurried by, but they didn't stop to offer any instructions or to ask why she was by herself.

The witch had ordered her not to move, insisting her knock would eventually be answered, but what if it never was? What if Sissy dawdled forever and no one came?

"Bec-Bec?" she whimpered. "Brother? Where are you?" Then she began to cry.

CHAPTER

1

Twenty-four years later . . .

"This is the place."

Sarah Robertson glanced over her shoulder at the teamster who'd conveyed her in his wagon. They were only a few miles out of the city, so the distance wasn't as great as she'd expected.

If she'd had the energy—which she didn't—she could have walked from town. Or if her life had been plodding on in its usual condition, she could have paid a cab to bring her. But funds were never abundant, and recent events guaranteed they would soon be in even shorter supply. It was vital to hoard every penny.

So . . . she'd stood on the road and had begged for a ride.

It was difficult to believe London was so close. The noise, crowds, and traffic had quickly faded, and they'd been spit out into pretty, rolling woods that meandered along the river. The trees were so green, the August sky so blue. Fluffy clouds drifted by, and the ambiance was soothing.

She was London born and bred, and she never ventured out into the rural countryside. Why didn't she? It was lovely.

"You just head down the lane," the teamster said. "It'll lead you directly to the manor. You can't miss it."

"Thank you."

She slid to the ground and studied the gate that indicated the entrance to the grand property. There were carved posts on each side and an arch over the top that spelled out the name of the estate: HERO'S HAVEN.

"That's a tad pretentious, isn't it?" she asked.

"What is?"

She gestured to the sign. "The Sinclairs aren't big on humility."

The teamster's jaw dropped. "There's no need for them to be humble. The whole nation agrees with me. For goodness sake, the Royal Family attended Sir Sidney's funeral. Who are we to quibble over their status?"

"Who indeed?" Sarah muttered.

Obviously, *her* opinion of the exalted Sinclairs was vastly at odds with the rest of the kingdom. She had to remember that fact and be more circumspect.

"Thank you again," she said, simply wanting to get on with her unpleasant mission.

"You're welcome, and if I may inquire, Miss, should you visit all by yourself?"

"I'm not a fancy lady, sir. I have no maid, and I am twenty-seven this year. I think I can knock on the front door without a chaperone to show me how."

"Yes, you seem very . . . *mature,* but young Mr. Sebastian Sinclair is in residence, having inherited from his father."

"Isn't he thirty? I'd hardly describe him as *young.*"

"Yes, but his adventuring friends are all staying with him. It's the men from Sir Sidney's African expedition team? They're a collection of rich, important fellows who have too much time on their hands."

"Meaning what?"

"Meaning there are rumors flying around the neighborhood that there's mischief occurring. I'd hate to see you land yourself in a jam."

"You imagine one of them might accost me with wicked intent?"

The teamster shrugged. "It's been known to happen."

"Not to me it hasn't."

She viewed herself as being fierce and independent. Her dear, deceased father, Thomas Robertson, had reared her to be. In her line of work, as sole proprietress of the Robertson Home for Orphaned Children, she had to project a tough, imperious air, and she could never allow herself to be worn down by negativity, failure, or strife.

Yet she was only five-foot-five in her slippers, and she was much too thin. Her white-blond hair and big blue eyes made her look like a princess in a fairytale, a damsel in distress who was caught in a tower and in desperate need of a prince to save her. She appeared frail, vulnerable, and helpless, when she was none of those.

If a determined rogue espied her when he was bent on mayhem, she couldn't defend herself, but at the moment, she couldn't worry about bumping into any potential cads. There was one cad in particular with whom she had to speak—that being Sebastian Sinclair—and he was likely the most despicable in the entire group.

"I'll be fine," she insisted, and she smiled her best smile, the one that calmed terrified urchins and encouraged patrons to open their purses.

"Are you sure?" he asked.

"I'm sure. I'll be meeting with Mr. Sinclair himself, and as he is Sir Sidney's beloved son, I am positive I'll encounter no problems."

"Mr. Sinclair might be a gentleman, but watch out for his companions." He leaned closer and murmured, "I hear they've been away from England for so long that they behave like natives. They've forgotten our British ways and habits."

She could barely keep from rolling her eyes. Didn't he read the newspapers?

Sir Sidney had died in Africa, and he'd received a state funeral where no expense had been spared to honor him. His team of explorers had been present at all of the events, and as far as Sarah was aware, nary a one had exhibited the conduct of a savage.

"I appreciate your concern," she said, "but you needn't fret over me."

She was anxious to continue on, and she waved to him and headed for the gate. He sighed and almost delivered another warning, but apparently, he seemed to recall she was just a stranger he'd picked up on the side of the road. If she wanted to imperil herself, what was it to him?

He whistled to his horses, and the wagon lumbered off. She tarried until he vanished around a corner, then she squared her shoulders and marched down the lane. Orchards skirted the route, the branches laden with fruit, and through the trees, she had occasional glimpses of the mansion.

She'd spent plenty of time with the affluent. Her orphanage was a private facility that housed the natural children of the famous and infamous. The wealthy scoundrels who sent their bastards to Sarah were required to pay the cost of raising and educating them, but if they refused, or if they stopped paying, no child was kicked out, so she constantly scrounged for funds.

If she'd been forced to clarify her employment position, she'd have described herself as a beggar. She solicited money from every available source, and she was shameless about it, so she was used to observing prosperity and opulence, but it annoyed her.

When a smattering of people could have so much, and the rest have so little, the world was a very unfair place.

She emerged from the trees and went up the curved driveway to the manor. It was three stories high, constructed of a tan brick, with dozens, or perhaps hundreds, of windows gleaming in the sun. An expansive lawn surrounded it, the river slowly rolling by behind. It was peaceful and bucolic, and though she hated to admit it, she was quite charmed.

What would it be like to live in such an extravagant, marvelous spot? She couldn't imagine.

A set of grand stairs swept up to the front doors, and they were wide open, as if the whole kingdom was welcome to enter without requesting permission. There were carriages parked haphazardly in the grass, a sign of many visitors, and she grumbled with frustration.

She needed to have a very frank, very difficult discussion with Mr. Sinclair who was son and heir to the exalted, deceased Sir Sidney, but if he was busy with guests, he wouldn't have time for her, and her message was dire.

His illustrious father, Sir Sidney, may have been a national hero, but his morals had left much to be desired. Currently, she cared for two of his illegitimate children, a boy named Noah, and a girl named Petunia, whom they called Pet.

According to gossip, he'd sired many others besides them, but she hadn't had the misfortune to have any of them dumped on her stoop.

Did Mr. Sinclair know about his father's less savory proclivities? Had he been informed that he had at least two confirmed half-siblings? If he didn't know, and she was the unlucky person to apprise him, how might he react?

Hopefully, he wasn't the type to lash out in anger.

She climbed the stairs, and as she reached the top, she could hear laughter and raucous conversation. It was just after one in the afternoon, but it sounded as if a party was in progress.

Her exasperation soared. The rich and notorious never ceased to amaze her with their antics. Didn't any of them have jobs? Didn't any of them have tasks to accomplish?

Well, no, they didn't. They thrived on their laziness and sloth, and it was accepted that a gentleman never worked. It was considered vulgar and common.

She strolled into the foyer, and a footman was there, but he was completely focused on the activities in a nearby parlor. It was packed with people, mostly men, but there were women scattered about too. They were perched on the men's laps in a very scandalous manner that indicated dissipation was condoned by their host.

There was a harpsichord off to the side, and a pair of gorgeous women stood next to it and were about to sing a duet. They looked like doxies, attired as they were in bright red dresses that exposed lots of bosom. Everyone was drinking hard spirits, their glasses full, servants hurrying about to be sure.

The footman was so fixated on the party that he hadn't noticed her. She tapped him on the shoulder, and he jumped and whirled around.

"I'm here to see Mr. Sebastian Sinclair," she told him.

The cheeky oaf rudely assessed her, then said, "You're very pretty. He'll like you."

She frowned. "I beg your pardon? He'll *like* me?"

"Yes. I'm to admit every female immediately." He gestured toward the parlor. "Make yourself at home."

"I assume Mr. Sinclair is in there?"

"Yes. He's seated on the blue sofa."

"Might you ask him to attend me somewhere quieter?"

"I wouldn't dare disturb him."

"It's very important. I'm afraid I have to insist."

He scoffed. "He's having too much fun, so if you're expecting him to take you upstairs, I doubt he will."

Sarah was appalled. "I wouldn't go upstairs with him if he paid me a hundred pounds!"

"He never pays for any tart, so don't get your hopes up."

Sarah blanched. Was Mr. Sinclair consorting with harlots? Were there loose women in the house?

She always claimed nothing surprised her anymore. With how she had to talk to children about their salacious fathers, with how she had to explain bastardry and illicit bloodlines, she thought she was prepared for any eventuality.

But . . . harlots?

"Just fetch him for me!" she furiously said.

"I'll try, Miss, but I don't understand why you won't simply join in the merriment. All the fellows would enjoy having you arrive."

At the comment, she almost stomped out, but she couldn't leave until she had a commitment from Mr. Sinclair on several pertinent issues regarding Noah and Pet. The most riveting one was that the orphanage was about to be shut down, and she'd been unable to find another home for them.

What might he do about it? She was terribly worried he might not be willing to do anything.

She had a powerful way of glaring at a man. She could cow and shame even the worst sinner into better conduct. She employed it now on the footman, and he scurried off to the parlor. He was gone for only a minute.

"Sorry, Miss," he said as he strutted up. "Mr. Sinclair advises you to participate in the festivities or to depart if they're not to your liking. He's too busy to speak with you."

She smirked with aggravation. Why keep pestering the Sinclairs? It was obvious they weren't interested in the children's plight. She'd spent weeks seeking an audience with Sir Sidney's widow, Gertrude Sinclair, but she'd finally received a cease-and-desist letter from an attorney, and she was running out of time.

What if she returned to the orphanage and there was a chain on the door? Would she live on the streets with Sir Sidney's children? Was it a conclusion the Sinclair family would be happy to allow?

Suddenly, the weight of the world seemed to press down on her until she could barely breathe. She was twenty-seven, a single female and spinster who was all alone and on her own except for her awful sister, Temperance, but having Temperance was very much the same as having no one at all.

Over the past few weeks, after her building had been sold out from under her, she'd found alternative places for every child in her care—but for Noah and Pet. She refused to accept that there might not be a solution for them, and her temper flared. It had been flaring ever since she'd first written to Mr. Sinclair's mother and had been ignored.

Now, after seeing him reveling with doxies in the middle of the day . . . well! It was the limit. It really, really was.

"I believe I'll tarry for a bit," she apprised the footman. "How will I know Mr. Sinclair? I haven't previously met him."

"Why, he's quite the grandest gentleman in the land. You'll recognize him on sight."

Sarah whipped away and went into the room. There were about thirty people present, and the duet had begun to sing. It was a bawdy tune with bawdy lyrics, and the crowd chimed in on the chorus.

She scanned the faces, and the footman had been correct. She recognized Sebastian Sinclair, both because he was simply the handsomest man ever, but also because he looked exactly like his half-brother, Noah: blond hair the color of golden wheat, striking blue eyes.

With Mr. Sinclair seated on a sofa, it was difficult to judge his height, but she was sure he'd be six feet tall or perhaps even taller than that. His shoulders were broad, his waist narrow, his long legs stretched out and crossed at the ankles.

He was sipping a brandy, appearing regal and magnificent, like a lazy king who was bored. There were two men standing behind the sofa. They appeared tough and dangerous, as if they were guards, though why he would need to be guarded in his own parlor in rural England was a mystery.

Maybe they were always vigilant, watching for trouble, and they never acted any other way.

The song ended, the spectators chortling and clapping, and he perused the room, finally settling his attention on her. He grinned a wicked, delicious grin and signaled for her to approach. She didn't move, and he patted his thigh, inviting her to saunter over and sit on his lap.

The whole incident was disgusting, and she couldn't decide the best course, but one thing was certain. She had to confer with him and wouldn't give up until she had. She marched over so she was directly in front of him. He didn't rise to greet her as was appropriate, being so disrespectful that she yearned to shake him.

He scrutinized her as if she were a harem girl sent to entertain him, his insolent gaze starting at her head and meandering down, lingering at several spots he had no business evaluating. She might have been parading before him without her clothes, and she could hardly keep from squirming, but she stood very still, being positive he would enjoy disconcerting her.

His stunning blue eyes were locked on hers, and she couldn't look away. He was waiting for her to state her purpose, but she—who was never discomposed by any situation—was utterly discomposed.

He was a celebrity, renowned for his spunk, courage, and daring-do. Since he was ten, he'd traveled the Dark Continent with his famous father, exploring the wildest, most isolated locales. He'd been honored by kings and commoners alike. He'd even written acclaimed accounts about his adventures, and his books were so gripping that they'd been serialized in the newspapers.

In journeying to Hero's Haven, she hadn't wondered what it would be like to actually confront him, and the reality wasn't like she'd imagined.

He oozed virility and power, much like an ancient god who could destroy worlds or fly to the heavens. It was like stumbling on an angel or a saint. Humiliating as it was to admit, she was completely agog.

They seemed bound together by an odd spell, as if the universe was marking their meeting. It was very strange, but she felt as if she'd always known him, and there was a peculiar sense in the air that it might be the greatest moment of her entire life.

But if she was a tad overwhelmed, he definitely wasn't. He was a pompous ass, and he wrecked the thrilling perception quickly enough.

"You're pretty," he said. "I'll give you that, but was it Maud who sent you out from town? I've notified her that I'm weary of all the blonds she's provided—even if you are more arresting. I hate to have had you come all this way for nothing."

"I'm so sorry to disappoint you," she churlishly snapped.

"I'm not disappointed. You're just *blond*." He waved over her person. "And you're dressed like a frumpy nun. How will you entice me when you're garbed like such a drab?"

"I'm not trying to entice you."

"That much is obvious."

"Is there somewhere we could speak privately?"

"I've apprised you that I'm not in the mood to fuss with you. Why would we traipse off?"

"I'm not here to ... to ... frolic, you dolt."

At her calling him a dolt, his two guards stiffened. They might have rounded the sofa and grabbed her, but he raised a hand, halting them in their tracks.

"If you're not here to revel," he said, "why are you here?"

"I told you: I need to talk to you."

"I never waste time *talking* to women."

"Well, I think you should talk to me. In fact, when you learn of my mission, I'm sure you'll deem it vital."

"I very sincerely doubt it, and I'm busy." He glanced over his shoulder and said, "Raven, this harpy is annoying me. Escort her out and spread word among the staff that she shouldn't be allowed to return."

The noise had diminished as people noticed they were quarreling. They watched the exchange as if it were a humorous theatrical play.

She'd been chucked out of rooms before by rich, important snobs. When pleading an orphan's case, she could be a bit of a nag, so it wouldn't kill her to be evicted. But she'd come for Noah and Petunia, and she wouldn't waver in her resolve merely because their older half-sibling was arrogant and unlikable.

"Should I voice aloud what I have to tell you?" she asked. "Would you like everyone to hear it? I can guarantee you don't want that."

"Raven!" He gestured toward the door. "Hurry please."

The man, Raven, towered over her. To match his name, his clothes were all black, which added to his sinister demeanor. His gaze was severe, his manner frightening, and he could probably be very dangerous if provoked.

In three hasty strides, he'd seized her and was pulling her away.

"It's about your father," she tossed over her shoulder to Mr. Sinclair.

"Isn't it always?" he snottily retorted.

Then she was yanked out, as behind her, the guests tittered and snickered.

"Did you let her in?" Mr. Raven asked the footman who'd initially greeted her.

"Yes, sir. She's quite fetching. I thought Mr. Sinclair would approve."

"Take a good look at her," Mr. Raven said, "so you don't forget her face. Don't ever admit her in the future."

"I won't, sir. I promise."

Mr. Raven stomped outside, his grip on her arm still very tight.

"You don't have to keep holding onto me," she complained. "I understand plain English, and I realize I've been thrown out."

"You're too stubborn to realize it," he scoffed.

"Release me, or when you're through, I'll likely have bruises."

"Be silent."

They reached the driveway before he finally relented. She rubbed her arm and, even though he'd warned her to be silent, she wouldn't be. "I am Miss Sarah Robertson."

"I don't care who you are. Mr. Sinclair has asked you to go, and I expect you will. Immediately."

"What if I don't?" Her tone was just as snide as his. "Will you send me to bed without supper?"

"I will count to ten," Mr. Raven said. "If you're not walking down the road by then, I will hog-tie you and drag you off the property."

"You're as awful as your precious Mr. Sinclair, so I'm certain you would behave just that despicably. Do you always manhandle females when he orders it? Or are you simply rude and horrid all on your own?"

"I'm horrid on my own, *and* I do whatever he tells me." He leaned down so they were nose to nose. "Now *go!*"

She never heeded overbearing, obnoxious men, and she wasn't about to start with him.

"I am proprietress of the Robertson Home for Orphaned Children," she announced. She wouldn't be for much longer, but for the moment, it was her title. "Inform Mr. Sinclair that I have custody of two of his father's bastards."

Mr. Raven blanched and lurched away as if she'd struck him. "What did you say?"

"Don't pretend to be deaf. Sir Sidney's clerk was paying their fees, but upon his death, the money suddenly ended, so I'm owed a small fortune in arrears. Also, the orphanage is closing, and they're about to lose their home. I'm sure Mr. Sinclair would hate to have rumors spread that they were tossed out in the street."

He studied her with a mix of revulsion and rage. "You're serious."

"Serious as a poisonous viper. My facility is in London. Sir Sidney's clerk knows where it's located. Mr. Sinclair may call on me at his earliest convenience."

She whipped away and sauntered off.

Mr. Raven actually shouted at her. "Hold it right there, Miss Robertson."

"I'd really rather not."

"You accursed shrew! Is there a man alive who can command you? Stop!"

She halted and glared over her shoulder. "I *never* listen to insufferable men, and I most especially don't parlay with bullies. Mr. Sinclair can find me whenever he has a free hour. It would be such a tragedy if I had to talk to the newspapers about his lack of . . . *concern* for his poor siblings."

She continued on, thinking it was an interesting threat—one she would never carry out—but it definitely had an effect on Mr. Raven. He spun and raced inside.

What would he say to Mr. Sinclair? How would Mr. Sinclair react?

She suspected, before too many minutes had passed, all of her questions would be answered.

CHAPTER

2

SEBASTIAN WAS SEATED ON the sofa in his parlor, drinking brandy and generally being as lazy as possible. Most of the funereal proceedings were behind him, but his father, Sir Sidney Sinclair, had been very famous, and the tasks associated with his demise were draining.

As his only son, the burdens of planning the memorials and executing the Last Will and Testament had fallen on his shoulders.

He wasn't a clerk though, so the menial chores were taxing. He was a man of action and adventure, of intrigue and danger. He liked journeying to wild places, confronting mysteries and perils and sliding through unscathed. He *didn't* like picking the sort of flowers to have on the stage as his father was exhaustively eulogized.

It was the kind of job a wife should have handled, but he wasn't married. Or his mother, Gertrude, could have done it, but she was wallowing in her new status as Sir Sidney's grieving widow. She was hardly grieving though, and in Sebastian's view, she was glad to be shed of her errant husband.

There was one more trial to weather: the final inquest into the debacle in Africa that had taken Sir Sidney from them. The National Exploration Society had paid for much of the trip, and they were entitled to a detailed explanation of what had transpired.

They would hear testimony, produce piles of documents, and render judgment on the actions of Sir Sidney, Sebastian, and their crew. Then the Society would disseminate an analysis on the causes of the disaster—all with the expectation that future expeditions would avoid a similar calamity.

Sebastian couldn't and wouldn't give them a full accounting, and he was working furiously with his team members to get their stories straight. At all costs, Sir Sidney's reputation and legacy had to be preserved.

Suddenly, Raven stomped in, and he looked angry and upset, which was unnerving. Typically, he was steady and steely. Nothing vexed him. Nothing rattled him. What could have happened?

"What's wrong?" Sebastian asked.

"We have a problem, but we shouldn't discuss it in here."

"Can't it wait?"

"No."

Now that Sebastian's friendship with Nathan Blake had been destroyed, Raven Shawcross was his closest advisor. The fiasco in Africa was like a vortex that had sucked everything into it. Sir Sidney was deceased, their time together abruptly terminated. Sebastian's bond with Nathan was severed, probably forever. There were lies to conceal, tales to alter, scenarios to invent, and Sebastian wondered how it would all conclude.

Raven was Sebastian's same age of thirty, and for the prior decade, he'd traveled with Sir Sidney's dedicated band of explorers. He would face any hurdle, fight any foe, and overcome any obstacle. In a battle, Raven Shawcross was the one you wanted guarding your back.

"Sebastian is busy, and he's having fun." This was from his other sentinel, Judah Barnett. "Leave him to it. Whatever it is, you can tell him later."

Judah was age thirty as well, and he'd been with them for twelve years, first joining when he was eighteen.

Where Raven was reliable, dependable, and brave, Judah was hesitant, cautious, and never eager to leap into the fray. He could be a bit dodgy too, and Sebastian had already decided—if he went to Africa again—Judah wouldn't be accompanying him.

Sir Sidney had liked Judah, but Sebastian didn't share his opinion or his patience. Plus, there was the issue with Nathan and what had really occurred in Africa.

Sir Sidney had been hacked to death by natives, and Nathan had been mortally wounded too. After the chaos had calmed enough to mount a search, Sebastian had sent three men to stealthily hunt for Nathan, in the hopes that he might have survived his maiming.

The trio—led by Judah—had returned to camp, claiming they'd found Nathan dead in the foliage, but with the situation so hazardous, they hadn't been able to retrieve his corpse. All three of them had sworn to it, and Sebastian hadn't doubted them.

Except Nathan wasn't dead. Much to Sebastian's stunned astonishment, he was in England and home at his Selby estate where he was Earl of Selby. Sebastian had no idea how he'd lived through his ordeal or how he'd staggered to England on his own.

He'd spoken to Nathan about it precisely once, and Nathan had heatedly insisted he and Judah had chatted on that fateful day in the jungle, that Judah *knew* he was alive and had walked away. Trauma could affect a man's reasoning, so what was the truth? Had Judah and the others lied to him? Or were Nathan's memories clouded by tragedy?

Would Sebastian ever have the energy to find out?

He hadn't dealt with the dilemma on his end. He'd been overwhelmed by family matters, so he hadn't pried any answers out of Judah, but it would have to be addressed. He was terribly afraid—after he accepted Nathan's version of the event—he'd have to lash out at Judah in a very brutal way.

Yet he couldn't exactly commit murder in England, could he? There were laws against it, but he'd spent too many years in places where there were no laws, and he'd been able to extract punishment like a violent king.

"It can't wait," Raven said. "Come out to the foyer."

The ladies at the front of the room were about to sing again, and Sebastian would rather have listened to them, but Raven was adamant.

He pushed himself to his feet and, his displeasure clear, he marched out and down the hall to his library. Raven followed, Judah too, a pair of sentries whose only job was to keep him safe. It was important in Africa, but—in his own home in rural England—it seemed silly. He had them continue with it though.

He'd never admit it, but he received enormous comfort from their hovering. After what had happened in Africa, he was suffering the oddest ill-effects.

He jumped at the slightest sounds, and his temper frequently exploded. He was surly and antagonistic, and he didn't trust anyone. His insomnia was rampant, and because he never slept anymore, he was drinking to excess, using liquor to force himself into a stupor so he'd get some rest.

He'd always viewed himself as a very manly man, and it was humiliating to realize he'd become a trembling ninny. He had to work very hard to ensure none of his crew noticed his deteriorated condition. If they did, how would he maintain his authority?

"What is it?" he demanded as they trudged in, and Judah shut the door.

"It's about that harpy I escorted out of the house," Raven said.

"Why am I not surprised?"

"You won't believe what she told me."

"Yes, I will. The vixen had a smart mouth and an even smarter attitude. She's capable of any nefarious conduct."

"She runs an orphanage."

"Well . . . ah . . . good for her." What other comment would be appropriate?

"Brace yourself."

"I'm braced, I'm braced," Sebastian snidely retorted.

"She claims she has custody of two of Sir Sidney's bastards."

"What!" Judah gasped.

Sebastian gasped too. "That's not possible!"

Raven shrugged. "The facility is about to close, and they might be tossed out on the street. You're to contact her about them."

"The cheek of the wench!" Judah huffed.

Sebastian waved him to silence and asked Raven, "Where is she now?"

"When I last saw her, she was walking down the lane toward the road."

"Where was she headed?"

"I suppose to London. I didn't inquire."

"What's your opinion? Was she telling the truth?"

"She seemed to be."

Sebastian was very rich, as Sir Sidney had been, and there were always schemers slithering in to declare they were owed money. Since Sebastian had returned from Africa, a dozen shady characters had approached him, insisting they'd been Sir Sidney's partners in various furtive ventures, and he never ceased to be amazed at the penchant of human beings to cheat and swindle.

"I probably ought to question her," Sebastian said.

"I think that's wise," Raven agreed.

"Don't bother with her," Judah countered. "You should beat her with a stick for her pestering you."

Sebastian rolled his eyes. "I'm not the sort to beat a woman, and besides, she'd likely enjoy any physical coercion. It would prove I'm a barbarian."

"She was brazen and sassy," Judah shot back. "You don't have to tolerate that behavior."

"No, I don't." Sebastian nodded to Raven. "Fetch her for me."

Raven hurried out, leaving Sebastian alone with Judah. It was the perfect opportunity to raise the subject of Nathan, but he couldn't bear to. Not when he was about to joust with the blond shrew.

"Why don't you head to the party?" he said. "I can handle this on my own."

"I should be here with you. I'll help you to set her straight."

"I'm sure I can manage her. She's a wee little thing. A stiff wind would blow her over."

"You're too nice to females. You let them run roughshod over you."

"I'll try to buck up."

He pointed to the door, indicating Judah should depart and not argue about it.

Though they weren't soldiers, they were organized like a military unit. Or perhaps like sailors at sea. Sir Sidney had been their absolute dictator, with Sebastian his second in command.

Out in the wild, infractions were dealt with in the same way they would have been on board a ship. Sir Sidney had had miscreants flogged for lying, locked in the brig for drunkenness or laziness. Their work had always been dangerous, and no reprobate was allowed to imperil the rest of them.

The malcontents were eventually cast aside and never permitted to rejoin Sir Sidney's hallowed circle of explorers. It was a cruel result, and everyone in his orbit was determined it not happen to them.

Judah bit his tongue and slunk out. Thank goodness. Sebastian was in no mood to spar with him. If a quarrel started, who could guess where it might end?

He poured himself a tall brandy and sat behind the desk, considering the disturbing information Raven had just imparted.

Though Sebastian was resolved to hide his father's base appetites, Sir Sidney had been a rutting dog. He'd had a fondness for native women, and ultimately, it had gotten him killed. It had nearly gotten them all killed.

In Africa, they'd been living with a local tribe for several weeks, and Sir Sidney had begun fraternizing with some of the wives. A very angry, very jealous chief had caught him and murdered him.

It was a humiliating conclusion that Sebastian and his crew intended to conceal. The decision was deceitful and very, very wrong, but they would conceal it anyway.

They'd all worshipped Sir Sidney. He was a national hero who was beloved by the entire kingdom. Sebastian wouldn't have his father's reputation tarnished over a moral failing. It was simply too awful to contemplate.

But . . .

He'd often wondered if Sir Sidney had misbehaved during his short jaunts in England. There had always been rumors of mistresses and illicit children, but Sebastian had never been confronted with hard evidence, so he'd chosen to believe his father had only pursued his vices while on the road.

Had Sir Sidney dallied with trollops in England? Was Sebastian about to learn the answer to that question? If he had some bastard half-siblings in London, how did he feel about it? On the spur of the moment, he couldn't settle on an opinion.

It didn't take much time for Raven to return with her, and it appeared she'd come willingly; he wasn't dragging her in. No, she marched in, bold as brass.

When she'd waltzed in a bit earlier, he'd assumed she was a doxy, so he hadn't paid much attention to her. He'd noticed her hair, but that was all. Now, he enjoyed a very lengthy, very potent assessment.

Yes, she was blond, but it was a white-blond, a silvery color he'd never observed on a woman before. It was curly and long, barely restrained with a ribbon. She seemed magical, as if she'd been hatched by fairies and wasn't an actual human being.

She was thin and petite, but curvaceously shaped in all the right places. And she was very pretty. Annoyingly pretty. Exhaustingly pretty. She had one of those faces that made a man look twice, that held him rapt. It was a face that made a man act like an idiot, that had him bumbling over to introduce himself, then botching it because he was tongue-tied by her beauty.

But it was her eyes that were the most striking. They were a brilliant blue, like the sapphire of the Mediterranean. They reminded him of his ex-friend Nathan's eyes. Yes, they were definitely Nathan's eyes. Perhaps she had a Blake ancestor buried in her family tree.

She stood like Nathan too, feet braced, as if she was balanced on a ship's deck in rough waves. She had his same air of self-possession, as if she ruled the world and lesser mortals should get out of her way.

Maybe it wasn't just a Blake ancestor in her family tree. Maybe there was a king or a prince thrown in too. She was that magnificent.

Before he could rise to greet her, she sauntered over and pulled up a chair—without being invited to join him—and she started first.

"Thank you for responding so quickly, Mr. Sinclair."

Was there sarcasm in her tone? He was certain there was, but he ignored it.

"You're welcome."

"I am Miss Sarah Robertson. It was so *kind* of Mr. Raven to bring me back."

"It's Shawcross," Raven said.

"What?" she asked him.

"It's not Mr. Raven. It's Mr. Shawcross."

"I'm glad we cleared that up," she snottily retorted. "Next time you're manhandling me, I'll be able to scold you by the correct name."

Sebastian had no idea what had occurred between them out on the lane, and he didn't care. Nor did he have the patience to hear them bickering.

He glanced at Raven and said, "Would you excuse us? I'd like to speak with her alone."

"You shouldn't."

"I'll be fine. I doubt she bites."

"I wouldn't be too sure of that," Raven said. "I don't trust her, and you shouldn't either."

"Don't discuss me as if I'm not here," she fumed.

"We wouldn't dream of it." Sebastian motioned Raven out, but cautioned, "Stay close. Once I'm finished with her, I'll need you to guarantee she leaves the property."

"Don't put up with any nonsense from her, and don't listen to any lies."

"I won't," Sebastian insisted.

Raven glowered at Miss Robertson, but his stern glare was futile. She glared back with an enormous amount of aggrieved offense. When Raven realized his posturing was having no effect, he stomped out and slammed the door.

As his strides faded, she mockingly said, "He seemed nice."

The scornful comment pried a laugh out of him, but he wasn't about to bother with small talk. Abruptly, he asked, "What's this about you having custody of Sir Sidney's natural children?"

The maddening woman replied with, "I'm dying of thirst. May I have something to drink?"

"We are not engaged in a social call, and I'm not about to ring for tea. We're going to wrap this up as rapidly as possible."

"You are the most inhospitable person I've ever met."

"You're right, but in my own defense, *you* are deranged, and I have no desire to confer with you."

She stared at his brandy glass, then her wily gaze flitted over to the sideboard where there was an array of liquor and wine. Was she hinting that she'd like some? What sort of wench was she?

"I'm not about to offer you an alcoholic beverage," he said.

"I haven't requested one."

"Well...don't."

"You've just made me think of my father, although with you being such an arrogant beast, I can't imagine why you would."

Don't ask, don't ask. He asked, "Why would I make you think of your father?"

"He and I used to share a whiskey every night before he went to bed—and we never told my mother. He viewed it as a terrible vice, so it was our secret."

"Your father is deceased?"

"Yes, both my parents are gone. My mother for over a decade and my father for three years now."

She sighed with regret, as if she was still mourning him. Having recently lost his own father, it was a fact that might have persuaded him to like her, but he was determined *not* to like her.

To his great disgust though, he proceeded to the sideboard and poured her a whiskey, then came back to the desk and slid it across to her. Of course she was ungracious and insulted and didn't reach for it.

"I won't imbibe of hard spirits with you," she said.

He wouldn't beg her, and he grabbed it and downed it himself. It was much stronger than the brandy he'd been drinking. His eyes watered, and he coughed and pounded on his chest.

She watched him with a jaundiced expression as if he'd behaved just as badly as she'd anticipated he would, and he was weary of her sharp assessment and even sharper tongue.

"You have exactly five minutes to state your case," he said, "then we'll be finished, and I will never grant you an audience again." He peered over at the clock on the mantle, marking the time, then he nodded imperiously. "Please begin."

But she didn't start as he'd commanded. Instead, she inquired, "Are you always so angry?"

"I'm not angry, Miss Robertson. I'm exasperated. I have guests, but you've dragged me away from them. I'm giving you a chance to play on my sympathies, and I suggest you take it." More severely, he added, "Tell me about my father and tell me at once! Stop stalling."

Without further hesitation, she announced, "You have a brother named Noah and a sister named Petunia. We call her Pet for short. He's twelve and she's six."

He wasn't certain what he'd expected, but it hadn't been that. He'd envisioned a nebulous story that might or might not be a lie. He hadn't been prepared for her to mention actual living, breathing children with names and ages. Suddenly, they seemed very real.

He shifted uncomfortably, hunting for the correct response, but he couldn't figure out what it should be.

Eventually, he opened his mouth, and what emerged was, "A brother *and* a sister? And you're positive they're my father's? You learned this ... how?"

"I have birth certificates."

He frowned. "You what?"

"I have birth certificates. Plus, Noah only moved in with me a few months ago, but he's always known who his father is."

"According to who?"

"According to his mother who was Sir Sidney's favorite mistress."

Sebastian felt as if he'd been turned to stone. No, no, that wasn't it. He felt that he'd been shot with a burning arrow. He was hot all over and practically bubbling with rage.

How dare this ... this ... tart, this stranger, stroll into his home and impugn his father so egregiously! How dare she level accusations based on unfounded gossip!

He studied her, his eyes narrowing to slits as he struggled to bring her into clearer focus.

She was very calm, her hands folded in her lap, her demeanor devoid of any cunning or deceit. She probably couldn't tell a lie if he threatened to tie her to a torturer's rack.

Could it be? Could she really have custody of his father's children? Had the worst finally occurred?

With rumors constantly swirling, wouldn't someone have come forward before now? Sir Sidney had had numerous enemies and rivals who'd have loved to ruin him, and envious people liked to tear down their heroes. Could one of them have paid her? Was this naught more than an extortion ruse?

"What do you want?" he asked, resolved to exhibit her same calm demeanor.

"First off, I'd like the money you owe me for the prior year."

He was almost disappointed in her reply. "You want money? You freely admit it? Why am I not surprised?"

"I don't run a public charity, Mr. Sinclair. It's a private facility for the bastards of the rich and notorious. Scoundrels have to help defray the costs. In exchange, we feed, clothe, house, educate, and raise the offspring they're trying to hide."

"And you're claiming you have two of them who were sired by my father."

"I'm not *claiming* it. I'm flat out saying they live with me. Pet always has. Her mother died when she was born, and she had nowhere to go. The woman wasn't a mistress of your father's though. Their encounter was what's referred to as a one-night romp."

"Miss Robertson! I won't listen to such denigration of my father. Please be more circumspect!"

But she ignored his request. "Noah had resided with his grandfather, but the man recently passed away."

Sebastian took a deep breath, desperate to rein in his temper, to not insult or shout at her. He had to get through the meeting without losing control.

"You feel I owe you money . . . why?"

"Pay attention, Mr. Sinclair. I run a *private* facility. Sir Sidney's clerk always sent Pet's fees, but this year, after Sir Sidney's demise, the funds never arrived. I inquired as to why, and I was apprised that my compensation was cancelled by a family member. Was it you? If so, I wish you'd have discussed it with me."

He searched his memory, but he couldn't recollect any revelations about an orphanage or illicit children. Then again, in the past few months, there had been so many decisions and arrangements to be made. It might have slipped his mind.

Or might it have been his mother? She was Sir Sidney's long-suffering widow who, he suspected, was secretly very glad to be shed of her domineering, wayward husband. Had stories reached her about her philandering husband? If so, what steps might she have implemented to conceal the truth?

She wasn't a kind or compassionate person, so any ending was possible.

"Sir Sidney's clerk paid?" He was particularly bewildered, as if he were a dunce who couldn't quite grasp the concept she was repeatedly clarifying.

"If you don't believe me, ask him. Or snoop in his ledger books."

"The other . . . child, the one you call Noah—"

"I don't *call* him Noah. It's his name."

"How did he suddenly show up on your stoop?"

"I swear there's something wrong with your ears, Mr. Sinclair. You ought to have them checked. I just told you: He was living with his elderly grandfather, and the man died. He sent Noah to me."

"*You* being an angel of mercy?"

"I like to think I am."

"I've never heard of your establishment."

"Most wealthy people haven't—until they need me. They quietly speak to their friends, and they learn about me."

She responded evenly, candidly, and it was so hard to discredit her account.

"You want money for the boy too?" he asked.

"Actually, what I'd really like is for you to find a home for them."

At the suggestion, he was absolutely aghast. "Me? Why?"

"My building has been sold, and once escrow closes, I'll be evicted." It was a difficult admission for her. She paused, but quickly regrouped and forged ahead. "For weeks, I've been contacting various families, so they could move their children to new locations." She shrugged as if she'd explained every problem vexing the world. "I need your help."

"I'll bet you do."

He leaned back in his chair, and he sipped his brandy as he scrutinized her over the rim of the glass. She was such a composed female. He could be a stern fellow, large in size, authoritative by nature, and a single glower was enough to give any woman a fit of the vapors.

Not her though. She looked as if she'd had a life of calamity and had faced it all down with nary a ripple of concern. She looked anciently wise, as if she had all the answers, as if she knew all the questions before they were asked. She carried herself like a goddess and made him feel like a clumsy fool.

"I'm very rich," he pointed out.

"Don't brag about it. It's annoying."

He snorted with disgust. "I don't suppose you considered that fact prior to soliciting me."

"Meaning what?"

"Meaning you could be running a confidence game so I'll buy your silence. It's called blackmail."

"I *am* trying to wring some money out of you," she brashly confessed. "I don't deny it, but it's merely the amount I'm owed for Petunia. I won't charge you for Noah. As I mentioned, he hasn't been with me very long."

"You talk as if I'll blithely toss my purse at you."

"Why wouldn't you aid me? When I'm evicted, will you permit Noah and Pet to be cast out onto the street? They're your father's children. You can't want that."

He sipped his brandy again, his thoughts jumping off assorted cliffs as he attempted to think of a pithy comment, one that would rattle her, one that might poke through her tranquil façade. She seemed so . . . *sure.*

How was he to guess if the two urchins were really his father's? She claimed she had birth certificates, but so what? Any fiend could print up a fake piece of paper.

He was so discombobulated he couldn't pick the best course. Ever since the debacle in Africa, it had been his usual condition.

The only thing he knew with any certainty was that he wasn't about to pay her a penny. Nor would he rescue any orphans. He wouldn't! And he didn't care how tenderly she shared her story or how prettily she batted her lashes.

"Thank you for coming," he said.

She studied him curiously, as if he were a strange bird in the forest. "That's it? After all I've told you, you simply *thank* me for coming?"

"Yes."

"What about Noah and Petunia?"

"I can't help you with them."

"Why not?" she had the temerity to inquire.

"Because I don't believe you."

She assessed him, then scowled. "Yes, you do."

"Are you a clairvoyant? Can you read my mind?"

"No, but I'm a good judge of character. You believe me. It's plain as the nose on your face."

"Miss Robertson, my father was a national hero. He was beloved in the kingdom. Can you picture him flitting about, siring a slew of bastards?"

"It happens all the time."

"Well, he *didn't* behave that way."

"A man can have many sides."

"Yes, and I assume you're an expert on men?"

"I'm an expert on *people*."

She evaluated him with those magnificent eyes of hers—Nathan's eyes—which was incredibly disturbing.

He pushed back his chair, practically leaping to his feet. She didn't rise with him, but appraised him meticulously. Her disappointment was exceedingly clear, and just as he started to feel ashamed and totally in the wrong, she stood too.

"I realize it's a lot to absorb all at once," she said. "Think about it for a few days."

"I don't need to think about it."

"You should stop by and meet them. I find—after family members are introduced—it can change everything."

"I have no desire to meet them."

She stepped to the desk where there was a writing tray complete with ink jar, quills, and paper. Without garnering his permission, she dipped a quill, penned a note, and sanded it. He watched, flummoxed by her audacity. He'd never encountered a woman quite like her.

"Here are the directions to my orphanage." She set the paper in front of him. "I live there. Visit us whenever it's convenient, but please hurry. I don't know when escrow will close, and I'm not sure where we'll be after it does. I would hate to miss you."

"I won't ever come."

She scoffed, as if his refusal was silly. "We'll see. You'd really like Noah. From what I hear, he's the spitting image of Sir Sidney, right down to the swagger in his walk. Anyone would notice the resemblance."

Sebastian thought of the inquest that was approaching, of the gossip he was working so valiantly to quell, of Sir Sidney's reputation they were all so desperate to protect.

"Are you threatening me?" he asked.

"Why would I threaten you? You have a half-brother and a half-sister too. She's the sweetest little girl ever—blond and blue-eyed, like all of you Sinclairs. Evidently, your father had strong bloodlines. All of you look exactly alike."

He was so taken aback by her remark that he was surprised he didn't faint.

She was very cunning, very dangerous. What might she ultimately say about his father, and to whom might she say it?

"In the next week," he said, "I'd like you to settle on a price."

"A . . . price?"

"Yes. How much will you require in order to be silent about this?"

"You couldn't pay me a sufficient amount to be silent about it."

"I doubt that very much. I predict you've already calculated the sum and that it's astronomically high. But you should know, Miss Robertson, that if you antagonize me, there will be consequences."

She tsked derisively as if he was being ridiculous. "Don't be so annoying. It's exasperating, and I don't have the patience for nonsense. Just come and meet your half-siblings. You'll like them. I guarantee it."

They faced each other as if on a battlefield. He yearned to dive over the desk and shake her until she admitted she was lying, or until she relented and swore she'd never spread any stories, or until . . . until . . .

"Raven!" he shouted.

Raven opened the door and asked, "Yes?"

"Miss Robertson and I are finished. Escort her off the property."

She threw up her hands. "We haven't decided a single issue."

"We've decided plenty," he said.

"Such as . . . ?"

"I don't believe you, I won't give you a farthing, and I've wasted every minute I intend to waste on you."

Raven stomped over, grabbed her arm, and marched her out.

She tossed over her shoulder, "This problem won't vanish simply because you wish it would. They're flesh-and-blood children, Mr. Sinclair. They're your *father's* children."

"Goodbye, Miss Robertson. If I'm lucky, which I haven't been so far, we won't cross paths again."

"Yes, we will," she snottily insisted. "I plan on it. I'll keep nagging at you until I wear you down. I'm exhausting that way."

"As she leaves," he advised Raven, "I'd like you to explain the sorts of penalties she might incur if she causes any trouble for me or my family. She should be especially concerned about the impact any rumors might have on my mother who is in deep mourning and would be terribly hurt by such despicable falsehoods."

"I will do that, Sebastian," Raven said.

He stepped into the hall with her, and she was gone.

For an eternity, he was frozen in his spot, listening to be certain she'd departed, then he went to the sideboard and gulped down another brandy.

"Bastard children indeed," he muttered to the empty room.

Then he headed out to join the party.

CHAPTER

3

"Did you like him?"

"Not really. He was pompous and absurd."

Sarah was talking about Sebastian Sinclair, and she flashed a wan smile at Noah and Pet.

She wished she was the sort of person who could lie with a straight face, but in light of the type of children she raised, she'd never seen a reason to prevaricate. It was important for them to know the truth about their various circumstances.

They were standing outside the orphanage, having just returned from running errands. There was as yet no chain on the door to keep them out, which had her shuddering with relief.

She wanted to believe—when the sale was final—she would be given a chance to remove her things, but her brother-in-law, Cuthbert Maudsen, was the fiend who'd sold the building, and he was a scurrilous villain. Merely out of spite, he might not let her retrieve her belongings.

"So we won't get to meet him?" Noah asked about Mr. Sinclair.

"I don't think so," Sarah told them. "I invited him to stop by, but he refused."

Petunia was always a budding optimist. "He could change his mind though, couldn't he? I would definitely like to meet *him*. It would be grand to have another brother."

Noah grinned at her. "One isn't enough for you?"

"One is very nice, but one *more* would be even better."

"We have another sister too," Noah said. "I wonder what she's like. Do you suppose she's as annoying as you are?"

Pet replied with, "She's likely pretty and kind as a princess."

Sarah had been so busy fretting over Mr. Sinclair that she'd forgotten about his younger sister, Ophelia. She was twenty-two and unmarried and still residing at home with her mother. She was another famous Sinclair who couldn't walk down the street or wear a new gown without the newspapers writing about her.

How would Miss Sinclair view the situation? It would require her to accept a negative fact about her precious father. If Sarah didn't make any headway with Mr. Sinclair, dare she seek out Miss Sinclair instead?

If she tried, she was sure Sebastian Sinclair would wring her neck.

Sarah was awash with worry. Noah and Pet were marvelous children: smart, polite, funny, considerate, generous, and selfless. Though they had different mothers, it was obvious they were siblings. With their golden blond hair, big blue eyes, slender frames, and confident demeanors, they were perfect little Sinclairs.

She recognized how hard it was for Mr. Sinclair to admit Sir Sidney had had character flaws. She could only hope, after some reflection, he'd calm down and contact her so they could have a sane discussion.

She'd like to keep Noah and Pet with her, to rear them herself, but she had no idea how she could. Yet the thought of separating from them was painful. She'd grown up at the orphanage, having been left on the stoop at age three, and ultimately, she'd been adopted by the Robertsons. Her mother, Ruth, had died when she was an adolescent, and she'd started managing the facility for her father, Thomas, when she was seventeen.

She was now a very elderly twenty-seven, her parents deceased, and her sole kin her awful sister, Temperance, with whom Sarah constantly bickered over their father's estate. Sarah had never lived on her own and couldn't envision what it would be like.

She was terribly afraid, should she find a place for Noah and Pet—her last wards—she might become invisible and simply float off into the sky.

"Might you approach Miss Sinclair about us?" Noah was speculating, as Sarah had, that Miss Sinclair might provide a path to assistance.

"I haven't decided," Sarah said.

"I think she'd like us."

"She might, but we can't be certain. Rich people can be very odd, and the Sinclairs have such a high opinion of Sir Sidney. It upsets them when bad stories spread."

"Everyone has a high opinion of my father." Noah nodded firmly. "It's well deserved too."

"Yes, it is," Sarah agreed, not meaning it, "but your half-siblings don't like to hear that he misbehaved with your mothers. It's distressing for them."

"If you arrange an audience with Miss Sinclair," Noah asked, "could we accompany you? I could speak for Pet and myself. Would it help?"

"I can't imagine it, Noah."

The entire debacle was so crushing that, suddenly, she felt as if she might burst into tears.

Her father—poor Thomas Robertson—had devoted himself to the orphanage. He'd spent his inheritance and had worked himself into an early grave in order to aid the children of strangers.

He'd been such a sweet, charitable man. How would he view what was transpiring? No doubt he'd be devastated.

He and Ruth had adopted Sarah when she was tiny, then, two years later, Ruth had birthed Temperance. She'd been born difficult and unhappy, and she'd hated the lowly existence their parents had offered.

When Thomas could no longer abide her tantrums, he'd sent her to live with his wealthy, pretentious mother. She'd coddled Temperance, and when she'd passed away, she'd bequeathed her house and a small trust fund to Temperance, so she'd wound up as a bit of an heiress.

Sarah had never been jealous about it. The woman was Temperance's grandmother, not Sarah's, and Sarah had been content with the life the Robertsons had bestowed. In contrast, Temperance was never satisfied with any situation and always protested that she wasn't receiving her share of what was owed.

At eighteen, she'd met Cuthbert Maudsen, a handsome gambler and wastrel, and she'd been determined to marry him. Their father had tried to dissuade her, so she'd gone to her grandmother and had convinced her to sign all the appropriate documents.

Temperance and Cuthbert had now been wed for seven years, and he was just as irresponsible and dodgy as their father had feared. Temperance's dowry was squandered, their home mortgaged to the hilt, and Cuthbert barely able to keep creditors from hauling him off to debtor's prison.

As Thomas's health had declined, his mental acuity had deteriorated, and Temperance had slyly persuaded him to change his Will, to leave his estate to Cuthbert—the *man* of the family—and Thomas had proceeded without Sarah knowing.

To her great astonishment and disgust, Cuthbert had ended up owning her building and, as his fiscal woes had worsened, he'd sold it. She hadn't found out what was occurring until a huge *For Sale* sign had been hung on the front door.

She'd beseeched Temperance not to allow it. She'd pleaded with Cuthbert not to do it. But Temperance would never defy her husband, and Cuthbert was desperate.

His cruel act—and Temperance's refusal to intervene—had been the final nail in the coffin of Sarah's relationship with her sister. Despite Sarah's repeated efforts to understand and tolerate Temperance, they'd arrived at a conclusion that was unforgiveable.

"Are you sad today?"

Pet's question interrupted Sarah's pathetic reverie.

"A little," she admitted, and Pet slipped her hand into Sarah's and squeezed it.

"It will all turn out for the best," Pet said. "You'll see."

"I hope so."

Noah added, "I won't let anything bad happen to you or Pet. I swear it."

Sarah smiled at him. "You're a good boy, Noah."

"Of course I am. I am Sir Sidney's son, and he was a hero. How could I not be one too?"

"You could practice some humility once in awhile. It wouldn't kill you."

"When I'm so wonderful, why be humble? What would be the point?"

Sarah chuckled and reminded herself to count her blessings, to stop flogging herself over what she couldn't fix or alter.

She opened her reticule and handed them each a penny.

"Buy yourself a candy," she said.

Noah frowned. "Are you sure we should? Can we afford it?"

"Two pennies won't make any difference." She gestured down the street. "Have some fun."

"We will, so long as you promise you won't sit in your apartment moping."

"I won't mope." But she probably would.

"Why don't you come with us?" Pet asked.

"I have some letters to write," Sarah lied, and she waved them away.

They hesitated and debated, but the pennies were too tempting. Ultimately, they skipped off, but they glanced back over and over, their concern for her extreme.

She'd been candid with them about their dilemma, but she'd framed her remarks in a positive way, insisting they'd be fine. She doubted it though. With each passing day, she grew more anxious, and as she entered the building, she decided she had to call on her friend, Nell Drummond.

She hadn't seen her in weeks, not since Nell had traveled to the country for a wedding. She had to be back in London by now, and while she wouldn't be able to supply any financial assistance, she'd definitely commiserate. She might even have some ideas that hadn't occurred to Sarah.

So far, she hadn't told anyone of the perfidy being pursued by her sister. Who could bear to confess it? But she had to cease her pretending, had to beg for help from those who could provide it. The problem was that she knew very few people who had the means to furnish much more than verbal advice.

She walked through the common room and up the stairs to her apartment at the end of the hall. She removed her bonnet and was hanging it on a hook, when suddenly, a man said, "It's about time you arrived. Where have you been?"

She jumped a foot and whirled around and there, on her dilapidated sofa, was the grand and glorious Mr. Sebastian Sinclair.

"Why are you in here?" she demanded.

"You ought to keep your doors locked," was his reply. "Otherwise, there's no telling who might wander in."

"Isn't that the truth?" she muttered.

As her pulse slowed to a manageable level, she had to tamp down a spurt of excitement. What could he want? What might he do? What might *she* convince him to do?

It had been three days since she'd visited him at Hero's Haven. While he was a blowhard and ingrate, he wasn't a dunce or a fool. She'd been mildly certain he'd seek her out—if only so he could yell at her again.

He was like a curious cat, and he'd pull and pull at the string of yarn she'd dangled in front of him until he was aggravated beyond his limit. He'd be determined to learn more about Noah and Pet. He'd chastise and blame Sarah for creating a situation he couldn't abide.

Well, he could complain incessantly, but so long as they were talking, there was a chance to push him into better behavior.

"Noah and Petunia just left to buy a candy," she said. "You missed them."

"I'm not here to see any of your stupid urchins."

"They're not stupid, they're not urchins, and they're your half-siblings. Don't be surly or you can leave."

She turned to hang her cloak on the hook too, and she was very deliberate about it, eager for him to realize that she wasn't impressed by him.

The reality was though that she'd been thinking about him constantly. He was very handsome, and with him being so famous, it had been riveting to meet him.

Her world was very small, filled with children who needed her. It was a rare moment when she crossed paths with a rogue or a scoundrel or a hero. She'd been overwhelmed by the encounter, wishing she'd have an opportunity to parlay with him again and wishing it would happen sooner rather than later.

The stories about his father read like tales out of an adventure novel. What must it have been like to be raised by him? What must it have been like to travel the globe with him? He'd been brutally murdered. Had Mr. Sinclair witnessed the hideous scene? How awful for him if he had. Who could ever recover from such a terrible sight?

She wondered what he'd do with himself now that his father had passed away, and she suspected he was vexed by that very same question. Clearly, he drank too much and was reveling to excess, and she figured it was simply him grieving.

Her own father had been dead for three years, and it seemed as if it had just transpired. From bitter experience, she'd found out that some wounds were very slow to heal.

"This apartment is my private home," she said as she spun to face him, "yet you felt free to bluster in. Tell me why I shouldn't be incensed."

He snorted with disgust. "I told you that you should lock your doors."

"Yes, but most people in this neighborhood are too polite to barge in where they're not welcome."

"I'm welcome," he absurdly claimed. "When you were at Hero's Haven, you specifically informed me to stop by whenever it was convenient."

"I stand corrected, but it still doesn't explain why you're sitting on my sofa."

"I've come to hear your price. I've been waiting to be apprised."

"Ah, yes, my price. I have a very high amount in mind."

"I'm glad you've pondered it. Raven thought you'd be difficult about reaching a deal, but I insisted you'd be sensible."

"Shall I make us some tea?"

"Gad, no. I hate tea."

"You hate tea? No one hates tea. It's very unBritish of you."

"Have you any whiskey?"

She had an old bottle stashed in a cupboard, but she wouldn't offer any of it to him. It was obvious he didn't need it.

"No, I don't have any whiskey—or any other alcoholic beverages—and if you're desperate to imbibe in the middle of the afternoon, you really ought to assess your condition."

"Thank you for the advice, Miss Robertson. I'm so delighted to be lectured by you."

She went to the stove and lit it, anxious to boil some water. She wasn't too enthused about having tea either, but she was disconcerted by his arrival, and she couldn't deduce how to act around him.

He was a very manly man, and he exuded a strength and vigor that were disturbing. It was a small room, and he took up too much space in it.

"What forced you to drag yourself to my paltry street?" she asked merely to fill the void. "Was it my stunning personality?"

"You're an intriguing woman, Miss Robertson."

"So I've been told."

"I didn't mean it as a compliment."

"It was an insult?"

He scowled. "Yes, I guess it was. You're bossy and annoying. You never listen, and you push yourself in where you're not wanted."

"Sort of like you."

"Yes, but I'm a man so I'm allowed to behave this way."

"And *I* am just a lowly female, a wilting flower who can barely walk through the world on her own."

She held a mocking hand to her forehead, as if she was about to swoon, and he chuckled.

"You still haven't stated your price," he said.

"You are so irritating. You saw the sign out front. This place is an orphanage. I'm not scheming on you. I'm trying to help you."

She'd never been domestically inclined, and she gave up on the fire. She couldn't get it going. Previously, she'd had several servants to take care of her, but she'd had to terminate everybody.

She came over to the sofa where he was hogging the entire piece of furniture, but then, he was so big. She sat down too, but ended up much too close to him. Their thighs, calves, and feet were forged fast, and it was immediately evident that she should have chosen a chair over at the dining table, but now that she'd picked her spot, she wasn't about to move.

He'd recognize how he overwhelmed her, and he'd gloat. She wasn't about to have him gloat.

He shifted toward her and asked, "You're trying to *help* me?"

"Yes. You need to make arrangements for your half-siblings, and I'm willing to assist you as you work out a viable solution for them."

He studied the room, the tattered curtains, the worn rugs, the threadbare décor.

Her father had been born into the gentry, and he'd used an inheritance to start the orphanage. He'd simply been kind and generous—a true Christian—who'd felt a strong duty to the less fortunate. His interest was based on a personal experience.

As a young man, he'd had a cousin who'd been seduced by a scoundrel. She'd birthed a bastard daughter, then passed away shortly after. No one had ever been able to verify what had happened to her baby, and the calamity had haunted him. He'd been determined that no unloved child would ever vanish as hers had vanished.

His benevolent leanings had left him estranged from his family who'd thought he'd tipped off his rocker. On originally purchasing the building, he'd filled it with his expensive belongings. Over the years, his possessions had begun to age, but he'd never spent money on new things. He'd spent it all on his orphans. In that, he'd been an absolute saint.

Sarah had never been rich, but she'd always had plenty. Yet her home was a pitiful sight, and with her having just visited the very opulent Hero's Haven, she realized that her own lodging would seem pathetic to Mr. Sinclair. But she wasn't offended to have him judging her.

After they died and went to Heaven, when they stood at the Pearly Gates and asked to be admitted, she'd hold up her good deeds against his any day of the week.

"You're a pauper." There was denigration in his tone.

"Well, of course I'm a pauper. I run a charity that's supported with donations."

"When you aid the poor, it simply encourages them in their poverty."

"Oh, be silent. Who told you such a miserable falsehood? Your vicar? Your wealthy mother? Don't spew your ill-informed, pious drivel at me."

"You are so sassy," he complained. "I was just *saying* that some people think the downtrodden are a burden and ought to tend themselves."

"*I* am not one of them, and I won't debate the issue with you. We should discuss Noah and Petunia."

"I'm not here to talk about them."

"Then why are you here? Is it merely to poke fun at my deplorable situation? If so, I wish you'd leave. I don't have the patience for your nonsense."

"Do you know who I am?"

She rolled her eyes. "Who doesn't know?"

"I am Sebastian Sinclair, hero of the nation, but you're not impressed by that fact. Why is that exactly?"

He was appraising her so earnestly, as if he truly couldn't comprehend her opinion and was eager to have her explain.

"Have you been drinking, Mr. Sinclair?"

"Yes, but apparently, I hadn't imbibed enough to keep me from coming over here."

For an instant, his pompous mask fell away, and he looked despondent and weary. She was surer than ever that he was grieving his father's death. The man had been his parent, mentor, and idol, and he'd been viciously murdered. That type of catastrophe would rattle any son, so perhaps she shouldn't be quite so vexed with him.

She rescued strays and lost souls and tried to find the value in everyone, no matter how wretched. Her father had taught her to live that way. Was it possible Mr. Sinclair could use some of her kind concern? Did he deserve it?

Probably not, but she'd provide some of it anyway.

"Why are you so sad, Mr. Sinclair?"

He frowned as if it was a bizarre question. "I'm not sad."

"I can see it in your eyes. Are you mourning your father? Is that it?"

He stared, but didn't reply. He was vain and proud, and he'd never confess a weakness. He'd view a bit of melancholia to be a failing.

They were sitting very close, and it was a potent moment, a stirring moment, where he might have uttered any profound comment. But when he finally spoke, he said, "Why is it so quiet and empty in here? Why isn't it bustling with activity?"

"I mentioned it at Hero's Haven. The building has been sold, and I've been busy, hunting for other accommodations for my orphans. Noah and Pet are the only ones left."

"Will you start another facility somewhere else?"

"I don't have the funds."

"How did you manage to open this one?"

"My father had an inheritance, but . . . ah . . . we didn't own the property."

She was desperate to confide how her brother-in-law, Cuthbert, had been keen to square some gambling debts, but it was too humiliating to admit that her sister would spit on their father's legacy in such a terrible manner. And if she *did* ever talk about it, she wouldn't explain it to a rich, snobbish hero's son who could never understand the burdens under which she labored.

"How many children were you housing?"

"Last month, we had two dozen. I contacted your mother about Noah and Pet, but—"

He lurched as if she'd poked him with a pin. "Don't drag my mother into it."

"She wouldn't meet with me, so I decided to pester you instead. Am I having any success?"

He scrutinized her, his glorious blue eyes digging deep, as if he was delving down to her essence to figure out what made her tick.

It wasn't difficult to discern. She was a simple woman, with simple tastes and simple needs, who struggled to be the best person she could be. In that, she constantly, humbly honored her father.

It seemed as if another profound comment was just around the corner from him, but evidently, his role in her life would be to ceaselessly disappoint her.

"You're very pretty," he said, almost in accusation.

"Thank you, I guess."

"Your hair is the most peculiar color. It's not blond. It's so white it's nearly silver."

"It can look that way sometimes."

"Who did you inherit it from? Your mother?"

"I didn't know my mother."

He scowled, his mind working it out. "You're an orphan too?"

"Yes, I was abandoned on the steps when I was three."

"By who?"

"I have no idea, but the Robertsons took me in." Sarcastically, she added, "I was so charming that they eventually adopted me."

"You? Charming?" He snickered. "I find that very hard to believe."

She never revealed her odd beginnings, and she'd lied to him when she'd claimed she wasn't sure who'd deposited her on the stoop, then raced away. Her birth father had been an aristocrat, Viscount Matthew Blake, and she had no doubt that someone from the Blake family had delivered her to the Robertsons.

Whoever it had been, they'd included her birth certificate, and no stranger would have had it in his possession. Apparently, she'd lived somewhere until she was three, then her Blake relatives had put her in an orphanage.

She had a few vague memories of that period when she'd been so small. Occasionally at night, when she was falling asleep, she would concentrate and dredge up old recollections. She thought she'd been happy. She thought she'd resided in a happy home.

And though it was very weird, there were always fleeting glimpses of another little girl who looked exactly like her and who she assumed was her guardian angel.

She wouldn't tell him any of that though, and she was surprised she'd admitted to being an orphan. People weren't aware that Thomas and Ruth Robertson had adopted her, and she never corrected any misconceptions. By every standard that mattered, they *were* her parents.

"Where were you the first three years of your life?" he asked.

"I have no idea about that either."

He studied her, then smirked. "You're lying."

"Maybe, but about what facts?"

"You're too impertinent. I don't like that in a female."

"I'm impertinent *and* bossy, so I'm brimming with traits for you to loath."

"Are you ever respectful of any man?"

"No, never. I've generally found them to be completely absurd."

"You've never learned your place."

"I've learned it, but I've never chosen to stay in it. Why should I? It's not as if the world will stop spinning if I'm too bold."

"That's a very dangerous attitude for a woman to hold. If all of you felt that way, it might send the entire planet rolling off its axis."

"I'll have to hope not."

Suddenly, he reached out and clasped a strand of her hair, and he wrapped it around his finger and used it as a lever to draw her to him so he could inspect it more closely. At the brazen gesture, she was absolutely transfixed. What was his intent?

Just when she decided he'd do something outrageous—kiss her? shake her?—he released the strand and eased back.

"I need to be going," he abruptly said. "How much money will you require to be silent?"

"I don't want any money. I simply want Noah and Pet to be safe after we leave here. It's vexing me."

"Where will you be once you're forced out?"

"I can't imagine."

"Aren't you worried?"

"Yes, I'm terrified."

"There's an inquest coming—about my father's death in Africa."

"Yes, your chum, Mr. Shawcross, told me about it."

"My family will be in the newspapers. There will be stories and articles and retrospectives. An enormous amount of attention will be focused on us, so I can't have you flaunting your bastards around the city. How can I get you to promise you won't?"

"Flaunting them! I never would! How dare you accuse me of bad conduct!"

"I will not have my father's reputation besmirched by you. Not now. Not after so much has happened."

"I understand."

"You couldn't possibly, Miss Robertson."

"Could you give me peace of mind with regard to their situation? Is there a cottage on one of your estates where they could live? The three of us could retire there, and I'd take care of them for you. We wouldn't be a bother. You wouldn't even know we were present."

"Trust me, *I* would know."

"If they wind up on the streets, will you be content with that ending?"

He leaned in so they were nose to nose. "I don't believe they're my father's children, so *no*, I'm not concerned about you or two children I've never even met."

It was a cold, cruel remark, and she was very hurt by it. It was rare for a person to be overtly horrid to her—other than Cuthbert or Temperance. Evidently, she'd had some silly, deep-seated wish that he would *like* her, that perhaps they would turn out to be friends.

She was such a fool.

He seemed startled by his remark as well, and his cheeks flushed with chagrin. "I was a tad harsh just then."

"I suppose I'll survive."

"I've been under a lot of pressure lately."

It was quite an admission for him, and she accepted it as an olive branch. She flashed a tepid smile. "You're forgiven."

He pulled away and stood, and he stared down at her, appearing stern and exasperated. "Don't contact my mother again, and please don't contact me. We can't help you. We *won't* help you."

He might have stomped out, but before he could, footsteps pounded up the stairs. Noah and Petunia burst into the room, Noah leading the way.

Prior to his living with Sarah, he hadn't been aware of Petunia's existence, but he was a wonderful, loyal boy. He'd instantly bonded with her, promising Sarah he would always be Pet's most steadfast champion. Sarah couldn't guess what would become of them in the future, but she had no doubt Noah would watch over his sister.

Mr. Sinclair whipped around and glared at them, and as Sarah rose to her feet, she peeked at his expression. He couldn't *not* know who they were, couldn't deny his connection to them. They looked like . . . well . . . his siblings.

He was dumbfounded and alarmed.

Noah immediately noticed Mr. Sinclair, and he staggered to a halt. Pet sidled over to him and slipped her hand into his. The three of them studied each other, their identical brows furrowing, their identical blue eyes searching.

"Noah, Petunia," Sarah calmly said, "this is Mr. Sinclair. This is your brother."

Mr. Sinclair blanched as if she'd struck him, and of course, he disappointed her yet again.

"Good day, Miss Robertson," he said to her. To the children, he spoke not a word.

He simply marched by them as if they were invisible. They listened as his booted strides faded down the hall. Shortly, the front door opened and closed.

Sarah sighed with regret and sank down onto the sofa.

"Shall we chase after him?" Noah asked. "Shall we try to talk to him before he leaves?"

"There's no need to talk to him, Noah. No need at all."

CHAPTER

4

"When will the inquest be held?"

"Two weeks from today."

Gertrude Sinclair stared at her son, Sebastian, and firmly nodded. It would be a relief to have the event finished once and for all.

"I trust you're ready with your testimony?" she asked him.

"Yes, we're all prepared."

"And Nathan?"

He shrugged. "I guess I'll have to try to talk to him again."

She wasn't certain what had happened in Africa to have resulted in her husband's murder, and she'd posed only the most banal questions about the incident. On some issues regarding Sir Sidney, it wasn't wise to seek too much information. She'd learned that lesson as a very young bride, when she'd been naïve about the ways of the world and where a wife was positioned in it.

Sir Sidney had been a handsome, dashing rogue, and with her large dowry, she'd snagged him for her husband. At the time, it had seemed like the grandest stroke of luck ever, but as the years had dragged by, as he'd grown richer and more famous, his flagrant character flaws had become more pronounced.

She'd spent quite a bit of her life ignoring his worst inclinations, tamping down rumors, and generally pretending he was a completely different man from the one he actually was.

He hadn't simply *died* in Africa. His body had been hacked to pieces in a violent melee. Sebastian's best and dearest friend, Nathan Blake, Lord Selby—who'd been like a second son to Sir Sidney—had been hacked at too and left for dead.

Somehow though, he'd survived and had staggered back to England on his own. When Sebastian had called on him earlier in the summer, they'd fought viciously, with the Africa debacle at the root of their squabble. Sebastian had come home bloody and pummeled.

During the altercation, Nathan had threatened to kill Sebastian, so obviously, there was a terrible secret at the heart of her husband's demise. The nosy idiots at the National Exploration Society were determined to pry the lid off the fiasco and, without her having to put her foot down, Sebastian understood that they couldn't be allowed to unravel the truth.

Sir Sidney's reputation was paramount, and at all costs, they had to protect it.

"Nathan will not betray Sir Sidney," she insisted, with a tad more confidence than was warranted.

"I hope not."

"Should *I* talk to him instead? He's furious with you, but not with me. I might have more success. I could remind him of how much he loved Sir Sidney."

"You needn't bother, Mother. I can square things with him. He's angry with me—for good reason—but I expect his temper will have calmed."

Sebastian was no more confident than she was about Nathan's appearance at the inquest. But she wasn't about to leave any detail to chance.

While she'd loathed her husband, she was enjoying her role as grieving widow. It made her a national icon in her own right, and she wouldn't have that lofty status jeopardized.

"You'll need to ride to Selby this week then," she said. "You have to find out what his testimony will be. You can't assume he'll behave as you wish. You're aware of what he's like."

"It will be fine. As you mentioned, he loved Sir Sidney. He would never imperil Father's legacy."

"I shall tell myself you're correct."

They were in her London house, having tea in the parlor. She'd been out running errands, and just as she'd returned, Sebastian had popped in without warning, which was pleasant. For the most part, he was a dutiful son, possessed of all his father's stellar traits, but few of his revolting ones. She was always glad to see him.

He was staying at their country estate, Hero's Haven, and it was his now that he'd inherited. The men of Sir Sidney's expedition team were all staying there too, and they were engaged in an unending bacchanal. But he was thirty—an adult male with his own fortune—and it probably wasn't any of her business if he was hosting an orgy.

Generally, she never went to the Haven. Over the years, Sir Sidney had used it as his den of iniquity, so she'd been happy to avoid it. As with so many issues surrounding her husband, it was better not to delve into his leisure activities. It was her habit to tarry in London, and it was more convenient for her socializing anyway.

"May I ask you a question?" Sebastian said.

"Certainly."

"Have you ever heard any stories about Father and perhaps . . . ah . . ."

His voice trailed off. They never discussed Sir Sidney in any genuine fashion. Their remarks floated on the surface where they were safest. Why dig into a hole that should remain filled?

He walked over to the sideboard to splash whiskey into his tea. He was very blatant about it.

"You're drinking too much," she complained, before she could bite her tongue.

"Yes, I am, but I'm still rattled by the catastrophe. It will pass." He toasted her with his cup. "It already is. I'm improving by the day."

She studied him, thinking he didn't look as if he'd *improved*. He looked sad and beaten down from his mourning Sir Sidney's death. Despite Sir Sidney being a failure as a husband, he'd been a wonderful father. It would be difficult for her son to move beyond such a gripping loss.

She wasn't the most maternal person though, so she had no idea how to comfort him. Nor would she toss out clichés. She shifted the conversation to more mundane topics.

"We shouldn't give credence to any *stories* swirling about your father," she said. "The lower classes like to gossip. Let's not join in."

"It's just that . . . well . . . occasionally, powerful men have secrets."

"Yes, they do, and Sir Sidney had many of them. Don't pretend to be surprised."

"Rich men have affairs. They have mistresses and sire illicit children."

For a moment, her pulse raced. She realized what he was suggesting, and her stern glare advised him to drop it. She would *not* parlay over Sir Sidney's penchant for trollops. He'd been content to dally with any tart—mostly actresses and opera dancers—who'd evinced the slightest interest.

None of it was a mystery to her. As the wife of the wealthy, notorious hero, she'd had many envious acquaintances. They'd all taken great delight in ensuring she was apprised of all the sordid rumors, but through every horrid fling—whether fleeting or lengthy—she'd insisted they weren't occurring.

Of course she hadn't *always* been able to wear blinders. Sir Sidney had spent most of their marriage out of the country, flitting home for brief respites, then flitting off again the minute his wanderlust struck. *She* had been forced to clean up his messes.

She'd paid for funerals of slatterns who had died birthing his bastards. She'd forked over money to women he'd left in the lurch. She'd succumbed to blackmail to silence harlots. And that didn't begin to describe the urchins who'd been brought to her door by idiotic guardians, vicars, or orphanage owners who'd presumed she would be thrilled to welcome them.

She had a method for dealing with his natural children. A clandestine associate sold them into indenture for her, so they were placed in service and whisked out of the country. It was a quiet and swift system guaranteed to hide a scandal, and while some people might have judged such conduct to be heartless and cruel, she declined to see it that way.

She wasn't about to support his bastards, but they couldn't be permitted to starve on the streets. *That* would be cruel. She helped them by sending them off to learn a trade and start a new life. It was the perfect ending for all concerned, and she never regretted the role she played in it.

"I'm too bereft to keep talking about your father," she blandly said. "I'd like to address a happier subject."

"Is there a happier subject these days?"

"Yes. I've invited Veronica to stay with me."

Their cousin, Veronica, was the bride Gertrude had picked for him, and he scowled. "I wish you'd asked me first."

"Why would I? You'd have simply refused my request."

"I'm not ready to think about matrimony. I *can't* think about it right now."

"No bachelor is ever ready."

"With the inquest approaching, I won't have time to dance attendance on her."

"She recognizes that you're busy, but after the inquest is over, I will expect that situation to change. We have to proceed to a betrothal."

Although he'd never been officially promised to Veronica, the family had an understanding about it. Veronica was twenty, and she had been waiting for four years for him to propose. She and her mother were beginning to protest the delay.

They were worried Veronica would become a spinster, and it was a conclusion Gertrude would never tolerate. Too much freedom put a fellow on a bad path, and Sebastian had to wed. He shouldn't continue to wallow in sin.

"Could we discuss this later?" He sounded irked.

"We don't have to discuss it at all. I merely need your assurance that we will get this arranged."

She'd aggravated him, and he downed his beverage and headed for the door.

"I have to be going," he said. "I have chores at home."

"After you visit Nathan, please stop by to confirm that his testimony is settled."

"I will."

He stomped out, and she sighed with exasperation.

He had no secrets from her. He was grieving—and drinking heavily in order to smooth over his woe. She despised weakness in a man. For goodness sake, he was Sir Sidney's son. He had to buck up and act the part.

———— ❦ ————

"I'M SO GLAD YOU'RE here!"

"I doubted your mother would ever invite me."

Ophelia smiled at Veronica. They were cousins, but old friends too, having been students at the same boarding school when they were girls. She was twenty-two and Veronica was twenty, both of them on the verge of being declared spinsters. Ophelia was unmarried by choice, but for Veronica, it was due to Sebastian's dithering.

In the past, Ophelia had had numerous swains, but she hadn't been interested in romance. She liked her status as Sir Sidney's daughter, and if she shackled herself to a husband, she'd become a boring, ordinary wife.

She also truly believed—if she remained single—she would eventually be allowed to accompany her father and brother on an expedition.

A husband wouldn't permit it. He'd demand she dawdle at home and knit by the fire, but she was possessed of all her brother's wanderlust. She couldn't imagine wiling away the decades in London when she ought to have been adventuring with the men in her family.

Her brother had initially joined their father when he was ten, and he was famous and acclaimed because of it. Why shouldn't Ophelia be granted the same chance? Why should her being a female matter?

Sir Sidney had never viewed it that way. She'd once broached the topic with him, and he'd nearly had an apoplexy. He was dead though, so he wasn't around to prevent it, and the minute she could, she would speak to Sebastian. She was positive he'd agree to let her tag along on his next trip.

"How is Sebastian?" Veronica asked.

"He's been tucked away at Hero's Haven. The inquest is coming, so he's been preparing for it."

"Will there be questions raised?" There was unease in Veronica's tone.

"Well, it *is* an inquest, so there will be all sorts of questions raised, but he wants to fully address everyone's concerns."

She stated the remark confidently, but she wasn't completely sure of what had transpired in Africa. The servants were whispering that there were issues surrounding the calamity that couldn't be mentioned aloud. What might they be?

Ophelia had hardly known her father. He'd traveled constantly, so he'd rarely been in England, and when he had been, she'd usually been at school. She was a lowly daughter, so she'd never been summoned to see him. Their sporadic encounters had occurred when she was home and he happened to be there too.

But still, he was her *father*, and she would hate for gossip to waft out. Not that there would be a reason for it to spread. In her eyes, he'd been perfect.

They were upstairs in a guestroom in her mother's London house, with Veronica having just arrived from the country. Ophelia had been instrumental in convincing Gertrude that Veronica needed to be in London. It was a terrible situation for a girl to be out of sight and out of mind. When Sebastian never socialized with her, he likely never thought about her.

Veronica had to be pushed into his path on every occasion they could manage.

Ultimately, Veronica would move from being her cousin to being her sister, and she couldn't wait for the wedding. She was the shining star that would bring it all to fruition and make her dear friend and wonderful brother happy forever.

"Shall we go down and say hello to Mother?" she asked. "She must have returned from her errands."

"I'm too tired from my journey. May I have an hour to freshen up?"

"Certainly."

Ophelia sauntered out, leaving Veronica to her servants and the unpacking of her trunks. From her huge pile of luggage, it was obvious she wasn't planning to depart London anytime soon.

Ophelia wandered through the large mansion. Typically, the halls were quiet, and she was used to it, but recently, all that silence had begun to grate. She kept telling herself it was due to her advanced age of twenty-two, as well as the fact that she hadn't wed as was the appropriate ending for a female.

She'd chosen to stay with her mother, fervidly and pointlessly hoping an exciting event would arise, but nothing ever did.

She reached the foyer, and her mother was in the receiving parlor, chatting with someone. When she recognized it to be Sebastian, she grinned. She hadn't realized he was in town. She nearly rushed into the room, but she was halted by the serious tone in his voice.

Have you ever heard any stories about Father and . . . perhaps . . . ah . . .

Her mother cut him off, her tone just as serious. *We shouldn't give credence to any stories swirling about your father. The lower classes like to gossip. Let's not join in.*

Then Sebastian added the most vexing comment ever. *Rich men have affairs. They have mistresses and sire illicit children.*

Ophelia felt as if her heart might quit beating. She skittered away in the opposite direction, and she hurried down the hall to an empty salon where she could hide and compose herself.

What had Sebastian meant? Clearly, he was hinting at reprehensible conduct by Sir Sidney, and at the prospect, she was absolutely aghast. Sir Sidney was proclaimed across the land as the epitome of British values and morals. He was considered a beacon of honor, decency, and all that was good in the world.

What if he wasn't? Should she have questioned a few details? Should she have been a tad less naïve?

Shortly, Sebastian exited the parlor and left the house. She hovered, wondering if she should chase after him, or if she should let him flee in peace, but she couldn't imagine doing that.

She had minimal opportunities to ever speak to him, and with his locking himself away at Hero's Haven, and his unruly crew being in residence, the intervals where she saw him were so infrequent as to be nonexistent.

Who could predict when he'd stop by again?

Besides, she had to ask him about the morning papers. If he'd been riding into town, she didn't suppose he'd have been apprised of the latest news.

She hastened down the hall and outside, catching him as he was about to climb into his carriage.

She waved and called out, "Brother! Hello!"

He turned toward her and smiled. He was so handsome, like a Greek god painted in a mural, and he was courteous to her in a way her father had never been.

She walked over to him. "You rat! How could you visit Mother, but completely ignore me in the process?"

"I just flitted in for a minute. I have to get going." He gestured to the vehicle, as if she hadn't noticed his driver was in the box or his servant was holding the door. "Did you need something?"

"Have you read the morning paper?"

"No. I'm not in the habit of reading it. You know that."

She didn't actually, but she didn't say so. She knew so little about him! "So you haven't heard."

"Heard what?"

"Nathan has married."

Her brother flinched as if she'd punched him. "He what?"

"There was an announcement. He was wed a couple of weeks ago—by Special License at Selby."

"To who?"

"Miss Nell Drummond? I have no idea who she is. How about you?"

"No." He frowned. "You're sure about this?"

"Yes, but I can show it to you if you'd like."

"I'm not doubting you. I'm just . . . shocked."

"And hurt too?"

"Yes, hurt. I admit it."

"He's always been selfish. I'm not surprised he'd treat you so badly, but he should be ashamed of himself."

"Yes, shame on him."

"I'm sorry," she said.

"Why would you be sorry?"

"I can't guess what happened between the two of you, and I won't inquire, but he should have told you about his wedding. You should have stood up with him at the ceremony. At the very least you should have been invited. It's cruel of him that you weren't."

"I agree." He stared off to the horizon, as if he could see Selby from where they were standing. "He's changed since we were in Africa. Maybe we're not friends anymore. Maybe I should get over it."

"Of course you're friends," she staunchly declared. "You always will be. You'll eventually fix what's wrong."

He snorted. "Some quarrels are too difficult to mend."

"Not this one. I'm certain of it."

"You're an optimist."

She pointed to the house. "Veronica has arrived. Would you like to come in for a bit?"

If she hadn't been watching him so closely, she wouldn't have noted the grimace of distaste that crossed his features. What did it indicate? Didn't he like Veronica? She refused to accept that could be it.

Veronica was the prettiest, most elegant girl in the kingdom, and she would soon be his wife. He had to *like* her. He was probably just irked over being delayed.

"I don't have time to chat with her," he claimed.

"I understand." Normally, she wouldn't have pestered him further, but she was feeling confounded by many issues. Dare she proceed?

"Could I talk to you about another matter?" she said.

"If you can promise to hurry. It likely seems as if I'm ignoring you, but I really am busy."

"It's rather . . . ah . . . private. Could we discuss it in the carriage?"

"Yes." He helped her in, then climbed in after her and shut the door. Once they were sequestered, he said, "What is it? Please assure me it's nothing horrid. I'm so overwhelmed these days that I can hardly think straight."

"It's not horrid. No, I take that back. I don't know if it's horrid or not. It's just that I heard you with Mother. I didn't intend to eavesdrop, but I walked up to the parlor as you mentioned Father."

"Oh."

"I was curious about your comments."

"Yes . . . ?" he pressed when she didn't continue.

Gad, it was so embarrassing to spit it out! She leaned nearer and lowered her voice. "Did Father have a mistress? Did he have other . . . other . . . *children* besides us?"

Sebastian studied her forever, then asked, "How old are you?"

"Twenty-two."

"Then you're no longer fresh out of the schoolroom, so I'll answer you as if you're an adult who can bear the truth."

"Just tell me. I'm always kept in the dark."

"Father wasn't the man you assumed him to be."

"Meaning what?"

"Meaning he had affairs, and yes, he had other children."

She gasped. "How many?"

"Two that I'm aware of."

"Two! How many might there be?"

"I couldn't guess."

"Where are the two you're aware of?"

"Here in London."

"Have you met them?"

"Yes."

"What are their names?"

"Noah and Petunia, and she's called Pet for short. He's twelve and she's six."

"My goodness. Does Mother know?"

"I'm betting she does. I doubt she could have been married to Father for so many years without having a clue as to his penchant for vice and fast living."

"When you traveled with him, you witnessed that kind of behavior?"

"Yes."

She felt as if she'd been sitting in a theater and the curtain had suddenly been raised to expose a hidden world. Her beloved, adored Sir Sidney had been a libertine? He'd had mistresses and had sired bastards? What was she to think of such an astonishing turn of events?

"Could I meet these children too?" she inquired.

"No." He shook his head quite vigorously. "You can't tell anyone either. It's a terrible secret, and I don't want it to spread, especially with the inquest coming. We can't tarnish Sir Sidney's reputation."

"I never would."

She was wishing she hadn't gotten into the carriage with him. Obviously, there was some information a person shouldn't ever discover. Wouldn't it have been better to *not* know about her father's proclivities? Now that she'd been apprised, it had changed her whole outlook.

"I hate to rush you," he said, "but I'm running late."

"There is one other thing."

"What is it?"

"Next time you go to Africa, could I go too? I've been waiting to ask you. Father refused to consider it, but I've been sure you'd feel differently. Will you think about it?"

He gaped at her, then rudely scoffed. "No, Ophelia, it's out of the question."

Her heart sank to her toes. "Must you decline immediately? Couldn't you ponder for awhile?"

"I don't have to ponder. I'm sorry, but Africa is not like you envision it to be. And you will *not* ever go." Like a death knell, he added, "Not. Ever."

She was so disappointed that he might have stabbed her with a knife.

"Yes, yes, that's fine." She was crushed and babbling like a fool. "I apologize for delaying you."

She feared she might burst into tears, and she slid away and scrambled out. She raced to the house.

"Ophelia!" he called.

But she didn't stop, didn't turn around, and didn't answer him.

—————⋇⋇⋇⋇—————

"TELL HER IT'S TO be Thursday or Friday."

"Can you be more precise?"

"No. Escrow will close when the papers are signed—and not a minute before."

Temperance nodded at her husband, Cuthbert. It was wiser to agree than to argue. He was the man of the family, and she was his wife. She'd vowed to obey, and that definitely included the burden of not annoying him, despite how she might yearn to.

"It will be nice to settle some of our debts," she said, trying to sound more supportive.

He smirked. "We're not paying off any debts."

"Then why sell the orphanage? I thought that's why we needed the money—to catch up on our arrears."

"We *will* catch up—eventually—but I have an image to maintain. I can hardly traipse about town looking like a pauper. A gentleman must have funds."

"Oh, right," she murmured, but she was incredibly confused.

When she'd convinced her father to bequeath his assets to Cuthbert—rather than place them in a trust—she'd truly believed it was for the best. A *man* should run things. A *man* should be in charge. It was how the world worked.

She and Sarah had no head for finances, but then, as Temperance had learned to her great detriment, neither did Cuthbert. Apparently, being a male didn't guarantee fiscal knowledge. The sad fact was that he spent much more than they had. She couldn't persuade him to cut back, slow down, or alter any of his habits.

"Hurry," he snapped. "I'm busy, and I don't have time to fuss with your sister. Talk to her—fast—so I don't have to."

"Yes, yes, I'm going."

"Don't dawdle and don't listen to any tales of woe. I gave her two full months of notice. It's not my problem that she's elected to linger instead of making arrangements for herself."

They were parked outside the orphanage in a rented hansom cab. Previously, they'd owned a carriage, but it had been seized by creditors, the vehicle having been confiscated while Cuthbert was riding in it. They'd deposited him in a ditch and had hauled it away.

In response, he'd come home and had smashed all her dishes.

She reached over and opened the door, and as she climbed down, she peeked in to where he was sprawled on the seat like a lazy, entitled tyrant.

He'd been twenty-three when she'd met him, and he was thirty now, but he appeared much older than that. Where he'd once been handsome and dapper, he'd grown very fat from his excessive diet. His curly blond hair, his pride and joy, had fallen out on the top, so he combed over the longer strands to hide the huge bald spot.

She tried to remember what had intrigued her so thoroughly when she'd been a naïve girl of eighteen. He had good bloodlines and was from a reputable family. Why wouldn't she have been enthralled? Why wouldn't she have been determined to win him?

Her father hadn't approved of her choice, but her grandmother had been more of a romantic, and she'd signed all the appropriate documents. By forging ahead when her father had specifically ordered her not to, she'd driven a wedge between them that had never been mended.

At the time, she'd been so *sure* that her decision was the correct one, but look where it had landed her! Not that she'd ever admit she might have been mistaken.

As her grandmother had warned when his gambling losses had mounted, no husband was perfect. Temperance just had to buckle down and figure out how to manage him.

"Go, Mrs. Maudsen!" he grouchily said. "Cease your woolgathering!"

He pulled the door shut, slamming it in her face.

She flashed a wan smile at the cab driver and asked him to wait, then she went to the orphanage and entered into the common room. It was always difficult to confer with her sister, and she hoped she could deliver Cuthbert's message and escape the building without quarreling. That probably wasn't possible though.

Sarah was like a thorn Temperance couldn't pluck out. She was beautiful and kind, smart and savvy, reliable and loyal. In other words, she was possessed of all the attributes their father had relished.

In contrast, Temperance—with her chubby physique, dull brown hair, and even duller hazel eyes—was *not* kind, was *not* smart or savvy, was *not* what Sarah was able to be without trying at all. Everything was easy for her sister, and Temperance loathed her for it.

Even though Temperance had fled the orphanage the minute she could, even though she'd been raised by her rich grandmother and had wed the man of her dreams, Sarah was the one who was happy.

It was so unfair!

The facility was very quiet, a general air of neglect and abandonment settling in. Momentarily, she wondered if Sarah might have already moved out without informing her. She couldn't deduce how she felt about it.

A boy of twelve or so walked in from the kitchen. He saw her and asked, "May I help you?"

"Is Miss Robertson here? Tell her that her sister, Temperance, has arrived, and I must speak to her at once."

She could have marched up the stairs to the family apartment, but she couldn't bear to be reminded of her humble beginnings. She'd come very far from those mortifying days.

"You're her sister?" the boy insolently inquired.

"Yes. Please fetch her." She clapped her hands at him.

"I will fetch her," he said, "but first, I should like to state that I'm glad I don't have a sister like you."

Temperance rippled with offense. "You cheeky devil! Get out of my sight before I have my husband whip you for being impertinent!"

"From what I hear, he's too lazy to brandish a whip. You shouldn't hurl threats you can't carry out."

The boy looked imperious and regal—as if he viewed himself to be very much above her in status.

"You little monster!" she fumed. "How dare you disrespect me!"

"It's quite simple, ma'am, and it's all deserved. You know it too. I can see it in your eyes. Don't pretend."

She'd never encountered such a brazen waif, and she wasn't sure how to react. Should she stomp over and slap him? She was terribly afraid he might slap her back! It was obvious he had no sense of his lowly place. What type of brats was Sarah rearing?

She couldn't predict what might have happened, but Sarah followed him in from the kitchen.

"What's wrong?" she asked the boy. "Are you bickering with someone?"

He rudely gestured to Temperance. "I was telling your sister that I don't like her."

"Thank you, Noah," Sarah said, "but there's no point in being awful to her. She's always been horrid. It's her genuine character poking through."

"Should I leave you alone with her?" he asked Sarah. "Would you like me to stay?"

"No. She can't do anything worse to me than she's already done."

The boy, Noah, shot a stern glower of disgust at Temperance, then sauntered off. Sarah waited until his footsteps faded, then she strolled over to where Temperance was standing by the door. She was definitely not in a rush.

"Why are you here?" Sarah sneered. "I told you not to come back."

Instead of answering, she said, "What a dreadful nuisance he is! If you're allowing that sort of sass, standards have certainly fallen."

"Noah has a very famous father, and he's inherited all of the man's traits, especially the ones regarding loyalty."

"He should be caned until he learns to shut his mouth!"

"Yes, I'll get right on that," Sarah sarcastically retorted. "I just love beating children. What is it you need? Please spit it out. Otherwise, I have chores."

"Cuthbert wishes me to inform you that escrow will close Thursday or Friday."

"Will that be all?"

Sarah was so calm and composed, and her unruffled deportment aggravated Temperance.

Temperance was wearing her very best gown, her velvet cloak and matching bonnet, while Sarah was attired in a tattered dress, an apron over top as if she was now doing her own cooking and cleaning. She had a kerchief covering her hair, her cheeks smudged with dirt, and *still,* she looked like a princess in a palace.

How did her sister manage her glamour? Why did she always appear so accursedly majestic?

Temperance never forgot that Sarah had been abandoned on the orphanage's stoop when she was three. With it being a private facility for the natural children of aristocrats—and her bill always being paid—it indicated she had a noble parent. Yet no matter how grand her countenance, deep down she was a bastard, and Temperance constantly gloated over that fact.

Temperance's parents—ordinary though they'd been—had been *married* when she was born.

She expected Sarah to expound on her plight, to complain about the situation or perhaps to beg Temperance not to let Cuthbert proceed. But they'd had that discussion months earlier, and Sarah never begged for anything. She didn't think she should have to.

The silence stretched out, Sarah's severe glare grinding her down, and Temperance couldn't abide it. Finally, she asked, "Have you made any plans?"

"Oh, yes, I have all kinds of plans in place."

"Well . . . good. How many urchins are still in your custody?"

"Two."

"Don't leave them here when you depart. I can't be saddled with them."

"I wouldn't dream of inflicting you on an innocent child."

Temperance ignored the insult. "When the new owner arrives, you have to be out."

"Yes, I've understood you from the very start, Temperance. You don't have to keep repeating yourself."

She was anxious to repeat herself though.

Sarah was very angry, and Temperance felt a powerful urge to defend Cuthbert, to talk until Sarah admitted that he'd taken the only viable course, one that would—hopefully—save Temperance from bankruptcy. But Sarah had never liked Cuthbert, as their father had never liked him, and Temperance was weary of explaining.

Sarah never listened anyway, so why bother?

"I'll just be going then," she muttered. "Once you're evicted, don't knock on my door."

"Believe me, I won't."

"I'd assist you if I could, but after how viciously you've been scolding Cuthbert, you're not welcome in our home."

"I would never come there."

Temperance nodded. "See that you don't."

When Cuthbert had first arranged the sale, they'd invited Sarah to supper, and she'd grudgingly accepted. After the meal, he'd told her what he'd done, and she'd called him hideous names, and since then, she hadn't ceased her harangue.

For better or worse—mostly worse—Cuthbert was Temperance's husband, and Sarah couldn't be permitted to malign him.

"In case I have to contact you," Temperance said, "where will you be?"

"Why would you care where I end up?"

"Don't be smart! I asked a valid question, and I demand a valid answer. You know we had to sell. You *know* it. Quit acting as if the world should stop spinning merely because you disagree with the direction it's turning."

"I'd kick the whole stupid planet off its moorings if I could."

"And that is precisely why you're in the predicament you're in."

Sarah frowned. "Is that why? Here I thought it was because your despicable husband sold my home out from under me. I thought it was because he's destroyed everything our father built."

"You will *not* disparage my husband in front of me!"

"You've delivered your message, Temperance, and you were very clear. I'm to be out by Thursday. Why don't you go? Isn't Cuthbert waiting? We shouldn't delay him. He gets so impatient."

Temperance might have shouted a thousand invectives, but it was impossible to win an argument with her sister. She whipped away to stomp out, and as she would have exited, Sarah said, "Temperance?"

She glanced back. "What?"

"Have you ever wondered if Father is watching us from Heaven?"

It was a terrifying notion that plagued her in the dark of night when Cuthbert was out gamboling with his friends. How would her father view their treatment of Sarah?

The idiotic man had been born rich, but he'd embraced a life of poverty and charity. He'd devoted himself to helping the poor, when it was common knowledge they couldn't be helped. How was any sane person to assess such deranged choices?

He would be devastated to have the orphanage closed, but his daughter needed the money from the sale. His son-in-law needed it. His *family* needed it, and they were more important than a bunch of orphans, weren't they?

Yet he would blame Temperance. He would be ashamed of her. He'd grieve over how she'd hurt Sarah—Sarah, who'd always been his favorite.

"No," she lied, "I don't think about Father. I *never* think about him."

She left before Sarah could annoy her with any other comments she refused to hear.

CHAPTER

---※·※---

5

It was a lazy Wednesday afternoon, and Sebastian was trying to enjoy some extended reveling at Hero's Haven, but he couldn't relax as he'd intended.

The house was once again packed with people. The members of the expedition team were all present, and his favorite brothel had sent a dozen pretty harlots to entertain them. It would be a day—and night—of disgusting behavior, then the doxies would leave, the servants clean up the mess, and a quieter group of guests would arrive.

He'd invited some of Sir Sidney's old friends to gather and reminisce before the inquest began. They were all explorers as his father had been, though none of them were so renowned as Sir Sidney, mostly because they didn't possess his flare for the dramatic.

Sebastian had asked his mother to serve as hostess, but she'd declined, so Ophelia would come instead, which meant Veronica would come too.

His mother and sister liked Veronica and considered him betrothed to her, but he'd never agreed to propose. At the moment, he had no desire to ponder matrimony or even some serious courting. He simply wanted to drink and carouse and stay two steps ahead of the demons that were plaguing him.

His mind was whirring with vexing issues. The inquest was front and center, and he'd be glad when it was finished, but he was overwhelmed too by Nathan getting married and Sebastian having had no idea. To add insult to injury, Nathan had wed someone Sebastian had never met, so he had to admit that the debacle in Africa had pushed them much farther apart than he'd realized.

Then there was the problem with Miss Robertson and Sir Sidney's bastards. He'd told her he didn't believe her story, but the bloody shrew couldn't tell a lie if her life depended on it. *And* he'd seen the pair as they'd burst into her apartment at the orphanage. Only a fool would deny their paternity.

Miss Robertson was about to be evicted. What was his opinion about that dilemma? Was he inclined to intervene? What was his obligation to the three of them? Did he have an obligation?

He still couldn't figure out why he'd visited her. She was just so different from every other female. She wasn't impressed by him, and while she'd begged for his help, it had been for the children, not for herself. Her conduct was odd and refreshing.

He was obscenely rich, with their journeys having pitched them into the business of diamond mining, so he was surrounded by sycophants and hangers-on. People constantly glommed onto him, but with dubious motives. Women in particular yearned to establish close ties.

Normally, he would have thought he hated the type of bold, unabashed arrogance Miss Robertson displayed, but it intrigued him to an insane degree. She carried herself like a goddess, like a warrior princess in an ancient fable.

She was shameless and exhausting, and he couldn't stop obsessing over her.

"You have to talk to Nathan," Raven said, pulling him out of his reverie.

"I know," Sebastian replied.

"And you have to do it soon."

"I *know*," he repeated more sternly.

A few weeks earlier, he'd ridden to Selby to inform Nathan's aunt that he'd perished in Africa, only to find him fit and hale and prancing about as if no calamity had occurred. For his troubles, Sebastian had been attacked by Nathan, in the process receiving two very painful black eyes and lucky his nose hadn't been broken.

Obviously, Nathan's trek home had been extremely difficult, and he was still very angry over what had happened there. Sebastian wasn't in any mood to be pummeled again, but at least he'd be better prepared. The prior occasion, he'd been too stunned to defend himself.

He glared at Judah. "Would you like to come with me? You have some topics to address with him."

"I can't accompany you," Judah said. "From how you've described him, he's mentally unbalanced. If I heard him telling lies about me, I can't predict how I'd react."

"Would it be pistols at dawn?" Raven facetiously inquired.

"It might be," Judah firmly stated.

Sebastian studied him, wondering what was true, and he wished there was some sort of machine he could hook to Judah to gauge his veracity. Wouldn't that be a neat trick?

The catastrophe in Africa had been chaotic and terrifying, with a native tribe chasing them through the jungle and hell-bent on murdering the whole crew. They'd barely survived.

With Nathan's fate a mystery, he'd sent Judah with two other men to locate him. They still swore he was dead when they'd stumbled on him, that they hadn't recovered his body because a group of natives had espied them, and they'd run for their lives.

Later, when matters had calmed, Sebastian had had emissaries attempt to retrieve his father and Nathan. He'd been given his father's corpse, but Nathan's had vanished, and tribal leaders had insisted they didn't have it. Sebastian had left for England without his friend, and it had turned out to be another bad decision in a long line of them.

His many vacillations were the best evidence of why Sir Sidney had been in charge of their expeditions, and Sebastian had simply been the favored son who'd followed him and obeyed his orders.

"Guess what Ophelia asked me yesterday." He was desperate to change the subject. "She wants to travel to Africa with us on our next trip."

Raven and Judah blanched, and Judah said, "As a member of the team? That's deranged. Africa is no place for a woman."

Raven snorted with disgust. "I hope you refused."

"I did, but she's furious about it."

"Well, let her be furious," Raven said, "and if she doesn't *stop* being furious, ignore her. You're an utter milksop with females. You always cave in."

"Not on this."

Raven never deemed Sebastian to be tough enough in any situation, but in light of Raven's temper and steely attitude, it was impossible to match him in rage or determination.

When he was a boy, his father had been duped in a swindle, and his family had lost everything. They'd been cast out of their home, and his father had died in prison. His mother had then died of shame. The bitter history meant he had scant sympathy for others, and you'd hate to have him as an enemy. He felt the slightest sign of weakness should be stamped out.

Sebastian switched his attention to Judah. "How should we mend your rift with Nathan? I'm curious as to how you think we should resolve it."

"You don't need to resolve it. He and I have to be the ones."

"I won't permit you to duel with him."

"Then he should shut his mouth and cease spreading stories that aren't true."

"If we can't fix it, how can I go to Africa with both of you?"

"Is that what's worrying you? Nathan loathes us now, so he won't be joining us on any future ventures. It will never be an issue."

"Probably not," Sebastian mumbled.

"Does your comment indicate there's to be a new expedition? Will we start preparing?"

The question was posed constantly. The crew especially was waiting to hear his opinion, but he couldn't imagine journeying to the Dark Continent again. Not when there was a potential for such violence and not without Sir Sidney. Not without Nathan. The very idea seemed like blasphemy.

Vaguely, he noted Raven was over by the door and talking to a footman. Suddenly, he bristled, then he marched over to Sebastian. His expression lethal, he leaned down and murmured, "Your presence is required in the foyer immediately."

"What is it?"

"Miss Robertson is here, and she has two . . . ah . . . young *friends* with her."

Sebastian was glad he was sitting down. If he hadn't been, he might have fallen down. "You're joking."

Raven never joked. "See for yourself."

"What's wrong?" Judah asked.

"Nothing's wrong," Sebastian claimed.

"Not yet anyway," Raven fumed.

Sebastian stomped out to the foyer, and there, seated on a bench, was Sarah Robertson. Petunia was nestled by her side, and Noah was standing, hovering over them in a protective way.

He looked magnificent and stout-hearted, but the two females looked beaten down and bedraggled. Miss Robertson was particularly bereft. He wanted to shout at them. He wanted to storm over and shake her, but she was so morose it would have been like kicking a puppy.

In the fleet minute since he'd emerged to confront them, at least three of his men had strolled by. There were never any children at the Haven, and everyone was peeking at them, wondering who they were.

Why couldn't the accursed woman have walked around to the servant's entrance? He'd explicitly warned her he couldn't have the children's identities being bandied. Why hadn't she listened? Why couldn't she—just once—behave as was appropriate?

Apparently, his past chastisements had had no effect on her. Was she deaf? Was she stark raving mad? Quite possibly so. It was obvious he needed to be much clearer with her, but before he could begin, Noah stepped between them.

"I recognize that we've surprised you," Noah said, "and Miss Robertson was convinced you'd be angry."

"Miss Robertson was correct," Sebastian irately replied.

"To prevent you from lashing out at her, I must clarify that it was *my* idea to come here. Not hers. I brought us."

"Is that right?" Sebastian's tone was dubious.

"Yes, that's *right,* Mr. Sinclair," Noah retorted. "I am not a liar and never have been, so I would appreciate it if you wouldn't accuse me of duplicity. Your temper is flaring, but you will not berate her. I'm sorry, but I can't allow it."

Sebastian was completely flummoxed. How old was the boy? Twelve? Yet he carried himself like a king, and Sebastian couldn't devise a suitable response.

The problem was exacerbated by the fact that the little ass was an exact replica of Sir Sidney. His haughty demeanor made it seem as if Sebastian's father had been shrunk down to a smaller size. Petunia so closely resembled his sister Ophelia that the same could be true of her. She was a small Ophelia. At the realization, he felt dizzy and disoriented.

What was he to do with them? He couldn't be the only one who'd noticed the similarities. If his drunken companions were too inebriated to figure it out, the servants certainly would, and they were the worst gossips in the world. News that two of Sir Sidney's bastards were at Hero's Haven would race through the kingdom like a wildfire.

"Raven," he said, "take the children down to the kitchen and have them fed."

Noah shook his head. "We won't leave Miss Robertson alone with you. Not if you intend to castigate her."

Sebastian had never spent much time around children, and those with whom he'd socialized had been quiet and polite. How was he to deal with such a fierce character?

A horrifying vision flashed in his mind—of himself quarreling with the boy and losing the argument—but Miss Robertson saved him.

"I'm not afraid of Mr. Sinclair," she said. "He would never hurt me."

"Maybe not physically," Noah said, "but he could verbally insult you, and *I* am the one who should be criticized. Not you."

She smiled a weary smile. "You haven't had any breakfast though, and Pet is starving. Why don't you eat while he and I talk?"

Noah scowled. "If you're sure?"

"I'm sure. You go on."

Noah pulled himself up to his full height and addressed Sebastian. "When you're done speaking to Miss Robertson, I should like to have my own conversation with you."

"There's no need," Sebastian told him. "Miss Robertson has been very open with me as to your situation."

"Yes, but she is a stranger to you, so she has no stake in what will happen to Petunia and me. *I,* on the other hand, am your—"

Before he could voice the word *brother,* Raven leapt over and clamped a palm over his mouth. Noah kicked him in the shin and attempted to wriggle away, but Raven held tight.

Raven leaned down, his manner very threatening. "Let's you and I escort Miss Petunia down to the kitchen and get her some breakfast. Don't sass me about it."

Noah yanked away. "I don't take orders from anyone—especially not from a man I've never even met."

"You'll take them from me," Raven seethed, and Miss Robertson saved them all again.

"Noah, please. I can't bear to bicker. I'm too sad."

At her plaintive remark, the boy relented, his shoulders sagging with defeat. "Fine. I'll stay with Petunia until you're finished."

"I won't be long."

Raven guided him away, Petunia walking behind. She cast a scathing glance at Sebastian, apprising him that she didn't like him, didn't approve of his treatment of them, and wouldn't countenance any rude behavior toward Miss Robertson.

Sebastian dawdled until they'd vanished, then he clasped Miss Robertson by the arm, raised her to her feet, and dragged her down the hall. Judah watched them and tried to follow, but Sebastian waved him away.

"What is it with the men in this house?" she grumpily asked. "Why do all of you think it's acceptable to manhandle a female?"

"We don't manhandle *all* females, Miss Robertson. Just those who are a nuisance."

He arrived at an empty parlor, flung open the door, and marched her in.

"How dare you come here!" he raged as he slammed it. "I insisted I couldn't help you, but you keep showing up like a bad penny."

"Yes, that's me," she snidely responded, "sweeping in like a plague of locusts."

He spun on her, ready to bellow at her, but before he could commence his tirade, she staggered over to the sofa and eased down.

She was still as a statue, her elbows on her knees, her head in her hands. She appeared so forlorn that he wondered if she wasn't crying.

He'd spent two decades with tough, brave, manly men and none of it with British females. He'd never tarried with one during a personal crisis and had definitely never comforted one when she was distraught. His fury waned. How could a fellow admonish a woman who was so clearly anguished?

Finally, she straightened, and she swabbed her fingers across her eyes, wiping away any evidence of tears. Then she stared up at him and said, "This has been the very worst day of my life—except for the day my father died. Might I have a whiskey?"

She was trembling. With regret? With fear? With a chill? He couldn't guess, but he went to the sideboard and filled a glass for her. He abstained from pouring one for himself. He'd had plenty, and he had to sober up and confer with her in a sane way. If he wasn't careful, what deranged assistance might he ultimately offer?

He delivered the beverage, and he'd brought the decanter too, figuring she might need more than a single shot. She proved him right, swiftly downing the first serving in a quick gulp, then she extended the glass, and he filled it again. She sipped the contents more slowly.

"What happened?" he asked. "And supply me with the shortened version. I don't require a drawn-out soliloquy."

"Could you sit down? It's exasperating to have you loom over me like a torturer."

He rather liked looming over her. From their prior encounters, he'd discovered that he had to stay on his toes or she would seize every advantage, and he had no intention of letting her.

But she was simply too miserable for words, so he decided to oblige her for once. He grabbed a chair and pulled it over, but of course, he positioned it much too close so their feet and legs were tangled together. Yet he didn't push it back. He didn't want her to assume she rattled him.

She didn't.

He glared, irked by her pretty blue eyes. They were luminous, shimmering with the tears she'd refused to shed, and for a moment, he felt as if he was drowning, as if he couldn't look away. He physically shook himself, jerking away from an unnamed abyss into which he might have tumbled.

He was struggling to keep his temper at bay. He'd previously learned that it was futile to shout at her, and if he raised his voice, he was certain she'd tattle to Noah. Bizarre as it sounded, Sebastian couldn't bear to be scolded by the boy. It would be too much like being scolded by Sir Sidney.

"Why are you here?" he asked in a more even tone.

"My building was sold," she said, "and the new owner came earlier than I anticipated. I thought I was prepared, but . . . but . . ." Her sentence trailed off, her woe too great to clarify.

"How long have you been there?"

"Since I was three—when I was left on the stoop."

"So it's always been your home. It must be very hard for you to lose it."

"Mr. Sinclair, you have no idea." She downed her slug of whiskey and shuddered with a mixture of dread and sadness. "I was too stunned to react, so they set the last of my things out on the street."

"You had to abandon all of it?"

"No. A neighboring business owner loaned me his wagon. We loaded my possessions in it, and we drove it to the Haven."

"Your belongings are out in my driveway?"

"Yes, sorry."

"I can see that you're distressed, Miss Robertson, but why didn't you make arrangements for yourself? You've known the sale was about to conclude. Why didn't you plan ahead? Why didn't you . . . ah . . . find another job or another building or another home? Why dawdle until disaster struck?"

"I don't have any money. How would I have moved precisely? And I *did* try to find a job. I've sought assistance everywhere, but there are so many people in the city who are searching for work too."

"I understand," he murmured.

Women flocked to London, anxious for employment, but there were too many of them and not enough spots. Most of them ended up toiling away in slaughterhouses or as seamstresses. The unlucky ones became whores.

She was so magnificent, and the prospect of her winding up in a brothel was appalling.

But was it his responsibility to rescue her from such a fate? The line of desperate females was long and growing longer, and she was a member of that tormented group. He couldn't save the whole world, but if he simply gave her a few pounds and sent her away, wouldn't he always be ashamed of himself?

"In my own defense," she continued, "I didn't have much time to fuss over my own plight. A month ago, I still had twelve children residing with me. I've been busy, hunting for lodging for *them*."

"Rather than for yourself." He clucked his tongue like a mother hen. "You are a do-gooder, Miss Robertson, which means you are the very sort of person who annoys me the most. Have you no sense of self-preservation?"

"I was born to help others," she said, "and if I wasn't born to it, my father led me into it. I couldn't turn my back on his legacy. I'm following in his footsteps."

"Look where it's left you."

"I apologize for bothering you, but when the door was locked behind us at the orphanage, I was in such a state, I really went quite mad. Noah was telling the truth that he brought us here. I was too despondent to decide on a destination."

"What is it you expect from me?"

"From you? I don't expect *anything* from you. Noah does, but not me. Before I met you, I'd hoped you might have some redeeming qualities, but I've had to accept that you probably have none at all."

He snorted with amusement. "I have a *few* positive attributes."

"I haven't witnessed them." She rubbed a weary hand over her eyes and, as if he wasn't present, she mumbled, "I'm such a fool. I couldn't convince myself that she'd proceed. Deep down, I was so sure she wouldn't. I can't believe she detests me that much."

"Who are you talking about?" he asked.

She didn't answer him, but kept on. "I constantly prayed for a miracle, that God would soften her heart, but it was pointless. Miracles never occur when people like me beg for them."

He clasped hold of her wrist, forcing her to look at him. Touching her, bare skin to bare skin, was like touching fire. He felt as if he'd been burned, and he whipped his appendage away, lest he leave it exactly where it shouldn't be.

"Who was it and what did she do to you?" he inquired.

"Don't pay any attention to me." She waved him away. "I'm being completely morbid."

He leaned in so they were nose to nose. "Who hurt you?"

She dithered forever, then admitted, "My sister and her husband. They inherited the building from my father. Actually, they coerced him into changing his Will when he was in declining health. They're in financial trouble, and they needed the money." She glanced down, as if she was embarrassed. "My brother-in-law is a gambler, so their debts are enormous. They're nearly out on the streets themselves."

"Gambling is a scourge in families." He was certain he could guess what her reply would be, but he posed his question anyway. "Can you stay with them now?"

She scoffed. "I'd camp in a ditch first. The orphanage was my father's pride and joy, his life's work, and they tossed it away. It's as if they've spit on his grave."

Sebastian didn't have to be told about fathers and graves and legacies. He was dealing with many of the same emotional issues himself.

"Who is your brother-in-law?" he asked.

"Cuthbert Maudsen. Might you know him?"

"No, but gad, just from his name, he sounds tedious."

He'd managed to wrench a smile from her. "He *is* tedious—and cruel and greedy and pompous. I hate him!" She blanched at her vehemence. "No, I don't *hate* him. I don't hate anyone, but if I could wrap my fingers around his throat and squeeze until he was dead on the floor, I might be inclined to do that."

"Remind me not to tangle with you when you're angry."

"I'm a fighter, and I don't like to lose or give up."

"I've noticed that about you."

She stared at him, and the strangest charge of energy was flowing between them. He'd never experienced a similar sensation, and suddenly, he felt very close to her, intimately connected, as if it was perfectly acceptable that she'd show up at the Haven, perfectly acceptable that she'd sought him out.

When had that happened? How had it happened?

"I should find Noah and Pet," she ultimately said. "They'll be wondering where I am."

"They can wait."

"You don't know Noah very well."

He thought of the little despot and how he blustered forward into places where he wasn't welcome. He was so much like Sir Sidney that it was uncanny.

"I probably know him better than you suppose," he said.

"I insisted we shouldn't come to Hero's Haven, but he wouldn't listen."

"I think a failure to *listen* might be a family trait."

"He intends to talk to you—man to man—before we go. I doubt he'll agree to depart until he has the chance."

Sebastian studied her, trying again to deduce what had happened. He was no longer incensed, so he was . . . what?

He couldn't decide, but he was suffering from the oddest impression that—if he permitted her to skitter away—he'd always wish he hadn't. He couldn't be shed of her. Was there some sort of fate drawing them together? Was there a destiny he was being urged to pursue?

Having spent twenty years wallowing in dangerous locales where it had seemed he had nine lives, and he'd recklessly used up several of them, he was superstitious as a sailor. He wouldn't ignore a potent sign, and it appeared Miss Robertson was meant to tarry for a bit.

Besides, he had one group of guests leaving and another arriving. Then he had to ride to Selby to speak with Nathan. After that, the inquest would commence.

He didn't have time to be distracted by her. Later on, he might throw her out, but just then, he couldn't pick a different conclusion.

"You're not going anywhere," he said before he could persuade himself not to intervene.

"I have to. The day's waning, and we should return to London. A friend of my father's runs a poorhouse. He offered to let us stay with him for a few weeks while I reflect on what to do."

Sebastian winced with dismay. "You're not staying in a poorhouse."

"I've exhausted all my other options, and it will be all right." She nodded vigorously, as if convincing herself. "While I'm there, I'll be able to rest and focus. I'll figure something out."

"No. You'll remain here. I have an empty cottage out past the lake. It's not fancy, but it's furnished and habitable. You and the children can have it."

"Until when?"

"Until . . . until . . . I have absolutely no idea, but you will lock yourselves in and try to be invisible. I won't have Noah and Petunia trotting about the estate and declaring their paternity."

"So you believe me then? You believe they're Sir Sidney's children?"

"I never *didn't* believe you." He pushed himself to his feet. "Let's find Mr. Shawcross."

"My favorite person in the world," she muttered.

"He'll escort you to the cottage and get you settled. I'll send some servants to tend you." They would be his most discreet ones too, the kind who could keep their mouths shut.

She stood too, and for a moment, he worried she might foolishly decline the shelter he'd proposed, but she wasn't stupid.

"I guess we can do that," she finally said.

"I guess you can too." She was so glum that he could only laugh. "I'm saving your sorry hide, Miss Robertson. Could you at least claim to be grateful—even if you're not?"

She chuckled, but miserably. "I'm very grateful, Mr. Sinclair, and you'll never regret helping me."

"I regret it already," he grouchily snapped, "but I'll pretend I don't." He gestured to the door. "Would you please adjust your expression so it doesn't look as if I've been flogging you? I'd rather not be scolded by Noah ever again."

She flashed a smile, and he felt it clear down to his toes.

"How's that?" she asked. "Any better?"

"It was quite grand."

He was aghast to have voiced the compliment, and lest he start to wax poetic, he whirled away and marched out. He didn't glance back to see if she'd followed him. He didn't dare. With how she overwhelmed him, there was no telling how he might behave.

CHAPTER

6

"I'VE NEVER LIVED IN a house," Petunia said. "It's nice, but quiet."

"The orphanage was loud, wasn't it?" Sarah asked.

"Loud—but in a good way. I miss all the other children. Do you suppose they're all right without us?"

Petunia had been delivered to Sarah when she was a baby, so she'd constantly been surrounded by a gaggle of children. Although it had been an orphanage, they'd structured their routines so it would seem their charges were part of a large family.

Over the years, orphans would come and go. They'd grow up and move onto apprenticeships or university scholarships or military service, but others would quickly take their place.

After Cuthbert had sold the building, it had been particularly trying for everyone. With each child whom she'd conveyed to another location, she'd grieved over the loss, but Petunia had felt them even more poignantly.

Sarah would worry forever about the children she'd abandoned. She'd also worry about those who might need her services in the future. What would happen to them? No doubt they'd wind up in public orphanages, which would be a travesty.

She sighed. As her father used to say, they couldn't save the whole world. They could only save little pieces of it. She'd provided what shelter she could for as long as she could, and if she was lucky, she'd reopen her facility someday.

They were in the cottage Mr. Sinclair had opened for them. It had been a hectic afternoon and evening after Mr. Shawcross had brought them to their temporary home.

The house was small with a main floor that had a cozy parlor on one side of the foyer, and a dining room on the other. There was a kitchen at the back, with a maid's closet behind it. Up the stairs, there were two bedchambers. She'd picked the maid's room for herself and had given Noah and Pet their own rooms. After living at the orphanage, it was a treat.

The residence had been shuttered for ages, the furniture covered with cloths, the air stale. As promised, Mr. Sinclair had sent over a bevy of servants to scrub, mop, and clean the hearths. They'd left coal and blankets and food.

When they'd finished and had traipsed out to return to the manor, they'd explained that a housemaid and footman would arrive to tend them in the morning. At the notion of having servants again, she'd nearly burst into tears.

All of it had transpired with a snap of Mr. Sinclair's fingers. It was as if he'd waved a magic wand and her most pressing problems had vanished. She never ceased to be amazed at how effortlessly a rich man could fix what was wrong.

It was late now, the sun having set, and they were weary from pitching in to get their new lodging in a habitable condition. They'd washed and dressed for bed, and they were in Petunia's bedroom, chatting, but not able to call it a night.

"How long will Mr. Sinclair let us stay?" Pet asked.

"I have no idea," Sarah told her, "and we won't fret over it. This cottage is a huge blessing, and we'll merely be grateful about it. And we'll have to work hard to not be a nuisance to him. We can't ever supply him with a reason to kick us out until we've figured out where we'll go next."

Noah was with them too. "Mr. Sinclair won't kick us out."

"We'll hope he won't," Sarah said, "but we shouldn't be surprised or hurt if it occurs."

"He won't behave badly toward us," Noah claimed.

"How can you be so sure?" Pet asked.

"He's exactly like our father, so it means he likes people to view him as being generous and kind."

"Was our father generous and kind?"

"Always."

Noah's mother had been a favored mistress of Sir Sidney, and she'd flooded Noah with stories about the great man. Sarah couldn't guess if the portrait his mother had painted was accurate. She might have simply created a fantasy in her mind to justify her infatuation. Or perhaps Sir Sidney had truly been wonderful to her.

"We should get to sleep," Sarah said. "We had a grueling day, and I'm exhausted."

"I'm afraid to be alone," Petunia said. "It's odd to be all by myself."

"You don't have to be afraid," Sarah insisted. "It's different here, but it's not scary."

"I'll be across the hall," Noah added. "Or—if you like—I can sleep with you. Would you like that?"

Pet hesitated, looking as if she wished she was braver than she was, but in the end, she nodded. "Could you tarry? Until I doze off?"

Noah was an excellent big brother, and the bed was wide enough for him to lie down. Sarah tucked them in, then blew out the candle.

"Goodnight, Miss Robertson," they said in unison, and they giggled.

"Goodnight, you scamps. Tomorrow will be better. I'm certain of it."

"Today wasn't so terrible," Noah said as he yawned. "Our brother helped us. It's the best conclusion we could have arranged for ourselves."

"Yes, it is," Sarah agreed.

She couldn't predict how their relationship with Mr. Sinclair would unfold, but for the moment, he'd guaranteed their security. It was an incredible boon.

She stepped over and rested a palm on Pet's head, then Noah's, as she murmured a silent prayer for both of them to always be safe. Then she eased away.

In every way that mattered, they were her children, and she was growing more and more attached to them. She'd spent weeks trying to find a home for them, but clearly, their *home* should be with her. Why not? No one else wanted them, but she did.

They quickly drifted off, and as she watched them, it dawned on her that they had her questioning whether she might like to eventually have a husband, so she could be a parent. She'd been too distracted to ever think about marriage, and in light of her reduced circumstances, it wasn't as if she ever met suitable candidates.

If she wed, her burdens would become her husband's burdens. *He* would take care of her rather than her having to take care of herself.

She struggled to envision that type of existence, but it was such a queer picture that she couldn't bring it into focus. She'd been on her own for much too long. What sort of wife would she be? Not much of a one, she figured. She was too stubborn and bossy. What man could put up with such a brash female? He would have to have a strong character to tolerate her brand of confidence.

She tiptoed out, and she said another prayer in the hall, one of thanks and relief. She didn't know what would happen the next week or the next month, but Mr. Sinclair had furnished her with some space to ponder her path. With how horridly the morning had started, who could have imagined the day would end in such a marvelous fashion?

She walked down the stairs, skirted through the dark kitchen, and entered the tiny maid's room she'd selected for her own.

"Hello, Miss Robertson."

She jumped a foot and pounded a fist on her chest, demanding her pulse slow to a manageable level so she didn't suffer a massive heart seizure.

Mr. Sinclair was sitting over by the window, on the only chair. Moonlight shone in, silhouetting him in shades of blue and silver.

"For pity's sake," she gasped when she could speak again. "You gave me the fright of my life."

"Why are you always tardy? Is it a habit of yours to keep people waiting?"

"You mad wretch! What are you doing in here?"

"I was curious as to how you settled in, and I decided I should check."

"You couldn't stop by at a sane hour? Such as tomorrow around eleven?"

"I'm busy tomorrow. I have guests coming."

"You always have guests."

"What can I tell you? I'm a popular fellow."

She'd expected to climb into bed, so she was wearing just her nightgown, and it was sewn from a summery fabric, the material faded from many washings. Her hair was down and brushed out, her arms bare.

If he'd been a gentleman—which he definitely wasn't—he'd have apologized for catching her in such a scandalous state, and he'd have left. But of course the notion didn't occur to him.

Manly aromas emanated from his person—fresh air, horses, tobacco—but there was a distinct odor of alcohol too. Was he a drunkard? In the times they'd interacted, she couldn't recollect him being particularly sober.

"Have you been drinking again?" she asked.

"What makes you inquire?"

"I can smell it on you."

"If it's that obvious, I won't deny it."

"Is it an addiction?"

"I only imbibe when I can't sleep."

"How often is that?"

"Constantly?"

"Why can't you sleep?"

"Because I have bad dreams. Why would you suppose?"

"Why do you have bad dreams?"

He stared at her, and just when she assumed he'd tell her, he asked instead, "How are the children getting on?"

"They're grand and very grateful."

"It's quiet here, and the upstairs windows are open. I could hear you tucking them in. You're so . . . *nice*."

He pronounced the word *nice* as if it were an epithet.

"Have you a problem with kindness?" she asked. "I view it as a positive trait."

"Kindness never took me anywhere," he absurdly insisted.

"You misjudge yourself. It was *kind* of you to let us stay in this house."

"No, it was deranged to let you."

"Probably," she concurred. "Are you having second thoughts?"

"Probably," he shot back.

She was amazed that they were conversing so casually, as if it was perfectly appropriate for him to be in her bedroom. Yes, it was *his* property, but still!

He was being extremely brazen, and she was nervous as to what had driven him over to see her, just as she was fretting over how she could persuade him to leave. While she wasn't afraid of him, it was late, and they were alone. The situation was a recipe for disaster.

What could he want? How could she provide it to him without stirring any trouble for either of them?

"You're good with children," he said, as if in accusation.

"I guess I am. It's my profession to deal with them."

"Why didn't you ever marry and have a few of your own? Why waste the years caring for the children of strangers?"

"If I hadn't done it, who would have? And as to my personal circumstances, why would I marry? In my opinion, men are fools."

"*All* men? Or just some of us?"

"All men. Why would I shackle myself to an idiot? It would simply hand him the legal right to boss me and beat me if I didn't obey."

"Why indeed?" he mused. "Don't you seek more for yourself than what you've been given?"

"Doesn't everyone? We're not all as lucky as you. We don't all have famous fathers who discover diamond mines."

He snorted with derision. "Your sister wed Mr. Maudsen. How did she manage it when you couldn't find anybody suitable?"

"She's always had a different path than me. She met Cuthbert at eighteen and was determined to have him."

"Would that be the same Cuthbert who has nearly gambled away her home?"

"Yes, that would be the one."

"She has no sense."

"Not much, no. Why would I hope for a husband when there's a chance I might end up with an oaf just like him? He seemed fine in the beginning"—a huge lie—"and his flaws only became noticeable after it was too late for her to escape."

"Don't you deem yourself to have better judgment than her?"

"Absolutely."

"You might stumble on a terrific choice."

"Perhaps, but why risk it?" She chuckled. "I can't believe you recall my sister's foibles. The details of my life are so boring. I must be making more of an impression on you than I realized."

"Yes, you're making an enormous impression, and it's bothering me."

"Why?"

"I can't stop thinking about you."

"I don't know whether to be delighted or alarmed."

"Are you a sorceress? Have you cast a spell on me? You've lodged yourself in my brain like a painful thorn, and I can't pluck you out."

"I'm a thorn in your brain? I would have thought I'd be located closer to your backside."

"That too."

She was hovering by the door like a frightened rabbit, which she hated.

There was a candle on the dresser, and she turned and lit it, moving slowly so she'd have something to do other than gape at him. She could feel him watching her, studying her feminine shape in a manner that was annoying, but thrilling too.

Once the candle flared, she spun to face him.

"Would you go?" she asked.

"No."

"I was afraid you'd say that. Please tell me what you want, so I can give it to you, then send you on your way."

"You shouldn't talk about *giving* me what I want," he told her. "You're a maiden, so you can't imagine how risqué it sounds."

Her cheeks heated. "I stand corrected."

"For the record, I have no idea why I'm here, so I have no idea when I'll be ready to depart."

"Maybe you'll be trapped with me forever."

"Maybe."

He pushed himself to his feet and stepped over to her. She was still next to the dresser, and he leaned in and crushed her against it. Their torsos were forged fast, chests, thighs, feet tangled together.

He was very tall, and she was only five-foot-five in her slippers. He towered over her, and she was mesmerized as the silliest debutante.

She considered herself to be a modern, independent female who had no romantic interest in men, but evidently, she'd been wrong. There was a palpable charge of energy flowing from him to her, almost as if their proximity was creating sparks.

Why was it happening? Where would it lead?

Before she grasped what he intended, he dipped down and kissed her. She was so shocked that she simply stood there and let it transpire.

It wasn't her first kiss. She'd attended boarding school for years, and there had been dances and other social events. She and her classmates had snuck into dark corners with the boys who'd been invited.

So she knew *how* to do it, but it had been a very long time since she had. She couldn't persuade herself *not* to participate, and she grabbed the lapels of his coat to pull him nearer.

Instantly, it became clear that kissing a boy when she was an adolescent girl, and kissing a man when she was a grown woman, were two very different experiences. Her body was alive and aroused in a fashion that was scary. Reckless thoughts were racing through her mind as she pondered activities she'd never previously pondered.

She loved how his hard male anatomy felt against her much softer female one. She was on fire with yearning, and the speed with which it had swept over her was disturbing. He was swiftly proving that there were facets to adult amour that she didn't understand and couldn't control.

She yanked her mouth from his, but he simply nibbled a trail across her cheek and down her neck, to nuzzle at her nape. Goosebumps cascaded down her arms, shooting waves of sensation out to her limbs. She was so overwhelmed that she was surprised her knees didn't buckle, that she didn't collapse to the floor in a stunned heap.

He wouldn't have allowed her to fall though. She was pinned tight, as if he might never let her go.

"Mr. Sinclair," she murmured, and she laid a palm on his chest and tried to ease him away.

"Call me Sebastian," was his reply.

"I can't. What are you doing? What are *we* doing?"

He glared at her. "We're kissing, Miss Robertson. Are you such an innocent that I must explain it to you?"

"I know we're *kissing,* but *why* are we? We don't even like each other."

"No, we don't, so I can't imagine what's driving me."

"It's been your response to my every question."

"I don't have a more specific answer for you, so cease your pestering."

He dipped in and kissed her again, and she sighed and joined in for a minute or two. All right, maybe three.

It was a rare occasion when someone held her. She couldn't remember when it had last happened. It was wonderfully sweet, but it was dangerous and foolish too.

He had no business seeking her out, and she had no business permitting him to tarry. He'd just extended a large amount of charity to her and the children. Was this his way of informing her he expected payment for what had been bestowed?

Oh, how she hoped that wasn't the case!

She pushed him away, saying, "We have to stop."

"Why?"

"I can't figure out what possessed you—or me."

"Must you evaluate every aspect of it? Are you the type of female who must talk every detail to death?"

"I'm worried there are strings attached to your generosity."

He scowled. "What kinds of strings?"

"You offered to let us stay in this cottage, then you immediately show up in an amorous mood. What am I to think?"

He muttered an epithet under his breath. "You suppose I'd demand physical compensation?"

She shrugged. "It's possible."

"You're being absurd. Haven't I mentioned that I have no idea what lured me here?"

"Well, you *did* claim I was a thorn you couldn't pluck out."

"Precisely."

"So . . . you're here for no reason at all?" she asked.

"There's a reason. It just remains a mystery to me."

He gazed down at her with an odd mix of affection and horror, as if he was perplexed over how he'd wound up in her bedchamber.

He placed his palms on her shoulders, and he stroked them down her back, over her bottom and thighs, then settled them on her waist. He touched her in a familiar manner, as if he was comfortable with her body and had every right to proceed.

"You make me feel better," he said out of the blue, "and now that I've told you, don't you dare gloat."

"I wouldn't dream of it." She leaned into him, liking how her torso fit with his, liking how sparks ignited when they were close.

"Are you sad tonight?' she asked him.

"What a perfectly idiotic suggestion. No, I'm not sad, and even if I was, I'm much too manly to admit it."

"Why are you drinking so much?"

"I never used to, but since I returned from Africa, it's worsened."

"Was it bad there? When your father was killed, was it terrible?"

For a moment, his mask fell. If she hadn't been watching him so intensely, she wouldn't have observed it. In that instant, she saw grief and heartache, a bit of shame and regret too, but it was swiftly concealed.

"I don't want to discuss it," he said.

"I understand."

"What should be done with you?" he inquired instead, deftly changing the subject. "I'm interested in hearing your opinion."

"You should allow us to dawdle indefinitely. Forget we've intruded."

"That's not an option."

"What *is* an option then?"

"I can't decide."

"Do you have a temper?" she asked.

"It's been known to flare occasionally. Why?"

"I would hate for you to grow angry and kick us out over nothing."

"I wouldn't."

She studied him, then nodded. "I'll tell myself to believe you, and I'll get busy, finding somewhere for us to go. I swear I will, but would you ever be willing to support us yourself? If you could chip in on our expenses, I'd have more alternatives, and we could depart quicker."

"You only just arrived. Don't push your luck."

She grinned. "I always push it."

He set a finger on the bridge of her nose and traced it down across her lips, her chin, her throat, her chest. He stopped at the bodice of her night-gown, perched as if to slip under the fabric and caress a breast. At the notion, her nipples hardened into painful buds, and her pulse galloped at a crazed speed.

She was agog with anticipation, wondering what he might attempt and what *she* might allow. He'd been in her room for a few short minutes. In that paltry amount of time, had she become a wanton? Could it be?

He came to his senses and pulled away, and she couldn't determine if she was relieved or disappointed. What if he'd begun disrobing her? Would she have let him?

She'd been told how men and women misbehaved when they were alone. Her widowed cook, who'd birthed a dozen children, had clarified the process. Sarah had been desperate to learn how babies were created, how unwed mothers landed themselves in such trouble.

Although she didn't exactly comprehend the physical mechanics of forni-cation, she grasped them well enough. She'd had passion explained, had had male lust and male drives explained.

If he'd removed her nightgown, he'd have done shocking, thrilling things to her that she likely would have enjoyed very much, and she'd always been curious as to what it would be like to be seduced. If he'd offered her the chance, might she have grabbed for it?

She could picture herself viewing it as a sort of scientific experiment. She liked to assume she'd never be that reckless, but what if she was wrong? Where would she be when it was over?

"I'll visit you tomorrow," he said.

"I suppose it's futile to tell you that you shouldn't."

"Yes, it's futile. It will be very late before I can sneak over here."

"You don't have to sneak. You could merely knock on the front door like a normal person."

"For what I have in mind, I'll definitely be sneaking."

"Should I be afraid for my virtue?"

He huffed with feigned offense. "You don't have to ever be afraid of me."

"If you plan to creep into my bedchamber after dark, how else should I feel about it?"

"You should simply consider yourself fortunate that I'm bothering with you."

She laughed. "You are so vain. How can I dissuade you?"

"You can't, so I'll see you tomorrow night. In the meantime, don't leave the cottage please. I have important guests coming, and I can't have any of them stumble on Noah or Pet."

"We'll keep out of sight, and I promise we'll behave."

He scoffed. "I doubt, Miss Robertson, that you have ever *behaved* a day in your life."

"Maybe not."

He stole another kiss, then headed for the door. At the last second, he tossed over his shoulder, "I still can't fathom why I came over here. I was hoping some conversation would get you out of my system."

"Did it work?"

"No. I'm more fascinated than ever."

The admission was strange and stunning. "I fascinate you?"

"Yes, bizarre as it sounds."

"You shouldn't be thinking about me at all."

"Isn't that the truth?"

The comment hung there between them, then he sauntered out.

She was frozen in place, listening as he exited the residence. It was quiet outside, and she strained to hear if he trotted away on a horse, but he didn't, so he must have walked from the manor.

It wasn't that far—just a fleet stroll across the park and around the lake—but it was much farther if he used the road, then turned up the lane.

Clearly, he was happy to take the shorter route, to show up without providing the warning of a horse's hooves on the gravel out front. He could furtively tiptoe in whenever he liked.

Would she let him traipse in without arguing?

The property was his, and she was staying at it because he'd permitted her to stay. If he chose to dally with her, and if he demanded she participate, what could she do about it?

He claimed he'd never expect compensation for them tarrying in the cottage, but it certainly seemed—on her end anyway—as if some sort of payment was owed.

How high might the price ultimately be? Would she be willing to pay it?

She thought—if she could kiss him again in the moonlight—that she might risk anything to make it happen. How had she arrived at such a perilous spot? And so rapidly too!

She blew out the candle and sank down on the bed, but she didn't lie down. His potent caresses had imbued her body with an energy she'd never be able to quell. Perhaps she'd never calm down enough to rest ever again. Perhaps she'd spend the rest of her life, staring out the window and anxiously watching for him.

My, my, but wasn't she in trouble?

CHAPTER

7

SEBASTIAN STOOD ON THE verandah at the rear of the manor and gazed across the park. Supper was over, and his guests were inside, chatting and playing cards. He was enjoying a quiet interval, staring out at the colored lanterns marking the paths in the grass.

He was drinking a whiskey, but not drinking it too quickly. His mother had noticed his excess imbibing, and Miss Robertson had commented too. She was nearly a stranger to him, and if she would perceive it, his habit had gotten out of hand.

It was just that, since surviving the ordeal in Africa, his mental state was quite chaotic. Often, for no reason he could discern, he'd be extremely anxious. He was relentlessly vigilant, as if an attack was imminent, and of course, insomnia was his constant companion.

Sleep was impossible. The minute he began dreaming, he'd once again be watching his father and Nathan being hacked to pieces.

The scenario always developed in the exact same fashion. He'd observe the calamity as it was bubbling up, and he'd try to shout a warning, but he'd find himself paralyzed and unable to call out. Then he'd try to run over and defend them, but his limbs would be turned to stone.

The assault would commence, the bloody blows landing in gory slow motion. Red droplets would pelt his face and hair and . . . ?

He'd lurch to consciousness. Who could slumber through a nightmare like that?

Liquor was the only thing that calmed him. He supposed laudanum might help too, but he wasn't about to walk down that road.

He glanced over to see Veronica approaching. She and Ophelia had arrived that afternoon, with Ophelia assuming the role of hostess, but Veronica was expending all the effort. They were eager for him to note that Veronica had the skills necessary to manage his home.

He *knew* she did, and he understood that she and Ophelia were fast friends, but he simply wished they'd leave him alone. His mother and hers were intent on their marrying, and he figured he'd eventually oblige them, but for the moment, everything annoyed him, and she was definitely on that list. So was his sister.

"Why are you hiding out here?" she asked.

"I can't abide all the stories about Sir Sidney. I've heard them a thousand times."

"If you were so certain this crowd of guests would bore you, why invite them?"

"The inquest is upon us, and it seemed important to acknowledge their connection to him."

"Will you need any of them to testify?"

"No, but they were his staunchest supporters when he was just starting out."

"We've come a long way since then, haven't we?"

His *family* had come a long way, but even though Veronica was a cousin, he didn't include her in that group. He and Sir Sidney were famous and revered, and they'd grown that fame into significant wealth with their diamond mines, but also with their travelogues and other items they'd used to spread their notoriety.

If and when he wed her, she would benefit from his riches, but for now, she couldn't lay claim to a single asset. He didn't mention it though. His mood was so low that he had to work hard to tamp down rude remarks he didn't mean to utter.

He studied her, struggling to imagine her as his wife. She was twenty, and he felt a thousand years older than her. With her blond hair and blue eyes, she was very pretty, but in a very typical British manner. There was naught that set her apart from any other debutante. She was petite and plump, which made her appear curvaceous, but a less generous person might have described her as fat.

He liked shapely women though, so he wouldn't be persnickety. No, his main issues with her were her youth and immaturity, her lack of life experience, and her not possessing the sophistication that journeying to foreign lands could supply.

How could they ever have anything in common?

He'd snuck out to the empty patio for the solitude it provided. Didn't she realize that fact? How long would she tarry?

"How was supper?" she asked. "You didn't compliment Ophelia, and she's worried you weren't happy with how it was arranged."

Ophelia and Veronica had rolled in after his chef had selected the menu and was preparing the food, so they'd had very little to do with it. And she wasn't actually inquiring about Ophelia's competence. She was inquiring as to how he viewed her own.

It was so exhausting, and he yearned to shake her.

"Supper was fine," he said. "The meal was delicious."

"I thought so too." She gestured to the house. "Will you come in? Some of the older gentlemen left a chair for you at one of the card tables. They're hoping you'll join them."

"Will they tell me more stories about Sir Sidney? Perhaps when he was a rapscallion at university?"

"Yes, I believe that might be their plan."

He grinned, attempting to look amused, rather than irked. "I'll be in shortly."

Could he be much more obvious?

Apparently, she'd gotten the hint, and she breezily stated, "Don't dawdle. It's supposed to rain this evening. I'd hate for you to catch a chill."

"I'll try to bear up."

Her comment was so *wifely*, and it irritated him beyond his limit. He forced a smile, then focused his gaze on the park again, bluntly apprising her that she'd been dismissed. To his great relief, she departed without another word.

He gulped his whiskey, placed the glass on the balustrade, then walked down into the garden. He strolled the various paths, leaving the mansion and the party far behind. He'd presumed he was wandering aimlessly, but when Miss Robertson's cottage became visible in the trees, he had to admit he'd had a destination in mind all along.

The prior night, he'd made a fool of himself with her. Why pursue the same course? Was he determined to show her, over and over, that he was an idiot?

Evidently yes.

He still couldn't figure out why he'd kissed her so vigorously. As she'd pointed out, they didn't even like each other, so how was he to explain his conduct? Maybe there was no explaining it. He was a man, and she was a woman, and they shared a hot, tantalizing attraction. Why ignore it?

She was much too old to still be a maiden, and it was an unnatural condition for a female. They needed to be wedded and bedded at a young age. She'd avoided matrimony, so she was brimming with energies that should have been slaked years earlier.

He was happy to be the lucky fellow who finally ignited her sexual passions. Was that his ploy? Would he seduce her? To what end?

A man couldn't ruin a woman without consequence. He always wound up owing payment, the biggest one being marriage if a babe was planted. At the notion, he shuddered with dread. A man of his station never wed of woman of hers. It was an absurd conclusion, so *no*, he wouldn't put himself in a position where he was required to fork over marriage or any other compensation.

Yet if that was his opinion, what was he thinking?

He had no idea. He was simply anxious to be with her again. She was unique and exceptional—like a white rose in a vase of red ones—and she had something he was desperate to receive from her. He wouldn't stop pestering her until he ascertained what it was.

It was late, probably close to eleven. She'd likely be in bed, and he suffered a rush of alarm at how delighted he was by the prospect. He went to the front door, and he didn't bother to knock. Why should he? Hero's Haven belonged to him. He could enter unannounced if he chose.

Still though, he slipped in quietly, like a thief in the night.

She was in the parlor, dozing in a chair by the fire. The flames had dwindled to embers, and they cast a pleasant glow around the room. From somewhere, she'd located a decanter of whiskey, and it was sitting on a table beside her, an empty glass too.

He was intrigued by her penchant for hard spirits, and it was just one more way she fascinated him. She smashed every convention about female norms that had ever been established.

She mumbled in her sleep, then frowned and reached out, as if she was trying to clasp hold of someone's hand. She gasped with dismay, then jerked awake.

For a moment, she appeared quite wild, as if she was confused as to where she was, but recognition gradually settled in, and she realized it had been a bad dream. She relaxed and breathed a sigh of relief.

She poured some whiskey into her glass, and as she did, she saw him standing in the doorway. They stared for a lengthy interval, a thousand unspoken comments swirling, but none seemed appropriate to voice aloud.

Ultimately, he came over, took the glass, and downed what she'd dispensed.

"I didn't offer you any," she churlishly complained, "and I consider it completely typical that you'd help yourself."

"It's my house, so I assume it's my liquor. I'll have some if I want."

"You're obnoxious."

"Not usually. You simply bring out the worst in me."

"I have that effect on people."

He snorted his agreement, then plopped into the chair next to her. He filled the glass yet again and put it on the table between them. They turned toward each other, watching each other's every move. They shared the beverage, sipping companionably, as if they were old friends.

After a bit, he asked, "What were you dreaming about when I walked in?"

She waved away his question. "It's a recurring memory. I think it's from my childhood."

"Before you were left at the orphanage?"

"Yes. I'm always very little, and I don't understand what's happening, but everything is ominous and scary. I'm being forced from my home. There's a ton of yelling and crying behind me, and a wicked witch is carrying me outside."

"My goodness."

"There's another little girl with me—who I'm guessing is my guardian angel—and I reach out to her so she'll protect me, but I can't find her anywhere. I start to call out to her, and then ... ? I wake up."

"That sounds incredibly traumatic."

"It definitely feels that way."

"Were you ever told who your parents might have been?"

"No. In fact, my adoptive father claimed he had no information about me, but after he passed away, I found my birth certificate."

"It means you learned the name of your real father. What a stroke of luck. Who was he? Is it anyone with whom I might be acquainted?"

"Why would you suppose you'd be acquainted with my father?"

"You're such an imperious shrew. From your haughty demeanor, I'm sure he was very grand."

She chuckled derisively, and he didn't know how he knew, but he was positive—when she replied—her answer would be a lie.

"You're wrong," she said. "He was no one of any account."

"I doubt that. I wouldn't be surprised to discover your father was a king."

She smirked. "He wasn't a king."

"What was he then?"

"He was just a ... man."

Because she wouldn't confide any details, his curiosity soared. Why would it be a secret? Was he a famous criminal or fiend? Sebastian was certain not. It had to be an elevated personage. He refused to believe she had a common lineage, and eventually, he'd pry the truth out of her.

"How was your day?" he asked her.

"It was very dull. How was yours?"

"Mine was boring and busy."

"How could it be both?"

"I had one group of guests leaving and another arriving. But the new group is much less amusing than the prior one."

"Why?"

"It's my father's old chums. They're telling stories about him and regaling everyone with tales of their glorious past."

"Did you love your father?"

"Yes," he admitted without hesitation. "He was the best father any boy ever had."

"Then you should cherish every memory his friends are willing to offer."

"You're correct. I should."

"There will come a time when no one talks about him anymore, and you'll be upset that he's being forgotten."

"Sir Sidney was a larger-than-life character. I'm betting he won't be forgotten for ages."

"Let's hope not—for your sake."

"Why for *my* sake?"

"A lot of your identity is wrapped up in being his son. If he fades from view, will you become invisible?"

He scowled. "What a ridiculous thought."

But she'd raised an issue that constantly vexed him. It was difficult to step out of his father's shadow. Would he succeed in his own right? Or would he merely coast on Sir Sidney's coattails?

What if he never mustered the temerity to return to Africa? At the moment, the notion of another expedition didn't appeal at all. It was dangerous to travel, dangerous to mingle with native tribes, to interact and strike trade deals.

When such disparate groups were congregating, misunderstandings could easily erupt. People could respond violently. People could even be murdered.

A pathetic picture flashed in his mind, of himself as an elderly codger, still bragging about his antics when he was twenty. Would that be his fate?

It didn't bear contemplating, so he wouldn't contemplate it. He changed the subject.

"I spent the day, chatting with my father's friends. What did you do?"

"The children and I worked in the cottage, unpacking our bags and fixing it so we're more comfortable."

"You're making yourself comfortable? It sounds as if you think you'll be staying forever."

"Yes, I plan to stay forever. I'm an optimist, Mr. Sinclair."

"You're not an optimist. You're a nuisance."

"That too." She grinned. "How long was this place shuttered before you opened it for us?"

"It's been a few years. The previous tenant was a retired valet who'd served my father for decades. I can't remember when he died, but it's been vacant since then."

"It must be nice to be so rich that you can have an empty house and no need to fill it."

"It is nice to be rich. I can't deny it."

She scoffed at that, and she noticed that they'd finished their drink. She rose, either to dispose of the decanter or to retrieve more of her secret stash, but as she scooted by him, he clasped her wrist and tugged her onto his lap. In a quick instant, her shapely bottom was perched on his thigh.

She scowled like a fussy nanny. "I won't sit on your lap."

"You already are, so I must point out that your comment is completely illogical."

"I realize we misbehaved last night, and I fear it's given you the impression that we'll misbehave again."

"I didn't arrive with wicked intent."

"Liar," she chided. "You want something from me. I'm terribly afraid I know what it is, and I'm sorry to report that you can't have it."

"I don't want anything." He stopped and frowned. "Or maybe I do. I haven't decided what it is."

"I *know* what it is. Don't you have some housemaids you can harass instead? Must you walk all the way across the park merely to harass *me*?"

"Would you call me Sebastian?"

"No."

"Why not?"

"Because we're not on familiar terms."

"We're not? I could swear you're snuggled on my lap, and you haven't tried to wiggle away. It seems awfully *familiar* to me."

At his remark, she made a feeble attempt to escape, but he wasn't about to let her. He dipped in and kissed her, and she allowed a swift embrace, but that was it.

"Why are you flirting with me, Mr. Sinclair? Please explain yourself so we can confront it in a sane manner."

"I missed you today."

She tsked with exasperation. "You did not."

"How about you? Did you miss me? Just a little?"

"If I did, I'm not about to admit it. It would simply stroke your massive ego."

"My ego is quite massive, and it requires constant stroking."

He pulled her closer, and for a fleet second, she refused to relax, but in the end, she relented. Her cheek was on his shoulder, a breast pressed to his chest.

He never cuddled with women. His encounters with them typically amounted to raucous carnal activity with doxies in port towns. He never carried on so tepidly, as if he had all the time in the world to nestle, and with her, he liked it very much.

"You're positively morose tonight," she said.

"You always assume you can read my moods."

"That's because I always can. Why are you sad now?" He didn't reply, and she said, "You can tell me. I'm very discreet."

"I'm sure you are." He sighed with a bit of melancholia. "I miss my father."

"Of course you do."

"And I miss everything that went along with being his son. I miss our expeditions and our camaraderie and our wild adventures."

"You don't have to relinquish it though. You can have your own expeditions, your own adventures."

He wrinkled his nose, reflecting on how the death of one man could bring so many futures to a screeching halt.

"I can't imagine going to Africa without him."

"It's too soon for you to ponder it."

"Yes, and with how he was murdered, I'm overcome with regrets. My men are anxious for me to arrange another trip, but I can't find the energy to proceed."

She laid a palm directly over his heart. "You're grieving, Sebastian. You need to give yourself some time to figure out how to move forward. Your road will become clearer when you're farther from the calamity."

"I think I might be . . . ah . . . *scared* to go back."

"You probably are, but after what you endured, it's a perfectly normal reaction."

It's how he'd convinced himself to view it, but he deemed himself to be a very brave fellow. He couldn't bear to consider that his courage might have fled.

"There's an inquest next week," he said. "The organization that funded our excursion? They have questions about what happened to Sir Sidney."

"Will it be hard to answer them?"

"Very hard."

"What did happen?"

He paused forever. It was on the tip of his tongue to blurt it out. If he revealed some of what plagued him, he thought she might absolve him for his failing to prevent the tragedy.

He felt so guilty about what had occurred, as if he should have been able to avert the disaster. Logically, he knew he couldn't have, but still, it seemed as if Sir Sidney's death was his fault.

"It's too gruesome to discuss," he murmured, "and I'd rather not describe it to you. There are some tales that should never be shared with an ordinary person."

"That's fine, but if you'd ever like to confide any of it, I'm happy to listen."

"Once the inquest is over, I won't be so forlorn." Then he shocked himself by confessing, "My memories have been distressing me."

"And it doesn't help that you'll have to divulge them all at an open hearing."

"It will be extremely difficult."

They were quiet for awhile, and he couldn't abide the tension in the air. There were too many things he wanted to tell her—things he didn't dare mention—and he was eager to walk a more enjoyable path.

There was a reason he'd visited her, and so far, she hadn't furnished what he'd hoped to receive.

He dipped down and kissed her again, and this time, she didn't balk. She participated with an enormous amount of vigor, and it was so enlivening to trifle with a pretty girl. She enticed him as no female ever had. It made no sense, but perhaps it didn't have to make sense.

They continued for an eternity, long enough that the embers in the hearth burned out, and the room grew dark and chilly. A hint of moonlight shone in the window and supplied the only illumination. And still, they didn't halt.

He sampled, nibbled, feasted, exploring her mouth, her taste, his busy fingers roaming over her body, imprinting her size and shape in his curious hands. He didn't slow until she shivered, and he realized it wasn't from passion. She was cold, but too polite to admit she was uncomfortable and needed a shawl.

He broke away and buried his forehead on her shoulder. He stayed there, inhaling her delicious scent. There was an essence about her that reminded him of flowers and sunshine and woman all rolled into one. It tempted him on an elemental level that was too thrilling to ignore.

"Take me to your bed," he suddenly urged, the reckless suggestion popping out before he could tamp it down.

She chuckled, but miserably. "I can't."

"You can," he insisted. "Take me there. I should depart, but it seems wrong."

"I know, but a relationship between us is impossible to fathom. You understand that, don't you?"

"Yes, but let's proceed anyway."

She snorted with disgust. "You would say that."

He sat back and studied her. When she shivered again, he said, "You're freezing. I can warm you under the covers."

"No." She flitted off his lap and stepped out of reach. "You have to go now, Sebastian. Please?"

He gazed at her, wondering if he looked as glum as he felt. "I don't want to go."

"You can visit me tomorrow. We'll chat more then—about the inquest and your father. You need some healing, and I'd like to provide it."

"I need *something* from you, but it's not healing."

"I'm sorry, but that's all I can give you."

He'd never been the sort to tumble his servants or force himself on lower classes of women as some men of his station were wont to do. She was a guest in his home, a destitute female who was experiencing great personal difficulties. He shouldn't have been bothering her at all, but he couldn't resist.

She was driving him mad, and he had to cease acting like an idiot. He wasn't a besotted boy who couldn't control his lust, but humiliating as it was to accept, that's precisely how he conducted himself around her.

He stood, hating how she was hovering across the room—as if he'd frightened her. He extended a hand. "Walk me out, would you?"

"As long as you promise you're about to say goodnight."

"I'm about to say it."

She came over and clasped hold, as if they were adolescent sweethearts. They went to the foyer together, and as she pulled the door open, Petunia spoke from up on the stairs.

"Miss Robertson, are you all right? It's so late, and I heard voices."

"I'm fine, Pet. Mr. Sinclair stopped by to see how we're settling in. He's just leaving."

"Hello, Mr. Sinclair."

"Hello, Petunia."

"Go to bed, Pet," Miss Robertson said.

They were locked in place as she tiptoed away, then they chortled like guilty miscreants who'd escaped punishment.

"I keep forgetting there are children in this house," he whispered.

"You have *siblings* in this house, Mr. Sinclair."

"I could claim it will make me behave better toward you, but it probably won't." He stole a final kiss, and as he drew away, he said, "I'll be away for a few days. I have to call on my friend, Nathan Blake. He's Lord Selby. Have I talked about him?"

She stiffened, then blandly inquired, "Isn't he one of your African partners? The one who was thought to have died?"

"Yes, that's him. He and I had a falling out, and I have to mend my quarrel with him before the inquest."

"I'm sure you'll work it out. Haven't you been friends with him forever?"

"Yes, forever. Swear to me you won't cause any trouble while I'm away."

"I never cause trouble," she ludicrously insisted.

"That, Miss Robertson, is a bald-faced lie." He shook a scolding finger at her. "I'll sneak over once I'm back."

She hesitated, then replied as he'd hoped she would. "I can't wait. Be careful on the road."

He stepped outside, and she shut the door.

He dawdled, staring up at the moon. He was already desperately missing her. But that was insane, and he couldn't figure out why she had such a potent effect on his miserable sensibilities.

He'd been away from the party for hours. No doubt his guests had given up on him and traipsed off to their beds. In the morning, how would he explain his absence? Ophelia would demand to know where he'd been, and Veronica would glare and fume, but not be able to interrogate him.

Good thing! For a man who people expected was about to become engaged, he was acting like a man who was free to philander.

He started for the manor, thinking how he would hurry to Selby to confer with Nathan. Then, apparently, there was a reason to hurry home. Sarah Robertson would lure him back. What was he to make of such a stunning development?

He had no idea.

CHAPTER

8

OPHELIA WAS IN THE village near Hero's Haven and tarrying in front of the mercantile. Veronica had lost a ribbon on her favorite bonnet, and she was inside, eager to find one that would match it.

They'd been bored at the manor, so they'd had a carriage harnessed and had gone for a ride. They'd coaxed Judah Barnett into squiring them about the neighborhood, so he was with them too. He was at the cobbler's, checking on the cost of a new pair of boots.

He was her favorite member of the Sinclair exploration crew. Other women might have picked Raven Shawcross, who was very attractive in a dark, sinister sort of way, but he was too brooding for her.

He never flirted with her or fawned over her due to her being Sir Sidney's daughter. Judah, on the other hand, was delighted to flirt. He was very tall, which she liked in a man, and his brown hair and eyes were deliciously enticing. When he focused his attention on her, she melted just a bit.

She was waiting for both of them and growing impatient to the point where she might have to enter the mercantile and nudge Veronica into hurrying. While Ophelia loved her cousin to death, she couldn't deny that Veronica could be very fussy.

It was a trait that would drive her brother mad, and occasionally, she wondered what kind of marriage he and Veronica would have. They didn't have anything in common, but as the negative notion arose, she shoved it away.

Sebastian was handsome and dashing, and Veronica was pretty and glamorous. Her dowry was huge too, and Ophelia couldn't comprehend why Sebastian continued to delay. Veronica had rebuffed several marvelous suitors while expecting to become Sebastian's bride, and with him out of the country so often, he likely wasn't aware of how popular she was.

If he was informed of how many boys had hoped to wed her, might he be in more of a rush?

She doubted it. Her brother was almost an exact copy of their famous father. No one had ever been able to tell Sir Sidney what to do, and Sebastian had the same obstinate streak. If he was pushed down the martial path, he'd delay even further merely to prove he couldn't be bossed.

As if she'd conjured Sebastian by thinking about him, he suddenly trotted by on his horse. She was surprised he was still at home. At breakfast, he'd mentioned he was headed to Selby to speak with Nathan, and she'd thought he'd already left.

His pending departure had cast a pall over the festivities at the manor. She and Veronica had intended to extend their visit so Veronica could slyly engage in more socializing with him. But with him flitting off to Selby, they were debating if they shouldn't return to town. It's what her mother would have demanded.

The men from the expedition team were in residence, so it wasn't appropriate for them to remain when Sebastian was away. Veronica wasn't too keen on the prospect, but Ophelia was thrilled to devise reasons to interact with Judah. Though she'd never admit it aloud, and couldn't guess what her mother's opinion might be, she was beginning to wish a closer acquaintance might be pursued.

Judah seemed to be wishing the same. Might they have a romance in their future? Ordinarily, she wouldn't have been interested, but with Sebastian flippantly rejecting her request to travel to Africa with him, she was angry and feeling very sorry for herself. An amour would definitely elevate her dour mood.

Sebastian hadn't seen her loafing, and she would have waved and called to him, but before she could, another female standing down the block—one Ophelia didn't know—greeted him instead. He reined in to chat with her.

Ophelia observed them, curious as to who the woman might be. She was attired like a governess in a plain grey gown, with long sleeves and black collar and cuffs, but she wasn't a governess. With her white-blond hair, she was much too beautiful and exotic for such a paltry role.

Sebastian was certainly intrigued. She uttered a comment that had him laughing, and Ophelia was startled. Africa had sucked the joy out of him, and she couldn't remember when she'd last heard him laugh.

Even though he'd earlier proclaimed himself to be running late, he dismounted to dawdle with the woman. They were toe to toe, and it was obvious they were intimately connected, appearing so attuned that sparks were practically flying.

Stunning her, Sebastian laid a hand on the woman's waist as if he was familiar with her person, as if he was allowed physical contact.

Was he smitten? Was he . . . he . . . in love?

It couldn't be. If he was involved in a significant liaison, she'd have had an inkling of it. Yet he was quite charmed. Ophelia had never witnessed such a shocking sight. No wonder he hadn't proposed to Veronica! He was too busy to consider it.

For an astonishing instant, Ophelia worried he might kiss the woman—right there on the street—but he drew away and jumped on his horse. As if he were a soldier in the army, he gave her a jaunty salute, then kept on to Selby.

The woman was overtly dejected to have him leave. She was frozen in place, watching with a forlorn expression until he vanished. She was terribly woebegone, as if she'd be bereft until he returned.

My goodness! What was happening?

Ophelia wanted to assume the woman was a doxy, but while Ophelia had never met a trollop, she was sure the woman wasn't one. She looked too magnificent to be a slattern. Who was she and how could Ophelia guarantee she stayed away from her brother?

She couldn't be permitted to distract him from his important decisions with regard to Veronica.

Judah sauntered up and asked, "What has you so transfixed, Miss Ophelia?"

"Sebastian just rode by."

"He must finally be off to Selby."

"Yes." She pointed down the block. "Do you see that woman?"

He scowled ferociously. "Yes, I see her."

"Sebastian stopped to speak with her. Might you know who she is?"

"Yes, I know her."

"Is she from the area?"

"No, she's from London."

"Why is she here in the village then?"

"She's...ah...an acquaintance of your brother's. She's been having a spot of trouble, and he's helping her."

"What sort of trouble?"

"She recently lost her home. He's...ah...letting her live in the valet's cottage out past the lake."

Ophelia gasped with offense. "She's living at Hero's Haven?"

"Only for a bit—until she can make other plans."

"What's her name?"

"It doesn't matter. Ignore her."

At Judah's determination not to say, she was determined to learn what it was. "I'm serious. What is her name?"

"Miss Sarah Robertson."

Just then, a boy and girl skipped up to Miss Robertson. Ophelia studied them, and an odd ringing clanged in her ears, and she felt horribly dizzy. They were incredibly familiar. Who did they resemble?

After a moment of intense concentration, it dawned on her. The boy was the spitting image of Sir Sidney! But the little girl bothered her even more.

Ophelia might have been staring at a tiny version of herself when she was five or so. There wasn't a whiff of difference between her and how Ophelia had appeared back then.

"And who are those two children?" she asked him.

He'd been gazing at Ophelia, and when he glanced over at them, he blanched with alarm. "They're not anyone at all, and they're not supposed to be traipsing around the neighborhood. Your brother wouldn't like it."

"Why wouldn't he?"

Judah didn't reply, but said, "Would you excuse me? I have to tell Miss Robertson something."

"Certainly."

"You remain where you are. Don't move."

Ophelia was agog with a dismay she didn't understand. Judah marched to Miss Robertson, and she bristled, her demeanor showing she didn't like him.

He was quite sharp with her, and he must have mentioned Ophelia because the children peered straight at her.

The boy was shameless and impertinent, and he must have wanted to talk to Ophelia because Ophelia heard Judah say, "You will not talk to her! Now get going."

He motioned down the road, insisting they depart. The boy argued with Judah, even though Judah was an adult. Clearly, the child had no manners.

Who was he? Why wouldn't Judah explain?

She had too much of Sir Sidney's blood flowing in her veins, and she might have blustered over and demanded to know what was occurring, but Veronica walked out of the mercantile.

Ophelia couldn't let her see Miss Robertson and the children or Veronica would be wondering who they were—as Ophelia was wondering.

Besides, Miss Robertson hadn't seemed keen to bicker on a public street. She'd herded the children away, and they were hurrying off in the opposite direction.

"Did they have your ribbon?" she asked Veronica, as she spun her away from the disturbing scene.

"No. They had several shades of blue, but none of them matched."

"Are you finished with your errands? Shall we return to the Haven?"

"Yes. Might your brother still be there?"

"No. He rode by while I was waiting for you."

"Drat it! I would have liked to chat with him. How long will he be gone? Is it worth it to tarry in the country in the hopes that he'll be back without too much delay?"

"Well, the last time he went to Selby, Nathan beat him to a pulp, so it might be a very short trip."

"They were fighting? Why?"

"I guess they have some unresolved issues over what happened in Africa."

"Will they mend their spat? Is that why Sebastian is calling on him?"

"He's *trying* to mend it. He needs Nathan to testify at the inquest."

"He will though, won't he? He loved Sir Sidney."

"Yes, I'm sure they'll work it out."

Ophelia led Veronica to the carriage, and Judah caught up to them as they were about to climb in.

"How was your visit to the cobbler?" Ophelia asked him, pretending he'd just arrived. "Were you able to order your boots?"

He shot her a hot look, informing her she was smart to refrain from discussing Miss Robertson in front of Veronica.

"Yes, I ordered a pair," he said.

"At least one of you was successful. Veronica couldn't find a ribbon to suit her."

Judah helped them in, then hefted himself in too. As they settled on the seat, he winked at Ophelia. They now shared a secret, and she arched a brow, notifying him he could bite his tongue for awhile, but not for long.

She wanted some answers, and the mysterious Miss Robertson would give her the perfect pretext to parlay with Judah much more intently than she should.

———⋄⋇⋄———

WHEN A KNOCK SOUNDED on the door, Sarah was startled. Two servants came over from the manor twice a day, but for the rest of the hours, they were on their own.

Mr. Sinclair was the only other person it might have been, but he'd ridden to Selby, which was extremely intriguing to her. He was best friends with her half-brother, Lord Selby, and she was so curious about him.

Was he as handsome as Mr. Sinclair? Was he as courageous and dashing?

She figured he probably was. He'd spent most of his life traveling to Africa with Sir Sidney.

Did he remember he had a sister? He was three years older than she was, and she'd like to meet him eventually, merely to discover what he recalled, but she doubted she'd ever be so brazen as to introduce herself.

If he didn't remember he had a bastard sister, or realize their father had been a philanderer, she didn't suppose he'd like to be apprised. A snooty aristocrat wasn't ever anxious to learn that sort of pesky detail.

Her friend, Nell Drummond, had grown infatuated with him over the summer when she'd stayed at Selby to attend a wedding. He'd been inappropriately flirting with her, and she'd been bowled over by him and had found it hard to resist his devious seduction.

Sarah hoped Nell had escaped his amorous advances. A girl like her, one who was poor and had no parents to guide her, could get herself into real trouble with a fellow like that, and Sarah hated to envision her half-brother as a libertine. Then again, Sarah's father had sired her out of wedlock, so her half-brother might be a roué too.

Nell lived with the rich Middleton family, and before Sarah had left London with Noah and Pet, she'd stopped by their mansion to tell her what had happened. But they'd been out of town, and no servant would explain when they'd return.

She'd written a desperate note to Nell, but as Sarah had had no forwarding address to include, there was no way for Nell to reply once she was home. The next time Sarah was in London, she would try to speak with Nell immediately.

The knock sounded again, louder and more firmly, and Sarah was yanked out of her reverie. She went over to the door, being shocked to see Ophelia Sinclair standing on the stoop.

"Miss Robertson?" she asked.

"Yes, I'm Sarah Robertson."

"I am Miss Ophelia Sinclair."

"I know who you are, Miss Sinclair."

"May I come in?"

Sarah would rather have poked her eye out than chat with the haughty shrew, but she forced a smile and said, "Yes, of course you can come in."

She waved Miss Sinclair into the foyer, but the girl strolled through to the parlor, without waiting to be escorted. She sat on the sofa, and she didn't shed her shawl or bonnet, so apparently, it would be a quick visit. Thank goodness!

Sarah followed her in, breathing a sigh of relief that Noah and Pet were outside playing. There was a stream behind the cottage that flowed into the lake, and they were throwing rocks and wading.

Earlier that morning, they'd been feeling housebound, so they'd walked into the village. Mr. Sinclair had ordered her not to prance about the neighborhood, but she had a bad habit of *not* meekly obeying. The minute they'd arrived, he'd ridden by.

He hadn't minded that they were out and about, but his henchman, Judah Barnett, had definitely been irked. He'd commanded Sarah—in no uncertain terms—to get the children out of Miss Sinclair's sight.

Normally, Sarah would have told him to stuff it, but she hadn't wanted to engage in a public quarrel. Nor would she jeopardize their spot at the Haven. She suspected Mr. Sinclair would be furious if his sister met Noah and Pet, and Sarah was happy to let him decide if overtures would ever be made.

"I've never previously been in this cottage," Miss Sinclair said. "My father's retired valet lived here for years."

Sarah had no idea how to respond to the comment or what, exactly, they ought to talk about, but she said, "Please pardon my manners, but I don't have any servants or any tea and biscuits. I can't supply you with refreshments."

"I don't need any."

"How can I help you?" Sarah was eager to cut to the chase and send her away before Noah and Pet blustered in.

"Mr. Barnett advises me that you've suffered some personal difficulties, so my brother is allowing you to tarry. I was very surprised and not aware he'd opened this cottage for you."

"I ran an orphanage in London."

"*You* ran it? A woman?"

"Yes, but the building was sold, so I've lost my home. I didn't have anywhere to go, and Mr. Sinclair is permitting me to use it while I figure out a plan for myself."

"How do you know my brother?"

"I just ... ah ... crossed paths with him recently." Sarah was a terrible liar, and she couldn't invent an innocent story to explain their association.

"The children who were with you in the village, are they *your* children?"

"No, they're orphans. As my facility was being shut down, I found places for all my wards except them. They don't have anywhere to go either."

Sarah was unnerved by Miss Sinclair. Obviously, she didn't like the notion of her brother opening the cottage, and he was on his way to Selby. While he was there, could his sister kick them out? What was her authority over the property? If she insisted they had to depart, had Sarah any option but to comply?

"I saw Sebastian with you," Miss Sinclair said. "You appeared to be very ... close."

"Yes, we've become good friends."

"I think you're *more* than friends." Miss Sinclair's tone was accusatory. "I think you might possibly be sweet on him. You seemed quite *fond.*"

Sarah chuckled as if it were the silliest observation ever. "If that's what you suppose, then you have completely misconstrued our relationship. It is simply one of charity, with him extending assistance to a woman who desperately needs it."

Clearly, Miss Sinclair didn't believe Sarah, and Sarah studied her, being uneasy over her purpose.

She was very pretty, twenty or so, with blond hair, blue eyes, and a slender shape. She was attired in very expensive clothes, sewn from the most elegant fabrics: a pink day dress and silk shawl, with dainty slippers that had been dyed to match the gown.

Sarah was wearing a functional grey dress. It was tattered and faded from too many washings. Her unruly hair was tied with a ribbon, her shoes scuffed and dusty from the walk to the village. In Miss Sinclair's presence, she felt dowdy and unkempt.

What must it have been like to be the daughter of the famous Sir Sidney? Her brother had gotten to travel the globe and have adventures, but *she* had had to dawdle at home with her mother. Did she ever chafe at the unfairness of her situation? Did she ever bubble over with fury that she hadn't been provided with the same chances as her brother?

Sarah would have raged and protested, and she could predict almost to the letter how dreary Miss Sinclair's life had been so far. Sarah might have been a thousand years older than the juvenile, spoiled girl.

"I thought you should know," Miss Sinclair said, "that my brother is engaged."

At the news, Sarah was shocked, but she managed to keep her expression carefully blank. "He's engaged? I hadn't heard. I'll have to offer my congratulations."

Miss Sinclair frowned, as if she might have overstepped. "You shouldn't mention it to him or anyone. For the moment, it's a secret. We haven't made any announcements."

"I understand, and I shall remain silent until I learn that it's official. Who is his fiancée?"

"Our cousin, Veronica Gordon. She was with me in the village. Might you have seen her?"

"Yes, she's stunning, and I'm sure she'll be a beautiful bride."

It was growing harder to maintain a calm façade. Yes, she'd espied the gorgeous girl who'd climbed into the carriage with Miss Sinclair and Judah Barnett. She'd been striking, but in an icy, harsh way.

Sebastian Sinclair was marrying *that* girl?

Sarah swallowed down any regret. She'd had a few brief days to enjoy their flirtation, but she should have known he'd be engaged. He was thirty after all. And she also should have known it would be to a cousin. Rich dolts like the Sinclairs kept their assets in the family so they didn't have to share with outsiders.

Why then—when the reality of his circumstance was so blatantly apparent—was she so terribly crushed? It wasn't as if they could have had a permanent bond. She wasn't that stupid. She wasn't Cinderella, and a man like Mr. Sinclair *never* married a female of her low station.

It simply hurt to realize that he'd been trifling with her when he was about to march down the aisle with someone else. Yes, he was a bachelor, so it wasn't technically wrong, but still, it was duplicitous behavior toward his fiancée.

She'd convinced herself that he was sweet on her, that he wanted a connection, and she was so pathetically lonely that she'd let him shower her with attention.

Why had she? Maybe she was as disgustingly fond as his sister had charged.

Well, she'd had a lifetime of parting from people with whom she was close, and she was good at it. The minute he returned from Selby, she'd nip any romance in the bud, *and* she'd start locking the door so he couldn't sneak in.

"I'm curious about your two orphans," Miss Sinclair said.

You shouldn't be!

"How have they intrigued you?" Sarah blandly inquired.

"They were very familiar to me, and I'm trying to figure out why. Who is their father?"

Sarah looked her straight in the eye and firmly stated, "I have no idea. They're *orphans,* Miss Sinclair. In my line of work, it's common that I wouldn't learn a child's parentage."

"I don't believe you, and I should probably inform you that my brother recently told me a distressing story about my father. He claims that Sir Sidney sired numerous bastards and that two of them have been living in London."

"That's very . . . interesting."

"And now, here *you* are with two children who resemble me exactly. So I ask you again: Who is their father?"

Sarah stared her down, struggling to deduce the best course. She hated to deceive Miss Sinclair or infuriate Mr. Sinclair, which she was positive would be the result of any revelation.

She couldn't guess how the encounter might have concluded, but to her dismay, the rear door banged, and the children tromped in. They were laughing, delighted to be in the country and viewing it as a sort of grand holiday away from the city.

Miss Sinclair cast a scathing glare at Sarah, then rose to her feet as the merry pair bustled in. Noah saw her first, and he beamed with excitement and strutted over to her. Petunia hung back, standing a bit behind Noah as was her wont. She was never as bold as he was.

"Miss Sinclair!" Being the little gentleman he was, he performed a perfect bow. "It's wonderful to finally meet you. No one would let us, and we've been so anxious about it."

Miss Sinclair scowled. "You've been hoping to meet me?"

"Yes!" He peeked over at Sarah. "Did you tell her about us? Is that why she's here? Or did our brother tell her?"

Miss Sinclair gasped, and she whirled on Sarah as if Sarah had tricked her. She was livid as she asked, "Are they my father's children?"

Sarah rose too, and she felt awful over how it had unraveled. Noah's smile vanished, and Pet appeared stricken.

With Miss Sinclair demanding to know if Sir Sidney was their father, was there any reason to lie? In light of how the secret had been pitched out into the open, she didn't think so.

A vision of Mr. Sinclair flashed in her mind, and she pictured him shouting at her, throwing things, kicking them out. It made her sad and left her very weary again. She'd thought they were safe, but perhaps—so long as Noah and Pet were with her—they simply couldn't be anywhere near the Sinclair siblings.

Once Miss Sinclair departed, they would pack their bags. If her brother arrived and tossed them out, they could leave without a fuss.

"Yes, Miss Sinclair, they are your father's children. This is Noah." She gestured to him. "And this is Petunia. We call her Pet for short."

They all froze, the moment so fraught with peril that it seemed as if they'd been turned to stone.

Then Miss Sinclair snorted with revulsion, as if she was offended to the marrow of her bones.

"My presence is required at the manor," she arrogantly said. "Miss Robertson, I expect you will attend me tomorrow morning at eleven. I have some questions for you to answer, and you will visit me *alone*." She peered scornfully at her half-siblings. "I don't wish you to bring anyone with you."

She swept out, and Noah hurled after her, "I apologize for upsetting you, Miss Sinclair. Please don't be angry!"

Sarah placed a hand on his shoulder, urging him to silence, and they listened as she stomped away.

After it was quiet again, Noah asked, "Will you speak with her tomorrow?"

"I suppose I'd better. I'm not certain about her authority over us, and I shouldn't antagonize her more than we already have."

"She'll calm down." Noah was a constant optimist. "Why is she so incensed? We can't change the fact that Sir Sidney is our father. It just . . . *is*."

"I doubt she views it that way."

Sarah glanced over at Pet, and the poor child was completely crushed.

"I always wanted to have a sister," Pet told them, "but she didn't even look at me."

"She was shocked, Pet," Sarah said, "and rude because of it. She didn't mean anything by it."

"She hated us," Pet said. "I could tell."

She burst into tears, and as Sarah sank down onto her chair, she felt like crying too.

What would happen now? She couldn't imagine, but she had an appointment the next morning at eleven. She had no idea when Mr. Sinclair would get back from Selby, but she could only pray it would be very soon.

CHAPTER

9

NELL DRUMMOND BLAKE, THE new Countess of Selby, was strolling down the lane toward Selby Manor.

She'd been to the village to attend a meeting of the church's Lady's Aid Society, of which her new position made her patron and chairwoman, and she was walking home. There were so many things she was expected to do now, so many tasks that had been dumped into her lap, and she felt dizzy with trying to keep them all straight.

She'd been married to Nathan for a few weeks, and she still couldn't believe it. Every morning, when she first opened her eyes and he was snuggled by her side, she'd pinch herself to be sure she hadn't dreamed it.

She'd become an orphan at age twelve and a ward of the very wealthy Albert and Florence Middleton, with Albert appointed as her guardian.

She'd grown up in their ostentatious mansion, and their daughter, Susan, was her dearest friend. She'd initially come to Selby for Susan's wedding, then she'd promptly misbehaved with Nathan. But he was handsome and dashing and so unlike anyone she'd ever previously known. How could she have resisted his wily seduction?

Susan had been a great heiress who'd been betrothed to Nathan's cousin, Percy, but that situation had collapsed into chaos when Susan had fallen in love with Percy's brother, Trevor. The negligent pair had eloped to Scotland, so Susan had been disowned by her rich parents. Percy, who'd been drowning in a sea of debt *and* who'd been a secret bigamist, had fled the country to escape his fiscal burdens.

Nell had returned to London in disgrace due to her being in the family way. In a pathetic attempt to tamp down any scandal, Mr. Middleton had arranged a hasty marriage for her to one of his clerks. Nathan had rescued her from that dire fate and had married her himself.

They were living happily ever after at Selby. Newlyweds, Susan and Trevor, were living with them too. Nathan was home for good, having vowed to abandon his adventuring to stay with her at Selby. She'd refused to have a husband who spent his life gallivanting across the globe, so it was a promise she'd extracted from him when he'd begged her to wed.

Of course he was never in the best of health. His final expedition had ended in tragedy, and he'd almost died in Africa, so he was still recovering. Even if he'd wanted to sail there in the future, he'd probably never be fit enough to proceed.

She sighed with gladness. All in all, matters had worked out perfectly.

Her only regret was that Susan's parents remained so angry over her elopement. They were upset with Nell too, assuming she'd assisted Susan in her disgraceful scheme. They were also incensed because Mr. Middleton had expended an enormous amount of effort to locate a husband for Nell, but after Nathan had arrived to claim her, she'd flitted off to Selby without a backward glance.

She'd resided with the Middletons for an entire decade, and she always hated to quarrel, so she wrote them once a week, hoping—eventually—they'd forgive her.

So far, she hadn't received a reply, and apparently, they'd shuttered their house and departed on a lengthy trip. Nell suspected their humiliation over Susan's elopement had driven them out of the city, but whatever the reason, they weren't home, so her letters weren't being opened. Yet she was an optimist, so she kept writing to them anyway.

Someone was riding up behind her, and she peeked over her shoulder to find a blond man approaching. She hadn't ever met Nathan's ex-friend, Sebastian Sinclair, but she recognized him immediately. She'd seen portraits of his famous father, and Mr. Sinclair resembled him exactly.

With their last journey concluding so disastrously, he'd visited earlier in the summer. Nathan had been mortally wounded in Africa and left for dead by his companions. Somehow, he'd staggered to England on his own, and he still declined to explain how he'd managed the extraordinary feat. He insisted the details were too disturbing to share, so she hadn't pressed.

After Mr. Sinclair was back in London, he'd traveled to Selby to apprise Nathan's aunt and cousins of his death. Nathan wasn't dead though, and Mr. Sinclair had been intercepted in the driveway by a lethally livid Nathan who'd sent Mr. Sinclair racing away, bruised, battered, and with his ears ringing from hurled instructions to never return.

If she remembered correctly, Nathan had threatened to *kill* Mr. Sinclair if they ever came face to face again.

So . . . she had no idea why he would dare to show up after such a short interval, but she was thrilled that he had. Obviously, he was determined to mend their rift. How could she help him accomplish it?

"Hello, Mr. Sinclair," she said as he neared.

He reined in. "Hello, Miss. Do I know you?"

"We haven't been introduced, but your reputation precedes you, and you have no secrets from me."

He flashed a charming smile. "I can't decide if I'm elated or horrified."

"Are you here to speak with Nathan?"

At her question, he hesitated, clearly wondering who she was. If she would refer to Nathan by his Christian name, then they were on familiar terms. Might he have read her wedding announcement in the newspapers?

He and Nathan had been friends since they were seven, and they'd been closer than brothers. It was odd for them to be estranged, but even odder that Nathan would wed, but Mr. Sinclair not be consulted or informed.

"Ah . . . ah . . . yes," he said, "I'm planning to speak with him."

"He's still furious. Are you sure you should risk it?"

Mr. Sinclair snorted at that. "I have to risk it. I need to talk to him."

"I'm Nell Blake."

"Are you a Blake cousin?"

Maybe he hadn't seen the announcement.

"I'm not a cousin," she said. "I'm a wife."

His mind whirred as he worked it out. "Nell . . . Blake? By any chance, were you previously Miss Nell Drummond?"

"Yes. That would be me."

He dismounted to bow politely. "I'm delighted to meet you, Lady Selby."

"You don't have to address me in a fancy way. Up until a few weeks ago, I was a very normal person, and I'm not used to all the pomp and circumstance. Please call me Nell."

"I will—if you'll call me Sebastian."

"I'd like that."

"As I'd never heard a whiff about you until your marriage was mentioned in the paper, I assume there is an interesting story behind you becoming Nathan's wife."

"I'll tell you about it someday." She leaned in and whispered, "Mostly, we had to proceed in a hurry because we're having a baby."

He blanched with astonishment. "Oh! My goodness."

She laughed and waved away his reaction. "Before I traveled to Selby over the summer, I viewed myself as a very moralistic female, but after my antics with Nathan, I've been forced to accept that—in certain instances—I'm no better than I have to be."

"Well . . . !" His jaw dropped. "I have no response to that."

"I could have pretended that we married quickly for no reason at all, but I expect you can calculate the dates on a calendar. You'd have figured it out pretty fast."

"I'd like to think I wouldn't have believed the worst."

"My husband *is* very fond of me too though, so he probably would have wed me even without the baby. In fact, I'd be so bold as to say he's madly in love with me, and we're annoyingly happy. Since you've been acquainted with him for most of your life, and I'm sure you deem him to be a huge grouch, I predict you're shocked."

Sebastian gazed down the lane toward the manor, looking as if he wished he had magical eyes that would allow him to peer inside its walls. "How is he?"

"He's healing and much improved. I doubt he'll ever be completely hale, but considering his condition when he first arrived, he's quite recuperated."

"I thought he perished in Africa."

"I know."

"If I'd suspected he was alive, I wouldn't have left him there."

"I know that too."

"We searched for him exhaustively, but he was nowhere to be found. We finally gave up and sailed without him—to my great shame."

He appeared so remorseful, and she hated how it had unraveled, how both men had ended up so wretched.

"It was a chaotic event," she said, "and you had your father and your crew to worry about."

"Has he told you how he made it to England?"

She shook her head. "No, he won't talk about it, so I'm guessing it was horrendous."

"I suppose it would have been." He gazed toward the manor again. "There's an inquest to be held about the incident. The expedition had financial sponsors, and they want answers about what happened."

"Nathan received a subpoena for it, and he's been debating whether to show up or not. It would be very difficult for him to be questioned."

"I *really* need him there, and . . . ah . . . I need to inquire about his testimony."

As with his miraculous journey to England, Nathan hadn't confided exactly why Sir Sidney had been murdered in Africa, but she had her suspicions. He'd been so revered, and his family would be anxious to preserve his status as a hero.

If they were plotting to bury unsavory details, what was her opinion about it? Should her husband be part of a duplicitous scheme to shade the edges of history?

It was likely best for her to stay out of it. Nathan should choose the correct path for himself. *He* was the one who'd have to struggle with his conscience.

"How angry is he these days?" Sebastian asked.

"Very angry."

"Could I convince him to converse civilly with me?"

"There's only one way to find out. Let's head to the manor, and I'll check his mood. We'll go from there."

— ❧ —

NATHAN WAS SEATED AT the desk in his library and wading through a stack of tedious correspondence. He'd never viewed himself as a farmer or a businessman, but with his swearing off adventures to remain at Selby, he'd become both.

In the years he'd been away on his wild escapades, he'd paid agents, lawyers, and bankers to handle the tasks associated with his enormous estates and fortune. Since he was home now—for good—he was trying to be more responsible, but he detested all of it. He was already thinking—at the earliest opportunity—he'd deliver it all back to his agents, bankers, and lawyers.

Nell was suddenly dawdling out in the hall, and without glancing up, he said, "Why are you lurking, Nell? Please interrupt me. I'm dying in here."

She bustled in, and her presence had him smiling—as always.

"How did you know it was me?" she asked.

"I'd recognize your stride anywhere."

She sauntered over, rounding the desk so she could snoop at the letter on the top of the pile. It was from a book publisher. There had been numerous inquiries about the possibility of his writing a book, but he couldn't imagine why any sane person would judge his comments to be relevant on any topic.

"What have you decided?" she asked. "Will you pen a memoire or not?"

"Who would want to hear about my life?"

"Everybody?"

"It's seems awfully pretentious."

"Well, you're a pretentious fellow, and your past has been so exciting. Why not entertain those poor souls whose existences are so dreary? They could live vicariously through you."

He rubbed his side, where old wounds continued to plague him. "It hasn't been all that grand."

"Liar. You wouldn't trade a minute of the adventures you've had."

"I might trade a few. Several of them turned out to be quite deadly, and I'd just as soon not reflect on them—*or* tell anyone about them." He riffled in the stack and handed her a letter. "I have some information about your friend, Miss Robertson."

Sarah Robertson had run an orphanage in London, and Nell had met her at church when she'd been shamelessly begging parishioners for donations.

Nathan was eager to be introduced to her because he was searching for his two half-sisters, Sissy and Bec-Bec, from whom he'd been separated as a boy of six. He'd grown up, not remembering he had sisters. His despicable relatives had persuaded him that he'd been an only child.

He was desperate to find them, and Sissy had been taken to Miss Robertson's orphanage when she was three. He'd intended to confer with Sarah to discover if she had any records from that long-ago period. But he and Nell had stopped by the facility shortly before their wedding, and it had been shuttered, a huge FOR SALE sign nailed to the front door.

"You found her?" Nell asked, looking overjoyed.

"No, but my clerk spoke to some of the merchants on her street. The building was sold, and she was evicted by the new owner."

"Oh, no! I thought she owned the building. I thought she inherited it from her father when he passed away."

"Evidently not."

"Where is she now?"

"No one had any news, but I've been given an address for her sister."

At the revelation, Nell was bewildered. "She has a sister? I had no idea."

"The woman has a home outside London. Next time we travel to town, we could visit her."

"I'd like that."

Nell was aware of how much he loathed paperwork, and she pointed to the pile.

"You've been very diligent in your efforts this afternoon," she said.

"Yes, and I deserve a reward."

He flashed a salacious grin, and she shook a scolding finger in his face. "You can't have a reward just yet."

"When *can* I have it then?"

"I have to talk to you about an important issue, and after I've finished, we'll see what sort of temper you're in."

"That doesn't sound good. What have you done?"

"Why would you automatically assume I've *done* something?"

"Because I know you."

He pushed back his chair and patted his thigh, and she snuggled herself onto his lap and riffled a hand in his hair. He'd lived his life around rugged, manly men, struggling through in dire circumstances. There hadn't been any women in that world, and he treasured her small ministrations.

"I'd like you to grant me a favor," she said.

"What is it? Before you inform me, I must remind you that I can't tell you *no* on any subject."

"I realize that fact, and I'm counting on it."

"You presume on my kindly nature."

"Yes. I'm quite brazen about it."

He snorted with disgust. "At least you admit it."

"You have to promise you won't get angry."

"I can't promise you that. Not without hearing what you intend to confide."

"Then you must promise you'll *try* to not get angry. Try to do this for me in a calm manner—to the best of your ability."

"You're terrifying me, Nell. Cease your coaxing and put me out of my misery."

She slid to her feet and gazed down at him with a great deal of affection.

"This matters to me," she said. "Remember that. I'm thrilled that this is happening. I think it will make you feel better."

"If you want to make me feel *better,* you could take me up to our bed-chamber."

"Not now, and don't you move. I'll just be a minute."

"Fine. Go."

He nodded toward the door, and she skittered away. As he watched her depart, he chuckled with amusement. While still a bachelor, if he'd been pressed for an opinion about marriage, he'd have categorically stated that he deemed it to be a horrid condition.

Previously, he hadn't understood why any male would proceed to matrimony, and he'd never pictured himself to be a viable candidate for a husband. With *her,* he became more besotted by the day. She intrigued him. She humored him. She amazed him. She delighted him in every way, and he suspected she always would.

She returned quickly, and there was someone with her, a man from the sound of the booted strides. He leaned back in his chair, braced for whatever mischief she was about to instigate. Yet when she entered the room, and he observed her companion, his smile vanished. Suddenly, he was so incensed he considered throwing the ink jar through the window.

Sebastian was standing with her, looking proud and imperious as ever. How dare he show up! How dare he coerce Nell into being his ally!

"This is your surprise?" he furiously demanded of her. "This is the favor you ask of me?"

"Yes," she firmly retorted. "Mr. Sinclair needs to speak to you about his father's inquest and other . . . *things.* I told him you would."

"And I told *him,* if I ever saw him again, I'd kill him."

"You're not killing him," she insisted, her tone exasperated. "You'll *talk* to him—like a civilized, rational person, like the old friend you used to be."

He glared at her, being so hideously disappointed, but he wouldn't bicker with her in front of Sebastian.

"I can't believe you'd do this, Nell," he quietly said. "You've gone too far this time."

"In my view, I haven't gone nearly far enough. I've let this quarrel fester, and I shouldn't have. I expect you to converse in a sensible fashion."

"We can't," he said. "It's not possible."

Of course she ignored him. "I'll be right outside. If voices are raised, I will have to act as your mediator. I'd rather not. You're adults, and you've known each other since you were boys. You have to settle this between yourselves."

Sebastian was still hovered in the doorway, and she urged him into the room and pulled the door closed. Nathan envisioned her dawdling in the hall, listening like the dedicated eavesdropper she could definitely be.

He yearned to leap up, march over, and pummel Sebastian again. He yearned to rail and accuse and toss him out of the house, but to his aggravation, she had asked him to remain calm, and he couldn't disregard her request.

She had that effect on him.

Besides, she'd mentioned the inquest, and he'd been wondering about it. He was anxious to attend so he could shout to the entire world what an immoral lout Sir Sidney had been. He'd frequently imperiled their crew with his licentious antics.

After two decades of traveling with him, Nathan had decided the major reason he journeyed out of the country so often was because carnal rules were more relaxed in foreign locales. He could fornicate with a reckless abandon and not worry about the consequences.

In light of how their last expedition had ended, Nathan would like every hero-worshipping idiot to discover the truth. But on the other hand . . .

Oh, on the other hand! He couldn't imagine betraying Sir Sidney that way.

He, himself, had worshipped the man—usually. He'd rescued Nathan from his brutal childhood. He'd treated Nathan like a second son. He'd replaced Nathan's father who'd been killed in an accident when he was six. He'd given Nathan a future and a purpose. By bringing Nathan along on their explorations, he'd made Nathan rich and famous.

Nathan had loved him, faults and all, and even though he'd passed away the prior year, in a distant land, surrounded by strangers, Nathan was still desperately grieving. He'd missed the numerous funerals and memorial services, and he couldn't bear to skip the inquest too.

Nor could he bear to utter a single derogatory remark that might dampen the memories people had of his mentor and idol.

What was the rest of the team planning to say? He'd been sure Sebastian would have had a false account devised, but Nathan had been too livid to contact him and learn what it might be.

Now, here he was: his oldest friend, the man he'd called his brother. The man who'd left him behind to die.

A fraught interval spun out, where neither of them could deduce the appropriate opening comment. Nathan wasn't about to start the discussion.

Ultimately, Sebastian pushed away from the door and walked to the sideboard. He filled two glasses with whiskey, then carried them to the desk. He slid one to Nathan, then seated himself in the chair across. Sebastian sipped his liquor, but Nathan simply stared, indicating Sebastian should get on with it.

Sebastian finally spoke. "An interesting woman, your wife."

Nathan wouldn't talk about her with him. "Why have you slinked in?"

"You didn't invite me to your wedding."

Nathan scoffed with derision. "As if I would have."

"She advises me you're on your way to being a father."

"My wife has a tendency to gossip too much."

"I like her," Sebastian said. "I'm glad for you."

Though Nathan had promised Nell he wouldn't lose his temper, it was flaring. "I'll give you five minutes to explain your purpose. Then, when your time has expired, if you're still sitting in that chair, I will bodily drag you out of my house."

He peered over at the mantle to check the clock, and Sebastian sighed with frustration. "Will you ever stop being angry?"

"No."

"Will you ever forgive me?"

"No. I'm meeting with you because why wife asked it of me. It's the only reason. Tell me what you want."

Sebastian bristled and stewed, then cast away his attempt at reconciliation. "You were subpoenaed to the inquest, and I have to know what you intend to say."

Another tense interval played out, and a vision of that terrifying day washed over him. It happened occasionally. He'd smell the jungle and hear the war cries. He'd feel his heart pounding in his chest, shoving the last drops of his blood into the dirt.

The longer he was home, the frequency and the virulence of his recollections were fading, but they still had the power to rivet him, to make him suppose he was back in the middle of that violent scene.

He inhaled deeply, tossing the ghastly sight away. "What would you like me to say? Just spit it out."

Sebastian nodded, accepting Nathan's olive branch.

"We've concocted a story." He reached into his coat, retrieved some papers, and placed them on the desk. "I wrote it down. You can modify it a little so it sounds more personal."

"What is the basis of our lie?"

Sebastian winced at the word *lie,* but that's what it would be. None of them could ever admit what had actually occurred. They wouldn't tarnish Sir Sidney's reputation, but also, they wouldn't humiliate Sebastian's mother. She didn't deserve to have such a salacious tale spread about her husband.

If rumors ever circulated, Nathan wouldn't be the one who circulated them.

"We'll claim it started over a mistranslated comment," Sebastian said. "We'll claim we thought we'd obtained passage across a tribal hunting ground, but we were mistaken about what we'd been allowed. When Sir Sidney tried to placate the tribal chiefs, a quarrel broke out."

It was a believable yarn, and Nathan could force himself to stumble through it, but it didn't clarify the hardest portion. "And my grisly part in it? How am I to smooth over the edges so it's not horrific?"

"Your part can be completely true. You intervened to quell the argument, but you were swept up in it instead."

Nathan tsked with irritation. "What about my being left behind? I'm certain the audience will listen to every detail with bated breath, but if I'm candid, you won't look too good."

"I didn't leave you behind!"

"Really? I'm quite certain I staggered home by myself."

"I sent a team of men to search for you."

"Yes, dear Judah. Such a *friend* to me."

"They insisted you were dead under some ferns. They swore it!"

"They lied."

"About which piece? They didn't find you? You never saw them? What?"

A wave of fury bubbled up, and he was eager to commit murder again. It was a crushing blow that Sebastian would question his description of the event, that he would accept Judah's version over Nathan's.

He could barely compose himself enough to continue. "I was mortally wounded, and they had a lengthy debate as to whether they should carry me to your camp or abandon me to my fate. If I was about to perish anyway, why bother rescuing me?"

"You heard them dickering over this? You talked to them."

"Yes, I *talked* to them, you idiot. Judah bluntly apprised me that you were worried I'd slow you down. He claimed your orders were—if I was beyond help—to let me die in peace."

"I never said that!"

"Then what did you say?" Nathan's expression was grim. "I'm surprised they didn't slit my throat to hasten my demise, but evidently, it didn't occur to them. They simply walked away."

"Swear it to me. Swear that's how it happened, that you're not confused or perhaps imagining things that never transpired."

Nathan felt ill. "Get out of my library."

"I never told them to leave you behind. I *told* them to find you! I *told* them to bring you back—no matter what."

"A likely story." He gestured to the door. "Get the hell out of here."

"You're aware of how trauma can affect a man's perception."

"No, I'm not aware of that, and my *perception* is perfectly clear. Judah and his two chums declared that *you* were afraid my feeble condition would imperil the rest of the crew."

"It's a damned lie."

"We'll never know for sure, will we? Maybe I should stop by the Haven and ask Judah what your orders were."

"If your memory is correct, there will have to be consequences imposed on my end. Big consequences. Men will lose their positions. They won't be able to travel with me in the future."

"Why would I care about that?"

Sebastian studied Nathan, apparently hunting for a hint of perplexity or vacillation. But Nathan could recount every detail, right down to how many heartbeats had pounded out before he'd crawled into the jungle. He'd been gasping for air, praying for a quick death. And he'd been all alone.

"Your five minutes are up," he evenly stated.

"I'm sorry," Sebastian murmured.

"You keep telling me that, but it doesn't change anything."

"I guess I'll see you at the inquest."

"Hopefully not. Hopefully, we'll testify on different days."

Sebastian stood, and he hovered, obviously eager to offer a parting comment, but Nathan couldn't abide another moment of the despicable meeting. His pulse was racing, sweat popping out on his brow. His insomnia was always bad, but after this discussion, he probably wouldn't sleep for a year.

He realized he was acting like a juvenile brat. Sebastian was *trying* to fix their quarrel, but Nathan wasn't interested in having it fixed. He'd been hurt in such a distressing way that he didn't think their rift could ever be mended.

Ultimately, Sebastian whipped away and headed out, and Nathan said, "Give Judah a message for me."

"I will. What is it?"

"I want my knife back. It was a gift from Sir Sidney for my eighteenth birthday. Remember it? When I was dying in the dirt, he cut it off my belt and stole it."

"I didn't know that."

"I want it back. If I have to come and *take* it back, it won't be pretty."

"I'll retrieve it for you. I promise."

"Thank you. Goodbye."

They shared a poignant look, then Sebastian yanked the door open. Nell was standing on the other side, and she frowned into the room.

"Are you finished already?" she asked Sebastian. "You can't be. You haven't been in there five minutes!"

"We're done," Sebastian replied.

"Are you positive?"

"Absolutely positive."

"At least there weren't any fisticuffs. I suppose that's progress." She sighed with exasperation. "Let me show you out."

She led Sebastian away, and Nathan sat in his chair, frozen with regret, with visions that wouldn't fade. He was once again being pummeled by a grueling sense of loss for what had been ruined in Africa. But he shook it away.

He wasn't a baby. He wasn't a weak-kneed dunce. He was Nathan Blake, Lord Selby, and he was busy. He picked up his stack of letters and started reading through them, but he couldn't focus on a single word.

He downed the whiskey Sebastian had poured, then went to the sideboard and downed two more. The liquor hit his stomach, and the quaking in his limbs gradually abated.

He walked to his desk, glared at his correspondence, and began again.

CHAPTER

10

"My brother is very old-fashioned."

"I've noticed that about him."

Ophelia grinned at Judah Barnett and asked, "How about you? Are you old-fashioned?"

"I'm not like Sebastian in even the slightest way."

"That's a relief. With the mood I'm in today, I would hate to hear that you share any traits."

Judah chuckled, happy to play the part of confidante. "How has he vexed you this time?"

"How hasn't he?"

It was barely past nine, and they were in the front parlor at the Haven and waiting for Miss Gordon to come downstairs. She was a sluggard and always late for every appointment. The two girls had decided to leave for town on the spur of the moment, and their bags were in the foyer and being loaded into their carriage.

He wasn't sure why they were departing so rapidly, but Miss Ophelia was practically dragging Miss Gordon away. It was probably for the best though. Sebastian was gone, so they shouldn't have dawdled at the Haven for a single minute.

The manor was full of handsome, randy bachelors, so it wasn't appropriate for them to be in residence too. If Sebastian's mother discovered the arrangement, she wouldn't be pleased. They were safe enough though. Miss Gordon was slated to be Sebastian's fiancée, so she was off limits to any flirtation. And Miss Ophelia was viewed as a sort of pesky little sister they'd watched grow up.

Judah, though, had an entirely different opinion about her. She ought to wed, and he was convinced that *he* ought to be her husband. By becoming a member of the family, it would cement his position with the expedition team, but it would also prevent any problems that might arise over Nathan Blake and what had happened in Africa.

Judah had traveled with the Sinclairs for over a decade, initially joining when he was eighteen. His father had deemed him to be a lazy wastrel who'd needed to toughen up and find a purpose, so he'd purchased Judah a spot on the crew.

He'd quickly adapted to the itinerant life Sir Sidney had supplied, and he didn't want it to ever end. Yet he didn't have the power to guarantee he be allowed to participate in the future. He could *get* that power by marrying Miss Ophelia.

Over the years, he'd worked to ingratiate himself to Sebastian and Sir Sidney, but he'd never felt his place was secure. They'd never been partial to him as they were toward some of the others such as Raven Shawcross. Judah had been tolerated and accepted, but he'd never been especially liked.

He was earning significant money from their trips and was determined to keep it flowing into his bank account. If he was kicked off the team, he had no idea how he'd support himself.

Plus, there was an enormous social benefit to being affiliated with the famous group. They were written about in the newspapers, recognized on the street. He reveled in the heightened attention, and that pompous ass, Nathan

Blake, couldn't be permitted to wreck what Judah had built for himself.

He'd persuaded Sebastian that he'd found Nathan dead, that there was no explaining how he'd survived. Judah's two companions had lied as vehemently as Judah, claiming trauma must have addled Nathan's wits, but Judah was no fool. Nathan and Sebastian had been friends since they were boys. No doubt they would eventually mend their rift, and when they did, where would Judah be?

At that very moment, Sebastian was at Selby, conferring with Nathan about the inquest, and Judah was in a panic. Each reunion between them might be the one where their relationship was restored.

If he was Miss Ophelia's husband, he would be Sebastian's brother-in-law. It would create a closer bond to Sebastian than Nathan could ever have. Nathan might tell tales and complain about what had occurred in Africa, but Judah would be *family*, and with the Sinclairs, family came first.

"I'm disappointed that you're leaving in such a hurry," he told Miss Ophelia.

"I thought we should. If my mother learned I had tarried after Sebastian left, she'd be incensed. I shouldn't have stayed at all. There are too many *incidents* transpiring that I shouldn't have witnessed."

"Such as?"

She didn't clarify, but asked, "How long has that woman, that Miss Robertson, been living here?"

"Just a few days. Why?"

"I had ordered her to stop by the manor to speak with me this morning at eleven, but I shouldn't bother with her. It's the actual reason for my departure. I don't believe she and I ought to ever converse."

"Why not? She can be a tad bossy, but mostly, she's harmless."

"She's *not* harmless. She's carting around a bit of . . . ah . . . *baggage* that she shouldn't be bringing onto our property."

Judah wasn't the sharpest nail in the shed, but he didn't have to be a genius to understand the reference. She'd observed Miss Robertson in the village—with Sir Sidney's bastards—and evidently, she'd figured out who they were.

Judah wasn't supposed to know himself, but he'd figured it out too, the minute he'd laid eyes on the pair. The men on the crew had been fully cognizant of Sir Sidney's less savory proclivities, and the children looked exactly like him.

There was no chance Sebastian could hide their paternity from anyone who was genuinely curious.

When Miss Robertson had shown up at the Haven with them, Sebastian had picked Raven to deal with them, without pausing to wonder if he should offer the responsibility to Judah. The snub was galling.

Judah was as loyal and reliable as Shawcross. Sebastian shouldn't keep secrets from him, and with Nathan off the team for good, Judah should be assuming a leadership role. Why hadn't Sebastian realized it?

"Were you intending to *discuss* her baggage with her?" he asked.

"Yes, but upon further reflection, it was apparent that I shouldn't. I'm sure she'll traipse in at eleven as I demanded, but please tell her there will be no meeting."

"I will tell her that, and I think it's wise that you avoid her. Your brother wouldn't like you talking to her."

"My brother!" She scoffed with derision. "Is it possible Miss Robertson has him besotted?"

Judah frowned. "I haven't really studied them when they're together."

"Well, *I* have. Yesterday in the village? He rode by while Veronica and I were at the mercantile. He saw Miss Robertson, and he reined in and chatted with her. They were quite friendly."

"I'll watch him. If I note any suspicious activity, I'll inform you."

"I'd appreciate it. She is a completely inappropriate female, and I hate that she's here and causing mischief."

"I feel the same," he agreed, anxious for her to consider him an ally. "I tried to dissuade him from extending any charity to her, but you're aware of what he's like."

"Just imagine if Veronica discovered he was engaged in a flirtation—right under her nose! It doesn't bear contemplating."

"No, it doesn't."

"I wish I could get rid of her, but I can hardly command my brother to better behavior. He never listens to me anyway."

"I've learned that about him. In fact, he was laughing about you the other day—in front of all the men."

"What was he saying? I'm certain he was thoroughly condescending."

"He was jesting about how you'd begged to come with us on one of our expeditions."

"I didn't beg!" she fumed.

"He still pictures you as a little girl, and he thought it was a hilarious request."

"I'm not surprised. You have no idea what it's like to be a famous daughter. Sebastian was permitted to travel with my father because he was a son. He started when he was ten! I waited until I was sixteen to ask Sir Sidney if I could go too, but he refused."

"I'm sorry to hear it."

"It was six years ago that I first approached my father. Six years! Since then, I've been impatiently hoping to ask my brother about it. I was positive he'd view it differently, but he was even more opposed than my father had been."

"That's too bad, but what did you expect? He wouldn't like you to tag along and suck up any of his glory."

"Too true, Mr. Barnett!"

"You *should* be able to accompany us. Why not?"

She smiled up at him, providing the distinct impression that he was coercing her correctly. She was an adult, but she was so incredibly gullible.

"If only I had the power to *make* him let me join the crew." She sounded especially woeful.

"There are other ways to garner what you crave."

She scowled. "What ways?"

"For instance, if you had a *husband* who was eager for you to go, your husband would decide. It wouldn't be up to your brother."

She cocked her head, looking mischievous. "Why, Judah Barnett! Are you suggesting what I think you're suggesting?"

He flashed a smug grin. "I might be. I've always been sweet on you. You know that."

"I haven't ever been interested in matrimony. I like my life as it is."

"Yes, but in this world, a woman can't carry on as she likes. Occasionally, she needs a spouse to open doors for her."

He brazenly reached over and squeezed her hand. "You should seriously ponder it. You're twenty-two. Will you waste away in a quiet parlor with your mother while Sebastian has all the fun in the family? How can you want that to be your path?"

"I don't want it."

"Well, if you don't wed, then you're stuck with your brother being in charge of you. He hasn't been inclined to give you what you desire. I, though, would spoil you rotten."

His gaze grew very intense, so his male regard was obvious. With her blond hair, blue eyes, and curvaceous figure, she was a beautiful girl who would be a beautiful wife.

If she was his bride, she'd bring him a social status and fortune he could never achieve on his own. *And* she'd protect his spot with her brother. She didn't like Nathan either. She thought he was pompous and rude, and if Judah married her, she'd have to side with him in any dispute over Nathan.

It was time to push them to a more intimate level, and he might have leaned down and kissed her, but Miss Gordon suddenly tromped down the stairs, her two fussy little dogs yipping at her heels.

Miss Ophelia stepped away, and he hurriedly murmured, "Tell me you'll consider a marriage between us. I'd like to have something to dream about after you leave."

She nodded. "I will consider it. It might be a perfect solution to many of my problems."

"I'll be in town next week. For the inquest? Perhaps we could get together while I'm there."

"Send me a note. We'll arrange a secret rendezvous."

It was the most thrilling comment she could have voiced. As she slid away and went to the foyer to greet her cousin, he breathed a sigh of relief.

⸻ ❖ ⸻

RAVEN SHAWCROSS STOOD ON the rear verandah at Hero's Haven. He was staring out at the park, trying to peer into the future, but he'd never been a clairvoyant.

He supposed, with Sir Sidney dead and Sebastian and Nathan having parted company, he was second in command of their group of explorers.

Sebastian had the strength of character to lead them, and it wouldn't necessarily be the wrong choice to continue on with him. He had much more common sense than his father, so he'd be much less likely to drag them into disasters.

But did Sebastian want to return to Africa? Raven didn't think so.

The men were pestering Sebastian to announce his plans so they could begin preparing. It was a huge task to raise funds, purchase supplies, and pack gear, but if they *weren't* going again, then the men needed to begin preparing for that eventuality too. Sebastian couldn't decide, but then, he'd been distracted by all the memorials and parades.

The inquest was approaching, then the diversions would be over. Hopefully, Sebastian would finally be able to focus.

Raven hadn't mentioned it to the others, but he was convinced Sebastian wouldn't be traveling anywhere ever again. He was exhibiting all the symptoms of battlefield trauma. He drank too much. He couldn't sleep. He was short-tempered.

He assumed no one noticed, but Raven noticed every detail. It had always been his job to notice. He'd been a scout for the team, the man who snuck into hostile territory to assess the area, the man who was expected to see what others never saw, the man charged with ensuring there were no surprises.

Sebastian simply wasn't behaving as if he was ready for another journey to Africa—or to any foreign locale for that matter. He might ultimately calm down and regain some of his aplomb, but it might be years before that day arrived.

Would Raven dawdle at Hero's Haven forever, waiting on Sebastian? Should he declare he was quitting to pursue his own course?

From the minute he'd joined his first Sinclair trip, he'd had a specific goal in mind. He'd been determined to earn as much money as he could, then use every penny to buy the retribution he craved. His deceased father deserved it. His dear mother, who'd died of a broken heart, deserved it too. If it took until he drew his last breath, they would be avenged.

Since he'd never wavered from that objective, wasn't it time to resign his spot and head off to accomplish it?

Footsteps sounded behind him, and he glanced over as Judah came outside. It was nearly eleven o'clock, and he was a lush who liked to spend his nights gambling. Raven was amazed to find him out of bed so early.

Raven suspected—if Sebastian ever returned to Africa—Judah wouldn't be invited. There was the whole debacle with Nathan, but his wagering and inebriation were gradually controlling him too. Who could trust the oaf when he had so many bad habits?

"The house is quiet this morning," he said as Judah sidled up.

"Miss Ophelia and Miss Gordon went back to town."

"That was a tad abrupt."

"Miss Ophelia had scheduled an appointment with Miss Robertson, but she pondered the situation and realized she shouldn't proceed."

Raven scowled. "She scheduled an appointment with Miss Robertson?"

"We were in the village yesterday, and Miss Robertson was there with her wards. Miss Ophelia was disconcerted by the sight of them."

Judah paused, eager for Raven to verify the children's identity, but Raven never gossiped.

"Why would their presence disturb Miss Ophelia?" he casually asked.

"They startled her. She was thinking they looked terribly familiar, and she was incensed to learn that Sebastian has them hidden away in the cottage."

"She shouldn't have an opinion about it. Hero's Haven doesn't belong to her. She has no authority."

"I agree, but Sebastian rode by as he was leaving for Selby, and he stopped to chat with Miss Robertson. Miss Ophelia observed their conversation, and they seemed closer than they should be."

"Again, Judah, she shouldn't have an opinion about it. Sebastian is barely acquainted with his sister, and he's a thirty-year-old bachelor. If he wants to chat with a pretty girl in the village, he probably ought to be allowed."

Raven yanked his gaze from the park and settled it on Judah, his dislike oozing out. They'd never been cordial, mostly because Raven couldn't abide him. If it had been up to Raven, he'd never have brought Judah on any of their expeditions. But he'd never been in a position to say so.

"If you have a problem with Sebastian," he said, "I suggest you discuss it with him. And if his sister has a problem, she ought to confront him directly, and you should butt out. As to myself, I'm not about to stand here and bandy rumors."

Judah's demeanor changed in an instant. He feigned an expression of perplexity as to why Raven would have taken offense.

"I'm merely telling you why Miss Ophelia left. I have no other motive. I'm glad she and Miss Gordon went to town. Without her brother in residence, she shouldn't have tarried."

Raven shrugged. "Her choices aren't any of our business."

Judah perched a hip on the balustrade, trying to appear relaxed and nonchalant. "Are those children really Sir Sidney's bastards? What's your guess?"

"I haven't given the matter any thought," Raven lied.

"What about Miss Robertson? Miss Ophelia is worried that Sebastian is sweet on her, and it's kept him from entering into his betrothal to Miss Gordon."

Raven rolled his eyes. "Judah, shut up."

The idiot never listened. "I mean, why would he stash her in a cottage out in the middle of nowhere? He must have a nefarious plan for her."

Raven wasn't certain how the argument might have concluded. He might have delivered a thorough dressing-down or he might have simply knocked Judah on his ass—just because it would have felt so good—but across the park, Miss Robertson burst out of the trees and marched toward them.

"There's the stupid wench now," Judah muttered.

"It looks as if she's headed to the manor."

"She has a meeting with Miss Ophelia, remember? I'm supposed to tell her it's cancelled."

Judah moved as if he'd traipse down into the grass to intercept her.

Raven couldn't figure out what game Judah was playing with Miss Robertson or with Miss Ophelia. He definitely shouldn't be talking about Miss

Robertson—or the children—with Miss Ophelia. It wasn't any of his concern, and Sebastian would be livid if he learned of it.

He put a palm on Judah's chest, halting him in his tracks.

"I'll speak to her," Raven said.

"I'm happy to do it. I have a few words to share with her."

"Stay out of it, Judah. This is none of your affair."

They were toe to toe, and for a moment, it seemed Judah might push down into the garden despite Raven's insistence that he not. Yet at heart, Judah was a coward. It was why Raven loathed him.

"Fine," Judah spat. "Deal with her yourself—if it's that important to you."

"Go find a card game where you can lose some more of your hard-earned money. Your presence on this verandah isn't necessary to anyone."

A muscle ticked in Judah's jaw, a thousand snide comments dying to spill out, but the cretin knew he was on thin ice with Sebastian due to the incident in Africa. So far, Sebastian had been too busy to tackle the issue, but he *would* tackle it.

Judah didn't dare stir trouble with another member of the team. He stomped away, and Raven watched until he'd vanished, then he stormed down the stairs and walked directly toward Miss Robertson.

She saw him, but didn't slow her pace. She was like a force of nature, like a hurricane whose route couldn't be altered. In a weird way, she reminded him of Nathan. She blustered into dicey situations—as Nathan constantly did—not afraid of anything. She wouldn't take *no* for an answer.

Raven couldn't abide such domineering traits in a female, and he felt strongly that there ought to be laws against women acting like men.

He stopped in the center of the path and glared at her. She glared back—as if they were equals, as if she might simply bowl him over if he didn't step aside. Her obstinacy was exasperating and infuriating.

"Move, Mr. Shawcross. I have an appointment at the manor, and I'm late for it."

"Your appointment is cancelled."

"Pardon me if I don't believe you. Ophelia Sinclair demanded I attend her, and I'd just as soon not be at odds with her."

"She went to London, and she asked me to inform you."

She studied him, searching for the truth of his statement, and ultimately stumbling on it.

"Oh, good. I wasn't keen to talk to her anyway."

She whipped away and headed for the cottage. Just like that. With no courteous parting remark.

"Miss Robertson!" he snapped more sharply than he'd intended, but the annoying shrew had that effect.

She glowered at him over her shoulder. "What?"

"Mr. Sinclair specifically told you he wanted those children out of sight, but you felt free to waltz into the village with them."

"We're not his prisoners, Mr. Shawcross."

"No, you're not, but you were blundering about in your usual reckless manner, and Miss Ophelia saw the three of you."

"Maybe Miss Ophelia needs to grow up and accept the reality about her father."

"Maybe that's not up to you."

"I'll keep that in mind," she snottily retorted.

She continued on, displaying a total disregard for the fact that he wasn't finished speaking to her. He could certainly comprehend why she was still single. Only a dolt who was completely emasculated would have dared marry her.

"Miss Robertson!" he said much too loudly, but she was quickly putting distance between them.

She whirled to face him. "Will you shout at me across the park, Mr. Shawcross? I must firmly state that I don't care for it. Why don't you stomp over here and manhandle me instead? It's what you're best at."

He tamped down a spurt of temper, determined not to have her goad him into lashing out. "Cease your flirting with Mr. Sinclair. His sister witnessed that too, but he's promised to her cousin, Miss Gordon. She's thick as thieves with Miss Gordon, and you'd gravely regret having either of them angry at you. You can't win a fight like that."

"Thank you for your wise counsel. I'm ever so grateful!"

"I'm trying to *help* you, Miss Robertson. I'm trying to make you see sense because you appear to possess very little of it."

"Yes, I'm renowned as a hysterical female."

It was a valid assessment, so he wouldn't debate the matter. "Stay away from Mr. Sinclair. I'm sure you have a wild idea in that deluded brain of yours about how you can charm him and latch onto him in a permanent fashion, but you never could. Take a piece of advice from me."

"I'm absolutely breathless waiting to hear what it is."

"You're too far beneath him to ever capture his notice, so save yourself some trouble. Remain in your cottage and behave yourself while you're there."

"Behave myself!" If she'd been standing next to him, she might have slapped him. "Mr. Shawcross, you are not my father, brother, or husband. You have no right to boss me, and if you don't like me being friends with Mr. Sinclair, that's *your* problem. Not mine!"

She flounced off, and he called to her twice more, but she ignored him. He would have bellowed a third time, but he realized he was embarrassing himself.

Why let her rile him? If she got herself into a jam with Sebastian, what was it to him? If she antagonized Miss Ophelia, hadn't Raven warned her?

It was simply that his loyalties lay with Sebastian, and he would never allow anything to happen that might hurt the man. No doubt about it, Miss Robertson was exactly the sort of wench who could bring disaster raining down.

When Sebastian returned from Selby, they would have to have a long, frank discussion. Miss Robertson and those children had to be sent away as swiftly as their departure could be arranged. Raven would personally dispose of her, and when he was escorting her off the property, he would smile all the way.

CHAPTER

11

SEBASTIAN WALKED UP TO the cottage, and as usual where Miss Robertson was concerned, he was trying to figure out his purpose.

It was late, and he probably should have spent the night in London, but he'd been overwhelmed by thoughts of her. He'd pushed on to Hero's Haven, suffering from an extremely illogical need to be with her.

After his awful conversation with Nathan, he required a huge dose of her fascinating personality to tamp down his doldrums.

He and Nathan had met at boarding school when they were seven. Nathan had been like a lost, angry puppy. He'd lashed out at every person of authority and had constantly gotten into fights. Sebastian had been amazed by his fearlessness and bravado, and he hadn't been able to resist their being friends.

Nathan's grandfather, Godwin, hadn't liked him and couldn't manage him, so he'd rarely been welcome at Selby. Sir Sidney had loathed Godwin, and he'd enjoyed tweaking the old man's nose with regard to Nathan. Nathan had been absorbed into the Sinclair family and had gradually seemed like one of them.

Godwin had died when they were ten, and with him no longer around to prevent it, Sir Sidney had started taking them with him on his trips. They'd grown up together on sailing ships, in desert caravans, in jungles where no Englishman had ever walked. They'd traipsed after his famous father and had become famous themselves.

They'd had the best childhood any two boys could have had, but it was clear that Africa would be their undoing. Nathan would never forgive him. His hurt was too great, his grievances too monumental.

Sebastian had to question Judah again, then send him packing, but he couldn't. Not with the inquest about to begin. At the moment, he wouldn't create an enemy who might spread negative stories.

But after the Exploration Society's findings had been disseminated, after Judah's testimony was set in stone under oath, he could raise whatever spurious claims he liked about Sir Sidney, but he'd be branded a disgruntled liar who was incensed over his spot on the expedition team being revoked.

No matter what else transpired, he had to search Judah's possessions for Nathan's stolen knife. If he had it, the discovery would mean Nathan was telling the truth and Judah wasn't. If that was the case, Sebastian was afraid he might murder Judah, and with those hefty topics weighing him down, he was in the mood for some merriment.

He could have stopped at the Haven, where there was likely a bevy of harlots entertaining his crew, but he hadn't wanted to revel with a bunch of loose doxies. He'd wanted to see Sarah Robertson.

It made no sense, but there it was.

The cottage was dark, the shutters closed, and he wondered if she was napping in front of the fire. Or might she have already climbed into her bed? The notion that he might stumble on her there was unbelievably thrilling.

He should just break down and ask her to be his mistress. Why not? He was rich, and she was desperate. There were worse ways for a female to support herself than by being spoiled rotten by a wealthy man. Plus, she was twenty-seven, so she was much too old to still be a maiden. She ought to learn about physical pleasure.

If he suggested that type of liaison, how might she react? She'd probably slap him and chase him out, but he'd suggest it anyway, and he'd cajole her until he wore her down.

He reached for the doorknob, eager to spin it and tiptoe inside, but...?

It was locked!

He was so stunned that he couldn't deduce what was happening. She'd locked the door? Why? She couldn't intend to keep *him* out. Could she?

Before he could dissuade himself, he knocked and murmured, "Sarah? It's me. Let me in."

She didn't answer, and he continued knocking and calling to her, growing more exasperated by the minute.

The entire journey home from Selby, when he'd been so glum, he'd pondered her incessantly and how he'd tell her all about Nathan. She had a pragmatic view of people, and she'd persuade him that the situation wasn't as bleak as he supposed. He'd been counting on her!

Ultimately, he was so livid that he kicked the wood—very hard—and it finally brought a response. A shutter creaked from the window in the parlor, and she leaned out.

"Be silent," she furiously hissed, "or you'll wake the whole neighborhood."

"Open up."

"No. You need to go back to the manor, and I need to go to bed."

"I have to talk to you."

"You do not, and there's no reason for you to be bothering me."

"Bothering you! I swear, if you don't open the door—right now—I will kick it in."

"You'd ruin a perfectly good door? For what?"

"If I decide to wreck it, I will. It's my house, as is every bloody thing on this estate. You should remember that."

"Don't be crude, and don't use foul language in my presence."

"I *have* to talk to you." He sounded almost frantic.

"You're being ridiculous, and if you don't calm down, the children will hear you. I refuse to have to explain why you're behaving like a lunatic."

At the snotty comment, he was so riled he was surprised the top of his head didn't blow off. He marched over, not sure if he planned to kiss her or shake her, but she lurched away so he couldn't grab her.

In her hasty retreat, she hadn't latched the shutter, so the window was wide open. He simply hoisted himself over the sill and scrambled into the parlor. In a tiny corner of his mind, it occurred to him that he was acting exactly like the lunatic she'd just accused him of being, but he didn't care.

No one was allowed to disobey him. No one was allowed to defy him or flout his wishes. He was Sebastian Sinclair and she was . . . was . . .

Well, he had no idea what she *was*. The accursed woman was destitute, friendless, and without a viable option for the future. She was lucky he'd ever glanced in her direction a single time, and she would not ignore him. If she thought he'd tolerate such insubordination, *she* was the lunatic.

She was over by the hearth, and she'd actually picked up an iron poker. She brandished it at him and warned, "Stay where you are!"

Of course he didn't listen. He stormed over and yanked the poker away, tossing it on the floor, where it landed on the rug with a muted thud. Then he placed his hands on her waist and pulled her to him.

He studied her and observed a great deal of rage and scorn. He'd been away for such a short period. What had left her so irate?

He dipped in to kiss her, and she wrenched away.

"Mr. Sinclair! Please!"

"Call me Sebastian. You're aware that I expect it."

"We are *not* on familiar terms."

"I determine those sorts of issues between us, Miss Robertson, so you will call me Sebastian. And I will start calling you Sarah. Don't argue about it."

"You're a bully, and I'm much too annoyed to put up with your nonsense."

"I've been away two days, and I arrive home to find you in a complete snit. What is wrong with you?"

She whirled away to light a candle. There was a fire burning in the hearth, but it had died down, so there was a bit of illumination, but not much. He gaped at her, watching, as she waited for the flame to flare, then she held it toward his face.

"I have a question for you," she said, "and I want to see your eyes clearly when you answer so I'll know if you're telling the truth or not."

"Fine. Ask away."

"Are you engaged to be married?"

He hesitated because he wasn't engaged, but he would be before too long. He couldn't keep evading the nuptial noose. Every bachelor was eventually ensnared, and his turn was approaching much more quickly than he'd like.

"No, I'm not engaged," he said.

She banged the candle down on a nearby table. "Oh, you liar! You are! You're engaged."

"Sarah, I am not. Who told you I was?"

"Your sister. The other day, when you rode by me in the village? She saw us together, and she felt compelled to visit me afterward. I was advised—in no uncertain terms—to avoid you like the plague."

"I'm sorry."

"She also saw Noah and Pet, and she demanded I admit the identity of their father."

"Did you?"

"Not at first, but she badgered me unmercifully, and I relented."

"It serves her right for being so nosy, I guess."

"In the brief interval you were away, I was shouted at by your man, Judah Barnett. I was insulted and abused by your man, Raven Shawcross. I was ordered about and chastised by your sister, and I am enormously aggrieved by all of their behavior toward me."

"I can tell."

She was magnificent when she was angry. Like a powerful goddess who could point her finger and destroy worlds. He wondered again who her father had been. Who might have passed on such imperious traits?

"I spent the day writing to acquaintances," she said, "and begging for assistance, so hopefully, I will be out of your hair very soon. Until I can make other arrangements, the children and I will sequester ourselves in this cottage, and we will not step foot outside it so we don't offend your companions. In the meantime, you will inform your cadre of tormenters that they should leave me alone."

"I will do that."

"Congratulations on your pending marriage, but as you are about to be a husband, there is absolutely no reason for you to be standing in this parlor. Goodnight and goodbye." She motioned to the window. "You found your way in, so I'm sure you can find your way out."

She huffed off and crossed the foyer, then the kitchen, then to the maid's room behind it. She slammed the door, and it grew very quiet.

He dawdled like a dunce, pondering his options. He'd have to scold several people for their interfering in his private affairs, beginning with Ophelia. How dare she claim he was engaged! As to Judah and Raven, they didn't have to pester Sarah for him.

He understood they would picture themselves as being very loyal, that they were protecting him from her, but he didn't require protection.

Despite her tirade, he was still eager to tarry with her. He was anguished over his meeting with Nathan and needed some cheering. Would it kill her to provide it?

Her fit of temper reminded him of why he hadn't betrothed himself to Veronica. He lived with virile, manly men, and he was perplexed as to how he should deal with the feminine impertinence Sarah freely exhibited, and he didn't want to deal with it.

He merely wanted to wallow in her presence until his mood improved. He glanced at the open window, then at the foyer that led to the other side of the house where her pathetic bedchamber was located.

His choice was easy. He blew out the candle and stomped off.

Sarah heard him coming, but couldn't prevent him from entering. The door to her bedroom didn't have a lock. If she'd been stronger, she could have pulled over the dresser as a barricade, but why expend the energy?

He was like a force of nature, a rich, cosseted brat who'd had the world handed to him on a silver platter, and she loathed his type of wealthy, domineering idiot.

They ruled the kingdom and assumed every lowly person in it should bow down, but the problem for her had always been that she wouldn't bow to anyone. She viewed herself as equal to any man, and in light of the fact that half her blood was from Viscount Matthew Blake, she had every right to feel superior.

If her father had wed her mother, Sarah would be far above Sebastian Sinclair in rank and station, and he wouldn't dream of disrespecting her. As it was though, he treated her like a servant, like a doxy who should be excited to give him whatever he desired.

He was a bully and a cretin, and she was still smarting from the humiliating experiences she'd had to endure from his sister and his men. They'd blithely berated her as if she should have to allow it. She wouldn't silently tolerate it though, and they harassed her at their peril.

As he blustered in, she was standing by the window and staring out at the night sky. It was dark and cloudy, looking as if it might rain.

For a moment, she thought about climbing out into the yard, but why bother? He'd simply follow her. He was that determined to be with her, and while she'd have liked to quarrel, the fight suddenly went out of her.

She displayed a tough façade, but in reality, she was a single female who constantly assisted others, but who had nothing to show for it. Not a home, not a relative she would acknowledge, not a friend who would aid her, not a penny in her purse.

How had she arrived at such a wretched spot? And how would she ever dig herself out of it? She was all alone, and only rude, overbearing Sebastian Sinclair had stepped forward to help her. The realization was the saddest ever.

"I could have sworn I asked you to depart," she said without turning around.

"I never listen to women, and I'm not about to start with you."

She snorted with disgust. "What is it you seek from me, Sebastian? Just tell me. Put me out of my misery, then go away."

He came up behind her, and he wrapped his arms around her waist. They were nestled together, her backside pressed to his front. Their proximity was thrilling in a manner she detested.

"I'm not engaged," he said. "I probably should be, but I'm not."

"But you're promised to someone."

"Yes, my cousin, Veronica."

"Why haven't you proposed?"

"Our mothers have pushed the match, but I'm not in any hurry."

"Do *you* want it?"

"Not especially. If I was keen to have her as my bride, I'd already be a husband."

"Is *she* expecting it to happen?"

"Yes, but only because my mother and sister egg her on. I have never uttered a word of encouragement to her."

"Swear it to me."

"I swear."

Dejection swept over her. "I don't believe you, but I'm so pitiful that I'll persuade myself to believe you. How nauseating is that?"

He leaned in and kissed her cheek. "Don't be angry with me. I had a terrible trip, and the whole way home, I thought about you."

"You did not. Don't pretend."

"All right, I didn't ponder you the *whole* time. I thought about you ninety percent. How's that?"

"Your lies grow more exhausting by the minute."

"I missed you," he claimed. She didn't reply with a similar sentiment, and he pinched her. "Tell me you missed me too."

"I didn't. I was occupied with fighting off your pompous sister and your obnoxious friends. I was too busy to miss you."

"I'm sorry they were horrid to you. I'll talk to them."

"Don't bother. If you mention it, matters will just get worse for me. They'll be more intent than ever to badger me—merely to prove they can."

"Poor, poor, Sarah," he sarcastically murmured. "So pretty and so unhappy and so dreadfully abused."

She elbowed him in the ribs. "Would you leave? Please?"

"No."

Her bed was behind them, and it was a narrow piece of furniture, little more than a cot really and certainly not large enough to hold two people. Before she knew what he planned, he lifted her, whirled her, and tossed her on the lumpy mattress.

She didn't have a second to protest or scoot away. He stretched out on top of her so, in a trice, she was in a position she never imagined she'd be with a man.

As always when she was with him, she sensed no menace. For reasons she simply didn't understand, she fascinated him, and he was anxious to fraternize in ways she should never permit. Unfortunately for her, but luckily for him, she was so lonely that she loved having him fixated on her.

He was handsome as a Greek god, like a hero in a storybook fable. How could she not fall under his spell? How could she avert disaster?

He kissed her, and when she refused to join in, he said, "Stop being a shrew. Kiss me back."

"You're a bully."

"Yes, I am, but I'm a *nice* bully. Don't be a grouch. I had a hideous day, and you make me feel better. Just be glad I'm here."

It was such a sweet speech. How could she discount it? When had anyone ever told her she made them feel better? She didn't think anyone ever had.

She moaned with dismay and pulled him to her, initiating a kiss of her own. He smirked, being completely convinced he could coerce her into illicit conduct, and he was correct. He likely could. Where he was concerned, she had no spine at all.

Their lips connected in a hot, searing manner, almost as if they were generating sparks. How heated could their embraces become? Might they ultimately set the world on fire? It definitely seemed possible.

He continued forever, tasting her, sampling her eager mouth, his hands roaming over her person, learning her shape and size.

Because she'd resolved to remain a spinster, she'd never tormented herself with dreams of marriage, so she'd never seriously contemplated what the physical side of matrimony might be like. Clearly, by forsaking that path, she'd missed out on something splendid.

In his arms, she felt young and beautiful, and she wondered—once she departed Hero's Haven and never saw him again—how she'd manage without him in her life.

Eventually, he slowed and drew away. He slid onto his back and shifted her around so she was partially draped across his chest.

"Have I calmed you down?" he asked.

"I guess."

"Vixen. Be kind to me."

"I'll try."

"Thank you." He sighed, his burdens heavy. "It's so good to be home. My visit to Selby was awful."

"That's too bad."

He'd called on her half-brother, Nathan Blake, who was Lord Selby, and she was desperate to pepper him with questions about their meeting. She was so accursedly curious about Lord Selby: what he looked like, how he acted, how he walked and talked, and if he resembled her in even the slightest fashion.

But she didn't dare pry. If she begged for a single detail, she'd babble incessantly, and how would she explain such blatant interest? She couldn't, not unless she was prepared to admit their relationship. She was silent, waiting for him to confide what he was content to share. If she was shrewd and cautious, she'd be able to dig out many intriguing facts.

"Why was it awful?" she asked.

"Have you read any of the accounts about what happened in Africa?"

"About your father, do you mean?"

"Yes, but about Nathan too. Sir Sidney was attacked by a group of natives during an . . . ah . . . disagreement. Nathan intervened, and he was struck down with my father."

"You thought he died, right? Isn't that the story that was in the newspapers?"

"Yes, I thought he'd died. At the time, matters were bloody and chaotic. I knew my father had perished, but I wasn't sure about Nathan. I sent some men—it was your great chum, Judah Barnett—to find him, but they returned to camp and claimed he was dead. They claimed they *saw* him, that they checked, but that it was too dangerous to retrieve his corpse."

"They were lying," she said.

"Yes. After the murder, we had emissaries negotiate for the release of the two bodies. Sir Sidney was handed over, but they couldn't locate Nathan." He paused, then said, "We left without him."

"How did he make it home on his own?"

"I have no idea. He's never told anyone."

"I can't blame him. I'm certain it must have been grueling."

"He can't forgive me for leaving him behind."

There was such remorse in the comment, and she scoffed. "I don't suppose I can blame him for that either."

"No."

"How is he faring? Is he fit and hale? Is he crippled? Is he recovering his stamina?"

"He's fine. He's thinner than he used to be. Mostly, he's just bitter and very, very angry."

"I can imagine." His heart was directly under her ear, and as she listened to it beating, she decided it was the most precious interval of her life. "Can I ask you a question?"

"I can't guarantee I'll answer, but you can ask."

"If you're positive Mr. Barnett lied about Lord Selby being dead, why is he still a member of your crew?"

"My only excuse is that I've been distracted by family issues surrounding my father's death. The inquest is next week, and I've been getting ready for it, so I haven't had the energy to worry about Judah."

"After it's over, you'll deal with him?"

"Yes. I have to cut him from our merry band of explorers, but it will be very hard. He's been with us for over a decade, and it will cause a huge rift among my men. I never like to quarrel with them."

They were quiet for a few minutes, both of them lost in thought. She wouldn't be sorry to have Mr. Barnett sent away, but he wouldn't relinquish his spot without a fuss. Also, the men earned money with the Sinclairs. She didn't understand how it was generated or how it was divided, but the loss of it would enrage him.

She didn't like or trust him, and she wondered if she should warn Sebastian to tread carefully in letting him go. But he probably didn't need advice from her on how to handle his affairs.

His breathing had slowed, and she peeked up, stunned to discover that he'd dozed off. Right in her bed!

She didn't wake him. Obviously, he'd had a long, unpleasant trip to Selby, and he was exhausted. She snuggled with him for an eternity, absorbing every detail of the encounter, until finally, a bird chirped outside. She glanced out. It was still dark, but there was a hint of light over on the eastern horizon.

"Sebastian," she whispered.

He roused with a start and jerked to a sitting position, an arm outstretched, as if he was warding off an assailant. A moment of terrified confusion flared in his eyes, then he gazed at her, and reality sank in.

"Was I sleeping?" he said as he dropped onto the pillow.

"Yes, it's been hours now."

"I never sleep."

"Well, you did with me."

"Aren't I lucky? Were you watching over me?"

"Every second."

He sighed with what sounded like contentment. "What time is it?"

"I believe dawn is about to break."

"I better tiptoe out before people are up to observe me sneaking away."

"Yes, you'd better."

Yet he didn't move until that stupid bird chirped again, a potent sign they couldn't ignore.

He kissed her, and she participated with an unbridled amount of joy, then he pulled away and staggered to his feet. He was swaying and off balance.

"Can you walk to the manor on your own?" she asked. "Should I escort you? I'd hate for you to be lost in the woods."

"I'll be fine," he claimed. He straightened his hair and clothes, then he grinned. "I was in your bed all night, and I'm such a cad that I didn't bother to take off my boots."

"You're forgiven."

"I have to go to town tomorrow. Or is it today?" He scowled. "Today, I mean, but I'll stop by once I'm back. It will be late."

"I'll wait up for you."

He bent down and stole a last kiss. "Don't you dare lock me out."

"I won't."

"I miss you already," he murmured, then he vanished like smoke.

The front door opened and closed, and she heard him striding away.

She relaxed onto the pillow, her mind awhirl as she tried to fathom what had happened, what she'd allowed, what she'd relished. He *missed* her already, and she felt exactly the same.

No doubt about it, she was in desperate trouble. How would she ever get herself out of it?

CHAPTER

12

"Sit down, Ophelia."

Sebastian glared at his sister and struggled to tamp down his fury.

They were in the library in his mother's London home, which was actually *his* home. She and Ophelia lived in it, but Gertrude considered it her own, and he was happy to let her. He didn't bother her and rarely stopped by. Usually, he wasn't even in England, and he much preferred Hero's Haven anyway.

Yet occasionally he used it, such as at the present moment when he had business to handle. It ruffled female feathers to have him on the premises and throwing his weight around. It reminded them of who was really in charge, who controlled them and all the money.

They crossed him at their peril.

He had an odd relationship with them and had never spent much time with them. His parents hadn't liked each other in even the smallest manner, and his father had dealt with the problem by never being in his wife's company.

Ophelia had been born when Sebastian was eight, so she'd been a toddler when he'd initially flitted off with Sir Sidney. He'd scarcely seen her after that. On each encounter, there were huge jumps as the years had sped by. First, she was a baby, then a little girl, then an adolescent, then a young lady. He'd missed all the periods in between where they might have established a sibling bond.

Now, Sir Sidney was deceased, and Sebastian had inherited everything, most particularly the diamond mines they'd accumulated during their many travels. His father's Last Will had left it all to Sebastian, with an admonition to *take care of* his mother and sister, but he hardly knew them, and what he *did* know, he didn't like.

His mother, Gertrude, was especially fussy and cantankerous. As for Ophelia, she was at a spot where she could continue on as she was, an unlikable version of Gertrude, *or* she could grow up a bit, garner some interesting life experiences, and become a better person.

She bragged about how she wouldn't ever marry, but should he start pushing her toward it? Should he arrange a match whether she consented or not? It was unnatural for a woman to shun matrimony, and he was acquainted with many honorable men who would love to have a connection to his family.

Then again, if she never altered her habits, if she remained a paltry imitation of their mother, he wouldn't foist her off on any man. Look at how miserable his father had been!

She appeared very pretty, her hair braided and curled, and she was wearing an expensive gown, as if she might be off to attend a musicale or theatrical play. Her expression was serene, as if she couldn't imagine that they might be about to quarrel. Had she forgotten her behavior with Sarah? Had it occurred to her that he might not appreciate her butting into his private affairs?

She'd overstepped her bounds so egregiously that he couldn't figure out where to begin in chastising her.

"I don't mean to rush you, Brother," she said, "but I'm off to an appointment. What is it you need?"

"Who are you meeting?" he asked, thinking he should learn more about her.

"Just . . . ah . . . some friends. You wouldn't know them."

"I have a difficult topic to address with you, and I have to be very clear about it."

"All right. What is it?"

"I'm not engaged to Veronica."

"You will be very soon though, won't you?" she cheerily inquired.

"Maybe. Maybe not."

His irked retort gave her pause. "But...but...she's counting on it. Mother and I are too."

"You shouldn't be."

"Are you claiming it won't happen?"

"I'm not claiming that. I'm apprising you that if and when I betroth myself, *I* will decide it. Not you or Mother."

"Of course you'll be the one."

"Since you understand that fact, would you like to explain your conversation with Miss Robertson when you were staying at the Haven?"

Her cheeks reddened. "None of my comments were improper."

"Nice try, Ophelia, but did you—or did you not—tell her I was engaged?"

"She had to be informed," she mulishly insisted.

"Why would you feel compelled to lie about my situation?"

"I saw the two of you together."

He was taken aback. "When?"

"When you were riding off to Selby. I was in the village, and you stopped to chat with her. It's obvious she's smitten, but you shouldn't encourage her."

He scoffed. "I'll keep that in mind."

"You'll only raise her expectations, and she's a completely inappropriate female to have glommed onto you. It seemed a word of warning was required. She had to realize you're promised elsewhere."

There were so many infuriating remarks buried in her statement that he had to inhale several deep breaths so he didn't lash out verbally.

"First off, Miss Robertson and I are merely friends."

She snorted. "If you say so."

"And second, she doesn't believe I'm all that grand, so I could never *raise* her expectations."

"If that's what you assume, then you are clueless about how women view these matters."

"Third, she's not *inappropriate*. I consider her to be quite extraordinary, and I won't listen to you denigrating her."

"She's a homeless shrew who's prevailed on your generous nature. I fail to comprehend why you deem her to be so marvelous."

"Ophelia!" He slapped a palm on the desktop. "Cease your disparagement."

"I'm sorry that you can't abide the truth. I was helping her, Sebastian. I was making her see sense so you don't break her heart."

"We don't have a romantic relationship," he lied. He couldn't deduce what sort of relationship they did have, but he wasn't about to call it *romantic*.

"She's distracting you, so you don't focus on important issues."

"Such as . . . ?"

"Such as your betrothal to Veronica! You flirt with the likes of Miss Robertson, so it means you ignore your responsibilities to our family."

"Miss Robertson has no bearing on whether or not I betroth myself to Veronica. I won't bother trying to convince you, but you should understand this: You are to stay out of my private business. I hope to never have a discussion like this with you again."

She didn't react to his admonition, but asked, "Who are those children living with her? Who is their father?"

"Who do you think their father is?"

"According to Miss Robertson," she snottily said, "their father is Sir Sidney."

"Yes, he is. Don't sit there and pretend you couldn't tell."

"If her story is true, then they're our half-siblings."

"Yes, they are."

"Why are they residing with her? How is it she has custody of them?"

"She previously ran an orphanage."

"Are you sure? Have you any proof that she ran one? A woman—all on her own?"

"I visited her there, so *yes*, I have my proof. She's extremely accomplished, and it's why I won't have you castigating her. She took care of the children at her facility, but the building was sold, and they were evicted. I've been assisting them until they can make other arrangements."

"You shouldn't have assisted them."

"I won't dignify that comment with a reply, and shame on you for uttering it. Like it or not, they are Father's children. Should we have left them to starve in the streets? Pardon me, but I'm not that horrid, and I pray you aren't either."

"Does Mother know about them? Does she know they're being lodged at the Haven?"

"No, and we won't inform her. The news would be needlessly upsetting."

"She wouldn't like it."

"So?" He shrugged. "She doesn't like anything."

Ophelia stared, her expression defiant, and her attitude was so exasperating. If she'd been a boy, he'd have whacked her alongside the head and told her to stop being so insolent. But she wasn't a boy, and he had no experience dealing with girls.

"I want to hear from you," he said, "that you won't accost Miss Robertson again. She's destitute and muddling through in difficult circumstances. As are our half-siblings. We should be more charitable toward them."

She glared at him forever, but it was a visual war she could never win. He returned her glare until she began to squirm in her seat.

"I won't approach her ever again," she ultimately mumbled, "and I apologize for my actions. I presumed I was right to intervene."

"I appreciate that, but I can handle my own affairs. I can't have you interfering."

"I won't. I promise."

"Good. I'm glad we cleared that up."

Suddenly, she looked much younger than twenty-two, and he felt like the bully Sarah often accused him of being.

"I hardly ever see you," she said, "and I've been dying to ask you a question. You're finally here, but you're in such a dour mood, I can't proceed."

"My *mood* is not dour. What is it?"

"I'm certain you'll be opposed, simply because I've irritated you. I'll try later."

"It's fine, Ophelia. I'm not angry. I'm just frustrated. Ask me your question."

She debated, then said, "I had always thought I'd never marry. I've enjoyed living with Mother and being independent, but I've been thinking I might like to wed after all."

"That's a grand idea. I've been wondering if you should wed too. Have you talked to Mother about it?"

"I wouldn't talk to her. She'd race off and pick some obnoxious oaf I couldn't abide."

He chuckled. "I'm sure you're correct, and I'm encouraged that you realize it about her. What's brought on this change of heart? Have you met someone who tickles your fancy?"

"Yes. I'm not positive he's who I want, but we've chatted a bit, and I'm interested enough to consider it. I'd like your opinion."

"Is he anyone I know?"

"Yes, you know him very well."

Two names flashed in his mind as men he knew *well*: Nathan, whom she couldn't stand, and Raven Shawcross. Raven had plans that didn't include shackling himself to a silly London debutante, so when she actually spoke the name aloud, he was so astonished he could have fallen out of his chair.

"It's Judah," she said. "Judah Barnett."

"Judah . . . ?"

He and his sister were perched at a very important fork in their road as siblings. She'd only ever previously sought one favor from him—to travel to Africa—and he'd emphatically refused to permit it. Now, here she was, posing another monumental subject and eager to receive his blessing.

He was devastated over what his answer would have to be. Would she ever forgive him? Probably not.

He'd like to have a cordial relationship with her. He'd like her to wed an honorable, steady fellow and live happily ever after, but it couldn't be Judah Barnett. It could *never* be Judah.

"Oh, Ophelia, I'm sorry. I can't be him."

She blanched as if he'd struck her. "Why not?"

"It's just . . . just . . . not possible."

"Why isn't it?" The mulish gleam was back in her expression.

"There are details about him that make him unsuitable."

"What are they?" she rudely retorted. When he didn't explain, she said, "Let me tell you this, Brother: You barely know me. Why should you get to control my future?"

"Maybe because I'm your guardian and I manage your dowry. *I* will select who you marry, and it can't be him. Ever." He sounded overly harsh, so he repeated, "I'm sorry."

She studied him caustically, then scoffed. "No, you're not."

She was right—he wasn't sorry—but he wouldn't admit it.

Judah was mostly a dependable crew member, but he had a chip on his shoulder and never thought he was valued as much as he should be. He had to be terrified over Sebastian's recent meeting with Nathan too. Even if they never reconciled, Sebastian would eventually dig to the bottom of what had occurred in Africa.

Judah had squandered his reputation with Sebastian, and he had to recognize that fact. He had to be worried that Sebastian was about to cut him loose. What better way to prevent it than to wed Sebastian's sister?

"How has this come about?" he asked her. "Did Judah approach you?"

"No. It sort of dawned on us together. We've always liked each other."

"Really? I'm surprised you've spent that much time around him that he'd feel comfortable conferring about matrimony."

"I like him. He's been kind to me."

"The notion simply popped up? Out of the blue. Judah didn't *suggest* it?"

"No! We *both* want it."

"You're not to talk to him about it again. You can't raise his hopes. I will never permit you to marry him, and if he raises the issue with you, please send him to talk to me instead."

"I should have guessed you'd act like this," she fumed. "You're exactly like Father. You don't view me as a real person."

"That's not fair. You requested my opinion, and I provided it to you. Don't complain because you don't like my response."

"Why are you so opposed to Judah? Give me one reason!"

"He's not the man you assume him to be. He's not trustworthy. He's not reliable. Just ask Nathan."

"Ask . . . Nathan? Are you joking? You cite *him* as a reason to reject Judah?"

"Yes, it's because of what happened in Africa, so I'm ordering you to stay away from him. If you won't promise me, I'll take steps myself to keep you apart."

She rose to her feet, her demeanor furious and condemning. "I shouldn't have discussed this with you. It's none of your business anyway."

"Your welfare is completely and totally my business. It's why *I* am in charge of you, to help you make good decisions."

"I repeat, Sebastian: You don't know anything about me. You have no idea what would be *good* for me."

She swept out, and he eased back in his chair, thinking how much he hated being head of the family, how he detested dealing with women's problems, and how he could avoid them all if he started preparing for another trip to Africa.

———————⋇⋇⋇———————

"Sebastian! How lovely to see you in town."

"Hello, Veronica."

She sidled over to him, attempting to appear willowy, as if she was gliding, and she breathed a sigh of relief that her dogs were up in her bedchamber. They could be excitable, and his mother, Gertrude, had warned her to hide them from him. Sebastian liked dogs, but he liked big, hulking, manly ones that could tend sheep or chase off wolves.

Her little darlings didn't fit the bill in even the slightest fashion.

Luckily, she was looking very fetching, wearing an exquisite sapphire gown that set off the blond of her hair and the blue of her eyes. Her hair was styled in a stunning array of curls and braids her maid had spent two hours arranging.

It was exhausting to constantly primp and preen, but they couldn't predict when Sebastian might show up. She had to be ready for his arrival every second.

They were in the foyer, and he'd been trying to slip out the door without being delayed, but she wasn't about to let him escape.

"Are you leaving so soon?" she asked. "I only just heard you were here."

"I'm needed at the Haven."

"You're so busy. Are you sure you can't have supper with us? We intended to eat at nine, but if you could tarry, I'm positive your mother would serve the meal earlier."

"Sorry, but I can't."

She flashed her prettiest pout, the one she practiced in front of the mirror. It never had any effect on him though. He always treated her precisely the same way. He was polite and friendly, but not really glad to have stumbled on her.

It was so difficult to be a female, to wait patiently for the man in the relationship to decide when to proceed. She yearned to seize him by the lapels of his coat, to shake him and demand, *What are you thinking? What are your plans with regard to me?*

But of course, she had to float along on his schedule, according to his whims. It was so unfair.

Every girl in the world would like to be his bride, and during her adolescent years, she'd flaunted her prestigious spot and had reveled in the jealous adoration of her acquaintances. If the marriage didn't occur, if they never wed, she'd die of shame.

He was pulling away from her, as if she wouldn't notice how eager he was to be off.

"May I walk you out?" she asked.

"Yes, certainly."

He smiled, but it wasn't sincere. There were so many rumors about him—that he had mistresses, that he'd had potent amours with the city's most beautiful actresses. Supposedly, it was the reason he'd evaded her marital noose. There were too many slatterns keeping him happy.

He hadn't offered his arm, but she took it anyway—as if he had—and they strolled out together. His horse was saddled and in the driveway, so there would be no dawdling as it was brought out.

"When will we see you again?" she asked.

"I'll be in town, starting Monday, for the inquest."

A thrill of hope ignited in her breast. "Will you be staying with us?"

"No. The Haven is close enough to the city that I'll probably go home at night."

"You always disappoint us."

Because the comment sounded like a complaint, she grinned, apprising him that she'd meant it in a teasing manner. In reality, she was completely frustrated by his lack of attention, and the minute he rode off, she would march into his mother's parlor and vent her ire. How much more vacillation could she endure?

"Ophelia and I would like to come to the Haven for a few days. We like the men on the expedition team so much. Would you mind if we returned?"

He stared at the house, suddenly very grouchy. "You and Ophelia can't come. I can't have you there now. Things are . . . hectic."

"Oh . . . ah . . . all right. Perhaps after the inquest is over."

"Perhaps," he said noncommittally.

He stepped away from her, grabbed his reins, and leapt onto his horse. He gave a jaunty salute in her direction that she figured wasn't even aimed at her. It might have been for any errant footman loitering in the vicinity.

He trotted away without glancing back, and she was *so* angry, but it was never a good idea to appear petulant. She smoothed her features and sauntered inside. She headed straight for Cousin Gertrude, determined to protest until Gertrude supplied answers that made sense.

"THANK YOU FOR SEEING me."

"I might not have, Mrs. Blake, but I was curious about your letter."

Nell Drummond Blake, Lady Selby, studied Temperance Maudsen, struggling to seem pleasant and affable, but it was hard. Nell had written to Mrs. Maudsen and had introduced herself as Mrs. Blake rather than Lady Selby, so as to keep Nathan out of it.

She found it easier to talk to others if they weren't aware of her true status.

She was a happy person who generally liked everyone she met, but Mrs. Maudsen might be the first one she didn't. The woman looked fussy and peevish, as if she'd never enjoyed a moment of contentment in her life.

She was unattractive too, with a round face and unremarkable hair and eyes. She was short and very chubby, the seams on her gown let out as far as they would ever go.

Nell was trying not to openly stare, but there wasn't the tiniest hint that Mrs. Maudsen and Sarah Robertson could be siblings. They were different as night and day. Sarah was gorgeous, powerful, optimistic, and commanding. With her sparkling blue eyes and striking white-blond hair, she turned heads wherever she went.

Nell was wondering if Nathan had incorrect information about Mrs. Maudsen. Maybe she was no relation to Sarah at all. Yet Mrs. Maudsen proved her wrong.

"In your letter, you asked about my sister."

"Yes, Sarah Robertson? I'm friends with her at our church. I visited her at the orphanage, but it's closed. I was so surprised, and I'm worried about her."

"Why worry? She's always fine. A stiff hurricane wind couldn't stop her."

"I agree. She can be quite forceful."

"It's an awful trait for a female to exhibit. She's bossy and unlikable, but what do I know?"

They were in Mrs. Maudsen's home, in her parlor. It was a three-story residence on a small acreage. According to Nathan, it was owned by Mrs. Maudsen's husband, Cuthbert. Nathan had inquired about Mr. Maudsen at his club, and the reports were all bad. The man was a gambler who was deeply in debt.

Though the house was nice enough, there was an air of genteel poverty about the place, as if the Maudsens were having financial difficulties. Mantles and tables had been emptied of clocks and other decorations. Furniture was missing—as if it might have been sold. The rugs and drapes were deteriorating, and clearly, there was no money to buy new items.

Although Nell had been welcomed appropriately and tea had been served, she felt as if she was imposing.

"I was amazed to discover Sarah had a sister," Nell said. "She never mentioned you."

"She wouldn't have," Mrs. Maudsen caustically stated. "We don't get along."

It was an odd tidbit to admit to a stranger, and Nell murmured, "I'm sorry to hear it."

"She's very jealous of me," Mrs. Maudsen claimed.

"Really? In my view, Sarah is very sweet. Why would you think that?"

"I didn't *think* it, Mrs. Blake. I'm very sure about it. I was raised here in the country by my grandmother, while my father insisted Sarah tarry at the orphanage with all his urchins."

"You and Sarah weren't raised together."

"No, and she hated that I'd been given so much, but she received so little from our parents. She resented how I'd been singled out, so it was hard for us to be cordial."

"What happened to her? What happened to the orphanage? Can you tell me?"

"Mr. Maudsen sold the building, so it was shut down."

"Sarah didn't own it? I assumed she did."

"No, my father owned it, but when he was dying, he signed it over to my husband. Sarah was vehemently opposed to the change, but Father recognized that a female couldn't be in charge, and Mr. Maudsen *is* the man of the family now."

"Sarah provided such a valuable service to the community. Your husband sold it ... why?"

Mrs. Maudsen huffed with offense. "That's not any of your business, is it?"

"No, of course it isn't," Nell rushed to concur. "Have you any idea where Sarah is?"

"No."

At voicing her curt response, Mrs. Maudsen was incredibly blasé, as if they were discussing the weather rather than her only sibling. What a peculiar woman!

"Have you any other relatives who might have taken her in?" Nell asked. "Might you recollect any friends who'd let her stay with them?"

"No. Mr. Maudsen and I are her sole kin, and she was too busy with her waifs to have had any friends. For all I know, she's living on the streets."

Nell gasped. "Aren't you ... ah ... concerned about her?"

"Sarah believes she's smarter than everyone else. My husband and I owned that building, and we needed the funds from the sale. Sarah refused to accept that fact, and she was horrid to us about it. When she chose to be so vulgar and ungrateful, further communication was futile."

"I understand."

Did Mrs. Maudsen realize how appalling she sounded? Well, Nell didn't have to listen to her, and it was definitely time to depart.

"I should be going," Nell said. "If you hear from her, I wish you'd send me a note. You may not be worried about her, but I am."

"Trust me, Mrs. Blake. She's too proud. She won't ever contact me."

"We can't be sure of that."

Nell reached into her reticule and pulled out a calling card that identified her as *Lady Selby*. She handed it over, but Mrs. Maudsen didn't grab for it, so she laid it on the table between them.

Then she stood and left. Mrs. Maudsen was a miserable shrew, but her staff was polite. A footman had her cloak and bonnet ready. She didn't bother to don them. After sitting through Mrs. Maudsen's vitriol, she felt as if she couldn't breathe, and she was desperate to get outside into the fresh air.

She flashed a wan smile at the footman and hurried out to her carriage. She'd just climbed in when the front door of the house was flung open, and Mrs. Maudsen waddled out.

She was holding Nell's card, and she waved it like a flag. "Lady Selby! Lady Selby!"

Nell peered out the window. "What is it, Mrs. Maudsen?"

"How are you acquainted with Sarah? I'm so astonished! How is it that she has such a lofty association?"

Occasionally, it was useful to be an elevated, important individual, and she was learning—from watching Nathan—how to be snobbish and pretentious when it was required.

"After meeting you," Nell told her, "I have decided that I shouldn't waste another minute in your presence."

Her condemning glare swept over Mrs. Maudsen, apprising her that Nell found her to be lacking in every way. She rapped on the roof, and the carriage lurched off. She didn't glance back.

———— ✻✻✻ ————

"May I tell you a secret?"

"You always should."

Noah grinned at Petunia. They were in the woods behind the cottage. A stream bubbled in the trees, and they were loafing on the bank, throwing pebbles in the water.

Pet leaned nearer and murmured, "I think Mr. Sinclair is sweet on Miss Robertson."

Noah frowned. "Why would you think that?"

"He visits her in the middle of the night."

"How do you know?"

"I've seen him leaving—twice."

Pet had trouble sleeping in the cottage. She'd been raised at the orphanage, surrounded by other children, so it had been hectic and noisy. She didn't like how quiet it was in the country, deeming it scary and unnatural. As to Noah, he slept like a log and dozed off the instant his head hit the pillow. He never heard a sound.

She fretted too about the future, but Noah never did. What was the point? He presumed matters would work out for the best, and he was usually correct. He was twelve already, and in another year, he'd be an adult. If he didn't like his circumstances then, he could change them, without asking anyone's permission.

His grandfather had been a very wise fellow, and he'd counseled Noah on how difficult it would be out in the world as a bastard. His father had made many mistakes in his personal life, so Noah would have to forge his own path and not expect much assistance from others.

Even now, at age twelve, he could find a job or begin an apprenticeship, but both routes seemed too *small*. A great destiny was percolating inside him. He merely had to figure out what it was and seize it as it passed by.

He was hampered though by his concern for Miss Robertson and Pet. He'd sworn to them that he'd always protect them, but if he left them to their own devices, he couldn't imagine what might transpire. Miss Robertson put on a brave front, but she couldn't manage her affairs. She was so bad at it.

Just look where they'd landed! If his half-brother hadn't offered them shelter, they'd have been residing in a poorhouse in London.

"If Mr. Sinclair stops by in the evening," Noah cautiously said, "it doesn't mean he's sweet on her. Maybe they had vital topics to discuss."

"It wasn't the evening. It was *night*, and the second time, he was in her bedchamber!"

"My goodness."

This was very serious.

His grandfather had supplied a hefty dose of advice on the amorous foibles of grownups. He'd been determined that Noah have no illusions about the sins his parents had committed, so Noah knew more about that sort of conduct than a boy ought to know.

Sir Sidney had been a handsome, dashing rogue, and Noah's mother, who'd been quite a famous actress, hadn't been able to resist him. She'd been madly in love with him, and he'd seemed to love her too—until he didn't anymore. After Noah was born, he'd moved on to greener pastures. His mother had died, supposedly from a lung infection, but people agreed the real cause was a broken heart.

She never recovered from the loss of Sir Sidney and had called his name on her deathbed.

Not that Sir Sidney had noticed. He'd vanished by then, with no support furnished. Noah had been sent to live with his grandfather, and he'd been lucky that he'd had somewhere to go.

He wouldn't want Miss Robertson to get herself into the kind of jam his mother had faced. She wrote letters to acquaintances every day, praying someone might write back and provide a miracle, but no one had even bothered to reply, let alone suggest a solution to their plight.

If his half-brother seduced her with wicked intent, then tossed her over, where would they be?

They were balanced on the edge of a perilous cliff, where the slightest ill wind could blow them over. Did Miss Robertson realize that fact? Well, of course she did, but as his grandfather had explained, females didn't choose the best path when they were misbehaving.

Should Noah speak to her? Should he speak to Mr. Sinclair? Had he the right to interfere? Was it any of his business?

"I hope they marry," Pet ridiculously said.

"They never would, and you shouldn't plan on it."

"Why couldn't it happen? It's obvious from how he gazes at her."

"How does he gaze at her?"

"As if he loves her."

"Men stare at woman like that constantly, but it doesn't indicate true sentiment. Especially when the man is a scoundrel."

"Are you claiming our brother is a scoundrel?"

"I have no idea, but I'm worried now."

"I won't think badly of him, and you shouldn't either."

"I won't, but Miss Robertson is too far beneath him. He's Sebastian Sinclair, and she's . . . ah . . . ah . . ." Noah wouldn't denigrate Miss Robertson, so he finished the sentence by saying, "He'd never pick her, and I'd hate for you to get excited about it. I wouldn't want you to be disappointed."

"I'm not a baby, Noah. If they don't end up together, I won't cry on my pillow."

"I'm glad to hear it."

"But I won't stop wishing for it. If they wed, we'd be safe. She'd be his wife, so he'd have to take care of her—and us. She wouldn't let him abandon us."

Noah couldn't bear to upset her, so he said, "I'll wish for it too. I'll cross my fingers that it occurs exactly that way."

Then and there, he decided he would have to have a frank talk with Mr. Sinclair. His half-brother couldn't be allowed to abuse Miss Robertson. He couldn't leave her in a dire condition, as Sir Sidney had left Noah's mother.

Noah wouldn't permit it.

CHAPTER

13

"You have a visitor."

"Who is it?"

Sebastian was at Hero's Haven, hiding in his library. He glanced over at Raven who'd just stuck his nose into the room.

The manor was silent for a change. There were a dozen men from the expedition team staying with him, but they were off on various errands and social calls. It was the middle of the afternoon, and he was drinking a whiskey and staring across the park, desperate to head over to Sarah's cottage and determined that he wouldn't behave so foolishly.

There was no reason to be so fixated on her. If pressed for an opinion, he'd have insisted he didn't like bold females. He was a very traditional fellow and thought women should be modest and unpretentious, that they should defer to men in all matters.

She was so removed from being that sort of person that it was laughable, so what was spurring his potent fascination? He had no idea.

"It's that little cretin, Noah," Raven said, "and he's demanded to talk to you."

Sebastian blanched. "Can't you send him back to the cottage? He shouldn't be over here. Tell him to go home."

"I told him precisely that, and he replied that I have no authority to order him about. He's quite a prick, and he won't take *no* for an answer. In that, he reminds me of Sir Sidney—and *you*."

"Don't even say it." Sebastian gaped at Raven, both of them vexed by the boy's arrival, then Sebastian asked, "What does he want?"

"I can't imagine, and I'd rather not debate with him."

"Are you afraid you'd lose any argument?"

"Probably." Raven shrugged. "You might as well speak to him. If you don't, I doubt he'll leave quietly."

Sebastian sighed. "All right. Bring him in."

So far, Sebastian had ignored the two children. Was he ready to become cordial with Noah? Why shouldn't he be?

He wasn't the first son in history to discover his father had sired other children, and he was actually curious about the boy's mother and her relationship with Sir Sidney. How had they met? When had they met? Had their affair been brief or lengthy? Why had they split? What details might Noah be able to provide?

"Don't wear out your welcome," Raven warned Noah as they neared, "and don't be a nuisance."

"I'm never a nuisance," Noah responded haughtily.

"If you upset Mr. Sinclair, I'll toss you out on your ass. Do you hear me?"

"Stop threatening me, Mr. Shawcross. I'm not scared of you."

They entered the room, and Raven glared at Sebastian and said, "I'll be out in the hall. If he annoys you, summon me. I'll get rid of him."

"You're excused, Mr. Shawcross!" Noah's tone was petulant, like an irked king.

Raven didn't follow commands from anyone but Sebastian, and he hovered, waiting until Sebastian waved him out. He closed the door, but he'd tarry outside as he'd promised. If Sebastian shouted for him, he'd rush in and deal with Noah, but Sebastian liked to assume he could handle a young boy on his own.

He was seated behind the desk, and he motioned for Noah to come over and sit down. Noah strutted over, the swagger in his gait an exact copy of Sir Sidney's. His mannerisms were so disconcerting!

"What can I do for you Mr. . . . ah . . ."

He was going to be polite and refer to Noah by his surname, but he didn't know what it was. Had Sir Sidney given Noah his name? Was he a Sinclair?

Noah was such a smart devil, and he realized Sebastian's conundrum.

"It's Noah Sinclair," he said. "Our father permitted my mother to put it on my birth certificate."

"Well . . . ah . . . good." Sebastian was at a loss for words.

"You needn't call me Mr. Sinclair though. I'm happy to have you call me Noah."

"Fine. How can I help you, Noah?"

Noah didn't explain, but asked instead, "May I call you Sebastian? I understand it's not entirely proper, and you are much older than me, but we're brothers. I ought to be allowed."

A muscle ticked in Sebastian's cheek as he began to grasp some of Raven's exasperation. What could it hurt to use their Christian names? Was it worth a quarrel? He didn't think so.

"You may call me Sebastian, but would you get on with it please? What is it you want?"

"I'm here to confer with you about Miss Robertson."

In the minute or two Sebastian had had to ponder Noah's mission, he hadn't wondered what the conversation would be about. He couldn't guess what would plague a boy like Noah. But . . . Sarah?

It was the very last topic Sebastian would have expected.

"What about her?" He managed to keep the astonishment out of his tone.

"It appears you've been sneaking over to visit her in the middle of the night."

"I haven't been," he firmly stated, "and I don't like to be accused of decadent conduct, so if that's all you needed to say, we can wrap this up."

"Our sister, Petunia, has seen you at least twice. She's not a liar, so don't pretend that she is."

Sebastian's impulse was to deny and deny and deny, but Noah was staring him down, practically daring him to impugn Petunia.

Carefully, he admitted, "I may have come by on occasion."

"In the middle of the night," Noah pressed.

"Yes." Sebastian's cheeks heated with embarrassment.

"I have to talk to you about it."

"What is it you'd like to tell me?"

"Miss Robertson seems very clever, but she makes bad choices."

"Really? I don't view her that way. She's been very successful in her life."

"Mostly, she has, but she believes the best about people, so she can't ever accept that they might have wicked motives."

"You think *I* have wicked motives with regard to her?"

"I hope not. I would hate for her to be hurt—as my mother was hurt."

"How was she hurt?" Sebastian stupidly inquired when Noah's very existence was the answer.

"She loved our father very much, and she was devastated when he left. She never recovered."

"How old were you when she passed away?"

"I was five. Our father liked pretty girls, but he was never too keen on them after they became mothers."

It was a shocking remark, and Sebastian asked, "How old are you now?"

"Twelve."

"How do you know all this about Sir Sidney?"

"After Mother died, I went to live with my grandfather. He told me stories about her and how Sir Sidney had burst into her life and wrecked it. My grandfather didn't like for there to be any secrets about it."

"That's a modern attitude."

"He was anxious for me to grow up to be a better man than our father was, to treat the ladies better than he did."

Sebastian was flummoxed by the comment. How was he to respond to it? He couldn't defend Sir Sidney's licentious habits. Since Noah was proof that their father had had low morals, any refutation would be silly.

"Are you worried about Miss Robertson being friendly with me?" he asked.

"Yes. She can't be involved with you. She's very lonely, and as I mentioned, she doesn't always make good decisions."

"What is your evidence of her poor decisions?"

"When her brother-in-law sold the orphanage, she had no plans for herself. She couldn't convince herself that her sister would kick her out, but her sister is a terrible person. The instant I met her, I realized Miss Robertson was doomed."

"You're an astute judge of character."

"Yes, I am. Miss Robertson is the only adult Petunia and I have in our lives, and if she's in jeopardy, then Pet and I are in jeopardy. You can't worsen things for us."

"Let me set your mind at ease, Noah. I like Miss Robertson."

"How much? I'm very afraid it might be *too* much. Would you marry her if you got her into a jam? I'm sure you never would, so there's no reason for you to stop by at night."

Out of the mouth of babes . . .

"You're correct, there's not, and in the future, I will refrain from nocturnal visits."

"Swear it to me," the little prick demanded.

"I swear," Sebastian breezily replied, not at all certain it was a vow he could keep. But did a promise to a child actually count?

"I'm glad we had this talk," Noah said.

"I am too."

"May I ask you another question?"

"Of course."

"What will happen to us?"

"I haven't given it much thought."

"Miss Robertson is working to find a solution, but even if she can, I have no idea how she'd support us, so I will throw myself on your mercy and plead with *you* to consider supporting us. Maybe out of Sir Sidney's estate? Petunia and I are his children after all. It's only fair. My grandfather previously sought financial assistance for me, but it was denied."

Sebastian scowled. "Who was contacted?"

"Your mother."

"My mother!"

"We had tried to reach Father, but he was usually out of the country. Finally, Grandfather wrote to your mother. He was dying by then, and he was very concerned about my fate."

"What was her response?"

"She called him a liar and threatened to send the law after him if he bothered her again."

Sebastian was flabbergasted. He'd wondered if his mother had an inkling of Sir Sidney's inclinations, and here was confirmation that, *yes,* she'd definitely known.

"I'm sorry for what my family has put you through," Sebastian told him.

"I've survived, with a huge dose of help from Miss Robertson, but *you* have a chance to fix some of the damage Father caused."

"I'll think about it," Sebastian tepidly said, not positive what he meant.

"And I was curious about another topic."

"What topic?"

"The next time you journey to Africa, may I join your expedition team?"

First Ophelia, now Noah. Was it the week for unlikely people to beg to join?

"You're awfully young, aren't you?"

"You initially went when you were ten."

"Where did you hear that?"

"I've read all your books. I've memorized whole passages."

"You have?" Sebastian was inordinately flattered.

"If I started traveling with you, I could earn an income that way, couldn't I?"

"Yes. We earn substantial income from our trips."

"Then I would be able to support Miss Robertson and Petunia on my own. I wouldn't have to depend on you, and I wouldn't have to fret about them."

The remark was very sweet, very dear, painting a clear picture of the kind of boy Noah was deep down. Who wouldn't want him on the expedition team? Who wouldn't want him for a brother?

"I'll ponder your request," Sebastian said, "but I'm not sure I'm going back. The last outing was incredibly traumatic."

"I'm betting you'll go again, once you've recovered a bit more."

"I'll keep you posted."

"Or, if you won't take me to Africa, might you buy me a commission in the army? That would be a splendid path for me as well, but I shouldn't enlist as a private. I really believe I should be an officer."

Sebastian snorted at that. "Yes, you'll definitely be a leader of men. I doubt you'd make a good private."

"And what about our living arrangements? Will you keep me posted on that too? Miss Robertson is so afraid for the future, but she doesn't always apprise us of what's occurring. She doesn't like us to worry, but I hate to have the weight of this situation on her shoulders. I'd like to carry some of it on mine."

"I'll meet with her—at a reasonable hour—to discuss it."

"Thank you." Noah stood and bowed. "And thank you for speaking with me. I appreciate it very much."

"You're welcome."

He walked out, and Raven was dawdling in the hall. On seeing Noah, he straightened and said, "Are you finished already? Please tell me you're leaving."

"I'm leaving, Mr. Shawcross, and you don't need to show me out. I know the way out of my own brother's house."

Sebastian winced, Raven too, both of them hoping no one was lingering nearby who might have overheard. Noah marched off, and after his footsteps faded, Raven came in and poured himself a whiskey. He sat in the chair Noah had just vacated, and he sipped his liquor, expecting Sebastian to comment.

When he didn't, Raven said, "That boy is dangerous."

"He's something, all right, but I wouldn't call him dangerous. He's so much like my father. It would be like calling Sir Sidney dangerous."

"The pot and the kettle," Raven muttered. "What did he want?"

Sebastian waved away the query. "He merely asked me to be nice to Miss Robertson and his sister, Petunia."

Raven looked dubious, as if he might have been eavesdropping. "Is that all?"

"He's a loyal fellow. He's concerned about them."

"Is he demanding you assume responsibility for them?"

"I've given them a place to live, so I'm staggering down that road."

"Before this is through, will you end up supporting them?"

Sebastian scoffed. "Absolutely not."

"We'll see, I guess."

Raven rose and stomped out, and Sebastian said, "What's that supposed to mean?"

"It *means* that Miss Robertson is pretty and intriguing, and a man could land himself in a load of trouble with a vixen like her."

"I imagine a man could," Sebastian cautiously replied.

"You should be careful. If a young boy has noticed your interest, it's gotten out of hand."

Then Raven was gone, and Sebastian slumped down in his chair.

Apparently, Raven had been listening from the hall. Apparently also, Sebastian had to keep better secrets. It appeared the whole bloody world had figured out the biggest one of all.

———⟶⟵———

SARAH WAS LYING IN her bed and staring out at the dark night. It was warm and clear, and she had the blanket kicked off and the shutters open so she could gaze at the stars.

Worries plagued her, and she couldn't sleep, which was odd. Usually, she worked so hard that, when evening arrived, she was exhausted and drifted off immediately. But not anymore.

With the orphanage closed, she'd lost her purpose in life, and she had no idea how to regroup. She was busy with writing letters and chatting with Noah and Petunia, but those two endeavors didn't require any energy, so she'd run out of ways to tire herself.

She wondered where Sebastian was, and pathetic as it was to admit, she missed him. She'd tarried in the parlor until eleven, thinking he'd sneak in, but she'd finally had to accept that he wasn't coming, and she'd trudged off to bed.

For a lengthy period, she'd tried to deduce her feelings about him and why she was pining away. In order to manage her father's beloved orphanage, she'd eschewed marriage, yet she'd let the facility slip away. The loss of it left her afraid that men were correct. Perhaps women oughtn't to be in charge of any enterprise.

Because she'd never previously engaged in a flirtation, she hadn't understood the type of strong emotion that would be stirred. She was yearning for boons she could never have and that sort of craving was futile and idiotic.

She wouldn't mope and brood over Sebastian Sinclair! It was ridiculous, and she was pounding the pillow with her fist, struggling to get comfortable, when a noise sounded out in the bushes. She propped up on an elbow, curious as to what was transpiring, when he emerged from the shrubbery.

She nearly spoke to ask what he was doing, but he put a finger to his lips, motioning her to silence. He clapped his hands on the sill and hefted himself inside. She'd like to claim she was irked by his audacity and that she gestured for him to depart at once, but the pitiful fact was that she was inordinately delighted to see him.

She held out her arms in welcome. He fell into them and stretched out atop her, and he began kissing her as if they'd been separated for years. The frantic embrace continued for an eternity, and when he ultimately slowed and drew away, they were giggling like naughty schoolchildren.

"I gave up on you," she said.

"I had decided not to come."

The news was terribly distressing. Was he growing weary of her already? His intoxicating presence in her dreary life was the only thing keeping her sane. He couldn't avoid her!

"If you'd stayed away," she said, "I'd have been so disappointed."

In response, he stood and went over to the window to pull the shutters closed. Then he tiptoed back and joined her on the mattress again.

"It seems, Miss Robertson"—he was whispering—"that your wards are aware of my clandestine visits."

"Oh, my. They never mentioned it to me."

"Well, they definitely mentioned it to me. Petunia has observed me skulking out—twice—and I've been thoroughly chastised by Noah. He forced me to promise I'd leave you alone."

"The scamp! He has so much nerve."

"I agree."

"I don't need protecting, and he's not my father."

"He thinks I have bad intentions toward you."

"Do you?" she saucily inquired.

"As I'm snuggled with you on this paltry bed, I have to admit he might be right."

"Maybe *I* have bad intentions too," she said. "Maybe I shall simply use you for illicit entertainment. Have you ever considered that?"

"Females aren't allowed to have bad intentions, so *no,* I haven't considered it." He grinned. "Now then, I swore to Noah that I would confine our conversations to business matters involving the three of you, so what would you like to discuss?"

"It's a tad late to be talking business. I'm too fatigued to voice a cogent comment on any topic."

"Let's deem the business end of our meeting to be complete."

She chuckled. "Let's do."

He shifted them around so he was lying on his back, and she was nestled over his torso, her ear directly over his heart. They dawdled in the quiet, and it was a perfect moment. Why had she never realized that an encounter with a man could be so precious?

Was it common for a couple to be so attuned? She imagined it was. Women constantly landed themselves in jams with men, and she'd always assumed—and was told—it was due to weakness of character or lack of morals.

But *she* had plenty of character and morals, so what was her excuse? She suspected that amorous conduct was addicting and could quickly spiral beyond a person's ability to manage. She was certainly in no hurry to slow the pace of what was occurring.

"I missed you," he murmured.

"If I tell you I missed you too, will you please not gloat?"

"No, but tell me anyway."

She sighed with disgust—at herself, at her deplorable infatuation. "I missed you, and I've been feeling sorry for myself because you didn't come to see me."

"We're a pathetic pair, aren't we?"

"Yes, and since you are a sophisticated fellow who I'm sure has engaged in many torrid affairs, will you explain to me what's happening?"

"We enjoy a physical attraction," he blithely said, as if it was the most common event in the world. And for him, it probably was. "Amour occasionally heats up to an incredible temperature, but it's rare for it to be this stimulating."

"What produces it?"

He shrugged. "It's one of the mysteries of the universe. Some people simply share a potent magnetism. There's no rhyme or reason for it."

"It's more than mere physical attraction though. I . . . I . . . *like* you much more than I should."

"Of course you should like me. I'm extremely likable."

"Sometimes you are," she said, "but most times, you're a pest."

"In your view, aren't all men?"

"Yes."

"So when I annoy you, I'm behaving exactly as you were anticipating."

"Yes," she repeated.

"Well, I *don't* like you, so I can't figure out why I keep sneaking over here."

"I think you might be fibbing a little. I *think* you like me just fine."

"Perhaps," he grumbled.

It dawned on her that she was very happy. She didn't know how long she'd hold his attention, but she was anxious to absorb every single detail about him so, later on, after he'd vanished, she'd be able to vividly recall every facet of their meetings.

"I'll be busy for the next week or two," he said.

"With the inquest?"

"Yes. I have to testify and all my men will testify too. I'm determined to have a good report disseminated after it's over. I can't have my father's legacy besmirched."

"What would the findings have to be for you to consider it a *good* report?"

"It would state that my father's death was terrible and unavoidable, and we couldn't have prevented it. I won't have questions lingering as to whether we could have saved him."

"Could you have?"

"No. It happened so fast, and my friend, Nathan? Lord Selby? He tried to stop it, and he was nearly killed for his efforts."

She relished his casual mentions of her half-brother, and she asked, "Will he testify?"

"Yes. It's why I rode to Selby the other day, to check that he was coming. Even though he detests me now, he'll do it for Sir Sidney."

"I doubt he detests you deep down."

"You have no idea how incensed he is."

"You were intimates for too many years. It might be cathartic for him to talk about the incident. Afterward, he might not be so angry."

"I'll hope for it, but I'm not optimistic."

She wondered when her half-brother would appear at the hearing. She'd never seen him in person—not that she recollected anyway—and she was desperate to catch a glimpse of him.

"Is the inquest open to the public?" she asked.

"Yes."

"Is there a schedule posted somewhere?"

"Not that I know of. Why?"

"I was curious as to who's been subpoenaed. I'd like to read through the list of witnesses."

"Mostly, it's the men from the expedition."

They were silent for a bit, to the point where she suspected he'd dozed off, but he inquired, "If you could have anything in the world, what would it be?"

"I'd restart my orphanage. It seems so wrong that it was closed. There are too many rich scoundrels like you, and they sire too many children."

"You'd really start it up again?"

"Don't be so shocked. It gave me a purpose. Why would I walk away without a fight?"

"It's precisely the response I should have expected from you, but it's too pragmatic. Pick something more interesting—even if you have to make it up."

"Maybe I'd like to get married and have my own husband and home."

He scoffed. "Every woman wishes for that."

"Not me." His sudden presence in her life was spurring all kinds of peculiar urges. "It's the first time I ever thought of it, and I can't believe the words just popped out of my mouth."

He laughed. "Neither can I. You're twenty-seven, so you're a dedicated spinster, and you'll likely stay that way. Try again."

"All right. I'd like to sail around the globe and tour all the castles in Europe and explore Italy to snoop out all the old statuary and murals. How's that?"

"Better."

In reality, she'd like to tarry by his side, but she didn't dare admit it. Instead, she switched the topic to him. Men liked to blather on about themselves.

"If you could have anything," she asked, "what would it be?"

"I already have all a man could want: money, fame, status, reputation."

"That's too predictable." She repeated his comment back to him. "Pick a more interesting choice."

"I guess I'd like to be happy."

"You're not happy?"

"I probably should have said *happier*. My life is quite grand at the moment, but it could always be improved."

"True, but you're not doing too badly just as you are."

Out of the blue, he announced, "Noah thinks I should support him and Petunia."

"He suggested it to you?"

"Yes, and I'm considering it. They're my father's children after all, but I can't decide what's best. If I rented a house and provided a stipend, would you like to live with them? Would you raise them for me?"

She pushed up on an elbow to stare at him. Was he serious? Or was he simply voicing ideas to hear how they sounded?

"I would love to raise them," she said. "We've been through so much that they seem like my own children. As matters resolve, if I had to part from them, I'd be devastated."

"I'm merely pondering my options, so don't get your hopes up."

"I always get my hopes up," she told him. "I'm an eternal optimist, remember?"

"Yes, I remember."

He snuggled her down and murmured, "What am I going to do with you?"

There were a thousand ways she might have answered—keep me, have me, wed me, make me yours forever—but she figured the question was rhetorical. His thoughts wouldn't be running on the path where hers were skipping around.

"It will all work out," she said.

"I like having you here—where I can hurry over whenever I'm in the mood."

"I like having you stop by."

"If you left the Haven, I wouldn't have a reason to see you anymore."

"If you wind up supporting Noah and Petunia, you could use them as an excuse to visit me."

"I hate that I'd need an *excuse*."

"Men like you don't have friendships with women like me. Actually, they don't have any sort of relationship with women like me."

She waited with bated breath, yearning for him to disagree, to declare that she was exactly the female he wanted, but of course, he didn't. What would happen between them? She was positive, in the end, she'd be brokenhearted.

When she jumped into a person's life, she jumped in completely. She imagined it was because of what had occurred before she was three, when she might have resided with her half-brother, Nathan. All of it had been yanked away, so when she bonded now, she latched on hard.

She'd give everything she had to please Sebastian Sinclair, then he'd waltz away when he was tired of her. When that terrible day arrived, she'd be . . . where? Nowhere she'd like to be, that was for sure.

It was quiet and late, and she felt so safe in his arms. Without intending to, she dozed off and fell into her old dream, the one where she was with her guardian angel—the girl who was just like her.

They were standing nose to nose, talking in a strange language she didn't understand. Was it the language spoken in Heaven? In the dream, they always recognized what their odd words meant.

Then ... without warning, the wicked witch swooped in and snatched her away.

Bec-Bec, Sarah called, realizing she knew her angel's name. Both of them were crying. She reached out, and Bec-Bec reached out too, but she was being carried off too quickly.

She sat up with a start, her pulse racing, a moan of despair on her lips. Frantically, she glanced about, requiring a few seconds to recollect where she was. She was in her bedroom, on her narrow bed, but Sebastian wasn't with her. Had he departed without a goodbye?

No, there he was, seated on the only chair.

"What are you doing?" she asked.

"Watching you sleep."

"Weren't you bored to tears?"

"You're so beautiful when you're resting. You look younger, less ... distressed."

"Flatterer."

She shoved her hair out of her eyes. "I had such a nightmare."

"Was it the one with your guardian angel?"

"I can't believe you remember such a paltry detail about me."

"I'm filling up a book of *Sarah* details. Was it the same as before?"

"Yes, the wicked witch dragged me away."

He stood and laid a palm on the top of her head, as if she were a child he was comforting. "It saddens me to think that any issue vexes you."

"I'm fine." She was embarrassed, and she eased away, anxious to feel less discombobulated. "What time is it?"

"I have no idea, but I have to go."

"Must you?"

Her tone was so needy and possessive, but she desperately wished he would tarry.

"Yes, I must." He sighed with regret. "I'll be busy next week, so I don't know when I'll be able to stop by again."

Her heart lurched in her chest. "Because of the inquest? Or not ever?"

"Just for the week," he hurried to say. "My schedule is full, and some nights, I won't even return to the Haven. I'll be staying in town. So don't pine away, wondering where I am."

"Vain bounder. I shall absolutely waste away without you."

"That's more like it. I'm wearing you down."

"Mortified as I am by it, I like you more than I should."

"Which I deem to be a very marvelous conclusion."

He bent down and delivered a luscious kiss. Before it could become too interesting, he drew away and straightened.

She gazed up at him, a thousand affectionate comments swirling that couldn't be voiced.

She couldn't abide the tension it created, so she said, "Good luck at the inquest. I'll pray it resolves as you're hoping."

"I'll take all the prayers I can get."

"I'll pray too that you and your friend, Lord Selby, mend your quarrel."

"You claimed you'd *pray* for me. I didn't realize you could work miracles too."

She chuckled at that. "I'll miss you. I really will."

"I'll miss you too. I imagine it's pointless to tell you to keep out of trouble while I'm away."

"I always *try* to keep out of trouble."

"Try harder, would you?"

He peered down at her with such tender regard that she was completely flummoxed. What was she supposed to do with that look? How would she ever survive without it?

"If I'm tied up longer than I expect," he said, "I'll send you a note."

"You would? Are you pretending to be the type of man who might sit down and write a letter?"

"You'd be surprised."

"No, I wouldn't."

He dipped down, stole a last, quick kiss, then went over to the window. He paused for a moment to flash an exasperated grimace over the need for stealth, then he opened the shutters, climbed out, and crept away.

She flopped down on her pillow and whispered the prayer she'd promised him—for his inquest to end beneficially. But she also added one for Noah and Petunia and the possibility that he might support them. Then, because she was feeling greedy, she included one for herself too.

She prayed for strength, for the fortitude required to deal with Sebastian Sinclair, and mostly, for the stamina to continue on once he grew weary of her and left.

———⊰⊱———

REBECCA BLAKE CARTER DRIFTED off to sleep. It had been a difficult day, and she was exhausted. Almost immediately, she fell into her old dream, the scary one she loathed. It had recurred—particularly during periods of stress—ever since she was little.

The other girl, the one who looked just like her, was with her. Rebecca assumed it was her guardian angel. They were standing nose to nose, talking in a strange language when, without warning, a wicked witch swooped in and snatched her angel away.

Sissy! Rebecca called.

It dawned on her that she knew her angel's name, and she thought it was a silly, common name for such a special, divine being.

She frowned and reached out, and Sissy reached out too, but she was being carried away much too rapidly. Rebecca couldn't catch her. They were crying, grabbing for each other. They never liked to be separated! What was happening? What was wrong? Why wouldn't any of the adults explain?

A boy was shouting. *Where are you taking them? Why won't you tell me?*

She called out to him too, but she couldn't find him, and . . . and . . .

She jerked awake, her heart pounding, a moan on her lips. Anxiously, she glanced around, needing a few seconds to remember where she was. Recognition gradually settled in, and she blew out a heavy breath.

She was in her bedroom, and she was all alone. In the minutes she'd dozed off, why would she believe her circumstances might have changed?

CHAPTER

14

"IT HAPPENED SO FAST. There was no way to prevent it."

Raven Shawcross sat in a rear pew, listening to Nathan's testimony.

There were a dozen men on the board of the National Exploration Society, and they were seated around a table. Nathan was in a chair at the end, staring them down.

Sebastian was in the front row, but Mrs. Sinclair and Miss Ophelia had stayed home. Raven didn't know if Sebastian wouldn't let them attend or if they'd decided on their own that the evidence would be too gruesome.

The hearing was supposed to have been held at the Society's headquarters, but public interest was so high that they'd required a much bigger space. They'd rented a church for the event, and it probably wasn't fitting, but every parish needed extra money now and again.

He figured the pastor had been happy to open his doors—for the right price. The altar had been pushed back and a large conference table brought in.

Nathan was the witness who had generated the most excitement. With his being left for dead, he'd become even more notorious. His part of the story was the one that truly intrigued the crowd. How had he survived? It was a tale too miraculous to be believed.

As Raven had waited for the afternoon session to begin, the spectators had whispered infuriating questions. They were tittering over such inappropriate facts as how many times Nathan had been stabbed, how much blood he'd lost.

They were eager for him to wax on and fill in the missing pieces, but they were about to be disappointed. According to Sebastian, Nathan had never uttered a word to explain his extraordinary feat.

Raven didn't want to ever be apprised, and he prayed Nathan wouldn't expound. Each detail was a condemnation of the Sinclair expedition team. In reality, they'd implemented a half-hearted search for his body. They'd been too distraught over Sir Sidney's death, and when the native tribe couldn't produce Nathan's corpse, they'd shrugged and sailed away without much of a complaint.

Judah had insisted Nathan was deceased when they'd found him, and the rest of the crew had accepted his version of the debacle. Why had they? Why had Raven especially?

He'd always thought Judah was an unreliable ass, and he wouldn't have trusted him in any other situation. Why hadn't he, Raven, checked? His only excuse was that he'd been overcome with grief.

It was humiliating to admit that he'd been such an awful friend to Nathan, and he owed the man an apology for his negligence. He hadn't ridden to Selby to beg his pardon, and he should have, but he'd been too mortified over their mistake.

Plus, Sebastian had been the first emissary who'd gone to Nathan, and he'd been beaten to a pulp. He'd suggested they avoid Nathan until he calmed down, so Raven hadn't tried to talk to him.

He craned his neck, yearning to get a better view, and wishing he'd arrived earlier, so he could have been closer to the action. Nathan looked healthy and fit, his comments lucid and clear. Sebastian had described his prior condition as thin and gaunt, so he was recuperating quickly.

"What was the argument about?" an interviewer asked Nathan.

"Sir Sidney had assumed—incorrectly—that we had permission to cross the tribal hunting grounds, but he'd received erroneous information. The chief was incensed, and a quarrel broke out. The translator couldn't keep up, and tempers escalated."

Raven sighed with relief. Sebastian hadn't been certain that Nathan would spew the lie they'd concocted. He was so angry with them, and he might have refused, but he'd testified precisely as Sebastian had requested he testify.

Normally, Raven would have decried such duplicity, and Nathan would have too, but none of them would tarnish Sir Sidney's legacy with the truth. Nor would they shame Mrs. Sinclair or Miss Ophelia by revealing the genuine reason the fiasco had devolved into murder.

The crew deemed themselves to be prevaricating for the greater good, to protect innocent females who didn't deserve to be hurt. Wasn't that sort of sin allowed and forgiven? He wasn't a philosopher, so he wouldn't try to guess.

Nathan was still speaking, providing a graphic account of how Sir Sidney had been hacked to pieces, how Nathan had been slashed at too, how—after Sir Sidney was dead at his feet—he'd fled into the jungle and had been shot by an arrow.

The church was so quiet. No one moved. No one breathed.

"It's my understanding, Lord Selby," the interrogator said, "that you collapsed under some ferns, and you were experiencing what should have been your last minutes on this earth."

"I was."

"Can you tell us what happened next?"

"No. It conjures difficult memories for me, so I'd rather not."

"But we're all so curious," the man said. "We'd like you to clarify subsequent events. We're agog to find you in England, and you appear very hale."

"I'm fine. A little less vigorous than I was in the past, but I'm fine."

"Can you tell us for the record—but also for posterity—how you made it home?"

"I'm sorry, but no. I really can't."

"We'd all like to hear."

"I'm sure you would, but I never discuss it."

The Society men cast furtive glances at each other, wanting a brave soul to step forward and press him to enlighten the crowd, but it wasn't a criminal proceeding, and there was no judge on the bench. They had no way to compel him.

Nathan seized the reins. "I've been testifying for over two hours, and I've shared every aspect I recall. If you have other questions about the initial portion of the incident, I'm happy to answer them. Otherwise, I'd like to be excused."

There was a shuffling of papers, and the committee members glanced at each other again. It was obvious he wouldn't delve into the juiciest section, the section everyone had been dying to have divulged.

Finally, the chairman said, "Are there any other lines of inquiry for Lord Selby? Or have we covered sufficient ground?"

There was a general murmuring of assent that he could be dismissed, and Nathan didn't wait for their approval. He simply stood and walked out.

He passed right by Sebastian, but didn't so much as peek at his old friend, and the realization was depressing. The audience had noticed the snub, and Raven supposed there would be articles in the newspapers about it. They were such famous fellows, like warriors in an ancient fable. People were in awe of them.

He came down the center aisle, and the spectators gaped at him, anxious to be able to describe him to their acquaintances later on. He ignored them and kept on through the vestibule and out the church doors. Raven slipped out of the pew and went after him.

As he exited the building, Nathan was already down the block at his carriage. An outrider was holding the door so he could climb in.

Raven flitted down the stairs, calling, "Selby!"

For a moment, Nathan stiffened, then he continued on.

"Selby! Nathan!"

The use of his Christian name had him spinning around. There weren't many men who would address him so familiarly.

He watched Raven approach, and his expression was inscrutable. Was he irked to have been delayed? Was he annoyed that Raven had hailed him? He and Raven had been companions for over a decade. After all that had transpired, had he no opinion about seeing Raven?

He nodded. "Shawcross."

"I wanted to say hello." There was a lengthy pause where it was clear Nathan wouldn't fill the void, so Raven said, "I'm glad you attended the hearing."

"I don't believe I had a choice. Sir Sidney was like a father to me."

"Sebastian wasn't positive you'd bother, so thank you."

Nathan snorted at that. "I appreciate it."

Another pause ensued, and Raven felt terrible about it. It seemed their ability to be cordial had evaporated.

"I should have visited you at Selby," Raven said, "and I regret that I haven't. Sebastian told us how angry you were, and I can't blame you. He thought we should give you an opportunity to calm down, so I heeded his advice, but I wish I hadn't. I should have come to talk to you anyway."

Nathan scowled. "Why would you have visited me?"

"To apologize. You and I both know what Judah is like. When he strutted into camp, insisting you were deceased, I should have checked for myself. I'll always be sorry that I didn't."

"Your being sorry doesn't change anything, does it?"

"No. How are you really? Inside at the hearing, you claimed you were fine. Are you?"

"I'm fine enough."

"What will you do with yourself now? Will you go to Africa in the future? I can't imagine you'd travel with Sebastian, but might you mount your own expedition? Or have you considered joining a different team?"

"I'm finished with all of it. Our last trip was too much for me. I've lost my enthusiasm for the endeavor."

"I understand. I'm trying to decide myself if I'll go again, and I doubt I will. It wouldn't be the same without Sir Sidney."

"No, it wouldn't." Nathan shrugged, looking more relaxed, as if he was remembering they'd once been friends. Then he stunned Raven by announcing, "I recently got married."

"Sebastian didn't tell me."

"I promised her I'd give it up. She wouldn't have wed me if I'd planned to traipse off and vanish for years at a time."

"She must be quite a woman if you'd quit exploring for her."

"She is, but I didn't do it for her. I'd already determined I wouldn't return." He smirked. "I just let her assume it was because of her."

It was the sort of conspiratorial male remark they might previously have shared, and Raven chuckled. "Your amour must have happened very fast. Who is she?"

"Her name is Nell. You wouldn't know her."

Nathan's tone indicated he wouldn't expound on his bride. Evidently, he viewed himself as being so separated from the Sinclair expedition team that he wouldn't provide even the smallest personal detail.

Raven was genuinely curious though, and he might have pressed for information, but suddenly, Nathan glanced over his shoulder and frowned.

"Excuse me," he said, and he took off like a shot.

Raven whipped around and blanched. "Dammit!"

Judah was strolling toward the church. What was the idiot thinking? Sebastian had distributed a copy of the schedule, so the entire crew was aware that it was Nathan's afternoon to testify. Judah couldn't have forgotten, so what was his intent?

He was incredibly vain, so perhaps he was simply eager to flaunt himself at Nathan merely to prove he could.

Nathan attacked like a shark in the ocean, his first punch brutal and precisely on point. Judah hadn't noticed him racing up, and at receiving the clout, his knees buckled and he collapsed. Nathan leaned down, grabbed him by his shirt, and hit him again.

Raven spun toward his carriage, and his servants were watching the altercation. "Help me!" he shouted to them. "We have to stop this!"

He didn't dawdle to learn if they followed. A crowd had gathered to observe the combatants, and as Raven pushed through the gaggle of spectators, Nathan had released Judah and stepped back.

"Traitor!" Nathan accused. "Coward! Thief!"

Judah mumbled an unintelligible comment, and Nathan kicked him in the ribs. Judah curled into a ball. His nose was bleeding profusely and likely broken.

"You have some gall," Nathan fumed, "to show yourself on the streets of London."

"It's a free country," Judah unwisely retorted.

The taunt infuriated Nathan so much that he delivered a flurry of blows, and Judah howled in agony.

"If I ever see you again," Nathan warned, "I'll kill you. The only reason I won't do it here is that there are too many witnesses."

"Bastard!" Judah muttered, and Nathan kicked him again.

Raven leapt in and pulled Nathan away, saying, "He's not worth it, Selby. Leave him be."

Nathan gaped at Raven like a wild man, then recognition settled in. He jerked out of Raven's tight grip and said, "Tell Sebastian that I'm still waiting for my knife."

He stomped off, and his outriders surrounded him. In a trice, he was in his coach and spirited away.

People knew who Judah was, and the story of how he'd declared Nathan deceased was all over the kingdom. He lay on the ground, a beaten, solitary figure with no friend to lift him to his feet. Raven certainly wasn't about to assist him.

Bystanders scoffed with disgust, then sidled away until it was just the two of them. Raven spat onto the cobbles and walked off too.

JUDAH WAS IN HIS bedchamber at Hero's Haven when a footman knocked and told him Sebastian was in his library and needed to speak with him immediately. But he couldn't go downstairs. He'd been desperately searching for Nathan's knife, and he couldn't find it anywhere. Where could it be?

When Nathan had been dying in the jungle, Judah had cut it off his belt and taken it. It was a magnificent weapon, sharp and heavy, with real jewels embedded in the handle. Sir Sidney had given it to him on his eighteenth birthday, and he'd always sauntered about with it attached to his hip.

Judah had been jealous of that knife. Sir Sidney had never given Judah anything, and he'd traveled with the man for twelve years!

He'd stolen it almost on a whim, and apparently, Nathan remembered the incident and had mentioned it to Sebastian. Who would have expected Nathan to survive? Not Judah, that's for sure. And with how Nathan had been hovering at death's door, why would he have recollected any details of their encounter?

Sebastian hadn't confronted Judah about the knife. Why not? What might it mean?

He should have pawned the bloody thing. Or sold it. He'd ordered himself to get rid of it so often, but he hadn't. He'd enjoyed having it hidden in his room, and he liked that he'd seized it from Nathan whom he'd always detested.

But where was it?

Judah hadn't planned to bump into Nathan at the inquest, but he had, and look where it had left him! His nose was so painful that it had to be broken, and he suspected a few ribs were broken too. His eyes were black and blue, and his right eye was swollen shut. He was a pathetic sight.

The assault had happened three afternoons prior, so his injuries had had plenty of time to throb and puff up. He was quite miserable, his thought processes muddled, his fury acute. He'd been battered on a city street, and no one had intervened.

Even Shawcross had been a prick about it. They'd never been particularly cordial, but for pity's sake, they'd worked together for over a decade. What kind of *friend* was he?

Judah grabbed his coat and started down the stairs, being especially careful to *not* peek at himself in the mirror. He couldn't abide his ruined face.

He wondered what Sebastian could want and yearned for him to exhibit some concern as to Judah's condition. It would be nice if someone would. Since his thrashing, not a single crew member had visited his bedchamber to check on him.

Judah intended that they realize how Nathan had become an unhinged lunatic. His behavior was so out of bounds—attacking a fellow with no warning—and Judah was determined that none of them ever mend fences with him.

He headed toward the library, and as he approached the door, Shawcross was perched there like an angry sentinel. He glanced into the room and said, "He's finally here."

"Show him in," Sebastian replied.

Shawcross didn't move, and because he was partially blocking the door, Judah had to wedge past him.

"What's your problem, Shawcross?" Judah grumbled.

"You don't look so good," the ass snidely retorted.

They might have quarreled, but Sebastian motioned Judah in.

"Ignore him, Judah, and sit down please."

Judah cast a glare at Shawcross, then trudged over. He'd like to presume he hurried, but he wasn't feeling spry enough to rush. He eased into the chair, finding it a relief to get off his feet.

Shawcross closed the door, and Judah was hoping he'd left so Judah could meet with Sebastian alone, but he came over and stood behind Sebastian, as if he'd been recently elevated to a higher position of authority. He and Sebastian glowered at Judah as if he was in trouble, and the notion was galling.

Why would *he* be in trouble? Nathan was the one who belonged in an asylum.

"What do you think of my injuries?" he inquired. "Nathan is completely deranged. He pummeled me for no reason at all."

"So I heard," Sebastian said.

Judah kept on as if Sebastian had denied the event. "If you don't believe me, ask Shawcross. He witnessed the whole thing. Just so you know," he blustered, "I'm considering having Nathan arrested."

Sebastian wasn't willing to have that discussion, and instead, he said, "I have to talk to you."

"About what?"

"About Africa."

"We've been over this a thousand times. The men who were with me verified my story. If you've decided to question it, bring in a Bible, and I'll swear to the facts."

Sebastian didn't accept the offer, but opened a drawer and pulled out an object wrapped in a leather sheath. At first, Judah couldn't discern what it was, but when he recognized it to be Nathan's knife, his eyes widened with astonishment—and no small amount of fear. He watched as Sebastian withdrew it from the sheath and placed it on the desk.

"Would you care to explain why this was tucked away in the bottom of your traveling trunk?" Sebastian asked.

"I've never seen that knife before in my life," Judah stridently said.

"Let me kill him!" Shawcross seethed. "Let me take him out into the woods."

Judah blanched. He had no doubt Shawcross would do exactly that. Of the entire team, he was the most dangerous, but Sebastian stayed him with a wave of his hand.

"My father gave this to Nathan for his eighteenth birthday," Sebastian told Judah.

"Oh, yes, I remember it now," Judah said.

"You cut it off him when he was dying. You cut it off and walked away with it."

Judah vehemently shook his head. "I didn't!"

"Stop lying to me."

"I'm not lying! I demand we ride to Selby so I can call Nathan a cur to his face!"

"I've been busy, so I haven't had the energy to deal with you, but I'm dealing with you now. We're through."

"I have no idea what you mean. You're speaking in riddles."

Sebastian tsked with exasperation. "Then I'll be clearer. You found Nathan alive."

"I didn't, Sebastian."

"Your actions cost me my best friend, but they also disgraced me. Because of you, I abandoned him."

"It wasn't just *me* who thought he was dead. Ask the others! They'll tell you."

Shawcross jumped in. "Shut your mouth, Judah, or I'll shut it for you."

"You chatted with Nathan," Sebastian accused. "You claimed *I* wouldn't have him slowing us down."

Judah would refute the truth forever. "You're wrong. You're *so* wrong."

"When he initially told me, I was sure he was confused about what had transpired. I assumed that trauma had addled his wits." A lethal calm settled in, then he said, "I am so ashamed. Both of myself *and* you."

Judah didn't understand. "Why would you be ashamed?"

"I'm a fool. I believed you. I believed *you* over him, so I allowed you to tarry in my home, and every minute of your presence has been an insult to him."

"I suppose you'd like me to apologize, but I won't—"

"You can't remain at Hero's Haven another second," Sebastian declared.

They were the most terrifying words ever uttered. The whole crew was residing at the Haven, reveling and waiting for Sebastian to announce his next venture. Judah couldn't bear to be excluded.

"I can't be barred from the premises," he said. "I'm one of you."

"Not anymore," Sebastian brutally stated. "You'll depart immediately, and you won't ever be welcomed back."

Judah forced a wobbly smile, as if it was all a big mistake. "It seems as if you're kicking me off the team."

"I am."

"But ... but ... I've been with you for twelve years!"

"By your reckless conduct toward Nathan, you've squandered your place."

"I didn't harm that pompous prick!"

The slur was too much for Shawcross. He marched over and whacked Judah. His head was throbbing from the beating Nathan had delivered, and he wailed in pain.

Shawcross said, "Your days of whining and complaining around me are over."

The logical response for Judah would have been to leap up and engage in a brawl, but if he threw a punch, Shawcross would punch back. The pathetic fact was that it would hurt too much to be hit again.

He shifted to Sebastian, and his gaze was beseeching. "How can I fix this?"

"You can't," Sebastian said.

"You're not serious!"

"I'm very serious. Even as we speak, footmen are packing your things. They're being loaded in my carriage out in the driveway. You'll be conveyed to town to whatever location you prefer."

"I belong with you. I'm *one* of you. You can't toss me out!"

"I already have."

"It's how I earn my living. It's my life!"

"I hope you saved some of the money you've accumulated."

"Sebastian, please!"

As his reply, Sebastian said, "My sister, Ophelia, informs me that you've been flirting with her."

"I haven't!" he insisted, as Shawcross said, "You're joking! Has she been encouraging this oaf?"

Sebastian ignored Shawcross and kept his focus on Judah. "I warn you away from her. You should never meet with her again, and if you dare, there will be consequences." Sebastian nodded at Shawcross. "Get him out of here."

There was a charged instant where they didn't move. Judah was frantically pondering, trying to think of how he could alter the direction they were traveling.

It had occurred too fast! It was ending too quickly! It wasn't fair!

"I was Sir Sidney's favorite," he said. "He wouldn't like you to treat me so badly."

"Sir Sidney might have favored you," Sebastian scoffed, "but when trouble was brewing, *I* viewed you as an untrustworthy coward. You were still on the crew because he constantly vouched for you, but I'm over it."

Shawcross grabbed Judah, lifted him up, and escorted him out. Judah dragged his feet, but he was so stunned he couldn't delay their exit.

They reached the door, and Sebastian called to him. "Judah?"

He suffered a spurt of excitement. Was Sebastian sorry already? Would he relent? "What?"

"Why didn't you just kill Nathan? I've been wondering. He was so grievously wounded. Why didn't you simply slit his throat and put him out of his misery?"

Judah could have answered in a hundred different ways, but Sebastian was staring at him as if he were vermin, as if he, Sebastian, had been soiled by Judah's presence.

His temper flared. "Why would I have bothered killing him? Why waste the energy? Who would have ever imagined the conceited ass would survive?"

Sebastian bristled with offense. "Just as I suspected."

Shawcross yanked him away, and Judah's legs could no longer support him. Shawcross half-carried him down the hall, through the foyer, and down the steps.

They stopped at the carriage, and Judah attempted to resist, to *not* climb in, but he was bewildered and off balance. An hour earlier, he'd been loafing in his bedchamber, a respected member of the Sinclair expedition team. Now he was no one at all. How had that happened exactly? He couldn't quite wrap his mind around it.

Shawcross had always been strong as an ox. He pitched Judah into the vehicle, but he thudded onto the floor and was huddled on his knees.

Shawcross leaned in and said, "Sebastian never liked you, and neither did I. I'm not sorry to see you go. My sole regret is that it wasn't much sooner." He slammed the door and told the driver, "Take him to town. Drop him at whatever spot he requests, and if he won't pick one, dump him off wherever you like."

The driver cracked the whip, and the horses lurched away so rapidly that, by the time Judah could brace himself and crawl up onto the seat, they were already down the lane, the manor swallowed up by the trees. He didn't catch a final glimpse of it.

CHAPTER

15

"It's finished?"

"Yes, all done."

Gertrude Sinclair stared at Sebastian and nodded. "How long will it take for interest to wane?"

"I think it will continue for quite some time."

She sniffed with offense. She loved her status as Sir Sidney's widow, but she hated to have her name in the newspapers. That kind of notoriety was never appropriate.

"Can't we tamp it down?" she asked.

"I don't wish to tamp it down," he maddeningly said. "I like it that people remember Sir Sidney. I hope they're fascinated for decades. In a small way, it seems as if he's still alive out there somewhere."

She too liked having him remembered—it elevated her own position—

but the public's obsession was focused on the lurid portions of what had occurred. The family hardly needed that type of gossip swirling.

"When will the report be published?" she asked.

"In about a month."

"Will there be any *problems* with the findings?"

"No."

They were in her parlor, having tea. For once, she was alone with her children, which she always enjoyed. Veronica was out on social calls, but Ophelia had stayed home. She was being a brat though and was in a snit over an issue she declined to clarify.

After Sebastian had shown up, Gertrude had requested Ophelia come down to chat with him, but she'd refused so vehemently that Gertrude had had to insist.

Ultimately, Ophelia had slinked in, but she wasn't happy about it. She was over on a small sofa in the corner, pouting and shooting rude glares at her brother. Were they quarreling? They rarely saw each other. What could they possibly have to fight about?

Was it because he wouldn't permit her to attend the inquest? She'd claimed, if Sir Sidney's son could be there, his daughter should be too, but Sebastian had rebuffed her demand to accompany him. Occasionally, she spewed the strangest nonsense, and Gertrude couldn't imagine how she developed such untenable, modern ideas.

As if a son and daughter were equals!

"How is Nathan?" she inquired. "I trust his testimony was acceptable?"

"He was terrific, but the spectators were disappointed because he wouldn't explain how he survived."

"I heard he hasn't ever talked about it," she said.

"And I doubt he ever will. He's been traumatized."

"How was he?"

"He was fine, Mother."

"Well . . . good."

"Did I tell you he married?"

"We read the announcement in the paper, but I didn't recognize the woman's name. I take it she wasn't anyone we would know."

It was a polite way of describing his wife as common, but Gertrude wouldn't voice that depiction. She'd tried to be fond of Nathan, but he'd been a difficult boy to like. Yet Sebastian and Sir Sidney had doted on him, so she had to tread cautiously in uttering any derogatory remarks.

"No, we don't know her," he said, "but when I went to Selby last week, I met her."

"What was your opinion?"

"She's extremely charming. I like her very much."

"You would," Ophelia mumbled.

"Were you commenting, Ophelia?" Gertrude sharply said. "If you would like to join our conversation, please feel free. But if it's your intent to mope and fume, then be silent."

"He just *loves* lowborn women," she said a tad louder.

Gertrude couldn't guess what her daughter was intimating. In the past, Ophelia had never exhibited any of the unsavory signs of adolescence, so perhaps her foul temper was merely a sort of delayed growth spurt.

Gertrude decided to ignore her, and she shifted her focus to her son. He was unfailingly civil and seldom in a bad mood.

"What are your plans now?" she asked him.

"I'm debating. My crew is bored, and they're pressuring me to arrange another trip to Africa."

She wouldn't argue that he shouldn't return to the Dark Continent. She'd often engaged in that battle with her husband—and always lost it. Africa was an addiction the Sinclair men couldn't shake.

Instead, she said, "What are you telling them? Will you go?"

He shrugged. "It wouldn't be the same without Sir Sidney or Nathan."

"You're suffering a few of your own ill-effects from the prior journey. As the months pass, matters will become clearer."

"It's what I'm hoping."

"In the meantime, Veronica is here."

He sighed. "Yes, she is, Mother."

She repeatedly wound any discussion to his betrothal, which he hated, but he had to be pushed. If he wasn't, someday he'd be fifty and still a bachelor.

"Before you ponder Africa, you must consider subjects a bit closer to home. You can't traipse off again and assume Veronica will wait for you."

"She doesn't have to wait. If she would like to find a beau who's ready to proceed—as I am not—I'm fine with that."

In any matrimonial deliberations, it was his trump card.

He'd never officially agreed to wed Veronica, and he would be happy to let her escape. If Gertrude nagged about it, he'd be even more recalcitrant simply to prove he couldn't be bossed.

In that, he was exactly like his obstinate father.

"If you depart on an expedition," Gertrude said, "where you might be away for years, you owe it to her *and* the family to resolve the issue before you leave."

"I suppose."

He downed his tea and stood, and she was so exasperated to see it. The minute she raised a topic he didn't like, he fled. Apparently, Veronica and marriage were on his list of what was forbidden.

"Must you go so soon?" she asked, when the answer was obvious.

"Yes, I'm weary from the inquest, and I'd like to sleep in my own bed tonight."

"When will you grace us with your presence again?"

"I have no idea."

"Veronica will be sorry she missed you."

"I'm certain she will be."

Was there sarcasm in his tone? Didn't he like the accursed girl? Was that the problem? She was beautiful, educated, trained, and gracious. If he hadn't wanted Gertrude to pursue the match, why hadn't he spoken up long ago? Was she expected to read his mind?

He marched to the door, but he paused to glare at grouchy Ophelia who was still pouting. So far, they hadn't conferred directly.

"Are you heeding me in that situation I mentioned?" he asked her.

"What situation would that be?" she snottily inquired. "Would it be the one where you think you can pick my friends for me?"

"Yes, that would be it. You haven't been meeting with anyone I would dislike, have you?"

She flashed a tight smile. "I've been an absolute saint."

"Keep it that way."

He sauntered out without a goodbye, and Gertrude could only shake her head. What on earth had that odd exchange been about? Was Ophelia socializing with unsuitable companions? Could it be?

"You have to stop badgering him about Veronica," Ophelia said. "He doesn't like it, and it simply makes him more stubborn."

"I wasn't badgering. Besides, I'm his mother, so it's perfectly appropriate for me to counsel him regarding matrimony. He's a dedicated bachelor, so he must be urged to get on with it. He won't travel that road on his own."

"He's too *busy* to contemplate matrimony."

The manner in which Ophelia pronounced the word *busy* was disconcerting, and Gertrude asked, "What is it you mean?"

"I *mean* he's distracted by someone who's prettier and much more interesting than Veronica, so he doesn't need to worry about her."

"What are you telling me? You're spewing riddles, and I can never figure them out."

"He has a mistress, Mother!" Ophelia brazenly declared. "What do you imagine I'm telling you?"

Gertrude was amazed that Ophelia would blurt out such a scandalous fact, but she wasn't surprised by it. After all, Sebastian was thirty, and he was Sir Sidney's son. But she *was* surprised that Ophelia would be aware of an illicit liaison.

"It's not proper for us to discuss such a sordid subject," she sternly said.

"I'm exhausted from listening to you pester him. I'm furious too that he's being so disrespectful to Veronica."

"Men have affairs, Ophelia. It happens." Her own husband had been the worst of the lot. "If Veronica never discovers it, he can hardly be accused of disrespect."

"The doxy is living at Hero's Haven!" Ophelia fumed. "He's opened the valet's cottage for her. Why, I was shopping in the village one afternoon, and she was there too. Veronica almost bumped into her!"

Gertrude felt faint. "She's living at Hero's Haven?"

"Yes! So don't pretend Veronica isn't being disrespected."

"What is the trollop's name? Were you able to learn it?"

"It's Miss Sarah Robertson."

"Sarah Robertson ..." Gertrude mused, and she scowled. "I know her from somewhere. Where?"

"She used to run an orphanage in London."

Gertrude blanched. "An orphanage?"

"Yes, and she brought two of her ... ah ... urchins with her. They're residing there too!"

A flicker of rage ignited as Gertrude vividly recalled how she was connected to the odious Miss Robertson, and she had no doubt as to the identity of the waifs she'd dragged to the Haven. Some of her dead husband's sins had come home to roost.

"Have you seen the two urchins?" she asked. "Have you learned *their* names?"

Suddenly, Ophelia was quite a bit less sure. "Ah ... I only observed them from a distance, so I don't recollect any details. And I never heard their names."

With a nauseating clarity, Gertrude remembered who Sarah Robertson was. The shameless woman had tried to pressure Gertrude into paying the support bills for a pair of Sir Sidney's bastards, and she'd ended the harassment by having her lawyer send a threatening cease-and-desist letter.

Gertrude thought she'd rid herself of the horrid harpy, but evidently, she hadn't.

"Would you excuse me, Ophelia?" she said. "I have some correspondence to write."

"On what topic?"

"It's nothing that would concern you."

"Ah ... ah ... I might have been too strident about Miss Robertson and those children. I wish you wouldn't fret over them."

"I'm not fretting, and I didn't find you strident at all. In fact, our entire conversation has been extremely enlightening."

She waved her daughter out, and when Ophelia hesitated, she flashed a severe glower, the one that always pushed Ophelia into obeying. It worked this time too. She skittered away like a frightened rabbit.

---·❦·---

Oᴘʜᴇʟɪᴀ sᴛʀᴏʟʟᴇᴅ ᴅᴏᴡɴ ᴀ deserted path in the park. She'd come in a carriage, then she and her maid had climbed out and told her driver to wait for them while they went for a walk. Once they were out of his sight, and he couldn't tattle to her mother, she left her maid behind and continued on to her secret spot. She'd snuck off with Judah twice now, and they were due for another rendezvous.

She was determined to chat with him on a sufficient number of occasions so she could decide whether to marry him. She was fond of him, but she certainly wasn't in love. Still though, as a young girl, she'd hoped to be swept off her feet by Prince Charming. Yet princes were few and far between, and she was a very sensible person.

If she broke down and wed, it would be because she'd been able to negotiate for the precise kind of life she was intent on having. If she was simply going to shackle herself to a husband who would command and boss her, what was the point?

She was living that meager existence with her mother and brother. She couldn't so much as open a window without seeking their permission.

Judah was the only man she'd ever met—ever—who pictured women differently. He viewed her as smart and perfectly capable of making up her own mind on vital issues.

Up ahead, she saw the secluded bench she'd chosen for their assignation. It was sheltered by several bushes, which was important. She was famous in London, and it would be a disaster to be noticed by an acquaintance, then have it reported to her mother. There would be no way she could explain it.

Judah hadn't arrived, but she hurried over and seated herself. She felt completely exposed, as if there were spies in the trees. Their relationship required too much stealth, and the furtiveness cast a shadow over their association, but their having to skulk about wasn't her fault. If Sebastian had behaved like a normal brother, there would be no need for a clandestine tryst.

She was early, so she had a quiet interval to reflect on the discussion with her mother about Miss Robertson and her father's bastards. She probably shouldn't have mentioned them, and briefly, she wondered if Gertrude might take action against Miss Robertson that would force them to depart the Haven.

Ophelia didn't necessarily want to cause trouble for them, but she was simply so upset with Sebastian and had wound up talking out of turn.

Judah was approaching, and as she watched him, she frowned. His face seemed askew, and he was limping, as if he'd been injured. As he neared, she gasped with dismay.

He'd been beaten to a pulp! He looked to be in great pain, as if each breath was torture.

"My goodness, Judah!" she murmured. "What happened?"

"You won't believe it."

"Sit down, sit down!"

She scooted over to make room for him, and he eased down next to her, moving slowly as if each little shift was agonizing.

"Who did this to you?" she asked.

He glanced away. "I shouldn't tell you."

"No, no, you have to say! Who was it?"

He hemmed and hawed, then admitted, "It was your brother."

"What?"

"I apologize. You're so close to him, and I hate to share bad news."

"Sebastian assaulted you?"

"Yes."

"But ... but ... why?"

He clasped hold of her hand and linked their fingers as if they were adolescent sweethearts.

"I went to him and asked to marry you."

A trill of excitement rushed down her spine. "You didn't!"

"I realize you wanted me to wait, but I couldn't bear any delay. I'm quite in love with you, Ophelia."

"Oh!" She'd never imagined a man declaring himself, and the words were exhilarating.

"Please don't be angry," he said.

"I'm not, but why would he attack you?"

"He claimed I couldn't have you. He claimed *he* was in charge of you, and he'd never let us wed."

"He can be so arrogant. I loath that about him."

"Despite his resistance, I didn't relent. I tried to flatter him. I tried to reason with him, but he wouldn't listen. Finally, I got down on my knees and begged to have you."

"Really?"

"Yes, but he merely laughed and called me hideous names."

"What sorts of names?"

"They're too vulgar to repeat, but he boasted that he had to teach me a lesson, that there had to be consequences for my pushing myself into his family when he refused to have me there."

Her eyes narrowed. "He beat you because you wanted to marry me?"

"Yes, and I'm so sorry."

"Why would *you* be sorry?" she asked.

"I can't see you ever again. And we certainly can't wed. Not with your brother being so adamantly opposed." He yanked away, appearing wretched. "I despise him for treating you like this! I wish I had a solution for us, but I'm afraid we have to part. It's why I'm here—to bid you farewell."

Ophelia was stunned—and very, very incensed. Sebastian was a bully, just like her father had been a bully. He liked to throw his weight around, liked to remind her that he had complete control of her future.

Would she allow him to have that control?

She'd only ever sought two favors from him in her life: to let her travel to Africa on his next trip and to consider a proposal from Judah. Yet he'd been obnoxious about both requests. Then Judah had tried to persuade him of their interest in marrying, and for his efforts, he'd been brutally battered.

How could she tolerate such an outrage?

"It doesn't have to be farewell," she said.

He frowned. "How can there be any other conclusion?"

"There are ways to wed without obtaining my brother's permission."

His frown deepened. "I don't understand."

"We could elope."

The words were out of her mouth so quickly she couldn't bite them down, but she wouldn't give herself time to contemplate.

An elopement was the most extreme, shameful act a girl could commit—short of finding herself with a babe in her belly and no ring on her finger. But it was the sole option for a female when her relatives didn't approve of her beau.

"My dearest, Ophelia," Judah said, "I couldn't dishonor you so egregiously."

"*I* am the one who suggested it, so I don't believe I'd be dishonored."

"I had pondered the same alternative myself, but I didn't dare hope. It never occurred to me that you might be amenable."

"Before I'd proceed, you'd have to promise to take me to Africa someday. If you swear you will, then my answer is *yes*. We'll elope."

"That's a problem for us now. Your brother kicked me off the expedition team for my having the gall to ask for your hand."

"Ooh, I could wring his neck!" She thought for a moment, then said, "You could sign on with another expedition, couldn't you? Sebastian isn't the only explorer in the world. We could join someone else."

"Yes, we could."

She had a fleeting vision of herself, standing at the front of a canoe and floating down a river, thick jungle on either side. She was scanning the horizon for danger, building her own reputation as a Sinclair.

Ha! Let Sebastian choke on that!

Her heart pounded with excitement, but with a second emotion she couldn't identify. If she'd paid too much attention to it, she might have recognized it to be fear, that she realized she shouldn't be agreeing to this.

She hardly knew Judah. Was it wise to flit off with a fellow who was practically a stranger? Was it wise to enrage her brother and devastate her mother? If Ophelia eloped, Gertrude would never get to host a grand wedding in the cathedral, and she'd blame Ophelia for denying her the chance.

Did she care? Would she regret it later on?

Probably, but she was past the point where she could back down. If she relented, she'd be surrendering power to her brother. She felt as if she was on a cart at the top of a hill, that it was rolling down and picking up speed. She couldn't stop it and didn't really want to.

Judah gazed at her and asked, "Will you marry me, Ophelia? Will you elope to Scotland with me and make me happy forever?"

For the briefest instant, she hesitated, aware that she shouldn't consent, but he seemed so besotted. No gentleman had ever looked at her so fondly.

She opened her mouth, and the comment that emerged was, "Yes, I will marry you, Judah Barnett. When and how will we accomplish it?"

CHAPTER
16

SEBASTIAN STOOD AT THE window of the library at Hero's Haven. He was staring at the waters of the lake that were shimmering in the trees. The sun was setting, and the colors were particularly brilliant, the greens so green, the blues so blue. The sight was so beautiful it nearly hurt his eyes.

The manor was empty, his men reveling in town. None of them had heard the news about Judah being cut loose or, if they had, they were discussing it amongst themselves. They hadn't rushed to ask him if the story was true.

There was no predicting what tales Judah might tell, and Sebastian had to be ready to counter them by branding him a traitor and a liar. He could only hope it would never come to that. It wasn't a fight Judah could win.

Sarah's cottage was just beyond the lake. He hadn't seen her in over a week. Throughout the days of the inquest, he'd stayed in the city. There had been a whirl of social activities to keep him busy, but he'd tarried in town for another reason too, that being Sarah and her presence at the estate.

She had a bizarre hold on his affections. He couldn't stop thinking about her. Every minute he was away from her was a minute he wished he was with her instead.

What did it mean?

Women threw themselves at his feet, being eager to garner his attention in whatever manner he would allow, but they'd never enticed him as she had. With how obsessively he was fixated, he was trying to figure out what it indicated.

Was he...he...in love with her? Could that be it? As he had no previous experience with the emotion and wasn't convinced he believed in it, he couldn't guess. Besides, how could a man love a woman he'd just met?

If it wasn't *love,* he had no idea what was happening, and he had no idea how to quash his swings of sentiment. He'd never suffered heightened feelings over any female, but with Sarah, there was something strange occurring.

Even though it made no sense, he was thrilled to have her in his life, and he was certain if she vanished, he'd regret it forever. It seemed that she'd been given to him for an explicit purpose. Would he muck it up? Would he ignore what Fate had bestowed?

How could he guarantee she never left? Would she agree to be his mistress? He doubted she'd be amenable, but then, she was desperate, so she might accept an arrangement she wouldn't normally countenance.

If she wouldn't be his mistress, there was one other way to latch onto her and that was to marry her. Could he actually be considering such an outrageous prospect?

He wasn't sure. If he wed her, it would drive a permanent wedge into his relationship with his mother and sister. His family—Veronica's branch of it anyway—would never forgive him. Veronica especially would be incensed, and she'd be entitled to her fury. When that would be the result, could he deliberately create such a rift?

Then there were Noah and Petunia to dump into the mix. If he formed a connection with Sarah, they would have to be included. It would thrust them under his mother's nose, and it would kill her with humiliation.

Was Sarah worth it? Was any female worth that sort of incessant trouble?

There were reasons a man's parents picked his bride. If a bachelor got a wild notion in his head, they stepped in and focused him on an appropriate match, which Sarah definitely wasn't.

He couldn't stand it. He had to see her. He'd been telling himself to avoid her, but why erect absurd barriers that wasted precious time they could spend together? He couldn't predict how the future would unfold, but for now, she was just across the park.

He downed the last of his whiskey and put the glass on his desk, and he'd turned to leave when the butler knocked and said, "You have a visitor."

Sebastian grimaced. Who would pop in as the sun was setting? "Who is it?"

"The woman who's residing in the valet's cottage? Miss Robertson? She was informed that you were home, and she's wondering if she could have a word."

Sebastian could barely conceal his wave of gladness.

Servants were the worst gossips in the world. They all knew she was on the property, and they'd be frantically debating over why he'd permitted it, but it wouldn't do to have them realize he was absolutely besotted.

"I'm not busy," he casually said. "Show her in."

The butler departed, and Sebastian dawdled behind the desk, struggling to tamp down the stupid grin stealing over his face, but he couldn't manage it. He was so happy!

He heard her coming, she and the butler chatting amiably, then the man peeked in again and announced her. She waltzed in, bold as brass, and the butler closed the door, obviously recognizing they should be left alone.

Sebastian vividly recalled how angry he'd been the day she'd arrived at the Haven, and it was interesting how a few weeks could change a fellow's path.

"Hello, Miss Robertson."

"Hello, Mr. Sinclair. The servants mentioned you were back, and I thought I ought to check on how you're faring."

"I was in a bad mood, but suddenly, things are looking much brighter."

He walked over to her, clasped her hand, and dragged her to the door. He opened it and peered out, finding the hall empty. She frowned and nearly inquired as to his intentions, but he held a finger to his lips, indicating she should be silent.

He whisked her out of the room, down the hall, and over to the rear stairs. They practically ran up to the third floor, and they reached his grand suite at the end without encountering a single soul.

Once they were sequestered inside, he fell on her like a feral beast, the embrace so fraught with passion and yearning that he was bewildered. He felt like a drowning man who'd been thrown a rope, a starving man who'd been seated at a banquet, a nomad wandering in the desert who'd stumbled on an oasis.

"What are we doing?" she asked between breathless kisses.

"I shouldn't have to explain it to you."

"I can't be up here in your bedchamber."

"You already are."

"What if someone sees us?"

"No one will, but if they do, I don't care."

He blazed a trail down her neck, to her bosom, to nibble at her nape, and she moaned with pleasure.

"I was just coming to the cottage," he said, "but you found me first."

"I couldn't keep waiting for you to climb in my window."

"You're such an impatient wench. I'm not sure I approve."

"The instant you returned, I expected you to slither over. What was taking you so long?"

"I was trying to avoid you," he said.

"Why, you deranged fool?"

"Because I'm terrified of you."

"Terrified, hm? I like the sound of that."

Usually, he'd have been aghast to have her appear uninvited. A sensible girl would have tarried in her own home until *he,* the man in the relationship, deigned to stroll in. Not her though. After meeting her, after developing such a ridiculous obsession, how could a silly, boring debutante ever appeal?

He was doomed. No doubt about it. She'd ruined him for every other female in the kingdom.

Without asking her opinion, he scooped her into his arms and marched through the sitting room and into the bedroom. The entire time, he was kissing her, and it dawned on him that he'd never be able to rid himself of her.

She was simply an addiction he couldn't shake.

He tumbled them onto his bed and rolled them so she was on her back, and he could stretch out atop her. The embrace grew more heated, more extreme, until he felt that he might burst from how exciting it was.

He forced himself to slow down, to gradually draw away.

Outside, the gloaming was settling in. It was that lovely period between evening and night when it was quiet and peaceful, but there was sufficient light to see her beautiful blond hair, her striking blue eyes. The shadows cast her skin in an odd silver color, so she looked magical, like a fairy.

"I can't believe you're in my bed," he said like an idiot.

"I can't believe it either. I'm positive I'm dreaming, and when I wake up—if I'm still in it—I'll be horrified."

"In my view, you've finally ended up right where you belong."

"In *my* view, you are unhinged."

"Very likely so," he concurred, "but if I am, it's your fault. You've pitched my world into chaos, and naught will ever be the same."

He kissed her again, more tenderly, then he shifted off her and onto his side. She shifted too so they were nose to nose.

"I missed you," he told her.

"I missed you too—every second—and it's so disgusting for me to admit it."

"What will become of us?"

"I have a few ideas."

"I have a few too," he said, "and I plan to share all of them with you."

"Should I be delighted or alarmed?"

"You should be both. You get to have me all to yourself, and I am wrapped around your little finger."

She smiled such a delicious smile that he could hardly stand to observe it. He suspected it was exactly the kind of smile Eve had flashed at Adam. No wonder the poor dolt had been destroyed. What man could resist a smile like that? What man was strong enough?

"I had the most depressing week," he said.

"Why? Was the inquest terrible?"

"It was fine. It concluded as I was hoping, but the whole thing was stressful."

"Of course it was. You had to sit there and have your father's murder recounted over and over."

"The worst of it happened away from the hearing. My friend, Nathan Blake, came face to face with Judah Barnett out on the street."

She blanched. "Did Lord Selby kill him?"

"No, but he assaulted him in front of a crowd of spectators."

"Good for him."

"In Africa, Nathan wore a knife on his belt. It was a gift from my father. When I visited him at Selby, he told me Judah took it that day in the jungle. He claimed Judah cut it off his belt and kept it as a souvenir."

"How shockingly awful."

He sighed, regret bubbling up. "I've known Judah for over a decade, and I couldn't conceive of him acting that way, but Nathan was so enraged about it that I rode to the Haven and checked Judah's belongings. Guess what?"

"You found the knife?"

"Yes, hidden in a trunk."

"What will you do about it? You have to respond somehow, don't you?"

"I already responded. I kicked him off the expedition team and tossed him out of my house. I've parted with him forever."

"I never liked him," she said, "and I'm not sorry he's gone."

He snorted at that. "It was difficult for me to send him away, and he was very upset."

"Might he retaliate? Should you be worried?"

"If he lashes out at all, he'll try to tarnish Sir Sidney's legacy by spreading bad stories about him. Then I'd be forced to remind everyone of how he left Nathan for dead. I'm predicting he's smart enough to avoid that type of quarrel."

She grinned an impish grin. "Are there bad stories about Sir Sidney?"

"Yes, and since you have custody of two of his natural children, you're aware of what some of them are, so don't expect me to clarify."

She riffled her fingers through his hair and said, "It's all over now: the hearing, the memorials, the issue with Lord Selby and Mr. Barnett. You can stop fretting and move on."

"It's not over with Nathan. I have to mend fences with him."

"I'm sure you will eventually."

"You haven't seen how livid he is."

"Other than his temper, what's he like? I've read so much about him in the newspapers, but the stories focus on his exploits, not his personality."

Nathan was such a complex fellow. How to describe him in a few words? "He's brave and clever and loyal, but he's very stubborn, and he can be extremely imperious. Most of the time, he behaves like a royal prince. Even as a boy, he was so annoyingly arrogant. He can be exhausting."

"I'd like to meet him someday."

"Well, you're not going to," he sternly told her. "You'd probably like him more than me, and he'd steal you away."

"Who says I like you in the first place? And I don't believe I'm *yours* for anyone to steal."

"You're mostly mine, and could we not talk about Nathan? I finally have you in my bed, and I'd like you to concentrate on *me* and no one else."

The petulant comment had her chuckling. "You poor baby. You never get the attention you deserve."

"Not from you anyway." He studied her, wondering how to begin, and he simply jumped into the fire. "I have to ask you a question, and you must consider your answer. You can't stomp out in a huff."

"Why are you certain I'll stomp out? If it's a horrid topic, why raise it?"

"I'm anxious for us to always be together."

She froze, then shook her head. "No, you aren't."

"Yes, I am. You make me happy, and it seems as if we're destined for a remarkable ending."

"For reasons I can't fathom, you've decided I fascinate you, and it's distorting your view of our relationship. I'm betting in another month or two, you'll be sick of me, and you'll be chasing debutantes again."

He scoffed with feigned offense. "I've never chased a debutante in my life."

"What about your cousin, Veronica?"

"I've definitely never chased her, and as with Nathan, could we not talk about other women?"

"If you insist, but it's important to point out that you're acting like a lunatic with regard to me."

"I've never felt clearer about what I want."

"And what is it you *want*?"

"I want you to be my mistress."

"Your mistress? Really?"

She started to laugh, and she was chortling quite merrily. It wasn't anywhere close to the response he'd anticipated. He'd predicted a range of emotions from a blunt refusal to grave moral outrage. He hadn't foreseen vast amusement.

"Why are you laughing?" he grumpily asked. "It was a serious suggestion."

"I'm so accursedly gullible. When you stated that you were anxious for us to *always* be together, I suffered a moment of insanity where I thought you were about to propose marriage."

"Oh." His cheeks heated with chagrin.

"I was frantically struggling to figure out how to dissuade you."

He frowned. "Why dissuade me? Every girl in the world would like to marry me. Why not you?"

"I'd love to wed, but I'm holding out for a husband who dotes on me *and*, since I'm an orphan, I'd like a family to call my own. With how your mother and sister despise me, they'd never accept me as your wife."

"Probably not." He wouldn't pretend Gertrude or Ophelia would ever like her. "I hate that you're so smart."

"Yes, it's an incredible burden. Now then, let me up."

"Why?"

"This discussion has yanked me to my senses," she said.

"What's wrong with your senses?"

"We have an odd attraction that bewilders me, and I've allowed it to flare. I can't help myself, but it's futile. We can't pursue it, and *I* in particular have to buck up, ignore you, and behave myself."

She tried to skitter away, so he rolled onto her, his larger body pinning her to the mattress. Nothing especially interesting had happened yet, and until it did, he wasn't about to have her leave.

"Why this sudden urge to behave?" he inquired.

"I could get myself into a great deal of trouble with you. You're too much *man* for me to handle."

"I'm too much *man* for every woman."

"You're humble about it too."

She relaxed, giving him the impression that he'd cajoled her into tarrying, but just when he wasn't paying attention, she scooted away and sat up. She appeared fond, but exasperated, and she laid a palm on his chest, directly over his heart.

"Thank you for inviting me to be your mistress," she said. "I'm flattered that you would consider me for such a role, but I could never agree."

"Why not?"

"There's no benefit for me to agree. You'd trifle with me until some other female caught your eye, then you'd toss me over. I'd be ruined and forsaken. I'm already forsaken, which is a hideous situation to be in, and I'd rather not be ruined too."

"I'm rich, Sarah."

"I know that about you, Sebastian."

"I could shower you with gifts and money. I'd buy you gorgeous gowns. I'd purchase a house for you and staff it with a dozen servants. You could even have a carriage. You'd live like a princess."

She scowled. "Do I look like the kind of person who's hoping for a wardrobe filled with pretty gowns?"

Where she was concerned, he was so clueless. He could only gape at her and ask, "Isn't that what every female craves?"

She tsked with irritation. "You don't understand me, and we have naught in common. The longer you talk, the more you're making me realize it."

He was irked that he'd mucked up his offer, but also because he couldn't bear to have her depart. He was eager for her to stay the night, and he had numerous intriguing ideas as to how they could wile away the hours.

He clasped her wrist and said, "If you don't desire what any sane, ordinary woman would choose, how can I tempt you? What tickles your fancy?"

"I've told you before. I'd like to reopen my orphanage. I also have to find a safe place for Noah and Pet, but I'll work to keep them with me."

"You seek advantages for others. You never request anything for yourself. How am I to entice you when you're so noble?"

"I'm generous and grateful because of the lessons I learned from my father when I was growing up. When he adopted me, he saved me from the sea of unwanted children. I honor his legacy by helping others. That's who I am. That's who you're attempting to seduce."

"I'm botching it too, aren't I?"

"Yes, and I should be going. I'm sure Noah and Pet are worried about me."

"Forget about them. At the moment, *I* need you more than they do."

She smirked. "What a ridiculous comment."

"I seem to be full of them."

She leaned down and kissed him, then she eased away and slid to her feet.

"I'm glad your stressful week is over," she said.

"So am I."

"What are your plans now?"

"I can't imagine."

"You'll have some leisure time to ponder. Will you return to Africa?"

"I doubt it."

"I'll be relieved if you never return," she said. "I'd fret too much."

"Then I'll definitely remain in England—just to keep you happy."

"Would you visit me tomorrow? I'd like to discuss Noah and Pet and your supporting them. Perhaps you could even fund an orphanage for me. We could name it after your father: The Sir Sidney Home for Orphaned Waifs."

Sebastian sputtered with amusement. "I can't believe you suggested it. You are such a brazen hussy."

"I always have been."

"Tell me who your father was. You know, don't you? Don't lie to me."

She paused, then grinned. "Oh, yes, I know who he was."

"Was he a king?"

"You can reflect on it until you drive yourself mad."

"Wench. Would you really rather spend the night at the cottage by yourself?"

"Well, I can't spend it with you. You're deranged if you thought I might, and I can't determine why I let you drag me up here."

"It was worth it."

"Maybe."

She winked at him and headed for the door, and he said, "It's dark out. I should walk you over."

"I'd never arrive. You'd constantly ambush me with compliments and kisses."

"How did you guess?"

"You are not a mystery to me, Sebastian Sinclair. And besides, I can't be observed strolling through the park with you."

"You're crushing my ego."

"Someone should."

Then she was gone, and he flopped onto the pillow and stared at the ceiling.

He'd led her to his bedchamber, had shared a passionate interlude, and then?

He'd asked her to be his mistress, and he'd bungled it. His lewd proposition had yanked her to her senses and had sent her fleeing.

It was so quiet without her, and his room felt positively claustrophobic without her in it. He dawdled in the silence, wondering what time it was, wondering how long it would be before he'd see her again. How long could he bear to be away from her?

He didn't think it would be very long at all.

CHAPTER

---✦✦---

17

SARAH WAS IN HER bedroom at the cottage. A candle burned over on the dresser, casting forlorn shadows. She was standing at the window and staring out at the stars, but it was cloudy so there was nothing to see.

Hours earlier, she'd crawled under the blanket and had tried to doze off, but she couldn't sleep.

She was wearing just her summer nightgown, her arms and feet bare. It was chilly, so she should have been freezing, but she was burning with torrid thoughts of what had nearly happened over at the Haven.

Sebastian had asked her to be his mistress! Had he actually presumed she'd agree? Did she appear that desperate?

Well, yes.

The pathetic fact was that she'd been tantalized by his suggestion. Sick as it sounded, she longed to remain with him in any manner she could arrange. If an illicit amour was the sole way to bind herself, why not proceed? Any other destitute female would probably have jumped at the chance. As he liked to point out, he was very rich. With a snap of his fingers, he could fix her problems. Why not let him?

But she could never participate in such an immoral relationship, and she'd have wound up with a broken heart. She already felt as if it was broken, and she hadn't yet misbehaved to any significant degree.

In her entire twenty-seven years, she'd never grieved over her low birth status. She'd grown up around children who were in her exact same boat, sired by wealthy, reckless men who pretended they didn't exist.

Suddenly, she was wishing she was a duke's pretty daughter. Why settle for a duke? Why couldn't she have been born a princess? Why not? Wouldn't it be marvelous to be precisely the woman he needed?

The door opened behind her, and for a second, she closed her eyes and a wave of gladness flowed through her. Had she conjured him merely from pondering him so intently?

When he wasn't being a pompous oaf, he could be so incredibly wonderful. Apparently, she wouldn't be spending the night by herself.

She grabbed the shutters and latched them, then she spun to face him.

"We have to quit meeting like this," she teased.

"I know, but I missed you."

"We've only been apart for a few hours."

"And every minute was torture."

The room was very small, and in two strides, he was across the floor. She figured he would kiss her, but to her great surprise, he clasped her hand and dropped to one knee. A gentleman only adopted that stance when he was about to propose marriage, so she was a tad startled.

"Over in my bedchamber," he said, "I insulted you."

"I wasn't insulted." She frowned, then said, "Maybe I was, but I hope you realize why I had to refuse."

"After you left, I was so lonely. I tried to deduce what was wrong, and finally, it hit me. I can't bear to live without you. Will you marry me?"

She scowled ferociously. "You're not serious. You had a difficult week, and you're not thinking clearly."

"I'm not confused about what I want. Say *yes*. Say you'll have me."

"I won't. Now get up."

She attempted to lift him to his feet, but he wouldn't budge.

"You can't decline," he said.

"Yes, I can. We're scarcely acquainted, and your family would never approve."

"Bugger my family," he crudely muttered. "This doesn't have anything to do with them."

"Don't be absurd. It has everything to do with them."

"No, it's about you and me and how happy you make me. It's all that matters."

She sighed. "If only that were true."

"I won't allow you to spurn me."

"I believe I already have."

"No. This was my initial salvo. I have until dawn to change your mind."

"You can't change it."

"I'll simply keep on until you stop being so silly."

"I'm saving you from the biggest mistake of your life, and *I* am the one who's being silly?"

"Yes, and I'm weary of listening to you complain. Please be silent."

He stood, and he was so tall that he towered over her. Was that deliberate? Would he intimidate her into it?

Before she suspected his wily plan, he clutched her by the waist and tumbled them onto her bed. It was quite a step down from the grand bed in the master's chamber at the Haven. It was barely wide enough for them to lie down, barely sturdy enough to hold their combined weight.

She didn't protest or wiggle away because she didn't want to escape. She'd never met a man like him and didn't suppose she'd ever have another chance like this. What could it hurt to misbehave a little?

She'd always been intrigued as to why females ruined themselves, and she was twenty-seven. Wasn't it time she learned some of what other women had learned?

From the strident embraces they'd shared, he'd tantalized her with hints of how delicious passion could be. Why not discover what else he might show her? She knew how babies were created, and if she never walked to the end, where was the harm?

He began kissing her and kissing her, but every so often, he'd pause to ask, "Will you marry me, Sarah?"

She'd shake her head, and he'd scoff at her foolishness and start in again.

Gradually, he was removing her nightgown. Would she let him? It seemed as if she would. He was pulling it up her legs, past her shins, her knees, until fabric was bunched at the top of her thighs.

She came to her senses and drew away.

"Wait, wait," she said.

"Wait for what?"

"What's happening?"

"I intend to get you naked."

"Sebastian Sinclair! You do not."

"You have to agree, Sarah, that so far in our relationship I've been a perfect gentleman."

"By what standard? You keep sneaking into my bedchamber, and I can't convince you to desist."

He shifted onto his haunches and stunned her by tugging off his shirt and tossing it on the floor.

"We're not disrobing." Her tone was scolding.

"I've simply taken off my shirt," he told her as he snuggled down. "I'd hardly call that disrobing."

"You're hoping to push me into conduct I shouldn't attempt."

"Yes, probably. If we walk down the path I'm eager to travel, you'll have to wed me."

"You'll coerce me into it?" she asked.

"No coercion will be necessary. You'll relish every minute of it."

"What brought this on? If you'd sought my opinion an hour ago, I'd have insisted you didn't even *like* me very much. Now, you're begging me to be your bride. Pardon me if I'm dubious."

"You don't think I'm sincere?"

"No."

"Can you imagine I would ever do anything I didn't truly wish to do?"

"Most likely not."

"Why would I propose if I wasn't earnest? What if I didn't really want you, but you accepted? I'd be stuck with you."

She chuckled, but miserably. "You should go back to the manor."

"No, I shouldn't."

She gazed into his mesmerizing blue eyes and murmured, "No, you shouldn't." Then she groaned with disgust. "Gad, I'm so weak around you! In every other facet of my life, I'm tough and strong, but not with you. You run roughshod over me."

"You're mad about me," he said. "Admit it."

"I'm mad about something," she retorted, "but I'm not sure it's you."

"It will work out. Don't worry so much."

She thought of how lonely she'd been before he arrived. Her existence was so small, her future so bleak. He delivered a tiny sliver of joy, and he was offering to attach himself to her. Why shouldn't she grab hold?

She would be a completely inappropriate wife for him, but she couldn't persuade him to care about that fact. It was *his* mother and sister who would be incensed. It would be *his* family and friends who would be shocked. If he wasn't concerned, why should she be?

He was very rich, and wealth smoothed over a lot of sharp edges. Maybe it wouldn't be awful.

"Look at me and tell me you're serious," she said.

"About what? About marrying you? I'm serious as a viper about to pounce on an unwitting victim."

"What are you envisioning? When would we wed? Where would we wed? Where would we live? Could Noah and Pet live with us too? How would you feel about that? I'm terribly afraid you haven't pondered any of the ramifications."

He raised a brow. "Do your questions indicate you're considering it?"

"I might be."

"We'll proceed tomorrow or the next day. I have to apply for a Special License, and it involves meetings with church officials and preparing documents."

"Your mother and sister would be livid."

"So? They're not the ones marrying you."

"What if you regret it later on? There's some sort of insanity infecting you, and I fear you'll recover your wits and realize your blunder. Then where will I be?"

"Answer me this: Was your father—your *real* father—an aristocrat?"

She hesitated, then cautiously said, "He might have been, but at this point in the discussion, why would it matter?"

"I've been certain I wasn't proposing to a fisherman's daughter. I was fairly sure I would be getting a grand prize with you."

"A grand prize? Me?"

His amusement faded, and his expression grew more somber. "I think you're extraordinary."

She snorted at that. "I'm very vain—vainer than you probably—so I won't argue with your assessment."

"I offended you by suggesting you be my mistress, and I apologize. The instant the words were out of my mouth, I was appalled to have uttered them."

"You're forgiven."

"But I don't want a temporary relationship with you. I want you by my side forever, and there's only one way to guarantee that conclusion."

"You're not joking?" she said. "You're not tricking me somehow?"

"You assume I'd trick you over such an important topic?"

"Yes. No." She wailed with dismay, feeling bewildered. "I can't predict what you might do."

"Take a chance, Sarah. Let's see what happens."

"What if I leap to my doom, and it ends in disaster?"

"It won't. It will be perfect. I swear."

He started kissing her again, and she jumped into the fray. He was on a peculiar trajectory, claiming they would wed. She was desperately anxious to believe him, so—for a few hours—she *would* believe him. For the sole occasion in her life, she would behave recklessly.

She would bluster forward and seize the opportunity he'd dangled. She'd never gambled, but what if this once, she placed her bet and won every hand?

WHAT A BIZARRE TURN of events!

Sebastian had proposed marriage, and she suspected he was jesting. He ought to be insulted. Well, he'd show her! He'd forge ahead, then he couldn't back out. If they fornicated, there could be no reneging. They'd have to wed—whether either of them wished it or not.

Although she didn't recognize it in herself, she was a very lusty creature. She'd revel in what he was about to teach her, and he pictured decades of merry sexual play where *she* constantly dragged him off to their bedchamber.

He dove into the passionate fire again. So far, he hadn't pursued much mischief. He hadn't unbuttoned any buttons or untied any ribbons, but it was time to push her to a new level of intimacy.

He'd already tugged the hem of her nightgown up her legs, and he'd removed his shirt. Very soon, they'd both be naked, and the notion was so thrilling he could barely stand to contemplate how beautiful she'd look without any clothes.

He was driving her up the ladder of pleasure, learning her size and shape. Through the fabric of her nightgown, he massaged her breasts. The garment had two tiny straps to hold it on, so it was easy to dip under the bodice and clasp a nipple.

He pinched and squeezed until it was clear she needed more stimulation. Then he nibbled a trail down her neck, to her chest. He yanked down the straps to expose her bosom to the cool air, and he sucked a nipple into his mouth.

The act caused such a response in her that—if he hadn't been lying on top of her—she might have leapt off the bed in surprise.

"What are you doing?" she asked.

"I'm tempting you."

"This is occurring too fast."

"There isn't a slow way to engage in it."

"It feels absolutely sinful."

He grinned at her. "It is, but we'll proceed anyway."

"I figured you'd say that."

"I'm a scoundrel. What can I tell you?"

She flopped down onto the pillow and sighed with resignation. "When I die, I'm going straight to Hell because of you, aren't I?"

"Probably, but I'll be there too, so you'll have a friend waiting to welcome you when you arrive."

He began again, sucking, biting, pinching as, gradually, his hand slithered between her legs to sneak under the hem of her nightgown. Without warning her first, he slid two fingers into her woman's sheath. He glided them in and out, in and out, but it was too much for her, and she tried to jerk away.

"You're scaring me," she said.

"I am not."

"I have no idea what I'm supposed to do."

"You don't have to *do* anything. You simply have to enjoy yourself."

"I never expected to have an experience like this."

"Some brave man should have pressed the issue with you years ago. You're twenty-seven! You're so far over the hill that I can hardly see you."

"I'm not over the hill," she complained. "I'm . . . mature."

"Ha! You're a spinster, and you should learn what you've been missing."

"What if I don't want you to?"

"Sarah! Is it your intent to talk me to death?"

"No."

"Then relax. It will be wonderful."

She glared at him, then flopped onto the pillow again. She was wet and ready, her body aroused and eager for what was approaching. He sucked on her nipple as he flicked his thumb on the spot where all her sensation was centered—once, twice—and just that quickly, she soared to the heavens.

She flew up and up. As she reached the peak, she moaned so loudly that he was afraid he might wake Petunia, so he captured her lips in a torrid kiss that went on and on. She finally tumbled down, and as she collapsed at the bottom, he was preening, thrilled with what he'd perpetrated.

"Oh, my," she murmured when she could speak again. "I think I've been struck blind. What was that?"

"*That* was sexual pleasure."

"Am I still a virgin? I thought there was more to it than that."

"Yes, you're still a virgin."

Her naïve question gave him pause. Was he taking advantage of her? No. He was marrying her the next day. No doubt they should have delayed until after the vows, but he was at the limit of his restraint.

"I can't move my limbs," she said. "I'm paralyzed."

"It means I can have my way with you now."

"Haven't you been having it?"

"Yes, since the moment we met."

"Vain beast," she muttered.

"I want to show you the rest of it. Has anyone told you what happens?"

"I have a fairly good idea."

"It's physical."

"I've heard that."

"After we're finished, I'll be yours forever. You'll never be shed of me."

She chuckled. "I can't decide if I like the sound of that or not. Are you worth having?"

"Am I worth having?" He scoffed with feigned offense. "Sarah Robertson, you are too, too cruel, and I can't figure out why I put up with you."

"Neither can I, and you have to always remember that I tried to talk you out of this."

"You can't dissuade me. You've driven me mad with affection."

"I'll convince myself that's true."

"I'll make it true. Just you watch."

She pulled him close so she could study his eyes, then she said, "Swear to me that you'll wed me tomorrow."

"You are such a hard nut to crack."

"My life is on the line here. If you're not sincere and you don't follow through, I will be in a terrible jam. You can't fault me for being cautious."

"No, I can't."

He wished she would trust him a bit more, but they didn't really know each other all that well. She'd grow to trust him though. He'd prove she could rely on him in every situation. From this point on, he'd be her staunchest friend.

"I swear I'm serious," he replied. "I swear I'll wed you tomorrow."

"I'll tell myself to believe you. I'll tell myself it will transpire."

"It will. I promise."

He gazed at her, and the oddest perception swept over him. He might have been peering down a tunnel, the decades flying by. There they were newly married. There they were as parents, then with a house full of noisy, rowdy children. There they were older, their children with children of their own.

There they were elderly, happy, the years having been as good to them as he'd imagined from the start.

"Sebastian?"

Her voice sounded as if from a far distance, and it drew him back into himself.

"What?"

"Where did you go? For a minute there, you looked as if you'd vanished."

"I was thinking of how contented we'll be together."

"I think we will be too."

"Will you spoil me rotten and obey my every command?" he asked.

"I'll let it be a surprise."

The most precious sense of *rightness* settled in, as if the universe consented to their scheme, as if they'd arrived precisely where they were supposed to be.

He began kissing her again, and he was overcome by the worst anxiety. This was her wedding night, but he doubted he could make it special enough for her.

She leapt into the embrace, and instantly, it became passionate and heated. Their physical attraction was so powerful that it seemed impossible to control or tamp down. And why tamp it down? She would be his for the remainder of his life. They could be as wild as they chose.

He was determined to see her naked, and with a few flicks of his wrists, he finally had her nightgown up and over her head. As he stretched out again, as their chests connected—bare skin to bare skin—he was amazed they didn't ignite. The feeling was that potent.

All the while, he was kissing her, his hands playing with her nipples, keeping on and on, until he couldn't stand much more.

Gradually, he unbuttoned his trousers and yanked them down around his flanks. He widened her thighs, positioning his cock where it was demanding to be. He wedged in the tip, and only then did she panic.

"Are we going to ... to ..." She didn't have the salacious vocabulary to discuss what he intended.

"Yes, we're going to behave exactly as we shouldn't, but we're marrying tomorrow. We're simply having our wedding night a tad early."

"I'm afraid," she said.

"Of what?"

"Of what I don't know."

"It will be over in a second."

"I hope it will last a bit longer than that," she teased.

"Maybe a *bit* longer, but I'm too overwhelmed by you, and I can't wait to finish this."

"Will it hurt?" she asked. "I've heard that it hurts."

"Just for a moment. You'll hardly notice it."

"I'm glad you'll be the one."

"I am too."

His heart was hammering furiously, and he was desperate to wax poetic. He was so totally and irrevocably besotted, and he was keen to apprise her, but he wouldn't embarrass himself by expounding.

He had to get to the end, and he started tormenting her. As her lust escalated, as she tensed and cried out, he gripped her hips and pushed once and again and again, and just that quickly, just that easily, he was fully impaled.

She huffed out a breath, and he froze, watching as she acclimated to her new condition.

"Is that it?" she asked.

"Most of it."

"I'm not a virgin anymore, am I?"

"No."

She grinned. "I'm delighted that I'm not."

"Believe me, so am I."

"Show me the rest," she said, "so I'll love it as much as you do."

"I will do that," he vowed. "Every occasion we're together like this, I'll try to make it perfect."

But he couldn't follow through on that promise. He was so stimulated that, almost immediately, his seed surged from his loins. There was no way to slow the pace or alter the route.

After several deep thrusts, he emptied himself against her womb, the experience so stunning that he felt as if he'd been pummeled, as if he'd been wrung tightly and hung out to dry. He collapsed onto her, his body heavy with satiation, as he thought, *You're mine now! You'll never be able to escape.*

It occurred to him that she was being awfully quiet, but she was never quiet. How had she viewed the event? He couldn't imagine.

He pulled away from her and slid onto his side. She rolled too so they were nose to nose.

"Why are you smiling?" she asked.

"I was thinking about what a cad I am."

"How are you a cad? I practically begged you to proceed."

"I deflowered you, and I was so anxious about it that I still didn't take off my boots. You should scold me for being so impatient."

She smiled too. "I'll remember that for future reference."

"What is your opinion, Miss Robertson? You've participated in the marital act, and you're no longer a maiden."

"It was very . . . interesting."

Her reply was terribly tepid, and hastily, he said, "The first time can be awkward."

"I didn't find it awkward. I found it quite thrilling."

"I'm elated to hear it. I'm so enamored of you that I blundered into it like a green boy with an innocent girl."

"I liked it anyway."

"Good."

"It was more physical than I realized, and I understand why people are only supposed to engage in it when they're wed. It was so intimate. I could never try it with anyone else."

He frowned. "Well, no, you won't—ever. You're about to be my bride, so get that insane notion out of your head."

"I'm happy."

"Not as happy as I am."

He shifted onto his back, and he drew her nearer so she was partially draped over his torso, her ear over his heart, a lazy arm across his waist.

"What now?" she asked.

"We nap for awhile, then we do it again."

"Can you do it more than once a night?"

"Yes, I can." He swatted her on the bottom. "And be careful with comments like that or you'll crush my poor male ego."

"Heaven forbid." A silence ensued, then she said, "Petunia will be so excited."

"Girls are wild for a romantic ending. How about Noah?"

"He'll be more relieved than excited. He feels such a duty to protect me."

"That job will fall on *my* shoulders."

"It will be nice to have you around to help me carry some of my load."

"My dearest, Sarah, I will carry *all* of your load. It's what a husband is for."

"Please tell me this won't cause too much of a fight with your family."

"Don't worry about them. You just need to show up for the wedding. Leave the rest to me."

"Will we hold the ceremony here at the Haven?" she asked.

"Yes. Are there any guests you'd like to invite? I hate to delay, but if you have relatives who'd have to travel, we can put it off for a few days."

"There's my sister and her husband, but after how they treated me over the orphanage, I wouldn't want them to attend. I have a friend in London too, but she's out of town, and I don't know when she'll return. I'll visit her after matters are more settled."

"Are you sure you wouldn't like to wait until she's home?"

"Are you joking? I'm not giving you an excuse for a postponement. You might come to your senses. Then where would I be?"

"Where you are concerned, I will *never* come to my senses."

They dozed off then, and when he roused, the sun was cresting the horizon, so he had to sneak out—and fast. While they'd be married soon, they weren't married *yet*. He couldn't have Petunia catch him tiptoeing out.

"Sarah?" he whispered.

She groaned and opened her eyes. For a moment, she was confused about where she was. She popped up on an elbow and frantically peered about, then recognition dawned.

He chuckled, wondering if she always awakened in such a disoriented state.

"Ooh, I was sleeping so hard," she murmured.

"The sun's up. I have to go."

"I miss you already," she said, and she eased down.

"I miss you already too."

He slid to his feet, and he tugged on his shirt and straightened his trousers. The entire time, he studied her, filling his vision with her and suffering from the strangest perception that if he glanced away she might vanish.

It was a chilly morning, and he pulled a blanket over her and tucked her in. As he did, she gasped and said, "My goodness! I forgot I'm not wearing any clothes!"

"I like you just like this," he told her. "From this point on, your job will be to make me happy. If you're naked, I'm happy."

"Bounder."

He braced his palms on the mattress and stole a quick kiss. It was luscious and delightful, and he yearned to crawl under the blanket again, but the sun had an annoying way of climbing higher and higher.

"Will I see you today?" she inquired as he drew away.

"I'm not certain. I have to ride to London to apply for the Special License, and I'll have some meetings too." Mainly, he had to talk to his mother and sister and warn them of his plans. "I can't guarantee I'll return tonight. If I don't stop by, don't fret."

"Can I tell Noah and Pet or would you rather I wait?"

"Why don't we wait? I'll inform people on my end, then we'll spread the news farther than that."

"That's fine."

"Might Noah like it if I went to him and asked for your hand?"

"He'd be over the moon, and he'd relish the chance to give you his permission."

"I'll speak to him then. It's how we'll apprise them. After that, we'll announce it to the whole world."

"I'm positive we'll send it spinning off its axis." She reached out and linked their fingers. "Are you still sure about this?"

"I'm very, very sure. Now you can sleep in, but *I* have to get out of here."

He couldn't decide which exit was safer—the front door or the window—but he had to hope he wouldn't bump into Petunia as he crept away. He chose the door.

"Hurry home," she said.

"I won't let myself be delayed a single second."

He paused to take a final look at her, liking how rumpled she was. She might have been a beautiful harem girl who'd just serviced her master. She appeared well-loved and contented.

He forced himself away, knowing—if he didn't depart immediately—he never would.

CHAPTER

18

"Where have you been?"

"Ah . . . at Hero's Haven?"

Gertrude glared at her son. She was so furious that she yearned to march over and shake him, but she managed to refrain.

"I sent for you hours ago!" she fumed.

"Really? I didn't know."

"Where were you? My messenger arrived at dawn, only to be apprised that you hadn't been home all night, and none of your servants could contact you."

His cheeks heated, providing plenty of evidence that he'd been loafing precisely where he shouldn't have been.

"I'm not a child, Mother," he said. "If I was out for the evening and delayed in returning, it's not any of your business."

"The sky has fallen on us, and I was desperate to find you. I ordered my footman to bring you with him, yet he staggered to London with no news as to your whereabouts."

"Well, I'm here now. What's wrong?" He glanced out the window. "It appears to me that the sky is still over our heads so perhaps you're exaggerating a bit?"

"You think this is funny, don't you?"

"As I have no idea what's transpired, I can't guess whether it's funny or not."

"After all the effort you expended to ensure no scandal ensued over the inquest, we have one brewing anyway. You can pretend you don't mind, but I won't be so blasé about it!"

"What are you talking about? Please spare me your theatrics."

She walked to her writing desk and retrieved the note from Ophelia's pillow.

Who could have predicted that Ophelia had such reckless tendencies? Then again, the foolish girl was Sir Sidney's daughter. Half her blood came from him. If she'd finally wanted to marry, why didn't she declare herself ready?

Gertrude would have been delighted to pick a husband for her.

She stomped over and handed Sebastian the note, and as he perused the words Ophelia had penned, Gertrude almost enjoyed observing the rush of emotions that crossed his face: confusion, shock, bewilderment, then rage.

"Ophelia has eloped?" he said like a dunce.

"Yes. Even as we speak, she's racing north to Gretna Green."

"With Judah Barnett? Oh, my lord. When did she leave?"

"It was during the night. The message was on her pillow when a housemaid went in to light the fire this morning."

He read it over and over, as if repetition might alter the import.

"Had you any clue about her plans?" he asked.

Gertrude tsked with offense. "If I'd had a clue, don't you suppose I'd have locked her in her room so she couldn't sneak away?"

"She sought my opinion about Judah," he stunned her by admitting.

"What do you mean?"

"She mentioned him a few days ago. Apparently, he'd been flirting with her, and she was curious—if he proposed—how I'd view a match between them."

"I hope you told her you wouldn't consider it. He's a completely inappropriate candidate."

"I agree, and she was very upset with me for telling her so."

"Is that why you've been quarreling?"

"Yes."

"Judah Barnett!" Gertrude was nearly wailing. "What is she thinking?"

"She isn't thinking; that's the problem. She doesn't know what *I* know about him. I tried to warn her, but she wouldn't listen. I kicked him off the expedition team."

She gasped. "You what?"

"He's involved in that whole mess with Nathan, and Nathan is correct about what happened in Africa. Judah stumbled on him alive, but left him there to die."

"What a hideous revelation." The story had her feeling faint, and she was struggling to unravel the threads of the sordid scenario. "Is this some type of revenge for his being cut loose? Is he using her as a bargaining chip to regain his spot? After all, if he's your brother-in-law, he might assume you'd change your mind."

"He could never change my mind. No matter what."

"Perhaps he's simply eager to glom onto her dowry."

"Yes, but I'm the trustee of the funds, and I'd never sign over a single farthing."

"Ophelia wouldn't have reflected on that possibility. She's always been a dreamer. She probably believes they'll support themselves with her money."

"They won't ever receive it from me, and I won't have him inflicting himself on us. Not after what he did to Nathan."

"Certainly not!" Gertrude huffed. "You have to stop them, Sebastian. We can't let him get away with this!"

"They've had such a head start. I doubt I'd be able to catch them."

Gertrude blanched. "Don't say so! You *must* catch them."

He crumpled the note and pitched it on the floor. "I don't *want* to go after them."

"Who else is there?"

"I have my own issues to handle today. I can't worry about how stupid Ophelia is being."

"I can't imagine a sole topic that would take precedence over this calamity. She is your only sister and my only daughter. We have to attempt to save her."

"What if I can't? What if they make it to Gretna Green? If she's become his bride, what's the point?"

"The point is that we have to *try*."

"He'll ruin her on the way—to guarantee the conclusion he craves. Even if he has to force her, he will. If that's the ending we're dealt, what then?"

Gertrude shivered with dread. "We'll cross that bridge when we come to it."

Their conversation dwindled to a halt, and he stared out the window, his angry thoughts wafting out. Finally, he sighed with exasperation.

"I guess I'll go," he furiously muttered. "I don't have a choice really."

"You can't travel alone."

"Raven Shawcross will accompany me. He's staying with friends here in town, and he never liked Judah. He'll be thrilled to assist me."

"We can't have rumors spreading. Can he be trusted with our secrets?"

"He'll never tell a soul."

He hurried to her writing desk and penned two notes. He sanded the ink and sealed them, one inside the other so she couldn't ascertain the second addressee.

"I need to have these delivered to the Haven," he said. "I have to inform the staff that I'll be away for a bit, and I had . . . ah . . . some other plans today. I have to be sure the concerned parties are aware they're cancelled."

"I will have them delivered immediately. When will I hear from you again?"

"I have no idea. I might find her right away or I might have to search."

"Keep me apprised."

"I will. If they're married once I locate them, I will abandon them to their fate. I presume that's your wish, yes?"

"Yes, that's my wish. If she's wed him, I'm through with her."

He nodded, then stormed out, and she walked to the window to watch him mount his horse and ride away.

Vaguely, she wondered what mission had brought him to town. It hadn't been her frantic summons. Evidently, his servants hadn't alerted him. He'd claimed his trip had to do with his own issues, and Ophelia's debacle had quashed any different path he'd anticipated.

After she was positive he'd departed, she went to the desk and picked up his letters. Without hesitating, she flicked at the seal. The outer one was to his butler, notifying the man that Sebastian would be delayed by important business and didn't know when he'd be home.

As a postscript, he'd asked that the second letter be conveyed to Miss Robertson at the valet's cottage. Gertrude tore it open, and her temper flared to a frightening degree.

I'm sorry, but we can't proceed as I intended. A family situation drags me away, and I'll have no opportunity to apply for the Special License. I will explain all the minute I'm back. It may be several days. I miss you already . . .

"A Special License?" she mused to herself.

The news was so shocking that she could barely remain on her feet. Was he thinking to wed the lowborn, mercenary tart? What else could it indicate? Ophelia had warned her of his infatuation with the horrid trollop, but Gertrude had assumed it was a passing fancy.

Was he in love with Miss Robertson? What other reason could there be for such a repugnant decision? He was Sebastian Sinclair, only son of Sir Sidney Sinclair. He could have any girl in the world as his wife, and Gertrude had selected Veronica for him. Had he forgotten?

Her children had become lunatics at the very same moment. Was there something in the air? Something in the water? Clearly, they were both insane.

Sebastian would sort out Ophelia and her ridiculous beau, but Gertrude would have to untangle this other madness. Sebastian could *not* be permitted to marry an up-jumped, greedy slattern. The notion was too bizarre to contemplate.

Veronica swept into the room and asked, "Was that Sebastian? My maid told me he was here. How am I to entice him if I never see him?"

"We have bigger issues to deal with than your matrimonial hopes."

She looked suitably chastened. "You're correct of course. What did he say about Cousin Ophelia?"

"He'll try and stop her."

"Thank goodness. I was so afraid he might refuse."

Gertrude had yearned to keep the scandal quiet, but she hadn't been able to prevent Veronica from discovering what had occurred. When Veronica had first come down to breakfast, Gertrude had been in the middle of the catastrophe.

"While he's away," Gertrude said, "you and I have to take care of a . . . *predicament* at Hero's Haven."

"What predicament?"

"Sit down, dear. I'm about to clarify a few facts of life with regard to Sinclair males."

"I have no misconceptions as to what they're like."

Gertrude harrumphed. "You haven't a clue about any of them—particularly Sebastian. They're much more shameful than you could ever fathom."

"Yes, he's treated me abominably so far."

"He hasn't begun to humiliate you, and if you plan to survive your marriage to him, you need to grow clever in tamping down various problems."

"What's wrong now?"

"Ophelia enlightened me as to why he's been too busy to propose. It's time *you* hear her story. It's pointless for you to be in the dark."

Veronica frowned. "Why am I certain I won't like what you're about to confide?"

"You *won't* like it, but if you ever expect to wed him, you have to do exactly as I say or, I'm aggrieved to report, it will never transpire."

NOAH STROLLED DOWN THE lane toward the cottage. Petunia was with him. Even though they were supposed to hide themselves away, they'd been bored, so they'd walked to the village. They were headed home.

It was a blustery afternoon, clouds whisking by as if the weather was changing. There was a chill in the air, reminding him that autumn—then winter—were on the way.

When those seasons arrived, where would they be?

"Have you seen our brother recently?" he asked Petunia. "During the night, I mean?"

"No."

"I spoke to him about Miss Robertson. I scolded him for calling on her so late, and I told him—if he's sweet on her—he should marry her. If he's not, he should leave her alone."

"Why can't they just be friends?"

"A man like him is never friends with a woman like her. My grandfather explained it to me. The woman simply winds up in a lot of trouble."

Pet grinned. "Well, I'll be positive about all of it."

Suddenly, a carriage lumbered up behind them, and the sound was startling. The lane led directly to their cottage, and it ended there. It didn't lead anywhere else. In the period they'd been in residence, no visitors had traveled down it.

As the vehicle neared, he studied it, deeming it ordinary, with no markings to indicate the occupants. It was small and enclosed, with two horses pulling it.

He and Pet moved to the side, figuring it would pass on by, but the driver tugged on the reins and halted. A man leaned out the window. He was rough-looking, dressed in common clothes, and he had a cruel face, as if he might have been a criminal or a pugilist.

He wondered what such an ominous fellow could want with them, and instinctively, he eased Pet behind him.

"Are you Noah Sinclair?" the man surprised him by asking.

"Ah . . . yes."

The admission was out before he could remember to be silent. They weren't to tell anyone their names, but the question had caught him off guard.

The man shifted his sinister gaze to Pet. "Then you must be Petunia Sinclair."

Pet never liked strangers, so she didn't respond. She glanced nervously at Noah, then nodded to confirm her identity.

The man talked to someone seated with him, then the doors flew open, and several ruffians leapt out. There was no time to react. They were surrounded, grabbed, and thrown into the carriage. The driver cracked his whip, and the horses sprinted off.

Noah managed a single shout for help, then he was whacked on the head and pressed down to the floor to prevent him from crying out again.

He and Pet vanished as if they'd never been there at all.

———※———

"NOAH! PETUNIA! WHERE ARE YOU?"

Sarah was in the woods and approaching the cottage. It was late in the afternoon, the sun over in the west and sinking toward the horizon, and she'd been searching for them.

The pair had left prior to the noon meal, and it wasn't like them to make her fret. At first, she hadn't missed them. She'd enjoyed the solitude and had used the interval to reflect on the night she'd spent with Sebastian.

It had been thrilling and lovely, but she still couldn't deduce why she'd ruined herself for him. Apparently, she was as foolish as any debutante. Yes, he'd proposed marriage, but what if he hadn't been serious?

She couldn't bear to suppose he'd be that despicable, but rich men constantly behaved in spurious ways, and the women they tricked never understood what was actually occurring until they were in a desperate jam.

Why had he proceeded? They were so different, and from centuries of trial and error, humans had learned that disparities in status and ancestry were too difficult to overcome. The world worked better when people stayed in their places.

What if he didn't mean it? What if she never saw him again? For hours, she'd dithered over it, and ultimately, she'd ordered herself to stop worrying.

If and when he tossed her over, *then* she would panic.

Her obsessing had kept her from noticing Noah and Pet's lengthy absence. When she'd finally glanced at the clock, she'd been stunned by how time had flown, and she'd begun hunting for them, but they were nowhere to be found.

"Noah! Pet!" she tried again, and she waited, listening, but there was no reply.

She exited the woods and rounded the house, and to her dismay, there were two carriages parked in the yard. One was very fancy, a coach-and-four complete with a crest and liveried outriders. The other was small and nondescript with no markings and only a lone driver in the box.

Her pulse raced with dread. Had the children suffered an accident? Was it bad news?

The outriders were loafing over in the shade, and as she hurried forward, they glared at her in a condemning manner.

No doubt the servants were gossiping about her. They'd be speculating over Sebastian's intentions. Well, when he followed through—she refused to accept that he wouldn't!—they'd all discover his intentions, and she'd be his wife. They wouldn't dare glare at her then!

She ignored them and rushed in the door, frantic over what was about to be revealed, but she halted in her tracks. There were numerous traveling trunks sitting in the foyer, as if her belongings had been packed while she was out.

There was a young lady seated on the sofa in the parlor. She looked very comfortable, as if she owned the residence. She seemed familiar, but on the spur of the moment, Sarah couldn't recall who she was.

With her blond hair and blue eyes, she was very beautiful, plump with good health, and definitely aware of the striking impression she made. Her hair was curled and braided in an intricate style, and she was dripping with jewels.

She was everything Sarah was not: gorgeous, wealthy, entitled. She glowered at Sarah as if she were a scullery maid who hadn't cleaned the ashes from the hearth as she'd been trained.

"May I help you?" Sarah asked.

"Miss Robertson, isn't it?"

"Yes, I'm Sarah Robertson. My wards are missing, and I'm growing concerned. Are you here about them? Please assure me that they're all right."

The woman rose to her feet, her movements graceful and elegant. "I am Veronica Gordon."

The name rang a bell, but with how afraid Sarah was over Noah and Pet, she couldn't recollect why it would.

"Hello, Miss Gordon. Have you come about Noah and Pet?"

Miss Gordon bristled. "You don't recognize me."

"No, sorry. If we've met, I don't remember."

"I am Sebastian's fiancée."

"I don't think so."

The words were out of Sarah's mouth before she could bite them down.

Miss Gordon's identity rammed into her with lightning speed. Ophelia Sinclair had claimed Sebastian was engaged to Miss Gordon. Sarah had immediately confronted him, and he'd sworn there was no betrothal. She'd believed him.

Suddenly, she felt weak with alarm. Who was telling the truth and, more importantly, who wasn't?

Miss Gordon scoffed with annoyance. "You don't *think* I am Sebastian's fiancée? Let me guess, Miss Robertson. You asked Sebastian if he was promised, and he insisted he wasn't."

"Ah . . . yes." Sarah was too perturbed to answer like a sane person.

"Then I hope you haven't ruined yourself for him."

Sarah scowled. "Miss Gordon, your comment hints at immorality on my part. I can't imagine what you've been told about me, but I'm not the type to blithely be insulted by you."

"I wasn't insulting you. I was *warning* you. Sebastian has a reputation as a scoundrel."

"Really? I've never noted any wicked traits."

Miss Gordon shrugged. "It's a burden we Sinclair women have to carry. The Sinclair men are disloyal cads. His mother explained it to me prior to my agreeing to wed him. She wanted me to realize what I was getting myself into so I wouldn't be surprised by his philandering."

Sarah struggled to exhibit a calm façade. "There must be a message for me in your remark. What is it exactly?"

"Sebastian will trifle with any female in a skirt. It's a failing of his, but I decided to wed him anyway. I'm eager to be Mrs. Sebastian Sinclair, so I thought it would be worth it, and—as his mother constantly states—trollops like you are a penny a dozen. You'll never have any bearing on my marriage to him."

"Mr. Sinclair and I are friends," Sarah said. "I'm having a spot of financial trouble, and he's been kind enough to assist me."

"Yes, I found out from the servants how he's rationalized your affair, but I'm not as gullible as they are."

Sarah blew out a heavy breath. "I'm in the middle of a crisis, and I need to deal with it. Would you excuse me?"

She went to the door and whipped it open, and she gestured outside, indicating Miss Gordon should depart, but she didn't budge. She extended her hand, and it sported a gold ring, with a huge diamond in the center.

"It became official two nights ago," she said.

"Congratulations."

"It was after the inquest was over. Sebastian's mother hosted a party at her home to celebrate. All of fashionable London was there, and he proposed in front of everyone. It was quite romantic."

Sarah tried to recall where Sebastian had been two nights earlier. Could he have been in London, proposing to another woman? Was it possible? Miss Gordon seemed so *sure*.

"If you're engaged as you claim—" Sarah started.

"I'm not claiming it, Miss Robertson. I'm stating it as a fact. Do you see this ring on my finger? It's a Sinclair family heirloom. The Sinclair brides all get to wear it."

"Fine. You're engaged to Mr. Sinclair. Why bother me over it?"

"Isn't it obvious? I want you to go away and never come back."

"I'm not hurting you by tarrying in this cottage. Why would you be upset?"

"May I be frank, Miss Robertson? Even if you wish I wouldn't be, I must be candid. Your presence is keeping Sebastian from moving forward with his life. So long as you're here, he can frolic and play, and he doesn't have to buckle down."

"I'm not keeping him from any task."

"Aren't you?" The question hung in the air between them. Then Miss Gordon said, "I can vividly picture it. He's been leading you on, filling your head with nonsense. You view yourself as Cinderella, and he's your Prince Charming!"

"It's not like that," Sarah contended, although it absolutely was.

"I suppose I was correct and you've ruined yourself for him."

"He and I are *friends*," Sarah repeated, but without much vehemence, "and I'm incensed by your accusations."

"You're a very bad liar, Miss Robertson. Have you any idea how many young ladies he's seduced? Have you any idea how often his mother has waded through this same scenario with various maidens?"

"Mr. Sinclair wouldn't act like that."

"He wouldn't?" Miss Gordon laughed viciously. "He is his father's son. Are you aware of Sir Sidney's licentious habits? Don't pretend you haven't heard about them."

"I've heard about them."

"Now then, I am a patient person, but I am also very possessive of what's mine. I have let Sebastian entertain himself with you, but your relationship appears to have progressed to an untenable level, so you must vanish from our lives."

"I'd have to speak to Mr. Sinclair before I could agree."

"Speak to Sebastian? How would you? He left for Scotland today. Didn't you know?"

Sarah blanched. "He's gone?"

"What? He didn't tell you?" Miss Gordon waved a breezy hand. "Well, he didn't have any duty to tell you. After all, you're just his latest . . . *tart*."

Sarah felt as if she'd been punched. He was on his way to Scotland? What?

"Why . . . ah . . . is he in Scotland?"

"That's not really any of your business, is it?"

"Probably not, but I . . . ah . . . how long will he be away?"

"Several weeks at least." The reply was so shocking that Sarah's knees gave out, and she lurched over to a chair and eased down. Miss Gordon ignored her and continued. "He's there on a family matter, but he'll also be scouting property for our summer residence. I used to spend school holidays outside Edinburgh when I was a girl, and I loved it there. He's buying me a house in the area as a wedding gift."

"I'm happy for you," Sarah managed to say.

"Whatever he might have promised you, Miss Robertson, he didn't mean it, and shortly—after I am Sebastian's bride—Hero's Haven will be my home. I don't regret to inform you that you have overstayed your welcome."

"I can't believe this is happening," Sarah murmured.

"Did you seriously think he would be interested in you? Who are you, Miss Robertson? As far as I can discern, you're no one at all, while *I* am his cousin and bound to him since I was a child."

The door opened behind her, and Sarah leapt up and whirled around, hoping it would be Noah and Pet or even Sebastian so he could strut in and call Miss Gordon a liar. But it was an older woman, about fifty or so, imperious in her bearing and irked in her countenance.

"Is it settled?" she asked Miss Gordon.

"No. She refuses to accept that Sebastian and I are betrothed, and I can't convince her."

The older woman marched over to Sarah and said, "I am Gertrude Sinclair, revered widow of Sir Sidney Sinclair."

Sebastian's mother? "Hello, Mrs. Sinclair."

The regal shrew stared down her nose at Sarah and announced, "I have taken your wards."

"What?"

"I have them in my custody. Would you like to have them back?"

"Where are they?" Sarah demanded.

Mrs. Sinclair didn't respond, and Sarah dashed by her and ran outside to peek in the two carriages, but they were empty. The outriders were still loafing in the shade, watching her with bored expressions.

"I'm looking for a blond boy and girl, age twelve and six," she told them.

They didn't answer or even seem to notice her. They might have been deaf, and she might have been invisible.

She ran in and stormed to Mrs. Sinclair who'd moved to the writing desk in the corner.

"What have you done with them?" she raged.

"Sit down, Miss Robertson," was Mrs. Sinclair's retort. She pulled out the desk's chair and motioned to it.

"Why should I?" Sarah asked.

"You will write Sebastian a letter of goodbye, then I will take you to the children." Mrs. Sinclair raised a brow. "If you won't, you'll never see them again."

Sarah studied the awful woman, then shook her head with disgust. "What is wrong with you?"

"*You* are wrong with me, Miss Robertson. You have inserted yourself into our lives, even though—in the past—I had to threaten you with legal action to rid myself of you. You were too stubborn though, weren't you? You thought you could wring concessions from my son that you couldn't wring from me."

"Your husband's natural children need some help from your family."

"My husband was a national icon. He sired no bastards, and we owe your wards no duty. You are obsessed with your deranged ideas, but you must stop pestering us, and I'm weary of this discussion. Miss Gordon and I would like to be on our way."

"I won't write anything for you."

"Fine." Mrs. Sinclair turned to Miss Gordon. "Let's go, Veronica. The afternoon has waned, and I'd just as soon not be out after dark."

They started for the door, and Sarah was totally bewildered. Events were spiraling out of control too fast.

"But . . . but . . . what about Noah and Petunia?" Sarah stammered. "How will I locate them?"

"I've notified you as to how you can retrieve them," Mrs. Sinclair said, "but I won't dawdle and allow you to waste my time."

"No, no, come back. I'll write the letter."

Sarah slid onto the chair, grabbed a piece of paper, and picked up a quill.

She gazed expectantly at Mrs. Sinclair. The woman halted, but Miss Gordon continued out into the yard. Shortly, the outriders tromped in and began hauling out Sarah's trunks.

Was she being evicted? Immediately? With evening about to arrive?

Mrs. Sinclair traipsed over and said, "My son will be away for several weeks."

"Yes, Miss Gordon told me."

"While he's away, you will have disappeared. I doubt Sebastian will remember you were ever here, and in fact, I wouldn't be surprised if he brings a new doxy home with him. I can't have you lingering, and I won't have *him* wishing you'd tarried."

"He wouldn't want me to leave," Sarah insisted, when she ought to keep her mouth shut.

Mrs. Sinclair tsked with exasperation, as if Sarah was exceedingly stupid.

"Miss Robertson, listen to me. Veronica has requested a Christmas wedding, and I intend to plan it for her. We'll have a month of balls and parties, then a grand ceremony at the end. Afterward, Sebastian and Veronica will retire to Hero's Haven. Will you still be present? Will you shame Veronica? Will you disgrace yourself? Will my son be sneaking out of his marital bed to engage in sexual relations with you when his wife isn't looking? Is that the future you envision for yourself?"

The horrid woman's comments were pounding into Sarah like dull arrows. Had she really thought Sebastian would marry her? Well, no, she hadn't thought he was serious. And his mother and his fiancée were verifying her worst fears.

"You can cease your harangue." Sarah focused her attention on the blank sheet of paper. "What is it you'd like me to say?"

"Write a simple note. You *can* write, can't you?"

"Probably better than you," Sarah fumed.

"Don't be impertinent. I don't have to tolerate it on my own property."

"Swear that you'll deliver Noah and Pet to me after I've done as you've demanded."

"Yes, I swear."

Sarah felt trapped, overwhelmed, and very scared. Mrs. Sinclair appeared fierce and resolved, but absolutely treacherous too.

"What should I say?" Sarah repeated.

"Be concise: You made other arrangements for yourself, and you left because you weren't about to let him ruin his life over you. He shouldn't search—because you'll never be found."

Sarah penned exactly that, then she sanded the ink, and gave the letter to Mrs. Sinclair.

She scanned it, then smirked. "You were telling the truth. You *can* write." She pointed to the door. "Come. There's a carriage waiting for you, and your things have been loaded. We're locking the house so don't think about slithering back."

"Where are Noah and Petunia?"

"They're in London. My man will take you to them."

Sarah was trembling so violently she could barely stand. She realized she shouldn't display any weakness, but she couldn't help it.

She didn't trust Mrs. Sinclair, and she yearned to declare that she had the right to remain in the cottage, that Mrs. Sinclair couldn't kick her out, but it wasn't her place to quarrel over any issue. She couldn't guess what authority Mrs. Sinclair had at the Haven. For all Sarah knew, perhaps it belonged to her rather than her son.

"I'll find the children in London, won't I?" Sarah asked as they walked out.

"You have my word on it."

Sarah's trunks were in the smaller vehicle. She went over and climbed in. None of the men assisted her. They merely glowered as if they'd been apprised of Sarah's transgressions and viewed her as a terrible sinner.

Mrs. Sinclair followed her over, and at the last second, she handed Sarah a letter, and it had been addressed to her.

"What's this?" Sarah asked.

"It's from Sebastian."

"What?" Sarah was incredibly confused, and with events so raw, she couldn't puzzle it out. "He was aware that I'd be departing?"

"Yes. Be sure to read it. He couldn't bear to inform you himself that it's over between you. He hates goodbyes and never participates in them."

Sarah scoffed. "So he had *you* deal with it?"

"I don't care if you believe me or not. Just don't ever show your face here again. Remember: You have your urchins to consider. If you cross me, any calamity could befall them. It's a very dangerous world, isn't it?"

Mrs. Sinclair nodded to the driver. He cracked the whip, and the horse lurched away so quickly that Sarah was nearly flung off the seat.

She steadied herself and managed a final glance at the cottage. Mrs. Sinclair and Miss Gordon were over by the door, watching as an outrider attached a chain to it. Then the sight was blocked as they raced into the woods.

She opened the letter that was supposedly from Sebastian.

I'm sorry for it to end like this, it said. *I hope you can forgive me someday.*

She was stunned. She was crushed. She was so angry she'd like to set the whole kingdom on fire.

She wadded his note into a ball and threw it out at the passing trees, and she blindly stared at the scenery, but she was too devastated to see anything at all.

CHAPTER

19

OPHELIA WAS HUDDLED IN a cold, damp room at a decrepit coaching inn. She shivered and wrapped her cloak more tightly around her body. She'd never been more uncomfortable in her life. In fact, she'd *never* previously been uncomfortable.

She was twenty-two, and in her memories, all of those years had been passed pleasantly, in elegant surroundings.

It was raining outside, and their carriage had gotten stuck in the mud over and over. Judah didn't have his own vehicle, plus there had been a need for stealth, so he'd rented one, and it had been operated by a hired driver and two hired men.

The driver hadn't been terribly competent, and the two men hadn't been overly keen on expending energy to repeatedly dig them out. Judah had been snappish, the three hired men surly and mutinous, and Ophelia freezing every second.

The weather didn't show any signs of improving, so they'd given up and had called it a day. If they'd kept on, they'd simply have continued to bog down, and she suspected their hired men would have vanished.

As it was, Judah had had to bribe them so they swore they wouldn't sneak off after it was dark. If they left, it would be absolutely typical of the debacle so far. They'd have to employ new people, which would slow them even further.

With the afternoon waning, they'd stopped at the nearest inn, and they'd rented rooms for the night. It was a seedy place, and if the decision had been Ophelia's, she'd have traveled on by, but Judah had been adamant.

He was constantly bossing her, and she'd bitten her tongue and had tolerated his disrespect, and she was beginning to wonder if he was actually the person he'd presented himself to be. Her brother had claimed he wasn't trustworthy. Was it possible Sebastian had been correct?

In her brief discussions with Judah about how their future would unfold, he'd insisted he wanted a bride who would be an equal partner, but to her great horror, they'd been bickering for hours, and they'd barely departed London. As they journeyed north to Scotland, how might their relationship deteriorate?

Their escapade should have been merry and exciting, but they were practically strangers. The tedious trip had been incredibly stressful, but stress and tension brought out true character. It was easy to be agreeable when matters were running smoothly. When they weren't, it was much harder to be civil.

He was downstairs, having announced that he needed a stout whiskey to calm his nerves. She didn't necessarily begrudge him a libation, but he'd refused to let her accompany him. She'd walked by the taproom, and she'd peered into it. Several women had been seated there, so it wasn't as if women weren't allowed. Judah had simply felt *she* shouldn't be allowed.

The realization was galling.

He was to have sent up a maid to start the fire, but no maid had arrived, and the temperature was frigid. There was a stove in the corner, and Ophelia could have figured out how it worked, but she was too incensed to fuss with it.

She yearned to march down and join Judah at his table. She'd have liked to have her own glass of wine, to tarry by the roaring blaze that had been burning in the large hearth. But she wouldn't lower herself. Besides, if she pranced in—after he'd specifically told her she shouldn't—they'd quarrel, and she'd had all the arguing she could abide.

A knock sounded on the door, and she went over and peeked out. The maid had finally appeared, and a footman was with her and carrying their bags.

"I'm here to light the fire," the girl declared, as if Ophelia might be confused as to her purpose.

"About time," she mumbled.

The girl ignored her churlishness and blustered in to complete her chore. The footman set their luggage on the bed, then strolled out without opening it or unpacking. Was Ophelia supposed to do it?

It dawned on her that she was so unprepared for real life! She'd always been doted on by servants, her every wish granted. Was she ready to become an ordinary female? If this was how she'd be required to live, she couldn't bear it.

The flames caught quickly, but Ophelia didn't remove her cloak. She suspected she'd never be warm again.

"Your clothes might be wet from the rain," the maid said. "Would you like me to drape them by the stove?"

Ophelia suffered a vision of her undergarments hung from the rafters, and it was too humiliating to consider.

"No, thank you," she murmured, and she shooed the maid out.

She sat on the bed, misery sinking in.

What was happening in London? Would her mother have found her letter? Was she livid? Or would she not care in the least? What about Sebastian? Had he been informed? Would he care? He'd warned her to avoid Judah, but she'd defied him and had proceeded anyway. Might he merely shrug and think, *good riddance!*

By eloping with Judah, she'd behaved scandalously. What if she was so unimportant to her mother and brother that they didn't bother to chase after her? What if they never even noticed she was missing?

Because of the muddy roads, she and Judah hadn't traveled very far. It would be easy for her brother to find her. She gazed at the meager, dilapidated room, and it occurred to her that she wouldn't mind if he burst in and demanded she leave with him.

Oh, she'd protest his domineering manner, but she'd swiftly obey.

Yet there was a genuine possibility he wouldn't come, so she might have to save herself. If she advised Judah she'd made a mistake, how would he respond? Would he let her depart? And if she staggered home, would her mother welcome her back? Or might she have burned her bridges with Gertrude?

At the dire prospect, Ophelia's pulse raced with dread.

Booted strides echoed out in the hall, then Judah entered, and it was a relief, but an annoyance too. When they'd snuck away in the night, it had seemed so thrilling. Now she was just cold and tired and afraid of what sort of ramifications might befall her.

"We didn't put many miles between us and London," he said. "It's lucky no one knows where you are or we'd have your brother showing up to stop us."

"My mother knows where I am," Ophelia stupidly mentioned.

He scowled. "What do you mean?"

"I wrote her a note—so she wouldn't worry."

"I told you not to tell anyone."

"Well, I didn't listen."

"Dammit!" he muttered. "Will she apprise Sebastian? Will he ride to your rescue?"

"I doubt it," she breezily replied. "With how he and I have been fighting, he'd probably be glad to hear I ran away."

"I'd rather not tangle with him."

"I'm sure you won't have to." She pointed to their bags. "A footman brought in our things, but he deposited yours here with mine."

"So?"

"We can't share a room. We're not married."

He scoffed in a crude way. "Grow up, Ophelia. We'll be wed shortly. There's no reason to waste money on two rooms."

"Are you intending that we will . . . will . . . cohabit before the ceremony?"

"Yes, so climb down off your high-horse. You've been a shrew all day, and I'm weary of your complaints. I'm trying my best to get us to Scotland, and you've criticized me over every little issue."

It was a hideous comment, one that encapsulated every wretched minute since she'd tiptoed out of her mother's house to join him in the alley.

"I want to go home!" she blurted out. "I never should have left with you!"

"You want to go *home*? I don't think so."

"I'm not your prisoner. You can't force me to stay with you."

"How, precisely, will you arrive in London? Will you saunter in your mother's door and announce that you're back? Can you actually be foolish enough to imagine you could?"

"She'd be delighted to see me," she said, but without much vigor.

"Your mother is a spiteful shrew, Ophelia. She'll never forgive you. You're stuck with me."

His coat was damp from the rain, and he yanked it off and hung it over the only chair. He rolled up his sleeves, revealing his forearms, giving every indication that he considered them to be on familiar terms, that he deemed it perfectly appropriate to disrobe in front of her. She was flabbergasted.

There was a mirror over the dresser, and he went to it and studied his injured face. The bruises from his earlier pummeling hadn't begun to fade and were still very visible. Ultimately, he said, "Nathan really battered me, didn't he? The prick has a nasty right punch."

She ignored his foul language and asked, "What are you talking about?"

"When he attacked me, he was determined to kill me."

She frowned. "I thought my brother assaulted you."

"I swear, Ophelia"—he glared at her—"occasionally, you are too gullible for words."

"Wait, wait. Nathan attacked you?"

"Of course it was Nathan. Saint Nathan, beloved friend of the pompous ass, Sebastian Sinclair."

She was absolutely stunned. He'd lied to her! He'd claimed Sebastian had thrashed him. And she'd believed him! It hadn't been Sebastian? It had been Nathan?

She was so flummoxed by the news that she wasn't paying any attention to him, so she was startled when he stepped to the bed. Suddenly, he appeared very large and imposing, and she could smell a strong odor of alcohol, as if he'd downed more than a few whiskeys. Was he a drunkard on top of all his other flaws?

"Let's get this over with," he said, and he leered down at her.

"Get *what* over with?"

"At the rate we're traveling, it will take an eternity to reach Greta Green, and I'm not about to delay my wedding night forever."

"You plan to have marital relations with me?"

"Why not? We'll be married soon. We're just jumping the gun a bit."

"I don't wish to *jump* any guns."

"Yes, well, I'm the man in this pathetic duo, and you're the woman, and you're not allowed to have an opinion about it."

It was the sort of infuriating comment he'd repeatedly hurled at her, and she leapt up and pushed him away.

"Are you drunk?" she asked.

"What if I am?"

"I can't abide inebriation, and I've had quite enough of you."

She meant to huff by him and march down to the lobby. She'd have begged the proprietor to aid her, to send a message to her brother, but Judah had other ideas.

He grabbed her arm and asked, "Where do you think you're going?"

"I told you: I've had enough. I'm going home."

"No, you're not."

In what would always remain the most terrifying moment of her life, he tossed her onto the bed, and before she could move a muscle, he lay down on top of her.

She cried out, and he clouted her alongside the head—so hard she saw stars. She winced in agony and might have called out again, but he clamped a palm over her mouth to silence her.

"You're mine now," he said, "and I guess I better make sure of it. Once I'm through with you, your mother won't take you in. I guarantee it."

He began tearing at her clothes as if he'd strip them off. She writhed to escape, but he was so much bigger than she was, and she couldn't shove him away.

Their grappling seemed to inflame him, and the more she wrestled, the more aggressive he became. He fumbled about and unhooked the clasp on her cloak, then he seized the bodice of her gown and pulled on it. Fabric ripped and a bare shoulder was exposed. The sight agitated him even more.

She bit his hand, latching on like a rabid dog, her teeth breaking the skin so he jerked away in pain.

"Stop fighting me!" he fumed.

"I won't stop!" she wailed.

"You stupid wench. I can do whatever I like to you, and you have to let me."

"Never!" She screamed and managed one loud shout of, "Help!"

He slapped her and pressed a palm over her mouth again, and he was partially covering her nose so she couldn't breathe. Gad, would he suffocate her? Would this be her end?

Then . . . ?

He was viciously yanked away. Just that fast, just that quickly, his body was pitched through the air. He crashed into the dresser, and the mirror tumbled to the floor and shattered.

She was incredibly befuddled, and she gaped about, not certain of what had happened. When she finally focused in, Sebastian was looming over her. Mr. Shawcross was with him, and he had a boot on Judah's chest to hold him down. There was a cluster of spectators peeking in from the hall.

"You came for me!" she said, and she burst into tears like the foolish child she was.

Sebastian didn't speak to her, but glared at Mr. Shawcross and ordered, "Get him out of here."

"Gladly," Mr. Shawcross replied.

He lifted Judah and stood him on his feet, and though Judah was battered and disgraced, he puffed himself up and said to Sebastian, "What's all the excitement about? She was eager to elope. In fact, it was her idea. Why are you in such a lather?"

Sebastian hit him so hard that his eyes rolled back in his head, and he collapsed. Mr. Shawcross, without missing a beat, dragged him out, the onlookers separating to create a path for him.

Sebastian walked over and shut the door in their curious faces, and Ophelia sank down onto the pillow. She wanted to die! And she wished a hole would materialize in the floor so she could drop into it and never climb out.

"I'M SORRY."

"I can't listen to any apologies for awhile. I'm too furious."

Sebastian frowned at his sister. Other than a swollen cheek from where Judah had slapped her, her condition wasn't too bad.

The dramatic episode was long over, the observers disbursed, bribes paid to buy the servants' silence over what they'd witnessed.

The proprietor had been suitably horrified, and he and his employees had kindly endeavored to smooth over what had occurred. Ophelia had been bathed and her gown mended as she'd been washing. She'd been coddled and dosed with several glasses of wine to calm her nerves.

They were in the yard of the coaching inn and about to leave.

When he'd departed London, he'd had a Sinclair coach follow him so— once he'd found her—he could send her home in it. Her maid was inside, and his most loyal driver and outriders were waiting on her.

He guided her up the step, watching as she settled herself on the seat. He should have been more sympathetic, but her reckless act ensured a violent ending was about to arrive for Judah. Sebastian would have to dole out his punishment. Did she realize it? Had the notion ever crossed her mind?

Judah couldn't be allowed to behave as he had without a severe consequence being imposed. If Sebastian didn't impose it, Raven definitely would.

Sebastian could have turned Judah over to the authorities, could have had him prosecuted and hanged, but Ophelia's name would have been dragged through the mud, which Sebastian would never permit.

No, this was a castigation Sebastian would have to implement all on his own, and he was irate with her for instigating so much trouble. Later, he'd forgive her. She was young and naïve and had never previously bumped into a snake like Judah. But for the moment, he was too livid for words.

"Judah told me *you* had pummeled him," she said.

"What?"

"His injuries? He told me you beat him up as a warning to stay away from me."

Sebastian scoffed with disgust. "I didn't touch him. Nathan attacked him, at the inquest."

"I know that now, but it's why I left with him."

"You should have trusted me," Sebastian said. "I was trying to protect you."

"What will happen to him?" she asked.

"Don't worry about it."

"I'm afraid of him. I would hate for him to show up in London. I'll always be scared he might."

"He won't show up there, and he won't ever bother you again."

He stared her down, conveying a potent visual message, but he doubted she'd ever understand what he intended. He wasn't about to explain it either.

"I'm sorry," she said again.

He breathed out a weighty sigh. "We'll chat more after I'm home."

"You're not coming with me?"

"No. I have to wrap up a few matters here."

"If you're not there to speak for me, how will I persuade Mother to let me in?"

"If she's difficult, tell her I order her to welcome you. Use me as your excuse."

"Thank you for rescuing me."

"That's what brothers are for, I guess."

She reached out and squeezed his fingers. "I mean it. Thank you."

"I hope you've learned a lesson."

"I have."

"I hope too that you'll heed me in the future. Occasionally, I know what I'm talking about."

"After I've recovered a bit, I consent to being thoroughly berated for being such an idiot."

"I'll take you up on it." He moved away. "I'll see you in town."

He closed the door and motioned to his driver, and the vehicle rolled away. He stood in place until they vanished down the road, then he spun away and went to the barn.

Judah was bound hand and foot, gagged too, and lying on the hay in a stall. Raven was guarding him.

"Is your sister safely away?" Raven inquired.

"Yes."

Raven gestured to Judah. "Have you decided about him?"

"I've decided."

The proprietor had offered to summon the local sheriff, to have Judah carted off to the village jail, but Sebastian had convinced him not to, claiming he'd transport Judah to London and have the law sort it out there. The proprietor was a smart man, and he hadn't asked any questions.

"I expect the conclusion you're considering will be similar to the one I'm considering," Raven said.

"I'm betting it's exactly the same."

"I'm glad I don't have to waste energy luring you around to my point of view."

Their horses were saddled, a third one rented for Judah, but he wouldn't be astride it. Raven was strong as an ox, and he lifted Judah and threw him over the animal's back, face down, like a sack of flour. Judah kicked and protested, but Raven secured him to the saddle without too much effort.

Once, when he grew too cantankerous, Raven whacked him with the butt of a pistol. It silenced him and slowed his wrestling.

They took off, riding away from the city, proceeding farther into the countryside and away from people who might recognize them. He and Raven didn't speak, but Judah was mumbling behind his gag. They ignored him.

Eventually, Raven found a spot he liked, and they left the road and were swallowed by thick forest. The sun was on the horizon, evening approaching. It was starting to rain, the clouds heavy, so the deluge would probably increase as the hours passed. It would wipe away any tracks.

"You should head to town," Raven said. "If this is bungled, you shouldn't be attached to it."

"I have to be here."

"Why don't you let me deal with it on my own?"

"No."

There was no more debate. They hobbled their horses, then Raven cut the ropes lashing Judah to the saddle. He slid to the ground, and with his wrists still bound, there was no way for him to break his fall. His landing was painful, and he moaned in agony, but his misery garnered no sympathy from them.

Sebastian watched dispassionately as Raven yanked him to his feet. They marched him into the trees, and he struggled to escape, but Raven's grip was too tight.

They stopped under a huge oak, and Raven told him, "I'm going to untie your gag. When I do, keep your mouth shut."

As Raven tore it away, Judah hollered, "Help!"

Raven hit him so hard he flew through the air, then collapsed in a heap. He coughed blood and whimpered.

"He never was any good at listening," Raven said to Sebastian.

He picked Judah up yet again and dragged him over to the tree. Judah was off balance, swaying, and Raven had to press a palm to his chest so he remained upright.

Sebastian stepped in so they were toe to toe and asked, "Is there anything you'd like to say to me?"

"Prick," Judah muttered.

"Mind your manners," Raven warned, and he clocked Judah on the head as he inquired, "How did you persuade Miss Ophelia to accompany you?"

"She wanted to come. She begged me." Judah sounded as if he was bragging.

Raven hit him again, and he slumped down.

"We intend to kill you," Raven said. "You understand that, don't you?"

"You can't kill me," Judah blustered, but it seemed to have just dawned on him that his life might be in jeopardy.

What had he thought was their goal? Had he supposed they'd walked into the woods for a casual chat?

"Why can't we kill you?" Raven asked.

"This is...is...England," Judah stammered. "We're not in Africa. You can't murder a fellow here. There are laws preventing it."

Raven glanced at Sebastian. "Will you be upset if we break a few laws?"

"No."

Raven continued. "Focus, Judah. We're about to kill you. What would you like to say to Sebastian before I slit your throat?"

"Let me back on the expedition team," Judah absurdly said. "We'll forget all about this little ... ah ... incident. I'll never tell a soul what happened between Ophelia and me. We'll carry on as if it never occurred."

"Are you mad?" Sebastian asked.

"It was cruel of you to cut me loose!" Judah insisted. "I was a valued crew member. I was always loyal."

Raven snorted. "You are so deluded. How were you able to hide your insanity for so many years?"

"I was loyal!" Judah vehemently repeated.

Sebastian said, "I wonder what Nathan would think about that comment."

"Bugger Nathan," Judah crudely stated. "I made one tiny mistake with regard to him, and I've been chastised ever since. Am I to be condemned by all of you forever?"

"No," Sebastian said. "I'm done condemning you."

He nodded to Raven, and Raven extracted the knife on his belt. Judah saw it, and he finally exhibited real alarm.

"Have you any last words?" Raven asked him.

"Sebastian, please!" Judah beseeched. "You can't want it to end like this! Not after everything we've meant to each other."

"You left Nathan for dead," Sebastian caustically said, "and you tried your best to ruin my sister. You almost succeeded on both counts so that's two strikes against you. I can't constantly worry over who you might harm next."

"Don't pretend Nathan is a martyr," Judah raged, "and your sister *begged* to marry me. How many times must I say it?"

"No more times."

Sebastian nodded to Raven again, and Raven told Judah, "You're really awful at choosing your last words."

He thrust his blade into Judah's belly and pulled it up into his heart. He was very efficient, very subdued. He twisted the blade for good measure, then he withdrew it and stepped away. Judah dropped like a stone, and he was gasping for air, blood pumping from his chest as the final beats pushed it through his veins.

It was over quickly, but they dawdled for several minutes to be sure. Raven riffled in Judah's pockets to retrieve his purse and timepiece. After his body was discovered, it would look as if he'd been robbed in the forest by brigands.

There was a stream nearby. Raven rinsed off his knife and washed his hands, then he stood and asked, "Are we finished?"

"Yes, we're finished."

"Shall I dig a grave?"

"No, the buzzards can have him. I'm fine with that."

"He'll be found, likely sooner rather than later."

Sebastian shrugged. "This place is deserted. It should be a few days."

They walked away without peering back, and Raven said, "Don't you dare fret about this. You always feel bad when you shouldn't. We abandoned Nathan because of him! If you start softening toward him, remember that fact."

"I will."

"And he destroyed your sister. Even though we rescued her prior to any genuine damage being inflicted, gossip will leak out. He wrecked her future. For that transgression alone, this was the appropriate conclusion."

"You're correct," Sebastian said.

"I wasn't about to deliver him to the courts. It might have been months— or even years—before he was hanged, and I couldn't stomach the prospect of him loafing in a jail cell and boasting about his exploits. This is Sinclair justice."

"You don't have to convince me, Raven."

"Good."

They reached their horses and mounted them, and as Sebastian yanked on the reins to proceed to London, Raven didn't turn with him.

"We should part ways for awhile," Raven said.

"We don't have to. Who would miss him? Who would search?"

"We were the only ones who might have, but he burned that bridge."

"He was such a fool."

"A dangerous fool." Raven shook his head with disgust. "You're not planning another expedition to Africa, are you?"

"Probably not."

"I'm tired of loitering and waiting for something to happen. I have to move on with my life."

"It's a wise decision."

"Will you *ever* travel to Africa again?"

"I don't think so," Sebastian said. "I *think* I'm getting married instead."

Raven laughed. "You? Married? Who's the lucky girl? Not Miss Gordon."

"You wouldn't believe me if I told you." Sebastian could see the question in Raven's eyes, and he waved it away. "If I need to contact you, where will you be?"

"I'll be out on the coast. I'm ready to take care of my old family business."

"I hope it resolves as you've always dreamed. You've been angry about it forever. Don't lose your temper. Don't murder anybody."

"Don't you mean, don't murder anybody *else*?"

Sebastian chuckled. "Yes, that's what I mean."

Raven spat in the dirt. "He deserved it."

"Yes, he did," Sebastian agreed.

Raven stuck out his hand, and Sebastian clasped hold. A paltry handshake wasn't a sufficient farewell though, so he leaned across and hugged the man.

"Keep in touch," Sebastian advised him as he drew away. "The instant you have an address, inform me of what it is."

"I will, and if you ever need help, call on me first. I'll come right away."

"I know I can count on you."

Raven gave a jaunty salute. "You better not sit here moping."

"I won't."

"You shouldn't feel guilty either."

"I never do."

"Liar!"

Raven kicked his horse into a trot, and as he raced away, he glanced back. "Get going! Don't make me tell you twice."

Sebastian saluted too, watching until he rounded a bend, then he rode off in the other direction. Home to London—and all the drama he'd find there.

He was distraught over events, worn down by Judah's grisly ending. Sarah was at Hero's Haven, and she would cure what ailed him. Sarah would fix what was wrong. When he was with her, life was nearly perfect.

He galloped away, eager to be with her as fast as he could.

CHAPTER

20

SARAH STOOD AT THE gate to the Selby estate. It was the one spot she never thought she'd see. Her true father had been Matthew Blake, Viscount Blake. The current earl, Nathan Blake, was her half-brother.

From the day she'd learned of her connection to him, she'd been intrigued. On a dozen different occasions, she'd nearly traveled to Selby to introduce herself, but she'd always refrained. What would have been the point?

If she'd visited and he'd been awful to her, if he'd been dismissive or had refused to meet with her, she'd have been crushed.

And for all intents and purposes, she *wasn't* a Blake. She was Sarah Robertson, beloved, adopted daughter of Ruth and Thomas Robertson. In the world where she'd previously resided—a world of discarded children and philandering fathers—it would have been pretentious to brag about Viscount Blake, so she'd convinced herself that her link to the Blake family didn't matter.

But she was sure, when she was small, she'd lived with Nathan Blake, and they'd been very happy. Might he remember that period too? He was three years older than she was. Might he recall that he'd once had a little sister? If nothing else, might he be able to tell her what had happened when she was three? How had she ended up in an orphanage?

Normally, she wouldn't have bothered him. Normally, she'd have solved her own problems, but she was out of options and out of the energy to keep fighting. Even despite her wave of unrelenting tragedies, she might have stayed away were it not for Noah and Pet. She was terribly afraid for them, and she desperately needed help from a powerful person who wouldn't be scared to intervene.

Nathan Blake was an aristocrat, and he'd been Sebastian Sinclair's dearest friend. Mr. Sinclair had described him as trustworthy, brave, and loyal. She was counting on that description to be accurate, to at least provide an opening where she could ask his advice.

The cruel witch, Gertrude Sinclair, had promised Sarah—if she wrote a farewell letter to Mr. Sinclair—that she'd return the children to Sarah. That horrible afternoon, she'd been so disconcerted that she hadn't been thinking clearly. If she had been, she'd have realized Mrs. Sinclair was lying, and she was being tricked.

Mrs. Sinclair's driver had simply delivered her to London and dropped her at her orphanage. She'd pleaded with him to take her to the children, but he'd claimed he had no information as to their whereabouts.

He'd leaned toward her and had said, "Forget about them, Miss Robertson. You'll never find them. Mrs. Sinclair has a way of making all of them vanish."

Then he'd raced away, leaving her standing alone in the street.

Ever since, she'd frantically dithered over what he'd meant.

It seemed as if other of Sir Sidney's bastards might have approached Mrs. Sinclair, and she'd made them disappear too. How was it managed? Were they conveyed to public orphanages where they would be swallowed into the sea of abandoned urchins? Were they arrested for vagrancy and transported to the penal colonies? Were they murdered, their bodies buried out in the woods?

Mrs. Sinclair was so vicious that Sarah wouldn't rule out any dire possibility.

Was Sebastian Sinclair aware of his mother's mischief? He must have been or why would he have penned that pathetic note to her?

As she'd been whisked away from the Haven, her first instinct had been to talk to him, to ask how he could have hurt her so deeply, and wasn't that the silliest notion ever?

He'd gone to Scotland so he could buy his bride a house for her wedding gift. Would Sarah have dawdled in the woods at Hero's Haven, foraging for roots and berries to prevent starvation while she waited for him? Then what?

She was a proud woman, and there was no reason to talk to him. From the minute he'd started flirting with her, she'd wondered why he was, and his mother had been very blunt about it: He was Sir Sidney's son, a chip off the old block, and he trifled with foolish maidens for sport.

She'd spent several days in London, having prevailed on a tavern owner who had a business next to the orphanage. For a few nights, she'd slept on the floor in his kitchen as she'd struggled to drum up some allies to assist her, but it had been futile.

When the proprietor had suggested she could be hired for an illicit job in the upstairs rooms, she'd decided to depart and had begun walking out of the city. After she was in the countryside, she'd hitched rides with various teamsters.

And now? She was at Selby's gate.

She marched down the lane, reminding herself that she was an optimist who assumed kindness and a good heart would take her very far in life. If Lord Selby was away, or if he declined to speak with her, she'd inquire about her friend, Nell Drummond.

Earlier in the summer, Nell had visited the estate with *her* friend, Susan Middleton, as Susan had prepared to marry Lord Selby's cousin.

Prior to Sarah fleeing London, she'd once again passed by the Middletons' home, but it was still shuttered, so she had no idea what had happened to any of them. Would Susan be at Selby? Might Nell be with her?

She burst out of the trees, and the mansion loomed into view. It was four stories high, with hundreds of windows. On one end, there were turrets, as if the original portion of the building might have been a castle.

A huge lawn swept up to the manor, the curved driveway constructed of expensive brick. There were orchards laden with fruit, pastures with horses frolicking. Servants strolled about, seeing to their chores.

It was like a scene out of a storybook, and she could only ponder how two children—sired by the same parent—had wound up living such disparate lives.

Though her knees were a bit weak—from hunger, she suspected, not from fear—she went straight to the main entrance. Her condition was so bedraggled that she probably should have scooted around to the servant's door, but she was Viscount Blake's lost daughter, and she wouldn't slink in like a mongrel dog.

Before she could knock, a footman emerged and bowed.

"May I help you?" he asked.

She flashed her best smile, praying she wouldn't be tossed out immediately. "I hope so. I realize I'm being very impertinent, but I've traveled such a long distance, and I should like to request an audience with Lord Selby. Might he be available?"

The boy was very sweet. He glanced at her unkempt clothes, but his polite demeanor didn't alter. "Who may I tell him is calling?"

She would have replied, but was distracted by a dapper older man appearing down the hall. He proceeded directly toward them.

The footman said to him, "Mr. Dobbs, this young lady would like to speak with the Earl."

Mr. Dobbs studied her, his astute gaze roaming over her person, and when it settled on her face, he blanched. "My goodness," he murmured. "You look exactly like him—except your hair is blond and his is dark. I'd recognize you anywhere."

He stunned her by clasping her hand, and he patted it so gently that tears sprung to her eyes.

"I am Lord Selby's butler," he said. "Please tell me your name so I can announce you. I can't wait to observe his expression!"

He was almost *excited* to meet her, as if she'd been expected, and she was completely flummoxed by his effusive greeting.

"I am ... ah ... Sarah Robertson. Sarah *Blake* Robertson."

"Of course you are," Mr. Dobbs agreed. "Come with me, my dear."

He led her off, and her confusion spiraled. "Is the Earl at home?"

"Yes, and when I present you to him, he is going to absolutely faint."

"Ah ... really?"

Then, from up on the stairs, a woman called, "Sarah Robertson, is that you? Where on earth have you been?"

Sarah and Mr. Dobbs stopped, and Sarah peered up to where Nell Drummond was leaned over the railing on the landing.

"Oh, Nell," she said, "am I glad to see you!"

"Not half as glad as I am to see you!"

Nell dashed down, and Mr. Dobbs stepped away, watching like an indulgent uncle as they fell into each other's arms. They hugged as tightly as they could, which was odd. They hadn't previously had that sort of fond acquaintance, but Sarah was simply so overwhelmed. Nell felt like a lifeline to all that was sane and good in the world.

Nell drew away and assessed Sarah's scruffy state. She scowled and asked, "What has happened to you? You're positively deteriorated!"

"I've been having the very worst time."

"That's obvious, and I'm so relieved you're here. We've been searching for you everywhere."

"You have?"

At the admission, Sarah was astonished. While she'd been forlorn and fretting, her friend had been hunting for her? It was the nicest news she'd ever received.

"Lady Selby"—Mr. Dobbs seemed to be addressing Nell—"you won't believe who she is."

"I know who she *is*, Dobbs," Nell responded. "She used to own the orphanage where his sister was taken all those years ago."

"No," Mr. Dobbs said, "look at her. Look *hard*. She's Sarah *Blake* Robertson. Can't you tell?"

Nell gaped at Sarah as if she'd suddenly grown a second head.

"You're Sarah *Blake*?" Nell's tone was accusatory.

"Yes."

"You never told me!"

Sarah's cheeks flushed. "I've never been eager to share my past."

"Well, here's a bit of information that will astound you," Nell said. "I married Nathan, so that makes me your sister-in-law."

"You what?"

"I married Nathan a few weeks ago. I'm his wife and the Countess of Selby."

Sarah might have tumbled into a peculiar fairytale. "You're joking."

"No. Let's find my husband. He is going to faint when he sees you."

Mr. Dobbs chuckled. "That was my exact comment, Lady Selby."

"Where is he, Dobbs?" Nell inquired.

"He was in the library."

Nell guided her down a gilded hall, Mr. Dobbs dogging their heels. The library had three walls with shelves of books that rose to the ceiling. The fourth wall was all glass, the windows framing the manicured park, the lake behind it.

There was a massive desk in front of the windows, a dark-haired man seated at it. He was busy with correspondence, and without peeking up, he asked, "What is it, Nell? When you interrupt me, I never finish my chores. What do you need?"

He glanced up, grinning affectionately and obviously expecting her to be alone. He frowned, his gaze shifting to Sarah. For a moment, Time stood still, and they were frozen in place.

Then he said the strangest thing. "Sissy? Is it really you?"

And Sarah answered in the strangest way. "Yes, it's really me."

"Oh, my lord," he muttered. "You're finally home where you belong!"

He leapt to his feet, raced over, and hugged her so tightly she didn't think she'd ever breathe again.

⁕

"Excuse me."

"Shut your mouth, you little cretin, or I'll shut it for you!"

"I have to speak with someone in charge."

Noah stared at the man on the other side of the bars, hoping his stern glower would bring the result he sought. So far though, it had had no effect. He'd been complaining vociferously, but no one would listen.

The dolt who'd delivered them to the facility, as well as the dolt who'd detained them in the large room, had claimed they weren't under arrest, but it certainly felt like it. They weren't free to leave, and the door was never opened unless more prisoners arrived. Newcomers were shoved in, then the door would be locked again.

In the beginning, there had been twenty-five people with them, but more staggered in by the day. There were forty-six squashed together now. It was a mix of old and young, men and women, boys and girls. All of them were bedraggled, their clothes tattered, their conditions grim, as if they were on their last legs.

Only Noah and Pet appeared to have been snatched from stellar circumstances, and they had been.

"We're not supposed to be here." He kept repeating the comment. "There's been a mistake."

"There's no mistake," their jailor huffed, "so be silent. Your constant caterwauling gives me a headache."

The oaf was seated at a desk and eating a plate of food, the smell causing all their stomachs to growl with hunger. They were fed twice a day, and supper was hours away.

"I am the natural son of Sir Sidney Sinclair." He pointed to Pet. "This is his natural daughter, Petunia."

Their jailor snickered. "Yes, yes, I've heard you a dozen times. You're the son of Sir Sidney, and *I* am the son of the bloody King of England."

Noah was undeterred. "We are the wards of Miss Sarah Robertson, owner of the Robertson Home for Orphaned Children. We've been kidnapped and brought to you against our will."

"A person is never brought against his will." The man waved some papers

in Noah's direction. "Your documents were signed and notarized. Stop protesting your situation. You're simply making me angry, and you wouldn't like
me to lose my temper."

"I'm not afraid of you," Noah said.

"You should be."

"When my brother, Sebastian Sinclair, comes to rescue us, you'll be sorry."

"Trust me, if Sebastian Sinclair strolls in, I will faint dead away."

Pet tugged on Noah's sleeve and begged, "Sit down, Noah. I don't want
him to hurt you."

"He won't hurt me," Noah insisted.

"I'm terribly worried he might."

One of the other men called to the jailor, "I met Sir Sidney once. I'll bet
this boy is telling the truth. He's the spitting image of that famous fellow."

"You're correct," Noah said. "I look just like him because my mother was
his favorite mistress."

Noah's boast enraged their jailor. "Shut your mouth! Sir Sidney was a
saint! A saint! You'll not spread sordid stories about him in my presence."

"He wasn't a saint," Noah mumbled, and he plopped down next to Pet.

As their ordeal continued, she was growing quieter and more frightened. For
a girl of six, she'd endured too many catastrophes. Did their half-brother know
what had happened to them? And what about Miss Robertson? She had to be
frantically searching for them. Who was there to inform her of what had occurred?

There had been no witnesses to their abduction, and it was the scariest
part of the whole debacle. He'd promised Petunia that Miss Robertson or Sebastian would save them, but they had no way to deduce what had transpired,
so how could they figure out where Noah and Pet were being held?

Noah ceaselessly fretted, trying to fathom who had ordered their kid-
napping. Might it have been Sebastian? He'd never been keen on the notion
of Noah and Pet showing up in his life, and if Noah eventually learned that
Sebastian had betrayed them, how would he ever recover from the blow?

"What will become of us?" he asked the jailor, but he was ignored.

The other man, the one who'd said he looked like Sir Sidney, answered
instead. "We've been sold into indenture."

"I keep hearing that," Noah replied, "but no one will explain what it means."

"It *means* we'll be sent to another country, and we'll work there at jobs."

"For how long?"

"Seven years."

"Then what?"

"Then, if you've repaid the fees that it cost to transport you to our destination, you'll be free to carry on as you see fit. If you haven't repaid them, you'll have to toil away until your debt is squared."

"What country will it be?" Noah asked.

"I was hoping for Australia, but there are rumors we're bound for America."

"When will we leave?"

"We'll be ready to depart once they have sixty people. With the pace they're arriving, I expect it will be two or three more days."

Pet appeared horrified. "I don't want to travel to another country, and I especially don't want to sail on a ship!"

The man flashed a weary smile. "It will be fun. Think of it as an adventure."

"I've had all the adventure I ever wish to have," she said.

"We can't go to America," Noah added. "We haven't finished our schooling, and I'm to attend university in the future. Besides, Miss Robertson needs us."

The man shrugged. "I don't believe any of those things will be possible now. You should forget about them. Otherwise, you'll drive yourself mad with memories of what might have been."

"Why would we be here?" Noah asked him. "Why were we locked in with all of you?"

"Someone with authority over you would have had to sign a contract. You've mentioned you're orphans. Did you have a guardian?"

"Yes, Miss Robertson," Noah said.

"She must be to blame then. She'd be the only one who could bind you."

Noah was stunned. Would Miss Robertson have arranged such a dreadful fate? Why would she have? He'd assumed she liked them, and she'd definitely deemed herself to be responsible for them.

Yet she'd been very worried about her ability to care for them. She hadn't been able to procure permanent lodging, and their Sinclair kin had declined to help.

Had she finally decided this was the best conclusion? Had she been too ashamed to confess it?

"Miss Robertson wouldn't have done this to us," Pet said as if reading his mind.

"I can't guess what's true, Pet," he told her. "Who else might have yearned for us to vanish?"

"Everyone but her."

He gazed at the man. "Will my sister and I be allowed to stay together? I've sworn to always protect her. Is there a way to ensure we wind up at the same location?"

"No," the man killed him by saying. "It will depend on who needs servants and what kind they need. If there's no employer seeking both a boy and a girl, you'll be split up."

They were the most alarming words ever uttered. Noah slid his hand into Pet's, linked their fingers, and squeezed tight.

SEBASTIAN TROTTED UP THE lane toward Sarah's cottage. He was physically exhausted, but mentally exhausted too.

He probably shouldn't have stopped to visit her. He should have proceeded directly to London to check that Ophelia was home safe and sound. His servants were competent and would have conveyed her without incident, but he was concerned about his mother and how she'd reacted when Ophelia rolled up in her carriage.

Gertrude was such a stern, unforgiving person. It wouldn't surprise him to discover that Ophelia hadn't been permitted to return—despite his command. It would be another family quagmire to ensnare him.

His temper kept flaring over Judah, and he was disgusted at having had the man on the expedition team for so many years. In light of his perfidy, what sort of fiend had he been deep down? His dangerous tendencies had been so well hidden.

As Sebastian emerged from the trees, the residence was very quiet, the shutters closed, no smoke wafting from the chimney. He dismounted and hurried to the door, and he was so excited to see Sarah that he was practically skipping like a happy boy.

He didn't bother to knock, but simply blustered in, and he was about to call out to her, to announce himself, but he quickly stumbled to a halt.

There was the oddest perception in the air that the house was deserted, as if it had been empty for ages, as if Sarah and the children had never been there a single day. He stood very still, listening, trying to figure out what the silence indicated.

Suddenly, footsteps crunched on the gravel outside, and he grinned, expecting it to be Sarah, but it wasn't. Instead, it was the housemaid from the manor who'd been charged with delivering their meals.

"Master Sebastian?" She dipped a curtsy. "We didn't realize you were back."

"I just arrived." He gestured around the parlor. "I had a message for Miss Robertson, but the place seems abandoned."

"Yes, they left."

He cocked his head, as if she'd spoken in a language he didn't understand.

"What did you say?" he asked her.

"Ah . . . they left?"

"When?"

"It happened immediately after you departed on your recent trip. I've been coming over anyway, but there's been no sign of them."

"My goodness."

"I interrogated the staff, but no one noticed anything amiss."

His pulse pounded with a bit of dread. "This is worrying me."

"As I approached just now, and the front door was ajar, I assumed they were back. I'd planned to ask Miss Robertson if she'd like me to bring supper."

"No need for that, I guess."

"She wrote you a note."

"A note?" he repeated like a dullard.

She motioned to the desk in the corner, and she wrung her hands nervously, as if terrified he'd blame her for allowing them to slip away.

What could have transpired? He'd been gone for the better part of three days. He'd ridden north, had dealt with Judah, then had ridden home. Their absence made no sense.

He'd penned a letter to her. Hadn't she received it? If she hadn't, she'd be angry, wondering where he was and why he hadn't returned with the Special License he'd promised.

He went over and seated himself, and he grabbed the missive and ripped it open. It was short and to the point: She hadn't deemed his proposal to be sincere, so she and the children had fled. She wasn't about to let him ruin his life over her, and she told him not to search—because he would never find her.

He read it three times, then he folded it and stuck it in his coat. If the fire had been lit, he'd have burned it. He should have crumpled it into a ball and tossed it on the floor, but he would hate to have the servants pick it up and discover how stupid he'd been with regard to her.

She'd left! He couldn't believe it! Then again, yes, he could.

Women never behaved as a man was hoping, and she'd been a peculiar female who'd tempted him as another female wouldn't have.

Why had she tantalized him so thoroughly? In the brief period they'd been together, he'd frequently asked himself that question, but he had no viable answer. Occasionally, he'd felt quite bewitched by her, as if she'd cast a magical spell to entice him.

What had it all been about? He wasn't sure.

He wanted to rail and weep over what was lost, but what had that been exactly? She'd been a beautiful stranger who'd seduced him with her shameless ways and brash attitudes. They'd had a wild fling, and he was glad they'd had it, but wasn't it for the best that it had ended? Wasn't she wise to have severed their connection?

He'd relentlessly pondered the ramifications of marrying her, and he'd persuaded himself that she'd be worth all the trouble she'd cause, but why had he thought that?

She'd recognized the horrendous mistake he'd been about to make, and she'd saved him from it. He ought to be down on his knees and thanking her. He ought to be shuddering with relief that he'd dodged a bullet. Except deep down, there was a tiny voice insisting he'd mourn the loss of her forever.

But he was a grown man, and he didn't have to listen to silly voices in his head that weren't imparting anything he cared to hear.

Movement caught his eye, and he realized the housemaid was waiting to be dismissed.

"Is it bad news, sir?" she asked.

"No." He waved away the query. "Miss Robertson was staying temporarily. She'd been hunting for accommodations in town, and she found them. So they departed."

"They're not endangered?"

"Gad, no." He tried to sound jovial. "They're fine, and you needn't continue to traipse over here."

"I didn't mind."

"Please tell the rest of the staff, especially the kitchen, that we're done tending them. I'll be closing the cottage again, probably until some other friend needs the place."

"I will tell everyone."

He shooed her out, and for a moment, she hovered. It was obvious he was overcome by whatever he'd learned in the letter, but it wasn't her role to pry into what was wrong. She spun and walked out.

He sat at the desk, feeling as if he'd been turned to stone. He dawdled for an eternity, but he couldn't imagine how long he tarried. An hour? Two? Three?

The afternoon colors faded as dusk settled in, and he understood he should leave too, but he couldn't force himself to go. He'd liked having her in the cottage. He'd liked knowing he could rush over to see her whenever he was lonely and out of sorts. He'd been ... been ... *happy* for once.

Well, he was Sir Sidney's son, so it was to be expected that a pretty girl could convince him to act like an idiot. It was ludicrous to be so perturbed. He was busy, and she'd been such a distraction.

He had to ride on to town to check on his sister, and he pushed himself to his feet and went outside. As he shut the door, he fleetingly wondered if he might not simply tear down the bloody house. Why have it standing? It simply represented a humiliating interval he'd rather not recall.

CHAPTER

21

"Can you answer a question for me?"

"I can answer a thousand questions."

Sarah and her brother were back in his library, and it was just the two of them. They'd pulled up chairs so they were facing each other, and they were holding hands, sitting knee to knee, their feet tangled.

They were so much alike! Same eyes, same nose, same cheekbones and chin. She couldn't stop staring.

Once initial introductions had been made and hugs exchanged, Nell had whisked her away. A bevy of housemaids had bathed, fed, and dressed her. The whole time, Nell had flitted about, clucking her tongue like a mother hen.

Sarah was so overcome with gratitude that she'd kept bursting into tears. Nell would look horrified, then a new round of cosseting would begin.

She'd been scrubbed clean and garbed in some of Nell's clothes, then she'd been escorted down to the library. Nell had locked her in with her brother and had told them to talk for hours if need be. A tray of food had been delivered, and Mr. Dobbs was hovering outside so they could summon him if they required assistance.

The entire staff seemed to be smiling. All because of her. All because she'd staggered to Selby—thinking it her last resort. But Nathan had been searching for her for months, and the servants viewed themselves as being part of the happy conclusion.

"What happened to me when I was three?" she asked.

"You don't remember?"

"No. I know I was left on the steps at the orphanage. There was a note in my pocket as to who should be billed for my expenses. My birth certificate was included too, but I never saw it until after my father died and I was clearing out his papers."

Nathan launched into a gripping story about their terrible grandfather, Godwin Blake. He and their father, Matthew, had fought constantly. Matthew's aristocratic wife had perished when Nathan was a baby, then he'd fled Selby and had set up his own home in London.

He'd hired a pretty, sweet nanny for Nathan named Mary Carter. In the process, he'd fallen madly in love with her, and she'd been Sarah's mother.

Then Nathan uttered the most peculiar comment ever. "When you and Rebecca were born, Father was delighted, but Grandfather was enraged."

She scowled. "Wait a minute. Who is Rebecca?"

He blanched with astonishment. "You seriously don't recollect?"

"No." She started to shake, and suddenly, her heart was pounding, her head throbbing. "Are you saying . . . saying . . . we have another sibling?"

"Yes, we have another sibling, and *you* have a twin sister."

The news was so shocking that Sarah felt as if her limbs had melted. For the briefest moment, she blacked out and nearly slid off the chair.

"Whoa!" Nathan grabbed and steadied her. "Take a deep breath."

"I have a twin sister?" she repeated like a dunce.

"Yes. You called her Bec-Bec because you couldn't pronounce Rebecca."

He stood and walked to the sideboard, and he returned with the whiskey decanter. He poured some in a glass, then extended it to her, but she couldn't lift her arm, so he wrapped her fingers around it and guided it to her lips.

"Have a big drink," he said. "It will calm you."

She downed the liquor in a quick swallow, and she laughed a tad hysterically.

"I dream about her, but I assumed she was my guardian angel."

"She's not an angel. She's a real person."

"Where is she?"

"I have no idea. I'm hunting for her too."

"Are you . . . ah . . . expecting she's still alive?"

"I won't accept that she might not be."

Sarah closed her eyes and mentally sought Rebecca, as she often had in the past—when she was troubled, when she was sad, when she was feeling alone and scared.

Are you there? she asked in her mind.

The reply floated in immediately. *Yes, I'm here.*

She gazed at him again. "I'm betting she's alive too. In fact, I'm sure of it."

He continued with his depressing tale: how their father and her mother had built a life with Nathan and their daughters, how they'd been killed in a carriage accident when Nathan was six and Sarah three.

"Our Aunt Edwina came to shut down our house," he explained. "I was brought to Selby because I was the new heir, but Grandfather wouldn't permit Edwina to bring you and Rebecca too. She persuaded your mother's relatives to offer you a home, but when your mother's cousin arrived, you were sickly, and she refused to take you."

"We were split up?"

"Yes."

Her recurring nightmares made more sense now. The wicked witch who always swooped in and carried her away must have been her Aunt Edwina. Sarah had been crying with dismay, and she must have been reaching out to Bec-Bec. Nathan must have been the boy shouting in the background.

"I recollect a few details from that day," she said.

"Rebecca went with your Carter cousins, and Aunt Edwina carted you off to the orphanage." He clasped her hands again and squeezed tight. "Were you all right there? Were they kind to you? Were you fed and clothed? Was there coal for the stove in the winter? What was it like?"

"It was wonderful, Nathan, so please don't fret."

"I *have* been fretting. Ever since I found out I had sisters, I've been so afraid you might have been imperiled."

"Mr. and Mrs. Robertson were generous people. I had a good life with them."

He shuddered with relief. "That's such a load off my shoulders."

"They thought I was so charming that they adopted me." She grinned, the first one she'd displayed. "How could they not love me? I was Viscount Matthew Blake's remarkable daughter."

He chuckled. "I see you have some of my same humility."

"I don't have a humble bone in my body."

"Neither do I. In that, we're exactly the same." He nodded resolutely. "You're staying here with me so Nell and I can watch over you. You understand that, don't you?"

"Are you certain?"

"It's what Father would have wanted, and it's what *I* want too."

"I would hate to impose."

"You never could. From this point on, I have to know you're safe."

Tears flooded her eyes. "I wish I'd come to you long ago."

"Well, I only recently remembered you. If you'd showed up any earlier, I'd probably have called you a deranged liar."

"I feel as if Fate delivered me at just the right moment."

"I'm starting to feel that way too."

"Can we find Rebecca?"

"It's my plan."

"Now that you've told me about her, I'm quite impatient to be with her again."

"It was much easier than I anticipated."

"It happened so fast too. There's nothing to distract him now, so I'm positive he'll propose."

Ophelia was walking down the hall toward her mother's boudoir. She was in the doghouse, ordered to remain in her room, have meals on a tray, and generally be invisible.

The door was open, and her mother and Veronica were inside talking. In the brief period she'd been away, Veronica and her mother had bonded in an odd fashion Ophelia didn't comprehend. They were thick as thieves, always whispering, their heads pressed close as if they were sharing secrets.

Veronica had replaced Ophelia in her mother's affection, and Ophelia couldn't decide if she was irked by their switching of roles. A silly, flighty girl had run off with Judah Barnett, but an older, wiser matron had returned. She was wary and distrustful and caught herself questioning every issue.

"If he still doesn't proceed," Veronica asked Gertrude, "what then?"

"I'll broach the subject with him again very soon," Gertrude said. "He simply needs to get her out of his system, then he'll be more amenable to my suggestions."

Ophelia strolled in and inquired, "Are you discussing Sebastian?"

They stiffened, as if with affront, then Gertrude said, "You're not welcome in my bedchamber, Ophelia. Go to your own room."

"How long will you ignore me?"

"It may be forever."

Ophelia marched out, muttering, "Why am I bothering with you?"

"Feel free to depart whenever you'd like!" her mother hurled as she retreated like a whipped puppy.

She was bored and out of sorts, and she'd like to engage in some interesting activities, but the thought of being outside left her incredibly anxious. She was suffering such peculiar effects from the calamity she'd endured.

The slightest sounds had her jumping. If she rounded a corner and someone was standing there, she'd lurch with alarm, and her nervous reactions were so annoying. It was galling to realize she was such a trembling ninny.

She trudged into her bedchamber and climbed into the window seat to stare out the window. It was a rainy, dreary afternoon that perfectly matched her mood.

As footsteps echoed in the hall, she glanced over to see Veronica entering. They'd been friends since they were tiny, and Ophelia had been excited for them to become sisters. Their mothers had plotted for Sebastian to wed her, and Ophelia had never pondered whether it was a good idea or not.

Yet as with so many topics, her view about it had altered—because her view of Sebastian had changed. She no longer envisioned him as being aloof and stubborn. With his riding to her rescue, she'd had to accept that he was very tough, very brave, and that he might be much smarter than she'd ever given him credit for being.

Would Veronica make him happy? She didn't think so. Did he recognize it too? Was that why he had delayed?

"Don't mind Gertrude," Veronica cheerfully said as she came over and nestled herself into the window seat too. "She's angry with you, but she'll get over it."

"I don't care if she gets over it."

"You have to admit your conduct was exceedingly reckless. What possessed you? Mr. Barnett was handsome enough, but honestly!"

"He promised to take me to Africa."

"Why would you want to travel to Africa?"

Veronica gaped at Ophelia as if it was the strangest notion ever voiced.

"Well, I *am* a Sinclair," Ophelia said, "and my family is renowned for its wanderlust."

"The *men* are renowned for it. How do you fit into that picture?"

Ophelia wasn't about to explain the yearnings that plagued her, how she wished she were a man, how she wished she could be allowed the exotic experiences men were allowed. She couldn't be the only female in history to crave a bigger path.

"You and Mother are quite chummy all of a sudden," she said, deftly switching subjects. "What brought about all this camaraderie?"

Veronica smiled slyly. "You won't believe what we accomplished while your brother went running after you."

"Yes, I will. What was it?"

"You have to swear not to tell anyone. Especially Sebastian."

"I won't. I swear."

Veronica leaned nearer and murmured, "Your mother told me about that . . . *woman* who was living in the cottage at the Haven."

"Miss Robertson?"

"Yes, and we chased her away. We pretended Sebastian and I were betrothed and planning a Christmas wedding. She was absolutely devastated, and she fled without a whimper of protest."

"It was cruel to lie to her like that."

Veronica waved away Ophelia's comment. "I agreed with your mother. She had to be forced out of his life. It was the only way to get him to focus on me."

Ophelia remembered the day she'd seen Sebastian chatting with Miss Robertson in the village outside the Haven. He'd looked so fond, almost as if he was in love with her. He'd definitely never gazed at Veronica like that.

When Ophelia had first learned about Miss Robertson, she'd been livid. Why had she been? There was so little joy in the world. Why should it bother her if her brother had found a girl who made him happy?

"We've rid ourselves of those two urchins too," Veronica said.

Ophelia frowned. "Her wards?"

"Yes. It was outrageous of her to have dragged them into our midst."

"You know who those children are, don't you?"

Veronica smirked. "I know who Miss Robertson *said* they were. Just because she claimed a certain paternity, that doesn't indicate it's true."

"Did they leave with Miss Robertson?"

"No, your mother sent them somewhere, and I'm so relieved to be shed of them. Once I marry Sebastian, I wasn't about to have them strutting about at the Haven. Can you imagine the scandal it would have stirred?"

"Yes, I can imagine," Ophelia mumbled.

Previously, she'd been shocked by the arrival of her half-siblings. Now, she was simply sad for them.

Where were they? What would become of them? Sebastian had felt a duty to aid them. What about Ophelia? Should she intervene in Gertrude's mischief? Should she start a quarrel and demand answers as to where they were?

No doubt any display of temper would merely exacerbate the problems she was having with her mother. And really, was it appropriate for the children to have been thrust on them?

She couldn't decide.

"If you had to guess about their location," she said, "where would you suspect they are?"

"Your mother has handled this type of situation before. She has a method for dealing with unpleasant waifs who show up on her stoop."

"Might they be imperiled?" Ophelia asked.

"Gad, no! They're just . . . gone."

Ophelia stared at her old friend, her cousin, trying to find her prior affection, but it had vanished.

"I'm terribly fatigued, Veronica," she fibbed. "I think I'll take a nap."

"Fine. I'll pop in to check on you in a bit. Perhaps we can curl each other's hair."

"I'd like that."

Veronica left, and as Ophelia watched her depart, her anger flared. She wanted to rail at the obnoxious shrew. She wanted to shake her, but she was too weary to fight over any topic. What could she do about it anyway?

She'd discuss it with Sebastian. He would know what was best. She turned back to the window and continued to study the rain, mesmerized by how it pattered on the glass.

<hr />

NELL WAS IN SARAH's bedchamber and seated on her bed. Supper was over, and it was getting late. Sarah was snuggled under the blankets, and they were gossiping like schoolgirls. They couldn't stop.

It was hard to believe she'd stumbled in only a few hours earlier. Nell had spent those hours observing her and Nathan, which was fascinating.

Over the summer, she'd visited Sarah at the orphanage, and she'd been struck by how much Sarah had resembled him. She'd teased Sarah about it, joking that she must have had some Blake blood flowing in her veins.

It was uncanny how she and Sarah had been friends, how Nell had fallen in love with Nathan, how Fate had delivered Sarah to them. The Good Lord was definitely guiding all their steps.

"Did I tell you I met your sister, Temperance?" Nell asked.

"No, and before you describe your conversation with her, let me categorically state that I apologize for however she offended you."

"I assume you won't be insulted if I mention she's a horrid person."

"I won't be insulted."

"She's positively ghastly. Was she adopted by the Robertsons too?"

"No. She was their very own daughter. She came along after they adopted me."

"That's why you're so different then. During the entire appointment, I tried to figure out how you could possibly be related to her."

"Temperance was embarrassed by my father. He was from a wealthy family, but they disowned him when he used his inheritance to start the orphanage."

"He must have been a wonderful man."

"He was." Sarah sighed and nodded. "I was lucky that he and his wife wanted me. It changed everything."

"It certainly did."

"His mother was rich, and for some reason, she really liked Temperance. She invited her to move to the country and be raised there. My father fought it, but eventually relented. Afterward, Temperance became even more awful."

"The house she lives in, she inherited it from her grandmother?"

"Yes, and when the woman died, she was bequeathed some money too, so when Cuthbert latched onto her, she was quite a catch. Her money's gone though. He gambled it away, and the house will be lost before too much more time has passed."

"If they're forced into foreclosure, what will happen to them?"

"I'd like to say I'm concerned about it, but if I don't say that, will you think I'm being unkind?"

Nell chuckled. "No. I'll think—if you've cut ties with her—it's what she deserves. She'll probably need your help someday, but she won't be able to find you."

"I just suffered a little thrill merely from imagining it. I'm afraid my trail of woe is making me cruel."

"Or maybe more astute."

"Maybe."

"When I called on her, I had myself announced as the very ordinary Mrs. Blake, but when I departed, I was so irked with her that I guaranteed she knew I was Lady Selby. She fell all over herself, trying to smooth over her boorish posturing, but I left in an imperious snit, apprising her that I wasn't impressed—and she wasn't forgiven for being so rude to me."

They grinned a complicit grin, and Sarah said, "I'm so glad I'm here. It's like a dream. I'm scared I'll wake up and discover none of it is real."

"I still feel that way, and I doubt I'll ever grow accustomed to it. Even now, when someone refers to me as Lady Selby, I occasionally glance over my shoulder to see who they're talking to."

Sarah laughed so merrily the bed shook, and as her mirth waned, she said, "It's marvelous to laugh again. I was beginning to worry I never would."

"It will all get better very fast. Nathan is adept at fixing what's wrong."

"Can I ask you a question? I would have asked him, but with my just staggering in, I couldn't bear to upset him."

"He's not easily riled. He was a bit short-tempered when he first returned from Africa, but he was physically ill, and his mental state was low. He's improved so much, and his rage has nearly vanished. He'll be delighted to assist you with any issue."

"It's regarding Sebastian Sinclair," Sarah bluntly declared.

"Mr. Sinclair! Oh, my. At the moment, they're feuding."

"I know, but Mr. Sinclair is why I'm here."

"How are you acquainted with him?"

"It's a long story. If I tell it to you, will you promise you won't hate me?"

"Hate you! Don't be ridiculous."

"Then you have to at least promise you won't be shocked."

Nell's mind raced as she struggled to deduce what Sarah was about to confide. A suspicion dawned, and she said, "Is this going to lead where I think it's going to lead?"

"If you *think* it's going to lead to an illicit affair between the two of us, then you'd be correct."

"Sarah Robertson! For shame!"

Sarah winced, and Nell hastily said, "I was teasing. Since I ruined myself with Nathan before I ever had a ring on my finger, I am not in any position to judge you. You haven't noticed that I'm in the family way."

"What? I thought you'd put on some weight! You look so healthy, and I didn't want to accuse you of being chubby!"

"Most people would claim I'm glowing, but it's because I'm having a baby. And don't you dare calculate any calendar dates that might indicate immoral tendencies."

"A baby! That's terrific news!"

"So I can't exactly chastise you for an ethical lapse."

"I was hoping that would be your opinion. If I don't hurry and confess my sins, I just might explode."

"I was never a priest," Nell told her, "so I can't be your confessor, but I am an excellent listener. Spill all, you lusty wench, and don't stop until you get to the end."

NATHAN WAS DAWDLING ON a sofa in a cozy parlor at the rear of the manor. He was sipping a whiskey and staring into the fire that was burning in the grate. It was a cool autumn night, the wind blustery, the seasons definitely changing.

And he was stuck in England.

It occurred to him that he was accursedly happy. At Selby! Who would ever have imagined it?

He'd had a traumatic childhood, and he'd spent his life running away from it, but he was home for good, and with Nell by his side, everything was perfect.

He couldn't believe his sister had strolled in the door. All summer, Nell had been talking about her friend Sarah Robertson, with neither of them realizing that *her* Sarah was *his* Sarah too. She was at Selby now, which was right where she'd always belonged.

On her arrival, her condition had been dire, so she'd shown up at the precise instant he could aid her the most.

His main gift to her would be to find Rebecca. He had several clerks scouring old records, interviewing parish vicars, and visiting various coastal towns. So far, they'd had no luck, but he refused to accept they wouldn't locate her. When they did, when she came home too, what a reunion they would have!

Matthew Blake's three children, together at Selby!

He heard Nell walking down the hall. For what seemed like an eternity, she'd been chatting with Sarah, so it was very late. He supposed he should have slinked off to bed without her, and she'd probably scold him for staying up, but he actually liked her scolding. Her green eyes were so pretty when she was angry.

"There you are," she said as she entered the room. "I went up to our bedchamber, and of course, you weren't in bed as you should have been."

"I'm not tired." Ever since the debacle in Africa, insomnia had been his constant companion. "Besides, you have to repeat your conversation with Sarah word for word."

"This was the best day ever," she said as she snuggled next to him. "Except for maybe the day you and I met."

"I agree. Was she calmed enough to fall asleep?"

"Yes, but it took forever. She had a hundred stories."

"I've been pondering how odd it is that she was your friend."

"Fate has been guiding our paths."

"I agree about that too."

They were quiet for a bit, enjoying the comfortable silence, then she said, "I have to tell you a secret she shared with me, but it's difficult, and I'm afraid you won't like it."

"I'll try to bear up," he facetiously retorted.

She tsked. "I'm being serious, and I need you to be serious too."

"I will be serious as a priest at a funeral."

He'd expected she would reveal some inane feminine issue about clothes or money or some other topic that wouldn't interest him in the slightest, so when she slid away and moved to the chair across, he was a tad disconcerted.

What could it be?

"I won't hem and haw," she said. "I'll explain what happened, then we'll deal with it in a sane fashion."

"Good. I can't abide dithering."

"Sarah is in a jam."

"What sort of jam?"

"It seems, dear Nathan, that she was seduced by a scoundrel."

He winced. "Is she increasing?"

"It's too early to be certain."

"Who is the scoundrel?"

Nell sighed. "This is the tricky part."

"Why is it tricky? If he toyed with her affections, he'll have to pay a price."

"I heartily concur."

"Is she in love with him? Would she like to have him as a husband? Even if she wouldn't, if she winds up with child, there will have to be a quick wedding."

"She might be terribly in love with him, but they separated on bad terms, mostly because of his family, so I can't guess how she'd view a marriage. I doubt she'd want to wed him when his relatives hate her."

"They don't get to have an opinion." He downed his whiskey and put the empty glass on the table between them. "Who is the scoundrel? Is it anyone I know?"

"Oh, yes, you know him, and before I provide his name, you have to promise you won't fly into a rage."

"I never fly into rages."

"Don't pretend with me," she scoffed. "You can't."

She stared him down, and finally, he asked, "Well? Are you going to tell me who it is?"

"I'm waiting for you to swear you'll remain calm."

"All right, all right, I swear. Who is it?"

"It's Sebastian Sinclair."

He cocked his head, confused by her comment. "Sebastian ruined my sister? Is that what you said?"

"You heard me loud and clear. The orphanage was shut down, and he let her tarry at the Haven so she'd be close by and he'd have plenty of opportunities to wear her down. Then—after he'd succeeded in seducing her—he kicked her out. It's why she ended up here."

"Sebastian kicked her out? He did that to her? Really? He can be a pompous ass, but I can't picture him acting that way."

"Both of you have changed since you returned from Africa."

"True."

For most of his life, he'd been a man who blustered forward and seized what he craved, so he'd never kept his promises. He was trying to behave better for his wife, and he never liked to upset her.

But...

Sebastian had ruined Sarah? He'd trifled with her, then kicked her out so she was alone and endangered?

Suddenly, he felt as if he might explode with fury. He leapt to his feet and hurled his whiskey glass at the fireplace. It shattered, the pieces crashing to the floor.

"I will kill him!" he fumed. "I will absolutely kill him!"

"You swore you'd remain calm!"

"I lied."

"I WOULD HAVE YOUR answer immediately."

Sebastian glared at his mother. "Why must you nag the minute I walk in the door?"

"You haven't just walked in. You've been here for half an hour."

"If you're about to start in on me, my visit is over."

"I assume you're planning another expedition to Africa."

He shrugged. "Maybe."

He was forlorn and out of sorts and missing everyone: Sir Sidney, Nathan, Raven, Sarah, even Noah and Petunia. Why not plan another trip? The details would occupy his mind so he wouldn't have the time or energy to mope.

"You're already thirty," she said, "and if you're gone for three years, you'll be thirty-three when you return."

"You were always very good at math."

"Or what if you meet with a dire fate while you're away?"

"I'll try my best to avoid it."

"Veronica won't wait forever," she warned.

"As you never cease to mention."

"Why are you so opposed? What is wrong with her?"

"Nothing's wrong with her."

"You're being fussy for no reason?"

"I guess."

He was being very impertinent, and she threw up her hands. "I give up. Stay a bachelor if you wish. Journey to the darkest corner of the Earth and get yourself murdered like your father. Leave us with no heir to inherit. Who cares about the future? You certainly don't, so why should I?"

They were in her front parlor again. She was seated on the sofa by the fire, and he was in a chair across from her. He'd only stopped by to check on Ophelia, but she was never home when he arrived.

Gertrude claimed she was recovering from her ordeal, but he hadn't had occasion to speak to her himself. It wouldn't surprise him to learn she'd been locked in a closet, with his mother never intending to release her.

He stood and went to the window to stare out into the garden. Veronica was hosting a tea party in the solarium, it being too chilly to hold it under a tent in the grass. A dozen ladies were present, and her annoying little dogs were yapping at her feet, her guests laughing gaily.

She was a beautiful female, but in an icy, aloof way. Gertrude had been set on her being his bride for so long that he couldn't remember a period when it hadn't been her great dream. It wasn't the worst idea. Cousins always married.

It kept the money and property in the family, without having to split acreage or share assets with outsiders.

She had a fantastic dowry and much of the land in it was adjacent to one of his biggest estates. It would double the size. With her delivering that type of benefit, why was he dithering?

His sole complaint about her was that she was too young and he didn't particularly like her. But what man *liked* his wife? None that he knew of. Nathan had seemed fond of his, but he was in the early stages yet.

In a year or two, Nathan would likely be as miserable as every other husband.

Veronica noticed him watching her, and she smiled and waved. Her acquaintances looked at him, and titters flew around the table. Did they all assume the match arranged? Why not make it a reality?

After having been so foolish over Sarah, he was feeling quite stupid. Why not behave rationally for a change? Why not wed the girl his mother had picked for him ages ago?

He spun back to Gertrude and, lest his courage fail him, he said, "I believe I will propose to Veronica."

Thankfully, she didn't gloat. She merely nodded. "Marvelous. When can we accomplish it? When would be convenient for you?"

"You're having a supper party on Saturday night. How about if we take care of it then?"

"That would be perfect. We can have the men lift a few toasts. May I tell Veronica what's about to transpire? Or would you like to surprise her?"

He glanced out to where she was gossiping animatedly with her guests. He tried to picture climbing into a bed with her, fornicating with her, waking up next to her, eating breakfast together, but he couldn't imagine any of it.

"You can tell her if you want," he said. "I don't mind."

"She'll be eager to primp and preen so she's especially glamorous."

He snorted at that. "I'll see you Saturday."

"Drinks at seven, supper at nine."

"I'll be here."

"Won't you walk out and speak with her? She hates it when you sneak off."

"I can't bear to meet any of her friends, and besides, I'll be speaking to her plenty on Saturday night. I'll be saying the only thing she's ever yearned to hear from me."

Suddenly, he felt extremely ill. His stomach was churning, his head pounding, as if with an influenza.

"What would you think if Ophelia stayed with me for awhile?" he said. "She likes it at the Haven, and the country air might invigorate her."

"I'd be relieved to get her out of my hair. All she does is mope. Perhaps you would alter her mood."

"Ask her for me, would you? She'd be welcome whenever it suits her."

He was suffocating and desperate to be away. He left without another word, and he hurried out to the foyer. He was frantic, the oddest bursts of anxiety pummeling him.

"Sebastian!"

He peered up as Ophelia was rushing down the stairs.

"How are you?" he asked. "I've visited a half-dozen times, but I've never been able to catch you."

"I'm fine." She paused, then chuckled. "I take that back. I'm not *fine,* but I'm fine enough."

"Why don't you come to the Haven for a bit? I questioned Mother about it, and she's amenable."

"I'll consider it." She frowned and peeked toward the parlor. Then, more quietly, she murmured, "Have you been chatting with Mother?"

"Yes. For a change, she has some good news to share. I've decided to propose to Veronica."

He'd thought the announcement would cheer her, that she'd squeal with delight or clap her hands or at least smile, but no flicker of sentiment crossed her face.

"Are you sure you should?" she stunned him by inquiring.

"I've been putting it off forever, and I have to move on with my life. I'll ask her at Mother's soiree on Saturday."

As he voiced the comment, his stomach churned even more violently, and he truly worried he might be ill all over his mother's expensive carpet.

Ophelia stepped nearer and said, "Can I tell you something? It's really important."

"Yes, of course, but ... but ... I'm afraid it will have to wait. I'm not well."

"Oh."

"Come to the Haven. You can tell me there. Or you can tell me on Saturday night! We'll talk then."

It was all he could manage.

He ran out the door, jumped on his horse, and galloped away. The farther he traveled from his mother's house, the more his condition improved.

CHAPTER

22

VERONICA PEERED AROUND GERTRUDE'S packed parlor, wanting to catalogue every detail so she'd always remember. The guests were a collection of aristocrats, political elites, and rich acquaintances. They represented the very cream of London society, and they would all witness her glorious achievement.

People were peeking at her, gossip swirling, and she supposed rumors about the engagement had filtered out through the servants. After Gertrude had spilled the beans, the entire household had been in a frenzy of preparation for the party, so word would have leaked out.

She was trying to appear very calm, as if she had no idea what was coming, but she probably wasn't hiding much from anyone who studied her too closely. She might have raised her fist and crowed in triumph over how she'd snagged the biggest marital prize of the decade, but a lady never behaved in such a crass way.

It was almost eight-thirty, and the meal would be served at nine. Sebastian had strolled in mere minutes before, arriving so fashionably late that she'd begun to grow alarmed. Had he decided not to propose after all?

But no, he'd entered, looking as handsome and dashing as ever, but treating her as he usually had—like a pesky little sister. It was how he treated Ophelia.

He hadn't dawdled by her side—as if they were a couple—but had immediately proceeded into the next room to drink brandy with some friends. His conduct was infuriating, but she refused to be annoyed. It was her grand night!

As she'd briefly welcomed him, he hadn't given her any hint of his intentions, hadn't winked or whispered an anticipatory comment in her ear. He hadn't asked her to sneak off so he could speak to her away from the crowd, and she was on pins and needles, wondering when he'd get on with it.

Would he wait until just before supper was announced? Would he do it as the meal commenced? After it ended?

She was so anxiously impatient she could barely keep from fidgeting.

Ophelia was over in the corner, glaring at Veronica. She'd been in a snit ever since Veronica had admitted how she and Gertrude had chased away that tart, Miss Robertson. Well, Ophelia could fume all she liked, but Veronica was delighted with how the incident had brought her precisely what she craved.

Miss Robertson had only been gone from their lives for a matter of days, and Veronica's destiny was so changed that a magic wand might have been waved to create the future she'd always envisioned.

Still though, it was exhausting to have Ophelia glowering. They'd been best friends forever, and she couldn't comprehend why Ophelia wasn't more excited that the betrothal was finally about to occur.

She went over to her, and she didn't beat around the bush.

"Why are you so grouchy? You should be celebrating! I certainly am."

"I can't forget how you tricked Miss Robertson."

Veronica rolled her eyes. "I shouldn't have mentioned it to you, and I wish you'd stop obsessing. *You* were the one who told your mother about her. It worked out exactly as you were hoping, so I don't understand why you're complaining."

"I think he loved her," Ophelia ludicrously said.

"He did not. He would never have suffered heightened emotion for such an inappropriate person."

"He's never looked at you the way he looked at her."

"So?"

"What if he learns how you and Mother treated her? Aren't you worried?"

"No, I'm not worried, and you're being ridiculous."

"I met with her once," Ophelia said.

"You shouldn't have."

"I was rude to her, but since then, I've pondered her a lot. She was actually quite remarkable. She owned her own business, and she was very independent. She didn't need some stupid man to tell her how to carry on. She was so lucky."

"Why would a woman want to live without a man guiding her actions? What an absurd notion."

"Sebastian admired her strong attributes. What can you offer him that might convince him to like you?"

Ophelia's query was so offensive that Veronica was flummoxed over how to respond. She glanced about nervously, eager to locate Gertrude, so she could deal with her boorish daughter, but she was nowhere to be found.

"If you're so miserable, Ophelia," she said, "why stay down here? I'm positive you'd be happier if you returned to your bedchamber."

"I have to talk to Sebastian, but he's been surrounded ever since he walked in."

"What is it you have to discuss with him?" Veronica's panic soared, and she leaned nearer and hissed, "I swear, Cousin, if you ruin this for me, I will absolutely kill you!"

"I have to ask him about my half-siblings. I'd like him to find out where they are, so I can be sure they're safe."

"Honestly, Ophelia! What is wrong with you?" Veronica furtively pinched her arm as she murmured, "You will not ask him about them! Do you hear me? You will not ask!"

Ophelia yanked away, and they might have broken out in a full-on quarrel, but suddenly, the butler stepped in and announced, "May I present Nathan Blake, Lord Selby?"

Every head whipped toward the door, craning so violently she was amazed people didn't topple over. They were all aware of the protracted dispute between Lord Selby and Sebastian, and they'd be thrilled to observe any encounter.

He marched in as if he owned the residence, and her initial thought was that perhaps Sebastian had secretly mended their feud, that he'd invited Lord Selby so the guests would be surprised. At the prospect, her tummy tickled with glee.

If that was the case, the articles in the newspaper about her engagement would be splendid. But on further appraisal, she doubted he'd been invited. He wasn't dressed for a fancy party, but was attired in his riding clothes—leather trousers, scuffed boots, a wool coat—as if he'd just galloped in from the country.

Gertrude instantly appeared to intercept him. Obviously, she'd noted his shabby garments and had realized trouble might be brewing.

"Nathan!" She beamed a fake smile. "We're so delighted you could come."

She tried to spin him around as if she'd shuffle him out before a dire incident could occur, but he shook her off and said, "I'm here to talk to your son. He and I have an important topic to address."

Gertrude's smile faded. "We won't address it in this parlor. Let me show you to a quiet room, and the two of you can chat there."

"No."

Gertrude furiously warned, "You will not make a scene, Nathan Blake. I forbid it! This is Sebastian's betrothal supper, and you will behave yourself or you will leave!"

Lord Selby frowned. "He's betrothing himself? I don't think so."

"Of course it's happening," Gertrude insisted. "He's been promised to Veronica for years—you know that—and it's about to become official."

"From what I recently discovered about Miss Gordon, he probably deserves her, but he's not proceeding with her."

Veronica might have protested his awful comment, but Sebastian pushed through the crowd.

He was grinning, looking as if he was elated to see the imperious oaf, but it was clear the sentiment wasn't reciprocated. Lord Selby was livid over some issue. Would they fight? In the middle of her soiree? On the spur of the moment, she couldn't decide if that would be hideous or fabulous.

If they brawled, it would stir even more stories for the newspapers. Then again, Lord Selby was so angry. Who could guess what he might divulge?

"Nathan," Sebastian said, "what brings you by? How's your charming bride? Is everything all right?"

They were toe to toe, and Gertrude wedged herself between them, and she was practically begging. "Nathan, it's apparent you're upset. You and Sebastian should confer privately."

"No."

"Don't harangue at him, Mother," Sebastian told her, and he turned to his old friend. "What's wrong?"

"Since our last meeting," Lord Selby said, "I've had a very interesting development arise. I found out that I have a pair of half-sisters—twin girls—sired by my father when I was a boy."

"My goodness!" Sebastian exclaimed, and the whole room tittered over the declaration.

"They were lost to me when my father died," Lord Selby continued, "and I've been searching for them. One of them just staggered to Selby. She's there now."

"I'm glad for you," Sebastian said.

"Well, I am *not* glad because her motive in seeking me out was that she was gravely imperiled and desperately needed my help."

"How was she imperiled?"

"She was seduced by a cad. He took her into his home and let her live with him until he wore her down and was able to ruin her. Then he kicked her out on the road."

"I'm sorry to hear it."

"Are you?"

Lord Selby's question had people squirming, and Veronica was suddenly afraid of what he was about to reveal.

"Gertrude!" she beseeched. "Can't you make him depart? He's wrecking my party."

But Gertrude had never possessed the power to make a man act as she wished—her domineering husband had been proof of that—and she definitely had no authority to command Lord Selby.

He asked Sebastian, "Would you like to know my sister's name?"

"Ah . . . yes?"

What other answer could possibly be appropriate? Yet when he voiced it, Gertrude, Ophelia, and Veronica gasped with astonishment. As to Sebastian, he was dumbstruck.

"It is Sarah Blake . . . Robertson," Lord Selby said.

"Sarah is your sister?" Sebastian inquired like a dunce.

"Yes, and I accuse you of ruining her." Veronica couldn't imagine how Sebastian might have replied, but Lord Selby didn't give him a chance. "Before you respond, I should inform you that if you deny your perfidy, I'll kill you—right here and now. I've dreamed about it for months anyway. Furnish me with a reason to finally carry out my threat."

"Selby! There are ladies present!" one of the male guests blustered, and several of them physically positioned themselves to prevent an altercation from erupting.

"I wouldn't utter a derogatory comment about her," Sebastian said. "I thought she was extraordinary. I still think that."

"So you admit your treachery?" Lord Selby asked.

The spectators were hanging on their every word, and Veronica was frantically trying to get Gertrude's attention. If Miss Robertson had told Lord Selby about being seduced by Sebastian, what else had she told him?

They'd agreed that Sebastian could never learn of their mischief. If Lord Selby disclosed it to him, she was quite sure she would never be Mrs. Sebastian Sinclair.

"Mother is correct, Nathan," Sebastian said. "We should confer privately. There's an empty parlor down the hall."

"I don't need an empty parlor to impart my message."

"I've been so worried about Sarah," Sebastian said. "Is she all right?"

"She is—no thanks to your mother and fiancée."

Sebastian scowled. "What do you mean?"

"I'll let them tell you what they did to her."

At the snide retort, Veronica quailed and sidled back into the crowd, eager to be shielded from Sebastian's furious gaze.

Ophelia stepped forward. "I'm relieved that Miss Robertson is with you, Nathan, but what about my two half-siblings? Are they with you too? I've been very concerned about them."

Sebastian looked at Ophelia. "What are you talking about?"

"Mother made them disappear, and Veronica assisted her in getting rid of Miss Robertson. I've been anxious to apprise you, but you're always so busy. You shouldn't marry Veronica, and could I come to live with you at the Haven? I can't stay with them another second."

Her speech shocked the room to silence, and Gertrude finally understood that they were in big trouble. She seized the initiative. "Ophelia is being ridiculous, Sebastian. She's been distraught lately, and she's confused."

"With all due respect, Gertrude"—Lord Selby was very short with her—"you should shut your mouth or you'll simply dig a deeper hole for yourself." He whipped his focus to Sebastian. "Here is what I demand of you. It's not negotiable."

"Fine. What is it? Before you tell me, I should point out that there's nonsense occurring in this house of which I am unaware. I'll deal with it immediately."

Lord Selby kept on as if Sebastian hadn't spoken. "It's Saturday, and I expect you to arrive at Selby by Wednesday afternoon with my sister's wards. They have vanished, and I believe them to be in grave jeopardy because of your mother. They are two of Sir Sidney's many natural children—"

Every person gasped, and Gertrude seethed, "Nathan Blake! How dare you disparage my dear husband's memory!"

Ophelia snottily said, "Put a sock in it, Mother."

Lord Selby kept on again. "They are Sir Sidney's natural children, and we recognize that your family doesn't want them, but my family does. They are to be delivered to my sister by Wednesday."

"Consider it done," Sebastian said.

"While you are at Selby, you will propose to her."

"What? No! Absolutely not!" Veronica shouted the words, rattling the crowd. "He's marrying *me*. He's been promised to me."

"Be quiet, Miss Gordon," Lord Selby said. "You've inflicted too much damage already, and I won't listen to you on any topic."

Sebastian cast a disgusted frown at Veronica, then he shifted to Lord Selby and said, "Ignore her."

"I intend to," Lord Selby said. "Now then, where was I? Oh, yes. While you are at Selby, you will propose to Sarah. I have no idea if she wishes to have you as her husband or not, just as I have no idea what your feelings are for her. I'll leave it up to her to decide if you're worth the bother." Like a threat, he added, "But you will ask her, and if she consents, you will wed her."

He stormed out, and they were frozen in their spots, watching him go. No one moved until the front door slammed behind him, then the crowd erupted in chaos.

"Gertrude!" Veronica wailed. "Do something!"

"That's enough, Veronica!" Sebastian voiced the command in a calm way, but it was so chilling she felt as if he'd slapped her. Then he addressed the guests. "I'm sorry, but this party is over. Obviously, my family has some issues to discuss. The butler will help you with your cloaks and hats."

He tarried like a statue in the center of the floor, his imperious gaze daring them to complain. People glanced at each other, then one person and another hurried out. In a quick minute, they were alone—just him, Gertrude, Ophelia, and Veronica—the detritus of her ruined soiree the only evidence anyone had been with them at all.

He went over and closed the parlor door, sealing them in, then he flashed an evil glower and asked, "Who would like to start?"

"I HAVE NOTHING TO SAY," Gertrude huffed, "except I've always thought Nathan was a lunatic, and his behavior this evening proves I was correct."

"Go to your room," was Sebastian's response, "and you are not to emerge until you have my specific permission."

"This is my house!" she fumed. "You can't send me there as if I'm a naughty child."

Ophelia had always viewed her brother as an even-tempered fellow, but suddenly, he looked so angry she wasn't sure how he might act.

"This is *not* your house, Gertrude Sinclair," he told her. "I own every brick and nail. Now go!"

He bellowed the last and—her lips tight with irritation—she stomped out.

Then he turned to Veronica. "What did you do to Miss Robertson?"

As her reply, she said, "You can't wed her! You can't! You've been pledged to me since I was a girl."

"I can't guess what mischief you've perpetrated, but it's crushed any plans I might have had with regard to you. I will not marry you. Not ever."

At the announcement, Veronica was so stricken that Ophelia wondered if she might faint.

"You can't mean it!" Veronica moaned.

"You will go to your room, as my mother went to hers, but while you are there, you will pack your bags. You're departing in the morning."

"To what destination?"

"You're heading home to the country, and you will not ever be welcome here again."

Veronica was desperate to change his mind, but she never could, and her sole ally, Gertrude, had slinked away. She glommed onto Ophelia. "He can't treat me like this, Ophelia. Tell him he can't."

Ophelia shrugged. "It's his house, Veronica. He can do as he likes in it."

Sebastian marched to the parlor door and yanked it open, and he called to the butler. "Veronica is leaving in the morning. Have a group of maids prepare her things and ask them to be thorough. She's never coming back, and I want no item left behind that would give her a reason to contact us in the future."

Veronica began to sob, fat tears dripping down her cheeks.

"Whatever I did," she claimed, "and I'm not admitting any duplicity, I did it for us, so you'd wed me!"

"Honestly, Veronica," Ophelia scolded, "you're making such a scene, and my brother and I are sick of you."

"Ophelia, please," Veronica begged. "Help me to convince him."

"You never will."

Veronica spun to Sebastian. "I'll languish in the country for a week or two, and we'll talk after you've had a chance to reflect."

"We won't talk ever again," Sebastian said. "How can I be any clearer?"

"Of course we'll talk." Veronica was practically cooing. "We can't let this little dilemma destroy what's been arranged."

"I'll unravel your perfidy," Sebastian warned her. "You realize that, don't you? If Miss Robertson or my half-siblings were harmed because of you, I'm not certain what penalty you'll pay, but I can guarantee you won't like it."

She stamped her foot like a spoiled toddler. "Stop being so horrid to me!"

"I haven't started being horrid."

She wasn't having any luck, and she tried a last gamble. "If you send me away, I'll never forgive you."

"I don't care."

His expression was cold and condemning, and she keened with dismay and staggered out. Once her strides vanished up the stairs, he turned to Ophelia and said, "It appears you have a few secrets to share with me. I'm sorry I've been too busy to listen."

"It's my own fault. I've been struggling to deduce my feelings about you marrying Veronica. I've been excited about it for ages, but since my ... well ... my ordeal, I've been distraught. I was afraid I wasn't assessing the situation as I should."

"I'm glad you stuck your nose into it. Perhaps you and I will figure out how to get along after all."

"Maybe I'm finally growing up."

"Maybe. Now what have you discovered about all of this? I'm in a hurry to receive some answers—when I hadn't even grasped that there were questions I should be asking."

"I can explain what happened to Miss Robertson," Ophelia said, "but I can't guess what happened to the children."

"For the missing pieces, we'll search Mother's library. She keeps extensive records. We'll see what we can find, and if we don't dig up the information we seek, we'll torture her until she reveals every detail."

"I might enjoy it too much," Ophelia said. "Here's what I know for sure, and here is what I suspect."

"I HAVE TO TELL you something."

"What is it?"

Sarah smiled at Nell. In London, they'd been good friends, but with Sarah being Nathan's sister, they'd become extremely close.

"You probably won't like it," Nell said.

"Why would you assume that?"

It was a pretty autumn day, but a bit cool. They'd bundled themselves in warm cloaks and had walked to the village to tour the cemetery behind the church. All of her Blake relatives were buried there, and she'd visited her father's grave.

They were on their way back to Selby, strolling up the lane toward the manor, and she contrasted her current circumstance with her earlier arrival. It was interesting how quickly a woman's affairs could change when a rich man stepped forward to assist her.

She snorted with disgust. It was exactly the attitude she'd had when Sebastian Sinclair had agreed to let her live in his cottage and he...

She pushed the thought away. She wouldn't ponder him! He was the past, and her brother and Nell—and Selby—were the future.

"Why are you scowling all of a sudden?" Nell inquired.

"I was thinking how dire my condition was when I stumbled in. I'm so much better."

"Nathan is adept at fixing what's wrong. I learned that lesson when he whisked me away from disaster and married me."

"We're both lucky."

"Yes, we are."

"What were you going to tell me?" Sarah asked. "You said I wouldn't like it."

"I tried to dissuade him so please don't be angry with me."

"Don't be ridiculous. I could never be angry with you, and by *him,* I presume you mean my brother. What's he done?"

Nell halted, and they faced each other.

"I told Nathan about Mr. Sinclair," Nell confessed.

Sarah's cheeks heated. "I hope you didn't confide *all* of it."

"I told him enough, and it's the reason he rode to town yesterday. He went to talk to Mr. Sinclair."

Sarah gasped. "Because of me?"

"Yes."

"Oh, my lord! They won't fight, will they?"

"He swore he wouldn't."

"Your response provides no comfort at all."

"He intends to order Mr. Sinclair to locate Noah and Petunia."

"Well . . . good. If anyone can make him tell us where they are, it's Nathan."

She suffered a huge wave of relief. She'd been vexed over how to mention the children to Nathan. They were Sinclairs, and he was feuding with Sebastian. Plus, he'd already showered her with a thousand boons, and she couldn't bear to place another burden on his broad shoulders.

"Thank you for asking him," she said. "I couldn't figure out how to ask him myself."

"He'll find them, and he'll bring them to live with us. We have plenty of space, and it will be fun to have some children running about."

"It would be wonderful to have them here. I'd be so grateful."

"But there is one other thing you should know."

Nell wrinkled her nose, and Sarah said, "Uh-oh. What is it? Just spit it out."

"Your brother felt Mr. Sinclair should wed you."

"What?" Sarah grumbled with frustration. "I never wanted that! I wish he'd discussed it with me first."

"He was too incensed. Are you sure you wouldn't like to wed Mr. Sinclair? Were you fond of him? Were you in love with him? Tell me the truth."

"I once assumed I'd be delighted to marry him, but if you could have seen how he treated me! His mother and his fiancée were so cruel, and he had them evict me because he didn't have the nerve to do it himself."

"Are you positive he's to blame? I've met him, and I liked him very much. I can't picture him acting that way."

"Neither could I, but if I hadn't traveled to Selby, I can't imagine what might have happened to me. He had his driver dump me in London with no money and night falling. Have I told you—when I was sleeping in that tavern kitchen—I was offered a job as a tavern wench? And the proprietor wasn't interested in having me serve ale to his customers. He had another type of service in mind."

Nell's jaw dropped. "Perhaps I'll have Nathan visit that tavern so he can pound the owner into the ground for insulting you."

"When I claim I was *imperiled* by Mr. Sinclair's conduct, I'm not joking. You observed my deteriorated condition when I arrived."

"I'm livid whenever I recall it."

"Who would want a man like that for a husband? Who would want to join such a horrid family? As I remember how his mother glared at me, I get shivers down my spine."

"I'm sorry you had to endure that experience, but what if you're increasing?"

It took Sarah a moment to understand what she was intimating. "Increasing . . . with a baby?"

"Yes. What if you're increasing? I don't believe you'll be able to refuse a proposal from him."

"Then I'll be in a dreadful jam because he *can't* propose to me. Even if Nathan threatened him, he's already betrothed to his nasty cousin. I hope he'll be miserable with her for decades."

Nell laughed. "Nathan convinces people to obey him. If he commands Mr. Sinclair to propose to you, then Mr. Sinclair will propose. It means he'll show up and demand to speak with you."

Sarah's pulse raced with numerous emotions she couldn't identify.

Sebastian might come to Selby? He might propose marriage again?

It had previously been her greatest dream, and he *had* proposed. She'd ruined herself at his behest. Afterward, he'd trotted off to Scotland on business, where he'd planned to purchase a summer house for Miss Gordon as a wedding gift.

That malicious shrew would never release him, and his relatives were counting on the match.

During their brief affair, she'd supposed he possessed some genuine affection for her, but any partiality he'd harbored hadn't been enough to stop him from becoming engaged to Miss Gordon. It hadn't been enough for him to inform his mother that he wouldn't proceed.

Sarah shook her head. "Sebastian Sinclair will never show up here."

"Nathan can be very persuasive."

"And Sebastian is rich and important and extremely stubborn. He would never stoop so low as to marry a girl like me."

"Don't sell yourself short," Nell said. "These days, you're not some paltry orphanage owner. You're half-sister to the Earl of Selby."

"It's the *half* part that will give the Sinclairs a collective fit of the vapors. He'd never consider it. He had a chance to bind himself to me, and instead, he sent his mother over to evict me. He didn't have the courage to tell me to my face that it was over."

"I can't predict what will occur, but you should prepare yourself. Nathan will be home for supper tonight. Mr. Sinclair might be with him, and if he isn't, I'm betting he'll strut in very soon."

"He won't!" Sarah sternly insisted.

"I guess we'll see which one of us is correct, and you should spend some time figuring out what your answer is to be. If you spurn him, and it turns out you're with child, what then?"

Sarah laid a protective hand over her belly. Might he have planted a babe there? She didn't feel any different, and most women claimed it was evident right away.

"I'm not increasing," she said. "I'm sure I'm not."

Nell snorted with amusement. "It's what I told myself too, but Fate can be merciless to a female." She patted Sarah on the shoulder and said, "Think long and hard. If Nathan drags him here, your brother won't let you reject him."

"He can't force me," she huffed.

"No, he can't, but he's very persuasive, remember? He always gets his way."

CHAPTER

23

"STAND IN A STRAIGHT line. No slouching, no lagging behind."

Noah stepped closer to Petunia and slipped his hand into hers. As the days had flown by, she'd grown quieter until she hardly talked at all.

They were at the docks and about to climb into a longboat where they'd be rowed out to the ship that would whisk them away from England. The small vessel had gone out and back twice already, and they were in the last group.

He kept glancing down the busy wharf, studying the people rushing by. He'd been so sure they'd be rescued, but they hadn't been. Once they were on the ship, the sails would be hoisted and they'd vanish. It would seem as if they'd never lived in England, as if they might be ghosts that had floated away.

Throughout their ordeal, he'd constantly whispered to Pet that they'd be fine, that someone would help them, but why had he thought that exactly?

From the minute they'd been seized at Hero's Haven, they hadn't experienced a single positive event. Now it appeared they were at the end of the road.

"Stay by my side," he murmured. "After we're on board, I'll demand we be sent to the same spot. We won't be separated."

She simply stared up at him with those big blue eyes of hers. Her poor mind was about at the breaking point, and it killed him that he couldn't provide a better conclusion. He'd never forgive himself for failing her, but then, adults were so powerful, and he was just a boy. How could he fight any of them and win?

He yearned to grab Pet and run off into the crowd, but their jailor had feared that very scenario. They'd been roped to the others, so even if they wanted to flee, they couldn't.

Well, he wouldn't always be a child. In a few years, he'd be an adult too, and he assumed he'd shoot up in height, that he'd become brawny and muscular as his father had been. He'd be tall and strong, and he'd be able to get even with every villain who'd hurt them.

"I am Sir Sidney Sinclair's son," he said to a man who walked by, but the fellow ignored him. He repeated the same declaration over and over. He added too, "This is his daughter, Petunia Sinclair. There's been a terrible error, and we're being forced away against our will."

Their jailor noticed him harassing the passersby. He stomped down to them.

"Shut your mouth, you little bugger," he said. "Why can't you be silent?"

"My half-brother is Mr. Sebastian Sinclair," Noah responded. "I ask you to have mercy on my sister and tell him what happened to us."

"Shut up! We're tired of listening to your stupid stories."

"He'll pay you a reward. Visit him at his rural estate of Hero's Haven. Inform him of how and when we left—so he doesn't worry."

Noah didn't suppose their brother would care a whit about their plight, but he was so disheartened. Was there no one in the world to fret or wonder over their fate?

Mere months earlier, he'd resided with his grandfather. He'd been a beloved grandson who'd been spoiled and showered with every kind of boon.

How could he have been yanked from that marvelous place and deposited in this desperate place? How could such an injustice have occurred?

"Sebastian Sinclair will *pay* me?" their jailor scoffed. "Yes, I'll visit him immediately. He'll probably fork over so much money that I'll never have to work again!"

The man laughed, then strutted back to the head of the line. Those surrounding them laughed too. They'd heard Noah's assertions, but they didn't believe him. They thought he was a braggart and a liar.

He peered down at Pet and said, "We'll always be together. I won't let us be pulled apart."

Suddenly, there was a kerfuffle down the wharf as a fancy carriage rolled toward them. It was a coach-and-four, with outriders on the corners, the horses being whipped into a vigorous advance that had people and animals scurrying out of its path.

The vehicle halted directly in front of them, and an outrider called to their jailor, "You there! Stop and attend my master."

Everyone turned to see the eminent person who would exit, and Noah suffered a spurt of excitement. It was a Sinclair carriage. The servants were wearing Sinclair livery, and the Sinclair crest was on the side.

The outrider jumped down and set the step, then the door was opened. To Noah's great surprise, his half-sister, Ophelia, emerged, and his excitement instantly waned. They'd met her once, and she'd been horrid to them.

Then Sebastian emerged too. His haughty gaze landed on Noah and Pet, and he marched over, Miss Ophelia dogging his heels.

"Are you all right?" he asked Noah.

"We've been very frightened, but we're much better since you arrived. Have you come to rescue us? If you haven't, I can't imagine how I'll survive my regret."

"Yes, we're here to take you home." Sebastian whirled around, his glare piercing the jailor. "Who is in charge? You?"

The jailor blanched. "Yes, I'm in charge."

Their brother stormed down to him, but Miss Ophelia stood with Noah and Pet, and she hovered over them in a very important way, as if she was protecting them.

She put a palm on Pet's shoulder and said, "Don't be afraid. You're safe now."

Sebastian announced to the jailor, "I am Sebastian Sinclair, son of famed explorer, Sir Sidney Sinclair."

There were gasps of astonishment, and the man next to Noah muttered, "I'll be damned. I guess you were telling the truth."

Sebastian continued. "These children are my half-siblings, and they were brought to you by mistake."

"I have a signed contract," his jailor claimed as he had all along.

"Yes, I know," Sebastian said, "but the woman who signed it wasn't their guardian, and she had no authority to bind them."

"A likely story," the jailor mumbled.

"You doubt my word?" Sebastian demanded. "Me? Son of Sir Sidney?"

"Well . . . ah . . . ah . . ."

"I thought you might be recalcitrant." Sebastian slapped some papers into his fist. "This is a writ from a judge, granting me permission to remove them from your custody."

"A what?"

"A writ," Sebastian repeated. "Find someone who can explain it to you."

He came back to Noah and Pet, and he grinned at them. "Let's get you out of here."

Noah raised their wrists, showing him that they were fettered to the nearby adults.

"Were they worried you'd run away?" Sebastian asked.

"Yes. We've been awful prisoners."

"Good for you!"

He winked at them, then he reached to his belt where he always carried a knife. He cut through the rope with a single slice, then he pointed to the carriage.

"Who wants to climb in first?"

Pet looked up at Noah, at the carriage, at Noah again, and she burst into tears.

"I told you it would be all right," Noah said to her. "Didn't I tell you?"

He hugged her tightly, then led her over to the vehicle.

"You're leaving at once."

"Ophelia! You're being ridiculous. So is your brother."

"You are being sent home in disgrace."

"Ophelia!"

Veronica tsked as if Ophelia was merely being difficult, as if they were having the type of argument they'd had as girls over hair ribbons or dress fabric. The gravity of her misdeeds hadn't sunk in, and Ophelia might have shaken her head in disgust, but her cousin wasn't worth the energy it took to be irritated.

She handed a sealed letter to an outrider who would escort Veronica to the country.

"Give this to her mother and no one else," Ophelia advised him. "Apprise her that she is receiving specific instructions from Mr. Sinclair, and he expects they will be strictly obeyed—or there will be consequences."

"I will tell her," the man said.

They were in the driveway at Ophelia's London residence, and the man stuck the letter in his coat, then went over to the coach to stand by the door. There was an entire team of men—guards really—waiting for Veronica to depart.

They were staring at her, their disdain clear, but she was a snob who didn't notice their contempt.

"What is Sebastian's message to my mother?" Veronica asked, appearing a tad nervous over the possible contents.

"He is determined that she have no illusions as to your conduct while you were with us."

"I didn't do anything wrong!" Veronica furiously insisted.

"You're wasting your breath on me."

"Those two urchins are back in the house."

"No thanks to you," Ophelia muttered.

"And they're fine! They weren't harmed, so these theatrics make no sense. Besides, their predicament was due to Gertrude's scheming. Not mine."

"Yes, you were a saint through the whole debacle."

"Miss Robertson is fine too. Lord Selby said so! Why are you being so horrid to me? I simply can't understand it."

Ophelia wouldn't bother explaining. She was too incensed.

"You will remain in the country for the next three years, and during that period, you will not show your face in town."

"I would never agree to such a restriction," Veronica scoffed.

"You will entertain no suitors. You will encourage no marriage proposals. You will live quietly with your mother and behave yourself. My brother orders you to reflect on your perfidy in the hopes that you'll mature a bit in your habits and attitudes. Then—and only then—will he allow you to move on with your life."

"He has no authority over me," Veronica blustered, "and if he assumes he can toss me over, I certainly have no duty to heed him on any issue."

"You've conveniently forgotten that he owns the property where your mother currently resides. If you defy him, he will be delighted to find new tenants."

"But...but...that would mean he'd evict us. We're family! He can't be serious."

"He's very serious, and he commands you to take this seriously as well. So far, you haven't, and he and I are weary of dealing with you."

"I demand to speak with him!" When Ophelia didn't reply, Veronica bellowed, "I demand it!"

"You are in no position to make demands of us."

Veronica's posturing wasn't having any effect, and she drew in on herself, trying to look smaller and more contrite. "Just let me see him, Ophelia. Please? I'm sure I can calm him down. There's no need for all this animosity."

"My half-siblings were fettered on a dock and about to be loaded onto a cargo ship bound for America, where they would have been sold into indenture."

"I wasn't part of that! It's how Gertrude buried your father's dirty little secrets."

Ophelia ignored the scurrilous comment, saying instead, "You were responsible for Miss Robertson's misfortunes. She was thrown out on the road, with no money, no friends to offer shelter, and night falling. We're lucky she wasn't grievously injured. She is Lord Selby's lost sister, and the entire city has learned how you treated her."

"Gertrude insisted we proceed with Miss Robertson. You're aware of how overbearing she can be. I couldn't dissuade her! I am perfectly innocent of every charge! Why won't you listen?"

"Get in the carriage, Veronica."

"I won't! I have to talk to Sebastian."

"He has no desire to talk to you. Not ever again."

"When will we complete my betrothal? It was supposed to happen at my party, but Lord Selby interrupted us."

Occasionally, Ophelia wondered if Veronica wasn't touched in the head. She was definitely carrying on like a lunatic. She refused to admit her role in their duplicity. She refused to admit any treachery. She even refused to acknowledge that people were imperiled. Because they hadn't been physically hurt, she believed herself free from any transgressions.

"Sebastian will never wed you, Veronica," Ophelia coldly informed her. "He is promised to another now. He will wed Miss Robertson—whom he loves beyond imagining."

"No, no, no, no, no!" Veronica trembled violently. "He can't pick her. You have to intercede with him for me."

Sebastian had been too disgusted to confer with her. He was so upset that Ophelia had been afraid he might have lashed out violently. As it was, he still had to bicker with their mother. How would he stomach it?

The sight of Noah and Petunia on that wharf, their wrists bound, was one that Ophelia would always remember, and it had ignited a fire of umbrage in her own breast.

She had stepped forward to handle Veronica—so Sebastian wouldn't have to. *She* would scold her cousin and send her packing. It was a tiny gift she could give to her brother, and she was eager to provide it.

By his allowing her to assume control of the situation, she felt extremely powerful for a change.

"Sebastian is finally going to be happy," Ophelia said. "It's all I want for him. He'll marry the woman he loves, and he'll be happy forever. Now *get* yourself in the coach, Veronica. We're exhausted by you."

Veronica seemed to realize her jeopardy, that this was no joke or lark. She fell to her knees, her arms outstretched to Ophelia, as she beseeched, "Ophelia, I'm so sorry! Let me speak to Sebastian. Let me beg his pardon."

"You will not inflict yourself on my dear brother."

Veronica started to weep, huge tears dripping down her cheeks, but Ophelia was unmoved. She was Sir Sidney's daughter. She was Sebastian Sinclair's sister. For the remainder of her life, she would protect him from the slightest arrow anyone might shoot.

"Goodbye, Veronica. I doubt I'll ever see you again."

"You can't mean it, Ophelia! You're my best friend! You always have been!"

"Use wisely your three years in the country. Try to figure out what matters to you—as I have. Try to atone for your sins, and perhaps Sebastian and I will be able to forgive you someday."

"Ophelia!"

Veronica kept repeating Ophelia's name as if repetition would bring her a different result.

Her cousin was still on her knees, and Ophelia was fatigued by her obfuscations and whiny diatribe. She gestured to the outrider who would lead the servants.

Two men came over to Veronica, lifted her to her feet, and marched her to the carriage. She struggled and wouldn't climb in, so they hefted her in and shut the door. The men leapt on board, and the driver gripped the reins. There was an inhale of collective breath as everyone expressed relief that the horrid scene was over.

The driver called to the horses, and the coach rolled away. Veronica leaned out the window and complained, "It was all Gertrude's mischief! Every bit of it! Tell Sebastian for me. Gertrude made me do it!"

Then the vehicle disappeared out the gate. The rattle and noise faded, and Ophelia dawdled for a moment, the significance seeping in, then she spun toward the house. It would be *her* house now. *She* would live in it. *She* would have the independent existence she'd always dreamed of having.

Her brother had offered it to her, and she had gladly accepted. If another waif ever showed up on her stoop, he wouldn't be turned away.

She glanced to the upper floors, and Sebastian was standing in the window, gazing down on the proceedings. He'd watched Veronica's departure from up above, being too livid to participate. What would his presence have accomplished anyway?

He'd let Ophelia handle it, and she'd handled it well.

"One down, one to go," she murmured.

She nodded, indicating it was over, and he nodded too. They were siblings, and it seemed they would learn how to act like it after all.

———✦✦✦———

"Sit down, Mother."

Gertrude tarried in the door to the library. She studied her son, conflicted over what bearing to project. Should she grovel? Should she flatter? Should she unleash her fury?

What attitude would be most likely to calm his temper so he'd head back to Hero's Haven and leave her in peace?

Her diabolical husband had bequeathed everything to her son, with the caveat that Sebastian utilize his inherited assets to *take care of* his mother. The angry oaf could impose any penalty, and she would have no recourse.

After spending three days locked in her bedchamber, she'd been abruptly summoned to confer with his grand self. She was spitting mad, but she didn't dare display any outrage.

He was seated behind the desk—*her* desk—and he'd definitely made himself at home. He'd been through the drawers, and her personal papers were scattered on the desktop. She bit her tongue over the invasion of her privacy, and she walked over and sat in the chair across from him.

"You asked to see me?" she evenly said.

"I've found Noah and Petunia," was his opening salvo.

She blanched, unable to hide a reaction. "I have no idea to whom you refer."

"Nice try, but you have no secrets from me so don't bother lying."

"Fine. I'm aware of who they are, and I have no comment."

"Indentured servitude? Really? That was your ploy? Seven years—where they might have been worked to death like slaves? What is wrong with you?"

"Your father had numerous bastards."

"So I've discovered." He motioned to the documents he'd pulled from her files.

"I arranged for them to have jobs, to train as apprentices, to get a firm start in life."

"By *selling* them to strangers? By sending them out of the country to an unknown fate?"

"What awaited them here in England? Poverty? Starvation? Death on the streets at a young age? Even though I had no responsibility to any of them, I *helped* them. I won't be castigated for it."

"We're very rich," Sebastian said. "If I live to be a thousand, I couldn't fritter away our money. We could have assisted these children in a genuine and compassionate way. You didn't have to sell them. You did it merely because you're malicious and spiteful."

"No, I *did* it because your father was an immoral wastrel who was constantly traveling, and I was left behind to clean up his messes."

"His natural children were his messes?"

"Yes. They are a stain on my marriage, a stain on your father's legacy, and a humiliation for our family."

"I'm sorry that's your opinion."

"What would you rather I'd done with them?" she asked. "Would you have liked to have them strutting about London and declaring their paternity? *You* toiled valiantly to ensure Sir Sidney's reputation was preserved during the inquest. Don't pretend you disagree with these measures. Not when you were so recently worried about the very same ones."

"I won't debate the issue with you."

"These two latest urchins will thrive in America," she said. "They'll have good endings. You needn't fret. I retain a very reliable company."

He stared at her as if she was babbling in a foreign language. "I guess I wasn't clear. I found them and rescued them."

"What are you saying?"

"At this very moment, they're upstairs. Ophelia is with them, and the servants are tending them."

"I don't consent to this!"

"It's not up to you."

"This is my home!" she fumed. "I haven't given my permission."

"Apparently, we have to review the facts again. This is *my* home. Not yours. Stop acting as if you're in charge. You're not."

"I demand to speak with my housekeeper! I demand that she remove those waifs at once."

He rolled his eyes. "Talking to you is like talking to a wall."

"If I am such a burden, you needn't dawdle in town. You're welcome to depart for the Haven immediately."

"Tell me about Miss Robertson. Tell me how you coerced her into fleeing."

The change of topic was so swift that she felt dizzy. "Miss Robertson? Why on earth would we discuss her?"

"Veronica claimed *you* concocted the plan to evict her."

Gertrude bristled. "She did, did she?"

"So you have one chance to confess your perfidy. If you refuse to be candid, it will only go harder on you in the end."

"You're treating me as if I'm a criminal on my way to a jail cell."

He slapped a palm on the desktop, the sound echoing off the ceiling so loudly that she flinched.

"Tell me what you did!" he commanded.

She sniffed with annoyance. "Veronica and I simply reminded her that you were promised to another. She took great umbrage at the notion that you'd been lying to her about your situation, and she packed her bags and scooted out the door."

"That's your story?"

"It's not a story. It's what happened, and I have no idea why you're in such a snit about it. She was a totally inappropriate person for you to know. We're lucky she ran off without a protest."

"I proposed marriage to her."

Gertrude waved away his remark. "Yes, I read the note you penned to her, and I can't imagine what possessed you. I saved you from making the biggest mistake of your life. You should be thanking me rather than scolding me."

She was so angry and had been so terribly abused by him that her thought processes were a bit muddled. She probably shouldn't have mentioned reading his note, but it was too late to retract the words.

A silence settled in, and it seemed to continue forever. He glared scathingly, and she couldn't abide his derision. She was his mother, and he needed to be more respectful.

"Summon Veronica," she said. "She'll verify my statement about Miss Robertson. The mercenary tart couldn't escape the Haven fast enough, and we weren't about to prevent her."

"Veronica is gone."

Gertrude scowled. "Gone where?"

"She's been sent home in disgrace. I've apprised her mother that she's not to return to town for three years. I won't have her dangling her dowry at any gullible young men until she's matured."

"Then how will we get your engagement to her accomplished?"

"I'm not marrying Veronica. I'm *never* marrying Veronica."

"I'm your parent, and I chose her for you! You will wed her, and you will do it gladly."

"No. I've decided to wed Sarah Blake—if she'll have me."

"Sarah . . . who?"

"Sarah Robertson Blake. I'm marrying her."

"That . . . that . . . orphanage owner?" She tsked with offense. "You are not."

"She is half-sister to the Earl of Selby, so she's suddenly quite a catch."

"I wouldn't necessarily believe her. Just because she's boasting of a connection, that doesn't make it true."

He ignored her. "It's a perfect conclusion, and it will work to patch up my quarrel with Nathan. He can't detest me when I'm his brother-in-law."

"Don't be ridiculous. I don't give you my permission. I will *never* give it."

"I love her, and it's not up to you."

"Love, bah!" she spat. "*Love* is for idiots and fools. Let's talk about important issues. What money does she bring to the table? What property? What's the size of her dowry? Calculate them all, then we'll determine whether she's a suitable candidate."

"I'm finished arguing about this."

"If you had no intention of listening to me, why drag me down here?"

"I called you down merely to inform you that you're leaving."

"I'm not leaving," she said.

"Yes, you are. For the next year, you will reside in a convent outside Edinburgh."

"Are you mad? We're not Catholics, and I wouldn't lower myself to consort with a bunch of pious busybodies."

"I view it as penance for the damage you've inflicted on so many people, and you should use the period to reflect on your conduct."

"I've never harmed a soul."

"After the year is up, you will travel to America to live with our cousins in Boston."

She whacked a hand on her ear as if it had been plugged and she was clearing it. "What? I could swear you said I'm moving to America."

"Ever since I learned how you dealt with Father's natural children, I've been struggling to devise an equitable punishment."

"I didn't hurt those children. I *helped* them!"

"You should suffer the same fate. You should have to abandon all that's familiar. You should have to journey to a foreign locale and wallow among strangers."

"You've tipped off your rocker," she said. "I'm sure of it."

"The nuns will let you have one trunk of personal belongings, but they'll search it for contraband so you're not distracted from your solitude and prayers."

"I'm not going to Scotland! I'm not going to America!"

"While we were chatting, I had your trunk packed. There's a carriage in the driveway, and you're departing in it."

She was absolutely flabbergasted. Was he jesting? He had to be. Or perhaps he was attempting to frighten her. If so, he'd definitely succeeded! A woman had no power against a man, so she was completely alarmed.

She was Sir Sidney's widow! She was one of the greatest ladies in the king-dom! She couldn't be sent away. The very idea was absurd.

"Sebastian! You're not doing this."

"Yes, I am, and I'd say I'm sorry, but I'm not. I'm marrying Sarah, so Noah and Petunia will be with us. There's no room for you in that world. I don't trust you, and you can't have further chances to imperil them."

"Why would I waste my energy? They're nothing to me."

"Well, they're *everything* to me, and you can't flit about on the fringe of the life I'll build with them. I also can't sit back and hope that no other of Father's children skitters out of the woodwork. You'll never sell another one of them into indenture."

"What will you—in your infinite wisdom—do with them instead?" she snidely inquired.

"From now on, Ophelia will live here. If any child knocks on the door in the future, she'll help them. She'll *really* help them, and that's how our family will behave from this point on. We won't pretend they don't exist."

There were a thousand replies she could have hurled, but when she opened her mouth, what emerged was, "You're giving Ophelia my home?"

"It's not your home, and it's *never* been your home."

The comment fell between them like a death knell.

He stood and rounded the desk, and he lifted her to her feet. They start-ed out, and she was so befuddled that she didn't bother protesting. It was happening in an odd kind of slow motion, as if she was in the middle of a nightmare and couldn't awaken.

They reached the foyer, and she glanced about for an ally who might intervene. Ophelia was up on the landing and staring down as if she didn't know who Gertrude was.

"Ophelia!" she called. "Your brother is making me leave! Tell him he can't treat me this way."

"Goodbye, Mother," was all her daughter said.

"Ophelia! Listen to me!"

"You shouldn't have harmed my half-siblings. I'm very ashamed of you."

"I don't agree to this!"

Ophelia didn't respond, and Sebastian simply yanked on her arm. "Don't dawdle, Mother. You can't avoid this fate."

He marched her out, and before she could blink, he'd hefted her into a waiting carriage and shut the door behind her. He secured the handle with a piece of rope, tying an intricate knot so she couldn't unravel it and climb out.

Two housemaids were already inside and impatiently watching for her to arrive. They were surly, younger girls who'd never liked her, and the notion of their being in charge of her was galling.

Sebastian leaned in the window. "The nuns will allow you to write me every quarter, but I wish you wouldn't. We should let matters settle between us. I'll visit you in a year, when it's time for you to sail for America. I'll put you on the ship myself."

"Sebastian, stop it! Just stop!"

"Use the next year wisely, Mother. Try to find some peace. Try to atone."

He stepped away and waved to the driver, and the vehicle lurched away.

"I've been kidnapped," she told the maids. "You must release me. I demand it."

"We're not employed by you, Mrs. Sinclair," one of them snottily replied. "We're employed by Mr. Sinclair, and we take our orders from him."

"It's a long distance to Scotland," the other said. "You should relax. We won't tolerate you caterwauling the whole trip. If you annoy us, we have permission to gag you."

"Who may I say is calling?"

"Mr. Sebastian Sinclair. I am accompanied by my young brother, Noah Sinclair. We're here to see Cuthbert Maudsen."

"Please come in, Mr. Sinclair. Mr. Maudsen is expecting you."

The butler showed them into the front parlor of the Maudsens' country home. Mr. Maudsen was slouched on a sofa and drinking a brandy even though it was barely one o'clock in the afternoon. They'd never met, and the buffoon didn't stand when Sebastian entered.

Sebastian wasn't normally fussy about his position in the world, but the snub aggravated him enormously. He'd arrived ready to loath Maudsen, and the rude oaf had instantly provided a reason to detest him.

"Hello, Sinclair." Maudsen started off the conversation by gesturing to the chair across. "Have a seat."

"No, thank you." Sebastian nodded to Noah. "Mr. Maudsen and I have a few issues to discuss. Why don't you look around? Tell me if you think it will be sufficient for my plans. Count the bedrooms especially."

Noah departed, and Maudsen frowned. "Where's the boy going?"

"Don't worry about him."

Sebastian couldn't decide if Maudsen was inebriated or simply lazy, but he didn't order the butler to escort Noah, didn't rise and stop him from snooping.

"What is it you want, Sinclair?" Maudsen inquired. "When your clerk contacted me and asked me to convene with you in the country, I was definitely intrigued."

"You shouldn't have been. I need to address a rather mundane issue."

Maudsen smirked. "I hope I haven't wasted an entire day at this rural pile of rubble over nothing."

"After I declare my purpose, I doubt you'll feel it was wasted."

Maudsen snickered. "Well, then, let me have it."

Sebastian studied him, trying to picture him inflicting himself on Sarah, selling her father's orphanage, forcing her to remove the children who'd lived there, evicting her afterward.

What must it have been like to have her sister and brother-in-law behave so hideously? What must it have been like to be all alone, with no allies or friends?

No, there had just been Cuthbert Maudsen, and the vain prick would deem it easy to terrorize and abuse a defenseless woman. Sebastian wondered how he'd fare when faced with a really angry, really powerful man who wasn't afraid of anything. They were about to find out.

"I'm very wealthy," Sebastian said.

"So I've heard. Your father was shrewd to glom onto those diamond mines of his."

A flicker of excitement flared in Maudsen's greedy eyes. He probably thought he was about to be offered some funds.

"You're in debt all over England," Sebastian bluntly stated.

Maudsen wrinkled his nose. "I don't suppose my personal affairs are any of your business."

"I've made them my business."

It finally dawned on Maudsen that the appointment might turn out a bit worse for him than he'd imagined. "What do you mean?"

"I've bought up all your markers."

Maudsen swallowed hard, then he regrouped and grinned. "Bully for you."

"I require payment immediately."

"I can't . . . *pay.*"

"I know, but I'm requiring it anyway."

Sebastian walked over to give him some legal documents. Maudsen refused to reach for them, so Sebastian grabbed his hand and wrapped his fingers around them.

"Consider yourself served," Sebastian told him. "With my demand note, I've also included my notice that I have been apprised of your inability to compensate me in the amount I am owed."

"Now see here, Sinclair! You've got some gall to stroll in and throw your weight around." Maudsen sipped his liquor as he dropped the papers on the floor.

"I am foreclosing on your home and property," Sebastian announced.

"What?" Apparently, Sebastian had captured his attention. "You can't foreclose! It's outrageous! How could it be allowed?"

"It's explained in the documents."

"But . . . but . . . where will we live? I have a wife, Sinclair. This was her grandmother's house. You can't take it from her."

"I can and I have. You have one month to be out."

"A month! You're mad if you think we'll depart."

"I'll be sending some guards to keep an eye on the place to ensure you don't wreck it or steal from me. Every item in it is mine: the furniture, the drapes and rugs, the figurines on the mantle, the silver in the drawers. It's *all* mine."

Maudsen looked confused. "It can't possibly be."

"You've wagered it all away, Maudsen, and the men who previously carried your debt were willing to twiddle their thumbs and let you dig a deeper financial hole. I, however, am not willing to delay."

"This isn't right." Maudsen shook his head. "I've never even met you before. You can't just waltz in and seize what belongs to me."

"I repeat: I can and I have."

A woman entered the room, and Noah was with her. She said to Maudsen, "Cuthbert, who is this boy? I found him wandering upstairs."

"Temperance," Maudsen replied, "come in at once."

On her being referred to as Temperance, Sebastian realized she was Sarah's sister. She was mousy and plain, and as with her husband, Sebastian loathed her on sight.

He ignored her to ask Noah, "What is your opinion of the residence?"

"It will be smashing," Noah said.

"How many bedchambers are there?"

"Six that I saw. I believe we could lodge twenty-four children in fine style."

"Wonderful." Sebastian shifted his irate gaze to Mrs. Maudsen. "I am Mr. Sebastian Sinclair."

"Yes, Mr. Sinclair! Cuthbert notified me he was having you as our guest, and I'm honored to host such a stellar dignitary."

"Don't gush, Temperance," her husband snapped. "Wait until he informs you of what's occurred."

"Why? What's occurred?" she asked.

"I'm foreclosing on you," Sebastian told her.

She chuckled, but wanly. "You can't be serious."

"Mr. Maudsen had extensive debts, and he signed promissory notes with each of his lenders. I purchased them."

"Why would you?"

"I wished to deliberately ruin him. I've requested full reparation, but your husband insists he doesn't have the necessary amount."

She frowned. "I'm certain this is just a misunderstanding. Mr. Maudsen will visit the bank in the morning. We'll make payment tomorrow."

"He could work for a thousand lifetimes," Sebastian pointed out, "and never earn the money I am owed."

She appeared alarmed, and she urged her husband, "Tell him, Cuthbert. Tell him he's mistaken."

"Don't look at me like that, Temperance," Mr. Maudsen fumed. "Don't you dare look at me!"

The little toad leapt up and stomped out, leaving his poor wife to deal with the mess. Sebastian might have pitied her, but he couldn't forget what she'd done to Sarah.

"Mr. Maudsen is a tad high-strung," she said as his footsteps faded up the stairs. "When he's upset, he flies off the handle. I apologize."

"I don't care about your precious Cuthbert—or you."

"Well! I never!" she huffed.

He picked up the papers her husband had dropped and put them on the table by the sofa. "The appropriate legal documents are there. You can read them at your leisure."

"I don't need to read them. Mr. Maudsen manages our business affairs."

"Good luck with that arrangement," Noah muttered from behind her.

Sebastian cast a scolding glower at him, and Noah grinned and bit his tongue.

"You have to be out one month from today," Sebastian advised her.

"Be out of where?"

"Focus please, Mrs. Maudsen. You have to be out of this house and off this property. I've foreclosed on you."

"My grandmother gave me this house. I inherited it, and it was passed to my husband as part of my dowry."

"I'm sorry to report that he gambled it away."

"He wouldn't have!" she loyally stated.

"Regrettably for you, he did."

"Where are we to live instead?"

"That's not my problem, is it?" He peered over at his brother. "Let's go. I can't abide it here another second."

They started out, and they were out in the driveway before she bestirred herself and caught up with them.

"Why are you treating us like this?" she demanded. "You seem to hate Mr. Maudsen, but we don't even know you. Why would you act this way?"

"Oh, didn't I mention? I'm about to be engaged to your sister."

"To . . . to . . . Sarah?"

"Yes, and this house is my wedding gift to her."

"It is not! I absolutely refuse to allow it!"

"It's not for her specifically. I'm turning it into an orphanage for her. Since you shut down the facility your father had built, I thought it only fitting that you supply the space for a new one."

Noah added, "I was one of her orphans. Remember me? I'm predicting the children she helps in the future will love this place."

They'd ridden to the country on horseback, with Sebastian delighted to learn that Noah was an experienced equestrian, his grandfather having provided him with all the lessons a gentleman required. They went over to the animals and mounted.

Mrs. Maudsen was gaping at them, her mouth opening and closing like a fish that had been tossed onto a riverbank.

"You're giving my house to Sarah?" she said when she could finally speak. "You'll have orphans living here?"

"In my view, it's a perfect ending," Sebastian said.

"Why pursue this drastic conclusion? You still haven't explained."

"I'm merely doing to *you* what you did to your sister. I have yanked your lodging out from under you."

"We have nowhere to go. What will become of us?"

"I'm sure Sarah must have once made a similar comment to you." He nodded to her. "Be out in thirty days. Isn't that the period you gave Sarah to move? It's a suitable length of time for you as well. Don't take anything. Even your clothes belong to me."

"You can't have my clothes! What a ludicrous notion."

"I suggest you discuss it with your husband."

"We can't find other accommodations in thirty days!"

"I'm positive your sister would have said that to you too. If you're in residence in a month, I'll kick you out on the road."

He tugged on the reins and trotted down the lane. Noah followed, and they didn't glance back.

———⁂———

TEMPERANCE WATCHED MR. SINCLAIR ride away. When she'd heard he would visit, she'd been so excited, but he'd scarcely noticed her. Nor had he bothered to introduce the boy who'd been snooping through their bedrooms.

He'd foreclosed on them? He was stealing her home? How could such a heinous event occur?

Yes, she understood Cuthbert spent more than he should. Yes, they had some debts, but on the rare occasions she'd pestered him about them, he'd promised her he had their finances under control.

He liked to gamble and gambol in town, but every gentleman had those same interests. It wasn't a crime, and it certainly wasn't the sort of endeavor that should cause a person to grow bankrupt.

They had a month to leave? It was simply incomprehensible.

She spun away and staggered inside. Cuthbert was stomping down the stairs, and he'd donned his coat and hat.

"Where are you going?" she asked.

"To town. Where would you suppose?"

"But you can't depart. We have to talk about Mr. Sinclair. You have to hire a lawyer and stop him."

"How would I do that precisely?" he sneered. "Lawyers cost money, and I don't have any."

"We have plenty. You've always told me that."

"If we're a bit short, whose fault is that? Your dowry was never sufficient to cover our expenses. If we're in a fiscal jam, you should look in the mirror. Don't blame me."

He constantly managed to garble her words so she was in the wrong. She mustered the courage to say, "My dowry was very big."

"I should have held out for a *real* heiress, not some shrew who filled her bank account with pennies."

She hated it when he called her names. "You used to assume I was worth having."

"Clearly, I was duped. We've never had enough to pay our daily bills, let alone enjoy a few frivolities. You should have warned me my life with you would be naught but misery and woe."

"Mr. Sinclair plans to take our house!"

"Weren't you listening? He's already taken it."

"There must be a way to prevent him," she said.

"How can two ordinary people fight such a famous fellow and win? It's not possible."

"Will you permit him to get away with it? What then? He's ordered us to vacate the premises in thirty days."

"How can I guess what we should do?"

"He claims he's about to marry Sarah."

"Your sister?" He scoffed with derision. "Trust me, Mrs. Maudsen. Sebastian Sinclair is the premier prize on the Marriage Market. He will *not* wed your rude, bossy sister."

"He's giving her our home so she can turn it into an orphanage!"

He scoffed again, with even more derision. "I find it completely typical that this would be our end. Your sister has ruined us forever!"

"How has Sarah ruined us?"

"She'll wind up living here with her urchins. Ooh, the infamy! Ooh, the gall! I can just imagine how she'll laugh."

"She wouldn't laugh."

She's not cruel like you, she nearly added, but she didn't.

"I suggest you contact her," he said. "If this monstrosity is about to be hers, then she's the only one who can help us. You'd best write her immediately."

He slammed his hat on his head and stormed out the door. She lurched after him, observing as he walked to the stables. Several minutes later, he cantered by on his horse. He would have left in his carriage, but it had been seized by creditors.

If she could yank him back with the power of her thoughts, she'd finally tell him what a disappointment he was, what an awful husband he'd been.

He'd received everything he'd demanded to have. She'd even schemed on her elderly father for him so he changed his Will. She'd handed over every portion of her life and her sister's life to him. Then she'd stood idly by, watching as he'd wrecked what her family had provided.

She'd even acquiesced to his insisting they sell the orphanage, that they shutter what her father had built, that they kick Sarah out on the streets.

Here she was now, on a cliff of calamity, and Sarah was the sole kind person she knew. Might Sarah forgive the hideous crimes Temperance's husband had committed?

If Sarah was really marrying Mr. Sinclair, then she could save Temperance. Could Temperance convince her of her duty to her only sibling? Could she remind Sarah that they shouldn't bicker? She had to try, didn't she?

She jerked away from the door and stumbled into the parlor to sit at the writing desk. She pulled out a sheet of paper and dipped a quill in the ink jar, then she paused. She had no idea where Sarah might be, and she gazed out the window at the autumn afternoon.

The road was empty, the sun drifting toward the western horizon. Cuthbert would never rescue Temperance, and Sarah was gone for good. The house was very quiet, and she was alone and on her own.

NATHAN WAS SEATED IN the library, once again grumbling over the paperwork that constantly piled up. Ever since he was ten, he'd traveled to Africa with Sir Sidney. How was it, exactly, that he'd abandoned that thrilling existence to become a sort of glorified clerk?

As the question flitted through his head, he shoved it away. When he'd persuaded Nell to wed him, he'd promised her he'd never stare at the horizon and wonder what was over the next hill.

If he was having trouble concentrating, it wasn't wanderlust plaguing him. It was Wednesday afternoon, which was when he'd ordered Sebastian to show up and propose to Sarah. What if he failed to appear? What then?

He was tired of fighting with Sebastian, and he'd never been the type who remained angry for long. He didn't carry grudges. Plus, with his marrying Nell, the tragedy had ceased to consume his every waking moment.

With the incident fading in the distance, he had to recognize that he'd never doubted Sebastian's word in the past, *and* he'd never liked or trusted Judah. He had to accept that his memory of the event might not be accurate.

Sebastian would *never* have left him behind.

There! He'd admitted it. It was the mature way to view it, and if he took that outlook to heart, there would be an opening to mend their rift.

If Sebastian wed Sarah, it would mean he and his old friend would be bound by marriage, and he couldn't continue to feud with his brother-in-law. Oh, how he hoped the stubborn ass arrived! If he didn't, Nathan would have to let his temper flare again, and he'd rather not.

He reached for another letter in the stack, and it was from his investigator. The man was out on the coast, searching for Rebecca, and he sent regular reports. So far, there had been no news.

Except this time, when he flicked the seal, the message was stunning: *I may have picked up her trail.*

Nathan's pulse raced, and he might have jumped up to locate Sarah, but his butler, Mr. Dobbs, poked his nose in the door.

"I need you outside, my lord," he said. "You have to see what's occurring."

"I'm busy, so it better be good."

Dobbs scoffed. "I know you, my lord. You're glad for any excuse to be dragged away from your chores."

Nathan smirked. "You have always been a master of understatement."

He tossed the note about Rebecca onto the desk, and he followed Dobbs out to the driveway. To his great relief and amusement, Sebastian was coming, and he'd assembled such an ostentatious caravan that it might have been the King and Queen popping in for a visit.

The lead carriage was the family's fancy coach-and-four, and a second, smaller carriage lagged behind. It would hold maids and servants, and it was loaded down with luggage. Both vehicles had outriders hanging from the corners, and there was a contingent of men on horseback in between. They displayed flags and banners, as if it was a parade.

The group was a mix of retainers in Sinclair livery, but it also included most of the men from the expedition team. Nathan hadn't seen any of them since he'd staggered home, and he hadn't realized he'd missed them. On observing them, he beamed with pleasure.

Nell bustled out and hurried over to stand beside him.

"What on earth is happening?" she asked.

"I believe Sebastian Sinclair intends to propose to my sister."

"Why all the pomp and circumstance?"

"I'm betting he assumes she'll be obstinate, so he'll have to work hard to impress her."

Nell laughed. "She's a Blake, so he'd bet correctly."

"He's not taking any chances on what her answer will be. With him prancing up in full regalia, she'll never be able to refuse him. It would be too embarrassing."

"Where is she?" Nell inquired.

"I have no idea. She's been hiding all morning."

"Maybe she caught one glimpse of this procession and bolted out the rear door."

He grinned. "Maybe."

"Don't you fight with him."

"I will be an absolute model of propriety."

She chuckled. "You've never been a *model* of anything."

"I wonder if he found his half-siblings," Nathan said. "If he can deliver them to Sarah, she's doomed to be his bride."

"I was thinking the very same." Nell turned to Dobbs and whispered hasty instructions that would send the staff scurrying, then she said to Nathan, "It looks as if we're about to host a large party."

"Perhaps he's brought along a Special License. Let's hope it's a wedding party."

"Yes, let's do."

The cavalcade rattled to a halt, and Selby servants rushed out to help with luggage and horses. The outriders leapt down to open the door of the main coach, and Sebastian emerged first. To Nathan's incredible surprise, his sister, Ophelia, climbed out after him. Nathan hadn't expected her to come and decided it was another nail in Sarah's coffin.

His grin widened, and he said to Nell, "That's your old nemesis, Ophelia Sinclair."

Nell elbowed him. "She wasn't my nemesis, and I shall be delighted to meet her."

Nell had once thought Nathan was engaged to Ophelia, and that notion had nearly kept them from marrying, but Ophelia couldn't abide him. The fact that she'd travel to Selby with her brother was an interesting development.

A boy and a girl jumped out next, and with their blond hair and blue eyes, they could only be Sir Sidney's children.

"It appears he located Sarah's wards," Nathan said.

"My goodness but that family has strong bloodlines. I'd recognize those children anywhere."

The four Sinclairs marched over, and they stopped in front of Nathan and Nell. They exchanged typical greetings, and it was all very formal, very ceremonial.

Then Sebastian said, "Lord Selby, Lady Selby, I'd like to introduce my half-siblings, Noah and Petunia Sinclair. And of course, Lord Selby, you know my sister, Ophelia."

More greetings were exchanged, and Nell gazed at little Petunia and charmed her by saying, "Aren't you the cutest thing ever!"

Petunia smiled at her as if she hung the moon.

Sebastian reached into his coat, and he pulled out a leather sheath and presented it to Nathan. Initially, Nathan couldn't discern what it was, then he noticed the jeweled hilt sticking out, and he blanched with astonishment.

His knife! The one Judah had cut off his belt in Africa! Its return raised a thousand questions, but they could wait until later. For now, he was simply thrilled to have it back.

He stared at Sebastian, and his friend said, "A peace offering."

"Thank you. I didn't think I'd ever see it again."

"I'm sorry it took so long to get it to you. The oaf who had it was a bit slow in relinquishing it."

They shared a blunt look that made Nathan suppose Judah might have suffered an *accident* and passed away. He didn't have feelings about it one way or the other, and if Judah was deceased, he wouldn't necessarily mourn.

Sebastian continued speaking to Nathan. "My brother, Noah, and I would like to talk to you privately about your sister, Sarah Blake Robertson. I've come to ask for her hand in marriage, and Noah will act as witness as to my wealth, station, and character."

Nathan glanced over at Nell. "Would you excuse us?"

"Yes, have your discussion while I settle our guests." She leaned in and whispered, "Don't you two muck this up. When everyone's journeyed such a distance, and Mr. Sinclair has gone to so much trouble, I'm planning to have a wedding at the end."

"I'm planning on it too, Lady Selby," Sebastian said.

Nathan studied his old friend, and though it was odd, the rage he'd carried seemed to float off into the sky. He smiled, apprising Sebastian it was over, that he was forgiven, and Sebastian smiled back.

Then Nathan said, "Would you gentlemen please accompany me to my library? I'm eager to hear your proposal, and I hope you can convince me."

"I'm sure we will," Noah Sinclair told him. "We've already decided that Miss Robertson doesn't always know what's best for her, and she can't make her own choice about it. We men will have to make it for her."

"I completely agree," Nathan said.

The three of them spun and went inside.

CHAPTER

24

Sarah strolled out of the garden and climbed onto the verandah, approaching a rear door of the manor. It was Wednesday, the day Nathan had demanded Sebastian travel to Selby to speak with her. She'd tried to ignore the possibility that he might show up, but as the morning had ticked by, she'd grown too unnerved, so she'd taken a long walk.

She'd dawdled for hours, being swamped by the worst sense of dread and eager to wring her brother's neck for interfering. She'd been struggling to figure out if she wished Sebastian would come or if he wouldn't. Either path was full of deep holes.

If he didn't arrive, she'd be crushed. Yet if he *did* come, how was she to assess his presence? If Nathan's threats had caused him to break off his engagement to Miss Gordon—if that's what had been required to end it—would she want him as a husband?

She couldn't decide.

Would she like to marry into a family with such awful members? What would it be like to have a mother-in-law who hated her? If he tossed over Miss Gordon, his relatives would be incensed. After that snub, how could Sarah ever attach herself to him in a sane way?

And what about Noah and Petunia? What if they were never found? Or what if they were found, but they'd been harmed? Why would she ally herself with such despicable people?

She entered the house, and as she went toward the foyer, the place seemed alive with activity, as if they were suddenly hosting a party. Servants rushed about, food and other supplies being carried to various destinations. When she'd left earlier, it had been quiet as a tomb. What could have occurred to create such havoc?

Nell appeared down the hall and said, "There you are! Where have you been? I've been hunting everywhere."

"I'm sorry. I didn't realize you were looking for me."

"Your brother needs to see you immediately."

Sarah frowned. "Is something wrong?"

"No. Everything is perfect, and he has a surprise."

Nell led her to the library, and as Nell shoved her into the room, she said, "I've got a thousand chores to manage. I'll stop back in a bit to check on how you're faring."

She pulled the door closed, and Sarah spun to the desk. Nathan was seated in his chair, but to her great relief, Noah was next to him.

"Noah!" she gasped, and she dashed over.

She hugged him and riffled his hair, but he was a boy and didn't relish displays of affection, so he quickly wiggled out of her embrace. She clasped his arms and turned him side to side, searching for injuries, searching for signs he'd been maltreated.

"Are you all right?' she asked him. "Even if you're not, lie to me and claim you're fine."

"I'm fine, and I mean it."

"Is Petunia with you?"

"She's upstairs settling in. She's fine too."

"Where were you? What happened? How did you come to Selby?"

"I'll tell you about it in a minute, but first, Lord Selby and I would like to discuss a very important topic with you."

"Yes, Nell told me," she said. "What is it?"

Nathan raised a brow at Sarah, humored by Noah's authoritative nature, and he gestured to the chair across from him. "Let's get more comfortable, shall we?"

She sat as Noah asked, "May I stand, Lord Selby? Would you mind?"

"No, I don't mind."

They glanced at each other as if they were involved in some completely inane male jest, and she said, "What are you dying to impart? Don't keep me in suspense."

Her brother started. "Noah was anxious to join in this conversation because he feels—through your shared experiences—you've developed a significant bond."

"That's true," Sarah said. "We have."

"He also feels a weighty burden to protect you. As do I."

She scowled. "You two are being much too serious, and you're scaring me. Will you just spit it out?"

"I will." Nathan winked at Noah, then announced, "We've received a marriage offer for you, and we have accepted it."

She wasn't sure what she'd been expecting, but it wasn't that.

"What are you talking about?" she asked.

This time, Noah spoke up. "It was too good to disregard, and we agreed that it was best if you wed."

"There's been a proposal of . . . of . . . marriage?" she stammered. "From who?"

Nathan tsked. "It's not as if you have a line of suitors. Who do you think it's from?"

She squirmed uneasily. "Mr. Sinclair is here?"

"Yes," Nathan said. "He brought Noah and Petunia to us, then he and I conferred about you."

"Isn't that precious?" she sarcastically seethed. The notion of them dickering over her like a mare at an auction was infuriating.

Noah chimed in again. "I requested to be present when Lord Selby explained it to you. You don't always choose the right path, and I wanted to clarify the benefits so you don't make a mistake."

"Why would you automatically assume I'd make a mistake?" she asked.

"My Sinclair relatives have been awful to you, and you're probably very angry."

"I am angry," she admitted.

"I felt I ought to mention that Sebastian is a very grand fellow. He's brave and loyal, and he saved Pet and me from certain disaster. I'll always be grateful to him."

"So will I," she said.

"By his conduct toward us, he's showed how devoted he can be, and a woman can't ignore that sort of attribute."

"You're correct."

"He's rich too," Noah added, "and a woman shouldn't ignore that attribute either. Especially not *you* when you've recently been in such dire straits."

Nathan smirked. "I couldn't have said it better myself, Noah." Then he gazed at Sarah. "I've been friends with Sebastian since I was seven, and he's a fine man. I'd be happy to give you to him. I'd never worry about you a single day."

She began to tremble; she couldn't help it. They were both grinning, merrily presuming her future was arranged, but Sebastian Sinclair had committed a hundred sins against her.

The small ones were of no account, but the big ones—lying to her, having his mother evict her, seducing her, encouraging her with a false proposal— were massive. She nearly burst into tears whenever she recalled how thoroughly she'd been duped.

Well, she didn't have to be so gullible. She didn't have to behave like a ninny. She could buck up and act like the mature, adult female she was. She'd never permit a man to trick her again. She'd never be such a fool.

Before she could comment, the door opened behind her. Nathan and Noah could see who'd entered, and from how their grins widened, she could guess who it was. She shifted in her chair and looked over too. And . . . ?

There he was, Sebastian Sinclair, the dashing cad, the riveting hero, the famous explorer. For the occasion, he'd dressed immaculately: tan trousers, blue frock coat, knee-high black boots. His cravat was snowy white, yards of Belgian lace tied in an intricate knot.

At Hero's Haven, he'd always donned casual clothes, almost like a laborer, so she couldn't recollect his ever being so stunningly attired. He was elegant and beautiful. Could a man be beautiful? The answer was undeniably *yes*.

"It's about time you slinked in," Nathan said to him.

"You had to wear down her defenses," he replied, "so I didn't think I should rush you. I figured it might take an enormous amount of cajoling."

Noah told him, "We tried our best. I shared a dozen positive facts about you."

"Thank you, little brother."

On hearing the affectionate term, Sarah was perplexed. Had they bonded? Were they fond siblings? When had that happened? How had it happened?

"Let's go, Noah," Nathan said. "These two have some important issues to discuss."

Nathan stood, and they headed out, but as Noah passed Sebastian, he said, "We already informed her that we've accepted your offer, so if she's difficult, please remember it's all just incidental details."

They exited, and she and Sebastian were alone. He appeared cocky and confident, but she was spitting mad. The three males had been talking about her as if she wasn't in the room, as if she was powerless and couldn't make up her own mind.

Ooh, the gall! It had her even more furious.

She leapt up and whirled to face him. She'd meant to hurl a scathing retort, but found she couldn't. Words seemed to have escaped her. What would she like to have transpire?

She was as confused as she'd been earlier while walking in the garden. She wanted to marry him. She didn't want to marry him, and she wouldn't be pressured into it by Nathan and Noah. She yearned to send him away merely to show them they couldn't boss her, but that was juvenile behavior.

Hadn't she just vowed to stop being an idiot?

"Hello, Sarah," he said, and he started toward her.

He had a ferocious gleam in his eye so he looked like a predator stalking its prey. And there was no doubt about it. *She* was the prey.

"Hold it right there, you bounder," she warned.

"No."

He continued his advance, and for each step he took forward, she took one back. They danced an awkward sort of dance, until finally, she bumped into the wall and could go no farther.

He swooped in and clapped his palms on either side of her, trapping her in his arms.

"You left me!" he accused. "How could you abandon me like that?"

She blanched. He thought *he* was the wronged party? He thought *he* had been deceived and abused? Her blood boiled!

"Of course I left," she fumed. "What was I supposed to do?"

"Stay put? Wait for me?"

"Why would I have waited? You proposed, then you flitted off to Scotland, where—I was apprised—you intended to buy a summer house for your fiancée as her wedding gift."

"Aah," he mused. "I was wondering how they convinced you."

"You also swore to me that you were *not* engaged. You swore you weren't! Yet I had to stand in that accursed cottage at the Haven as your betrothed waved her engagement ring in my face."

"She was wearing a ring?"

"Yes!"

"I was never engaged to her," he claimed.

"That's not what your mother told me. That's not what your fiancée told me."

She scooted under his arm and hurried across the room, using the desk as a barrier to keep him at bay, but he simply marched around it, approaching until they were toe to toe. He leaned in, pinning her to it.

"Move!" she said.

"No."

She placed her hands on his chest and shoved him, but pushing him was like pushing a boulder. He wouldn't budge.

"Would you like to hear why I raced off to Scotland?" he asked.

"Your mother explained it for you. You had to manage some family business, and you'd be gone for weeks. You had her evict me when you were away because you were too much of a coward to kick me out yourself."

He rolled his eyes. "Do you really believe I would treat you that way?"

"How would I know? We're practically strangers, and I'm still trying to ascertain what possessed me to become involved with you. Why was I so ridiculously besotted? I must have been temporarily insane."

He grinned. "So was I. You drove me quite mad."

"If you're mad, it's not my fault. In my view, you've always been a lunatic."

He ignored her jibe. "I went to Scotland because my sister eloped with Judah Barnett."

"Ooh, I never liked that man. What was she thinking?"

"She wasn't thinking; that was the problem. My mother begged me to chase after them and stop them if I could."

"Were you able to?"

"Yes, and she's home safe and sound."

"What about Judah? How will you keep him away from her in the future? He's the kind of fellow who would strike again merely to prove you can't thwart him."

"It was my feeling exactly." He shrugged. "He'll never bother her again."

He appeared positive the matter was concluded, and she struggled to deduce his message. Had he made Mr. Barnett vanish? How, precisely, would he have accomplished it? With how determined he could be, she wouldn't be surprised to learn he'd murdered the stupid oaf. Would he have? Might he have been that intent on protecting his sister?

Sarah wouldn't consider the notion. It was too preposterous. Instead, she asked, "And your sister? She must have been rattled by the ordeal. Is she recovering?"

"She'd doing well. In fact, she traveled here with me."

Sarah scowled. "Weren't Noah and Pet with you too? How was she persuaded to be civil?"

"Since her foolish escapade ended, she's had a change of heart on many issues. She's grown up a bit too. She was incensed by my mother's conduct toward Noah and Petunia, and it's tamped down much of her snobbery."

"What did your mother do to them? Noah didn't have a chance to tell me."

"She had sold them into indenture."

Sarah gasped. "She what?"

"They were bound for America. Ophelia and I caught them at the docks just in time."

"Oh, my goodness."

She was afraid her knees might give out, and she staggered over to a chair and sank down. She stared at the floor, assessing the dreadful news. What sort of person behaved so despicably? In a detached manner, Gertrude Sinclair was their grandmother. What sort of fiend would imperil her grandchildren so egregiously?

"Indenture!" she eventually murmured. "What if you hadn't located them? What if the ship had sailed before you arrived?"

"I've been asking myself the same question."

Tears flooded her eyes, and she worried she might simply break down and weep. She gazed at him and inquired, "Are they safe from her? Will I constantly have to fret that she might sneak up and kidnap them again?"

"She'll never have another opportunity to harm them."

"How can you be sure?"

"For the next year, I've locked her in a convent."

"You didn't!"

"I did," he blithely admitted. "While I was trying to figure out where she'd hidden Noah and Pet, I learned that several other of my father's natural children had shown up in the past. It seemed to occur when my father was out of the country, so she had to deal with the situation herself. She sent numerous of my half-siblings into a life of indenture."

Sarah blew out a heavy breath. "I realize she's your mother, but may I say she's a witch of the highest order?"

"You can say it because it's true. When she's released in a year, she'll be transported to America to live with some cousins. I deemed it fitting that she be forced to head off to a foreign land and start over among strangers."

"That's positively diabolical." Sarah beamed with delight.

"I thought so, and it means Noah and Pet are protected from her."

"Good."

"Now ... as to you and me," he said.

She scoffed. "There is no *you and me*. You're engaged, remember?"

"I'm not engaged. Must I summon Nathan and my sister to verify it?"

"Miss Gordon was quite certain. I think a girl would know if she was betrothed or not."

"Miss Gordon has left too."

"Left for where?"

"I conveyed her to her mother in the country—in disgrace—and she won't be allowed in London for three years."

"Three *years*? Why so long?"

"She has a large dowry, and I won't have her entice some poor boy with it until she's matured a bit."

"That's very wise," she said.

"So my mother is gone, and Veronica is gone. I've punished them for hurting you, and they're out of our life forever."

"You keep talking as if we're together. We're not."

"Not *yet* anyway." He reached in his coat and pulled out a key, and he dangled it in front of her. "This is for you."

"A key? To what?"

"It's my marital gift to you."

"You're awfully sure you'll convince me, but I haven't heard a proposal from you." She paused, then snickered. "I take that back. I heard one previously, and it was completely false."

"It wasn't false. I had to chase after Ophelia, and although you aren't aware of it, I wrote you a note that explained my abrupt departure. My mother found it and burned it, so it was never delivered."

She gaped at him. She was still seated in the chair, and he was leaned against the desk, his legs stretched out, looking as if he hadn't a care in the world.

He'd penned a letter about his sudden trip? His mother had burned it?

Could the story be true? Could it be that her troubles had been caused by such a paltry misunderstanding? Had his mother and Miss Gordon watched him trot away and viewed it as an opening to be shed of her? Could it have been that simple?

"I might believe you about the burned note," she cautiously said.

"Ophelia discovered what Mother and Veronica had done, and when she apprised me of their duplicity, I figured you'd be livid so I ought to present you with a bribe that would make you like me again. Or at least one that would force you to consider whether I was worth the bother."

"You bought me a gift?"

"I didn't actually *buy* it. It came into my possession, and I'm giving it to you."

"You're speaking in riddles, and I've never been adept at unraveling them. What are you telling me?"

"I've met your brother-in-law, Cuthbert Maudsen."

"I'm sorry for you."

"I didn't like him."

"Who does?"

"He has a gambling problem, but I recall that you're cognizant of the situation."

"I am."

"I went around town and purchased his markers—then I foreclosed on him and your sister."

At the announcement, she was elated and alarmed. "You foreclosed?"

"Yes, and they have a month to vacate the premises. Your sister's house is mine now, and I'm turning it into an orphanage for the natural offspring of the rich and notorious."

"But . . . but . . . that's the sort of facility my father built in London."

"Yes, I know. I had Noah investigate the bedchambers, and he thought we could easily accommodate twenty-four children. I've already commissioned the sign we'll hang over the gate."

He reached into his coat again, and he pulled out a sketch of the sign: *Robertson Home for Orphaned Children.* Beneath it were the words: *A Sir Sidney Sinclair Charity.*

"It's the name of my father's orphanage," she said like a dunce. "It's where I grew up."

"Since you'll be my bride, and we'll be living at the Haven, you won't be able to run it yourself, but we can hire some competent people. It will probably be better, won't it, to have the children raised in the country? They can learn to ride and garden. I think it will be quite a grand endeavor."

"You did all that for me?"

"Yes."

"But why?"

"Can't you guess?"

"I have no idea."

"I love you, you silly woman. Why would you suppose?"

She shook her head. "You don't love me."

"Yes, I do! Don't tell me how I feel about you."

She stared at him, at the sketch of the sign, at the key he was still holding. She took it from him and traced her fingers over the smooth metal, and she burst into tears. She'd never been a watering pot, but honestly! How much more wooing could a girl abide?

"What's this?" he gently asked. "Tears? You can't be sad. Not when I've exerted such effort to make you happy."

"I'm not sad, you thick oaf."

He was a very typical male, and he glowered at her. "You look miserable to me."

"I'm not. I'm ... I'm ..."

She stumbled, too overwhelmed to voice her sentiment. She was so pleased, so grateful, so relieved. Noah and Pet were safe. His sister, Ophelia, had had a change of heart about them. His wicked mother and terrible fiancée were vanquished for good. He and Nathan seemed to have mended fences.

She was ensconced in the middle of both families. She was no longer alone.

He dropped to a knee and clasped her hand in his. With the other, he tugged a kerchief from his coat and dried her eyes.

"I'm going to propose again," he told her, "and I absolutely refuse to have you weeping when I do."

"I can't stop. I'm just so glad about everything."

He dipped in and kissed her, just the slightest brush of his lips to hers. She smiled, and he smiled too.

"I love you, Sarah Blake Robertson, and I want to marry you." He must have thought she'd decline because, before she could answer, he said, "I won't claim to be much of a catch."

"Don't denigrate yourself to me. I won't listen."

"Well, I've spent most of my life around swashbuckling, swaggering men. I've traveled in foreign locales and lived with native tribes. My manners are often lacking, and I can be bossy and domineering. It's simply my nature."

"I've noticed that about you," she said.

"But I'm rich, and my reputation is one of the best in the land. I offer you what I have: my name, my family, my home. I swear I will always protect and cherish you. I will love you until I draw my last breath. Will you marry me?"

She didn't have to ponder, didn't have to reflect.

"Yes, I'll marry you."

"Are you certain? Once you agree, I won't allow you to back out."

She studied him, reveling in how handsome he was, how dashing. Yes, he could be bossy and stubborn, but he could also be kind and generous and remarkable. He'd given her shelter when she'd had nowhere to go. He'd saved Noah and Pet from his cruel mother.

He was her brother's friend, the one man in the world Nathan would choose for her above all others. And to her great delight, *he* had chosen her— as Nathan had hoped he would.

"I'm certain, Sebastian. I love you so much I'm dying with it."

He raised a cocky brow. "I like the sound of that."

"Did you really kick my sister out of her house?"

"Yes. I've been extremely busy, doling out penalties to every villain who harmed you. Your sister and her husband were at the top of my list."

"What will become of her?"

"I don't care. Do you?"

She was too inundated with joy to think straight, let alone worry about Temperance. Was that a horrid attitude to have? Would she feel guilty later on?

At the moment, she couldn't decide. She could only gaze at Sebastian and wonder why she'd ever doubted him.

"I'm sorry," she murmured.

"Why would you be sorry?"

"I didn't believe in you. Your mother fed me a pack of lies, and I swallowed them all."

"Yes, and as penance, you should have to make it up to me. I shall expect you to spoil me rotten each and every day until I'm old and decrepit."

She grinned. "I promise I will do exactly that."

"Aren't I lucky?"

He leapt to his feet, and he scooped her off the chair and into his arms. Then he was kissing her and kissing her, and they were laughing, twirling in circles, careening round and round until they were crashing into furniture and could barely keep their balance.

Vaguely, she noted that the door had opened, and her brother said, "What's going on? Are you fighting?"

"This is not us fighting," Sebastian told him. "This is us *agreeing*."

"Lord have mercy," Nathan muttered.

He marched in, and a group of people entered behind him until the space was very full. Nell was there with Ophelia. Noah and Pet were there too, as were Mr. Dobbs and the upper level servants. It also appeared that most of Sebastian's expedition team had arrived.

"Have you asked her?" Noah said to Sebastian.

"I asked."

"And . . . ?"

The whole room held its breath.

Sebastian puffed himself up. "And . . . she said *yes*."

A rousing cheer went up, the spectators shouting and clapping.

"What's happening?" she said to Sebastian. "Why has everyone come?"

"We're having a wedding," he responded.

"Who is getting married?" she inquired, not understanding.

"You and I are getting married," he informed her.

Her jaw dropped in surprise. "You and I? Now?"

"Yes. There's no reason to wait, is there? I'm not about to give you a minute to deliberate where you might change your mind."

She smiled with exasperation. "You were definitely sure of yourself."

"Ha! You've never been able to resist me."

"No, I never stood a chance."

"Will you have me, Sarah Blake? Will you marry me, right here, right now?"

Had there ever been any real choice?

"Yes, I'll marry you right now, and could we please hurry? I suddenly find myself eager to be a bride."

He kissed her again, in front of the crowd, as they cheered and clapped even louder.

She hugged him as tightly as she could—Sebastian Sinclair, the man of her dreams, the one who'd always been meant just for her—and she would never let him go.

THE END

Don't miss Book #3 of Cheryl Holt's
ALWAYS trilogy

Always Mine

The story of
Miss Rebecca (Blake) Carter
and
Mr. Raven Shawcross

NOW AVAILABLE!

ABOUT THE AUTHOR

CHERYL HOLT IS A *New York Times, USA Today*, and Amazon "Top 100" bestselling author who has published over fifty novels.

She's also a lawyer and mom, and at age forty, with two babies at home, she started a new career as a commercial fiction writer. She'd hoped to be a suspense novelist, but couldn't sell any of her manuscripts, so she ended up taking a detour into romance where she was stunned to discover that she has a knack for writing some of the world's greatest love stories.

Her books have been released to wide acclaim, and she has won or been nominated for many national awards. She is considered to be one of the masters of the romance genre. For many years, she was hailed as "The Queen of Erotic Romance," and she's also revered as "The International Queen of Villains." She is particularly proud to have been named "Best Storyteller of the Year" by the trade magazine Romantic Times BOOK Reviews.

She lives and writes in Hollywood, California, and she loves to hear from fans. Visit her website at www.cherylholt.com.

CPSIA information can be obtained
at www.ICGtesting.com
Printed in the USA
LVHW111530180719
624531LV00003B/339/P